WILD HEART
of the
CROWN

WILD HEART
of the
CROWN

ERICA SEBREE

SQUIRRELED AWAY PUBLISHING
AUSTIN, TEXAS

First Edition: May 2023

Book Cover design by MiblArt

ISBN 979-8-9866118-3-9 (paperback)
ISBN 979-8-9866118-2-2 (ebook)

Squirreled Away Publishing
Austin, Texas

To every reader who took a chance on my debut novel,
Wild Heart of the Storm, *and decided to continue the journey.*

Thank you.

Contents

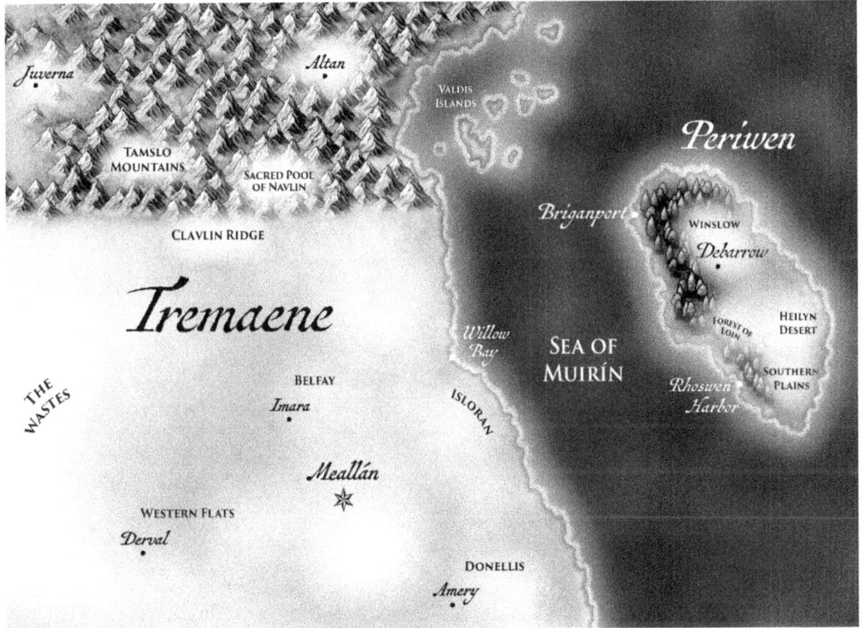

Juverna
Altan
TAMSLO MOUNTAINS
SACRED POOL OF NAVLIN
VALDIS ISLANDS
Periwen
CLAVLIN RIDGE
Briganport
WINSLOW
Debarrow
Tremaene
HEILYN DESERT
FOREST OF EOIN
Willow Bay
SEA OF MUIRÍN
BELFAY
Imara
SOUTHERN PLAINS
THE WASTES
Rhoswen Harbor
ISLORAN
Meallán
WESTERN FLATS
Derval
DONELLIS
Amery

PRONUNCIATION GUIDE

People

Abaigeal: Ab-ah-gail

Aeveen: Aa-vEEn

Aindreas: AHN-dree-ahs

Ainsley: AYNZ-lee

Alastar: AEL-aa-staar

Alpina: Al-pee-nuh

Ambros: AEMBRowS

Armel: AR-mell

Athdara: Aeth-DAAR-AH

Audris: Ow-DRIYS

Beglan: BEG-lahn

Bradach: BRA-daakh

Brighid: BrEEJ-id

Bryna: BRIHN-aa

Cace: KaaS

Cadwyn: KAD-wayn

Cahir: KAW-heer

Cian: KEE-uhn

Cora: Kaw-ruh

Derin: DEHR-ihn

Dougal: DOO-guhl

Drummond: DRUH-muhnd

Dwyer: DWY-ur

Edlyn: EHDLihN

Erena: EHR-ae-nah

Esme: EZ-may

Finbarr: FIHNBaa-R

Finley: FIN-lee

Gareth: Garr-UHTH

Genvieve: Jhehn-VIY-V

Gilian: JIL-ee-uhn

Grady: GRAY-dee

Griselda: Gruh-ZEL-duh

Gwen: Gwehn

Hagen: Haa-gn

Harlow: HARR-low

Hazel: HAY-zl

Jaime: JAY-mee

Keelin: KIY-lihn

Kelton: KEL-tuhn

Killian: KIL-ee-an

Kyla: Kai-luh

Leenan: Lee-NAN

Lennox: LEN-uhks

Liffey: LIF-ee

Luxovious: Luhx-o-vee-uhs

Madoc: MAAD-aak

Mairtín: MER-tn

Marta: MAAR-tuh

Molly: MOL-EE

Muirín: MWIR-in

Myles: MYLZ

Olan: OH-len

Olwen: OW-LWehN

Orianna: Aw-ree-ON-AH

Padraic: Paw-RIK

Pallya: Pahl-yah

Pearce: Pih-RZ

Quinlan: KWIN-luhn

Roderick: RAHD-rik

Rosaleen: RO-ze-leen

Shawndrell: ShAWhn-dryl

Sheridan: SHEHR-i-dehn

Sullivan: SUL-uh-vuhn

Tahra: TAE-rah

Tearlach: TCHAR-lakh

Tomas: TAWM-es

Torin: TAOR-ahN

Tuireann: TEER-ee-auhn

Winifred: WIN-e-frid

Places

Altan: AWL-tin

Amery: AM-e-ree

Belfay: BEHL-faye

Briganport: BRI-guhn-pORt

Clavlin: CLAh-vlihn

Debarrow: DEH-bah-row

Derval: DUR-vel

Dogherty: DOOR-ur-tee

Donellis: DOH-nel-lis

Imara: Iy-MAAR-aah

Iola: EE-O-lah

Isloran: Ees-LOH-rehn

Juverna: Joo-VUR-nah

Kearney: KAR-nee

Meallán: MEL-awn

Navlin: NAH-vlin

Periwen: Peh-ri-when

Tamslo: TAHM-sloh

Tremaene: TReh-meyn

Other

Loinnir: LUN-neer

Mios: Mhee-os

Neve: NEEV

Triskele: Tris-keel

Chapter One

A BLADE CUT through the air, forcing Esme back. It clashed with hers, the impact vibrating down her already shaking arm. She couldn't lose any more ground. Fragments of her training filtered through her mind. But Cahir fought differently than Killian. More likely, Killian never gave her his all when they sparred.

Esme gritted her teeth and tried to push Cahir back. He leveraged his formidable weight against her, sliding his blade down the length of hers.

Her breathing shallowed, and she barely had the strength to deflect his attacks.

When he pulled back, Esme lunged, thrusting her sword.

Cahir only smiled. His crystal blue eyes shimmered with delight as he pivoted easily out of range.

He advanced again, casually brushing his flaxen hair from his face.

Esme's energy was almost depleted, and Tearlach's advice of running and hiding no longer seemed like an insult to her fighting ability but a rather sound idea. Though, even if she could manage to outrun her guard, there was nowhere to hide.

Not for the first time, Esme fought the urge to call on her storm magic. But Cahir had never witnessed her magic—nor had the other warriors in the yard—and she planned to keep it that way, no matter how tempting it was to unleash crushing winds, battering rains, and bolts of pure crackling light. She was too physically exhausted to summon that kind of power anyway. Conjuring a single drop of rain might very well fell her before she could gather a decent storm cloud.

Cahir's blade forced her back again, and Esme retreated toward the edge of the ring. When she felt the catch of grassy turf behind her heel, she knew the tree line wasn't far.

Her sword locked with Cahir's. She tightened her jaw, funneling all her strength into her arm. Sweat prickled at her hairline, and the loose strands at her temples clung to her skin. Her muscles trembled in protest, but she braced her hand against her forearm and managed to shove their crossed blades aside. Grinding the dirt beneath her boots, she bolted for the barrier of trees.

Esme gulped down a desperate breath and glanced over her shoulder, narrowly avoiding the silver arc aimed at the unprotected space between her shoulder and neck. As the breeze of the blade's path grazed her heated skin, she angled her sword low, slicing at Cahir's muscular thigh. He sidestepped, causing it to strike the armored plate strapped around his shin. She took the marginal advantage and followed the momentum, spinning back around, her blade aimed high.

But Cahir was gone.

She sucked in a breath. Keeping her weapon raised above her head, her eyes darted from tree to tree, searching for a flicker of movement against the rough bark. Within the bark.

An arm took shape, unblending from the tree. Then a blade—shifting from the natural texture of the bark into cold, hard metal.

His arm lassoed her.

Esme bucked against him as her back connected with his torso. He formed a vise with his unyielding forearm and chest plate. Esme fought to take a breath against the building pressure. Her left arm was pinned at her side, but her sword arm was free. She grappled with her hold on it, struggling to keep it out of Cahir's reach.

The distraction was enough. She lifted her foot and stomped down hard on his instep.

With a grunt, Cahir loosened his grip. It was only a split second, but it was enough. Tucking her head, she rolled out of his reach. The moment her feet were under her, she ran for the center of the ring.

Anticipating Cahir's imminent pursuit, she spun around to parry. But her blade hissed through empty air.

Cahir hadn't moved. He stood watching from the grassy edge, the corner of his mouth twisting up into a wicked smirk.

Shit.

A rumble emerged from the ground, vibrating through the thick soles of her boots.

Feeling cracks spiderweb beneath her, Esme ran. As futile as it was, she broke to the right. Then left.

The cracks followed, biting at her heels, dirt sifting through the widening fissures.

"Cahir!" Tearlach shouted.

Esme knew he'd already siphoned the magic from her opponent, but it was too late.

The ground opened.

Esme's arms shot out, her sword sailing through a cloud of dust.

Her chest slammed into the jagged edge of a yawning abyss, forcing the air from her lungs. Her nails dug into the loose dirt as she clawed for a handhold. Her foot found purchase for only a second before that, too, crumbled away.

Hold on! Tearlach's booming voice thundered through her head. Pounding footfalls followed.

Her heartbeat hammered in her ears, drowning out the sounds from above. She was losing her grip. Her legs swung uselessly. But through the din, she felt a familiar sensation slithering toward her.

Just as her hold gave way, a thick root shot out, coiling instantly around her outstretched arm.

She fell only a foot before the vine jerked her to a stop. Pain streaked up her arm.

"She's fine," Cahir scoffed with far too much confidence.

Esme looked up as he peered over the edge. Powder-fine mica glittered in the rays of sunlight. She breathed in the smell of cool soil and damp clay, then spat the grit from her mouth.

"Get her out. Now!" Tearlach barked from somewhere beyond the edge of the giant pit. She didn't need to see his face to know he was giving Cahir a murderous look.

The root drew back, gliding soundlessly into the severed earth as it lifted her closer to the surface. Cahir reached down to grab her other hand, then hauled her up. The movement sent a cascade of pain through her as she became acutely aware of her many injuries.

"You okay?" he whispered as he set her gently on her feet.

Esme winced, rotating her shoulder. She surveyed the rest of her body, but felt only dull, throbbing pain.

"I'm okay," she croaked, wiping her face on the sleeve of her equally dirty linen shirt. "That was...something."

He gave her a cocky grin. When Cahir had first joined the royal guard, Esme had been told that his particular variant of earth magic tended toward the dramatic. But even hearing the unbelievable stories about him breaking the ground apart, she hadn't truly believed.

"Cahir," Tearlach growled. They both turned.

She'd been right about the look on Tearlach's face. It also appeared they'd drawn an audience.

"I'd better..." He angled his head toward Esme's overbearing personal guard. At Cahir's silent command, the ground stitched back together.

Esme allowed herself a few steadying breaths, then tentatively stretched her arms overhead. *Not too bad*, she decided. With a roll of her neck, she went in search of her discarded sword. It lay several feet away. Luckily, she'd had the soundness of mind to toss it, or it would've been nothing more than a lost relic, trapped inside the ground.

She brushed the dirt from her clothes, vaguely aware of Tearlach voicing his disapproval of Cahir's fighting methods, and knowing full well she'd be on the receiving end next.

Deciding not to wait, she found her guards and made for the palace.

———

"Oh my," Cadwyn murmured when Esme walked into the room, her eyes going wide at her charge's bedraggled appearance and the dirt she tracked in.

Esme swung her armor from her shoulder, but Cadwyn sprang forward, catching the items before they could hit the floor.

"Wait." She held up a hand, forbidding Esme from stepping anywhere near the plush, white carpet, then pulled over a chair.

Esme dropped down gracelessly to remove her boots. She flexed her bare feet and rubbed the tight muscles above her ankles. As soon as she rose, Cadwyn took her by the shoulders and aimed her toward the bathing chamber.

"I'm going. I'm going." Esme laughed. "No need to push."

Though Cadwyn had once been her lady-in-waiting—and Esme selfishly assumed she'd retain the title—Cadwyn had taken it upon herself to serve as her maid as well. And Esme knew full well how much more committed her friend's attentions could have been. It'd taken serious convincing before Cadwyn had agreed to occupy her old room, rather than sleeping beside Esme's bed each night. And while Cadwyn's presence was preferable to the nightmares that kept Esme from sleep most nights, she refused to add that burden to the many Cadwyn already carried.

Esme stepped down into the steamy, rose-scented water. Only it wasn't rose, she realized after soaking for several minutes. It was something floral and familiar, yet not. Slightly mossy, with the sweetness of a peach. It'd probably been grown in a hothouse at the hand of an artisan, blended with some exotic bloom she'd never heard of—not for its beauty, but for the unique oil it produced.

She breathed deeply and tried to enjoy the alluring aroma, but it only made her miss her garden in Debarrow all the more. Cadwyn's voice drifted in before her longing could turn to sadness, reminding her that she was to meet with Jaime later that afternoon.

Esme didn't need reminding. Meeting with Orianna's sister wasn't something she'd forget.

Chapter Two

ESME WAS GOING to wear a path in the floorboards if she didn't
stop pacing.

When Orianna's sister had first come calling, Esme had been wary
about facing a woman who might bear stark resemblance to a certain
high-priestess who'd attempted to kill her just one floor below. The
throne room remained a wreck of crumbled marble, fractured tiles, and
broken glass from their epic battle. She hadn't set foot in it since.

When Esme declined to meet with Jaime initially, the woman had
politely agreed to return to the palace at a later date. Esme could only
hope that the news hadn't been terribly urgent.

A rap at her door startled her from her thoughts. Cadwyn rose from
her seat and gave her a look. Esme nodded in understanding. Cadwyn had
made her instructions quite clear: *Remember every word she says.*

"I'll be right outside," Cadwyn reminded her.

"I know. Thank you."

A private meeting had been requested. Esme was under the
impression that Jaime was shy, and hoped her insistence of such was
due only to the woman's nerves and not the nature of the information
she held.

When Jaime entered the room, she bent into a low curtsy so quickly Esme only had time to notice the woman's hair—pale blond, nearly silver.

Esme clenched her hands at her sides and pulled a slow breath into her lungs. When the woman rose, Esme was relieved to find that hair color was where the resemblances between the sisters ended.

Esme led her to one of the low-backed sofas once introductions were made. "Please, do be seated," she insisted at the woman's hesitancy. "Can I offer you some tea?"

Jaime looked around like she was taking in the room, then brought her inundated gaze to the tea set. She nodded her head after a moment's consideration. "Yes, please. Thank you, Your Majesty." She took the proffered cup with unsteady hands.

Esme waited, giving her time to settle. Though an appointment with a commoner was sure to be vastly different from the council meeting she'd preside over in a matter of days, Esme felt the weight of new responsibility nonetheless. "So," she began slowly. "You wished to discuss something with me."

Jaime dipped her head forward, avoiding eye contact. "I apologize for arriving unannounced when I did, Your Majesty. It's just...I didn't think you'd agree to see me if I sent a letter, given who I am—who my sister was."

"I understand your concern for prejudice. Now, what is it you need to tell me?"

"It's..." Jaime ran the end of the ribbon belted around her waist through her fingers. "Well, I'm not sure it's anything, really, Your Majesty."

Esme was fairly certain no one had ever used her title so many times in so few minutes. She folded her hands in her lap, hoping the relaxed posture might help Jaime feel more at ease.

"I don't know anymore," the woman admitted, finally looking up from her restless hands. "It all happened so long ago, Your Majesty. It could be nothing. But then, it could be something. And I didn't want to keep quiet about it. Do you see?"

Esme nodded reassuringly, as though the person seated before her were a small child and not a woman many decades older than her. "Why don't you tell me what you know, and we'll decide together."

Jaime took a deep breath, as if summoning her courage. "It was many years ago, when we were just girls—Ori and me. The two of us were outside in the heather, running to reach the creek before twilight. That's when the fireflies come out, and we didn't want to miss them, Your Majesty," she explained. "There's something magical about spotting the first glow afore the others join in. But before we could reach the water's edge, Ori stopped. I watched her turn slowly in place, like she was looking for something. When I came up beside her, she asked if I'd heard it too. 'Heard what?' I asked her. 'The voice,' she told me. I asked her whose voice she'd heard and looked into the darkening trees, searching for the source. Then she turned to me with a disoriented look in her eyes and told me it was nothing, that it must've been the wind."

Jaime paused, leveling Esme with a confiding look. "Before that moment, Your Majesty, I'd never known my sister to lie. But there was something she wasn't telling me. I was sure of it. And let me tell you something else, Your Majesty, there wasn't a lick of wind that day in the field."

"I see." Esme nodded, though she didn't see. Not exactly. Orianna had heard something out in a field of heather. Was that what Jaime had come to tell her?

"A few days later, I awoke to Ori's voice. She was out of bed, speaking in hushed tones. I rolled to my side and saw her standing in the corner talking to...well, nothing. There was nothing there—nothing but darkness."

"You didn't see anyone else in the room."

"Just the darkness, Your Majesty. A...murky kind of darkness."

"What do you mean?"

"The lights from the night sky always illuminated our room, giving it a soft, green glow. Gray outlines of the furniture and the like, Your Majesty. But whatever—or whoever—Ori was talking to that night, the darkness swallowed even the shadows."

"What was your sister saying?"

"I couldn't hear anything more than whispers, Your Majesty. When she finished speaking, I closed my eyes and pretended to be asleep. After she crawled back under the covers, I glanced over at her. She was staring up at the ceiling, wide eyed with a strange smile on her face."

"Did it ever happen again?"

"That was the only time in the night, at least that I witnessed, Your Majesty. But then, years later, when her magic began to manifest, I found her out near the stream. Ori had water magic, you see, and she was directing the water when I came upon her. She didn't notice me. But then, all of a sudden, the water fell back into the stream, and her arms hung limply at her sides. I hid behind a tree, waiting to see what she'd do. Her gaze turned up slightly. Not toward the sky, more like she was looking up at someone taller than her—someone I couldn't see. That time, I heard what she said."

"What did she say?"

Jaime seemed to sort through her memories as she twisted the ends of the ribbon around her fingers. She lifted her gaze to Esme a moment later. "She said, 'I'm here. Yes, I understand. It will be my honor to serve you, Master.'" Jaime nodded resolutely. "Those were her words, Your Majesty."

Esme waited for her to continue, but Jaime's raised brow implied she was expecting a reaction. "You didn't hear any other voice? Anyone who might have been speaking to her?"

"No, Your Majesty," she assured, then hurried on with the story. "But I approached her on her way back. I wanted to know what it was about. She had this strange air about her. Almost like she was floating. And her eyes, they were different. Not deep blue as they'd always been, but almost... violet. When I asked about what I'd seen at the stream, she turned and looked down at me—though I wasn't but an inch shorter than her—and told me she'd been chosen by the gods, that she'd been called to serve."

Esme furrowed her brow, trying to make sense of the peculiar events, then nodded for Jaime to continue.

"I believed her, Your Majesty. I had no reason not to. I'd never received a call to become a high-priestess. Perhaps that's how it works; I'm not familiar with their ways. Though it did seem odd that she'd address the person doing the calling—or one of the gods, rather—as Master. I can't say I've ever heard a high-priestess use that term."

"Nor I," Esme agreed.

"Still, I dismissed it. I wanted to believe her, and our parents were so proud that she'd been called to join the Order. But something changed in her that day by the stream. You see, Your Majesty, Ori was always a caring, attentive, protective sibling"—Esme struggled to keep her expression neutral at that revelation—"but after that day, she barely looked at me. Even when she did, it was like she couldn't see me. She just...looked through me.

"I thought that perhaps she was experiencing some kind of transformation as she acclimated to her new power. I hadn't gone through it myself at the time, Your Majesty, but now I know how temperamental and sometimes frightening it can be to come into one's magic. A few weeks later, she left to join the Order in Imara. I hoped that being around others like her would help her settle into her true purpose. She never came home after that. We'd receive letters now and then, but I never saw her. And then, after the king and queen..." Jaime met Esme's eyes, then dropped her gaze, leaving Esme to wonder just how much people knew about the things Orianna had done.

Jaime's fingers moved on to fidgeting with the folds of her skirt. "The stories I heard of Ori's reign...the things she did, the executions...Like I said, Your Majesty, that wasn't the Ori I knew, the one I grew up with."

Esme watched her for a moment. Anger and confusion warred within her. Anything relating to Orianna set her on edge. She silenced the tremor that ran through her, and carefully picked up her cup of tea.

Could high-priestesses hear the gods? Perhaps that was how one was called to join the Order. Esme couldn't know for certain. Even if she wished to find out, there were no high-priestesses alive to question— Orianna had seen to that before she'd stolen the crown.

Esme glanced down at her cup. The cream had separated from the cold black tea. She set it back on the saucer and looked over at Jaime. "Thank you for the information," she managed in a calm, steady voice.

Jaime nodded in earnest. A look of profound relief spread across her face. She was likely glad to be free of the knowledge.

"Should you think of anything else—no matter how small—please keep me informed."

"Of course, Your Majesty."

Esme showed Jaime out, then told Cadwyn she needed a moment before closing the doors softly behind her.

Standing in the center of the room, she stared into the distance for a long moment. She shook her head, trying to keep herself there, in the room, away from the memories Orianna occupied. She tried to rub away the phantom sensations at her temples, but the feel of hooks digging into her skull—into her mind—wouldn't cease. Orianna had possessed a vast arsenal of magic—more than any Fae should possess. But most of those gifts had been absorbed from others, thieved through the act of killing.

And yet, Jaime believed Orianna to be kind and caring. Protective even. Esme couldn't reconcile that image with the woman who'd brought so much death and destruction to her kingdom. Had Orianna's call to join the Order changed her, corrupted her in some way? Maybe she'd been too weak to handle such immense responsibility.

Or perhaps too powerful.

Chapter Three

"I'M SURPRISED YOU'RE not planning to sew all my clothes yourself," Esme teased Cadwyn as she emerged from her dressing room wearing only a silk shift. She would've preferred to wear her loose linen shirts, tunics, and soft woolen leggings, but had to concur that a queen ought to have a few finer ensembles. Aside from the female guards, every woman in the palace wore a dress. Even Cadwyn. Esme supposed she should too.

"You're certain she can be trusted?"

With a huff, Cadwyn shoved the heavy chaise against the wall. "Do you not remember Leenan?"

"Should I?"

"She designed gowns for your mother."

Esme didn't remember Leenan. The palace had been disorderly, to say the least, after she'd claimed her throne. She was only beginning to reacquaint herself with the staff from her parents' reign. Some had endured Orianna; others had returned after she'd been deposed. Learning the name of every maid, cook, dishwasher, footman, stablehand, laundress, groundskeeper, and page had subsequently fallen through the cracks.

So, no, Esme did not recall a dressmaker from the city named Leenan.

"That's not the only reason I summoned her," Cadwyn added. "She'll be valuable to us in more ways than clothing design."

"Ah." Esme nodded. Cadwyn already had numerous eyes and ears within the palace. Leenan, it seemed, would provide the city beyond.

Cadwyn moved to the door, then threw a confident smirk back at Esme, her long scarlet braid whipping over her shoulder with the motion. "Because I most certainly *can* sew your gowns myself."

Esme chuckled as the doors swung open.

A footman stepped in, then immediately averted his gaze. His cheeks blushed a bright shade of pink at seeing his queen in so little clothing.

"May I present Her Majesty, Queen Esme of Tremaene."

Esme stood tall, trying to add a few inches to her height—and her dignity—as a woman entered and bent one knee behind the other.

"Leenan." Cadwyn took the woman's hands as she rose, leading her into the room.

Leenan gestured for two others to join, and began directing them before Esme could offer a greeting.

Bolts of fabric, a small wooden case, and a stool were brought to the center of the space Cadwyn had cleared. The stool, Esme realized as one of the attendants opened the folded top, was a low platform.

"Your Majesty, if you would."

Esme stepped up, bringing herself eye level with the dressmaker— and not even that with Cadwyn.

The other two women remained silent as they arranged their mistress's items. Leenan was quick as she wound measuring ribbons around Esme's body, commenting on every angle and curve as she went.

Esme pursed her lips, and was more than grateful when Cadwyn engaged the forthright seamstress to divert her attention somewhat.

Muslin bodices were pulled across Esme's chest, skirts swathed around her waist and pinned with swift, dexterous hands. Fabrics of all colors were strewn across the chaise, then held up one by one against Esme's cheek and the bare skin of her arms. She was asked to turn several times, the swatches angled this way and that, taking in the play of light across the weave.

She liked the purple velvet—the color of warm raspberry compote. *Plum*, Leenan had called it. Plum it most certainly was not, though Esme kept that thought to herself. Best not to challenge the woman holding the pins.

"The indigo brocade will suit her well." Leenan raised an eyebrow at Esme's golden hair. "But only in evening light," she amended, then blatantly scrutinized Esme's features as though she were nothing more than a seamstress form. "Those dark eyes...so unusual. We might need to try—"

"The indigo is lovely," Cadwyn agreed. "Though I think the emerald would better complement the amber highlights in Her Majesty's eyes. Perhaps in a charmeuse?"

A fold of dark green silk was quickly brought forth.

"Very fitting." Leenan nodded. "Now for day dresses, I was thinking..." She snapped her fingers. "Bring me that bit of raw silk in gray stone and the lavender organza. And whatever we have in coral and wild rose."

The less timid of the attendants came forward, head bowed, offering the requested fabrics.

"A crepe might work as well. Bring me the aqua or turquoise. Either one." Leenan shooed the woman. "And I wonder"—she brought her hand to her chin, circling Esme—"would Her Majesty be open to wearing something a bit brighter, perhaps a citron? For morning, of course."

Esme caught Cadwyn's eye before she could answer for her. Cadwyn hid a smile. Or perhaps a laugh.

Surveying the bolts of fabric, Esme spotted one she liked. Facing Leenan, she replied, "No. I don't believe *Her Majesty* would be open to citron. I would, however, like to see something in the ruby." She gestured to the red fabric. To Esme it was the color of a ruby gemstone, though she wouldn't be surprised to find that the name of the color was something obscure, like beet juice or crimson sunbird.

"Yes, Your Majesty. Of course. That color will look divine." Leenan curtsied, and fetched the intended swatch herself.

———

Esme pulled on a soft, loose-fitting shirt. Slowly. She finally felt warm and clean, but her skin was overly sensitive from the afternoon of bony fingers poking at her, and the slide of cold pins against her flesh. She'd scrubbed every inch of herself, then soaked in the bath for an hour trying to rid the unpleasant sensations. The wide-legged pants she'd selected barely grazed her skin as she settled them high on her waist. If only she could wear such comforts all the time.

She stepped back into her room, letting the steamy air of the bathing chamber escape. The wall sconces had been lit for evening, and something on her bed caught the flickering light.

Garments—a fitted shirt and matching pants with…Were those copper threads glittering throughout?

No, not thread, but a fine, delicate chainmail that had been woven into the fabric.

Esme knew instantly that it wasn't something Leenan or her seamstresses had fashioned. Even before she opened the note tented beside the shirt, she knew who'd left them.

Leave it to her personal guard to gift her something that would further protect her. Given the chance, she knew Tearlach would prefer to keep her tethered to him at all times.

You are to wear these anytime you step foot in the ring, the note demanded. *If you do not, I'll know.* Esme almost laughed at how Tearlach could convey such an ominous tone in so few words. She wasn't sure *how* he'd know if she forwent wearing the garments, but she didn't doubt he somehow would.

And she could tell, gazing down at them, that they'd fit perfectly. When her fingers touched the fabric, she hummed at the feel. She'd expected something stiff or abrasive, but even with the fine mesh, the garments were smooth and silky.

Esme glanced around the room, noting that her dinner tray had been cleared. Her maids wouldn't be coming back that night. Tearlach had left the garments knowing only she would see them.

Quickly, she disrobed and hopped onto the bed to pull on the pants. The fabric flexed and gave as she shimmied it over her knees and up the curves of her thighs. They molded to her legs like a second skin.

She stood and cinched the laces up the sides of her hips. The top fit just as well, hugging her modest curves, and stretching down the length of her arms, looping over each of her middle fingers to protect the tops of her hands.

She skimmed her palms down her sides, marveling at the fit. Feeling something warm against her skin, she unlaced the right side of the pants and folded over the waistband to find a small octagon of polished metal with a *T* stamped into its center—lest she forget who'd given the garments to her. Her fingers grazed the faint imprint of his initial outlined on her skin. She stared at it for a long moment, watching it fade into soft pink flesh.

A knock startled her, and she yanked the fabric back into place.

"Just a moment," she called, hurrying into the privacy of her dressing room.

Carefully, Esme undressed, folding the garments like they were precious and delicate, as if they weren't designed to stop the edge of a blade from slicing through her. She cleared a space for them in a drawer, then looked at the note that had accompanied the gift. She wasn't sure why, but she had an urge to keep it. To hide it.

After debating her reasons for far longer than was reasonable, she tucked it into the back of her dressing table drawer, then ran into the other room without a lick of clothing. Gathering her discarded clothes, she threw them on as she made for the door.

"Killian," she greeted breathlessly.

He wet his lower lip before answering with a smile. "Did I catch you at a bad time?"

"No, of course not. Come in. I was just...finding something to put on."

Killian swept an appreciative gaze over her. "I see."

The way his voice deepened—the way those two words seemed to hold countless unspoken meanings—reminded Esme that they hadn't seen each other for days. With her new obligations, and Killian's preference for night shifts as a royal guard, they hadn't found time to be alone together. Her heart sped up, and her skin prickled with awareness at his renewed proximity to her.

"Are you coming in, then?"

"Thought you'd never ask." He swept in, producing a pair of swords from behind his back.

"What—" Esme laughed as Killian set about moving the furniture from the center of the room.

Once he was satisfied, he tied back his thick blond hair and took up a starting position.

Esme mirrored him. A smile tugged at the corners of her mouth. She felt a thrum of pleasure run through her. When she'd first met Killian, she'd immediately marked him as the carefree, flirtatious member of their group. But as her sword training with him had commenced, she'd quickly discovered the kind, compassionate man beneath the coquettish facade.

Yet she couldn't deny the effect those knee-weakening smiles had on her.

He flashed one such smile as he held his sword at the ready. Right before he attacked.

Esme pivoted away and riposted. They moved across the room, attacking and parrying. It came easily to her, either from endless hours of training or because she'd learned to anticipate Killian's moves.

"This is serious, Esme." He cleared the playful expression from his face. But he could never hide the look in his cerulean eyes. She could read everything in those eyes.

"Right." Esme attempted to do the same, biting her lower lip.

His eyes darted briefly to her mouth before he lunged.

Esme blocked with a turn, then countered.

He caught her blade and grabbed her wrist, locking them together. "What if we made this a touch more interesting?"

"Am I boring you already?"

"Never, Your Majesty."

She laughed at the title. Killian was the last person who should be formal with her.

He released her blade and struck again. She blocked the attack, retreated, then thrust her sword low.

"I was thinking of a wager," he continued, pivoting easily from the point of her blade.

"I hardly see how that's fair." Her breath was coming faster. "I've never once bested you in a duel." She retreated past the bed as he advanced.

"You're not up to the challenge?"

Esme feinted an attack aimed high, then dipped when Killian moved to block, angling up to strike from below. Killian chuckled as he caught her sword with ease. He'd taught her that move, after all.

With her next retreat, Esme rounded the table, giving herself a moment to slow her thundering heart. Though it wasn't just from sparring. "And what would the terms of this wager be?"

"If I win..." He pinned her with a heated stare, then tossed his sword, spiraling it into the air before catching it. Without taking his eyes off her. "I get the pleasure of your company for a walk around the lake."

"Such a gentleman," she joked, conjuring images of what they'd done out on the balcony late one night. At the same time, her heart swelled at Killian's endeavor not to rush anything. "And if I win?"

"Well…" He seemed to consider her question as he effortlessly twirled the blade at his side. "What is it the lady wants?"

Esme skirted the table, coming to stand before him. Taking a deep inhale in an effort to keep her cheeks from blushing, she replied, "If the lady wins, then she deserves a kiss." Esme backed up a step and took a starting stance, raising her blade.

Killian yielded a step and mirrored her posture. "A kiss?"

They sparred across the room, their gazes clashing. Esme didn't register her position until Killian was one pace away from trapping her in the corner.

"That seems like an honorable wager." He slid the edge of his blade slowly up hers, then whipped it around to catch the other side. He pushed her sword arm out, leaving her body exposed.

When he took a step closer, Esme ducked under their crossed weapons.

Spinning around to face him, she said, "I'm not sure what's honorable about it. I've no chance of besting you."

"Oh, no?"

Esme only managed to put one more pace between them before she felt the bed press against the backs of her legs.

"Always be aware of your surroundings," Killian reminded with a playfully reproving shake of his head.

One more step and she'd be at his mercy. "I always am." Her voice lowered to a whisper.

With a clank, Killian dropped his blade to the floor. "You win."

"Cheat," she murmured just before his lips met hers.

Chapter Four

WATER SURROUNDED ESME'S body, twisting her until she couldn't make up from down. Panic clenched her insides as she remembered the dark depths of the underground lake that had almost taken her life.

She caught a glimpse of light in the distance—taunting her through the cold, gray ripples—but lost it as another wave yanked her away.

Spreading her arms wide, she pushed through the water until she faced the shrinking light again.

Her lungs burned. She struggled not to take a breath as she swam toward the surface.

But her will finally ceded, and her body overruled her mind.

She sucked in a lungful of water.

Her body seized. The light faded.

Then her back slammed against solid ground, forcing the water from her lungs. She rolled to her side in a fit of coughing, until she finally managed a desperate breath.

After three slippery attempts on the slick marble floor, she got to her knees. And met Orianna's violet eyes.

Beyond, Esme could see the throne room, intact—light filtering in from the glass dome above.

And they were alone.

She risked a glance over her shoulder to where her companions should have been kneeling—bound by Orianna's invisible restraints—but saw only the tall pillars that ringed the room. Orianna's guards were absent as well.

Esme swallowed the dread that rose in her raw throat, then faced her enemy again.

Her senses filled with the charged energy of a storm. The feel of pelting rain on her skin. The smell of wet earth in her nose. The chill of harsh wind at her back.

But the storm failed to converge.

She called on it again, expecting the familiar sensation of magic working through her body, into her fingertips, pressing against her skin before she released the torrent force upon her foe.

Nothing. It was beyond her reach.

She tried to summon invisible vines as she'd once done in that room. But they felt trapped beneath her feet.

Her hand twitched at her side, only the sheath that held her dagger was empty. She had no weapons.

Orianna grabbed her. Too fast for Esme to react. The woman's grip tightened around her throat.

Esme clawed at her wrist, trying to pry it off. A scream caught in her throat as her feet left the ground.

Orianna's icy cold hand squeezed, digging sharpened nails into Esme's neck, crushing her windpipe.

Wild purple eyes stared at her, filling her field of vision before everything went dark.

She was trapped, her body bound by something. Esme struggled to loose an arm just as a hand gripped her shoulder.

She jerked away, but when her face pressed into the soft surface of a pillow, clarity emerged. She peered over her shoulder and saw Tearlach leaning over the bed, reaching for her again.

"A dream?" she managed through her foggy mind.

He nodded as if assuring himself as well, then pulled away. A sword hung at his side. He was still dressed for the day.

Esme unwound from the sheet she'd managed to bind herself with, then rolled over to see the open door beside her bed—the secret passageway between her room and her personal guard's. The sound of it banging open must have wrenched her from the dream.

Coming to sit, she pulled the sheet higher, tucking it under her arms to cover the thin material of her nightdress. She glanced at the silk coverlet folded at the foot of the bed and thought about reaching for it, but paused when she saw Tearlach run his hands through his raven hair.

His chest was heaving, as though he'd been prepared to run into battle. Even in the dim light of the room, she could see his pulse pounding at his throat. His gaze raked over her, like he needed to convince himself that she hadn't been hurt. He turned away without meeting her eyes.

There was no physical danger. Volatile magic no longer bit at the heels of her tempestuous dreams. But when a dream felt as real as that one had, her unconscious fears flowed unchecked through the connection she shared with Tearlach—indiscernible from a physical threat. Much as she disliked that aspect of the Lifeblood Oath that bound them together, Esme was grateful he'd felt her distress and pulled her from the dream.

Not all thoughts and emotions lived so near the surface. Some dwelled deeper, in hidden places. With practice and concentration, she'd been able to keep most of her private thoughts concealed, just as Tearlach did.

Esme had never heard a single word, nor felt a flicker of emotion from Tearlach, that wasn't intentionally projected. He likely had an impenetrable stone wall protecting every inch of his innermost thoughts—wide as a redwood trunk and taller than the Clavlin Ridge. She imagined a deep ravine cut around it, teeming with ferocious monsters to keep even the most tenacious of intruders out, and the stealthiest of emotions trapped inside.

His posture was the only indication of the thoughts running through his mind. Tearlach stood rigid, his powerful body silhouetted against the rippling lights of the night sky filtering through the sheer, amethyst curtains. His fists were clenched at his sides. And even as he exhaled a long-held breath, the tension in his shoulders remained.

"Tearlach?" Esme's voice seemed to call him away from the threats his mind perceived. He turned and locked eyes with her. "It was only a dream. I'm safe."

"I know." His voice was raw and angry. "I know," he said again with a hint of guilt. He moved closer, coming to sit on the edge of the bed.

"Tearlach, I'm okay. She can't hurt me anymore." The words were as much for her as they were for him. Tearlach blamed himself for Esme facing Orianna alone. She knew he felt like he'd broken his vow, failed to protect her. And it didn't matter what she said about the subject, he'd continue to hold himself responsible.

And seeing him so unsettled made her wonder if a legendary warrior who'd lived through the horrors of the Dark War could feel as powerless as she often did.

He stood and gripped one of the bedposts. Again, his eyes traveled over her sheet-covered form. When their eyes met, he nodded once and moved toward the concealed passageway.

Esme slid back under the covers, but couldn't bring herself to shut her eyes.

"Wait." Her voice broke, and Tearlach was at her side in an instant.

She pulled herself up. "Will you stay?" She could feel her cheeks flush, but hoped Tearlach wouldn't notice in the hazy, purple light. She wasn't sure why she felt nervous for asking such a thing; they'd slept in close proximity since the night she'd been forced to flee the mortal realm.

And while she'd never admit it to her stubborn—and often infuriating—bound protector, she felt safer in Tearlach's presence.

Without a word, he carried over one of the high-backed chairs that circled the dining table.

Esme didn't look at him, just rolled onto her side, curling her knees to her chest. Her heartbeat returned to a steady rhythm. But even as exhausted as she was, when her eyes closed, she found herself back in the throne room staring into Orianna's crazed, violet eyes.

Maybe if she told Tearlach about the dream—if she confessed what it felt like to be trapped under the weight of crushing waves, to have her mind scratched by invisible claws—she might be able to cast aside the lingering nightmare.

After a moment, she turned to him. Tearlach stared back. His face was a mask of unreadability, but she knew his mind was filtering through the attacks of the past several months, wondering which one she'd been forced to relive.

Before she could tell him anything, Tearlach spoke. "Sleep, Esme. You're safe now."

And with her next breath, the familiar blanket of Tearlach's sleep magic settled over her.

Chapter Five

ESME SURVEYED THE information strewn across the table and groaned inwardly. Cadwyn and Sully had spent nine years making plans for Esme's eventual return to Tremaene, but it was apparent that their plans hadn't stopped at her claiming the throne. They were prepared to do everything in their power to ensure Esme *kept* her new title.

"Now, there are two vacancies that need to be filled," Sully told her. "You'll take care of the first one tomorrow."

"Vacancies? What do you mean? I thought everyone in the council made it safely into hiding after Orianna took over."

"They did. But the lordship of the Tamslo Mountains was already vacant for a number of years."

"My father never named another?"

"He didn't, and I can't say I know for certain why. There were candidates vetted, but it's possible he wanted to keep the voting members of the council at an even split."

Esme nodded, wanting to unravel that bit of information, but knowing they had more pressing matters to cover.

"And the other vacancy?"

"Minister of Defense," Cadwyn offered.

Esme scrunched her brow, thinking back on the person who'd held the position when she was a child. A general, but she couldn't remember his name.

"General Dwyer took to the Isloran coast instead of the mountains," Sully explained. "He was…executed a few years ago. It appeared as though he'd been working with someone inside the city to relay information. It's likely there were other factions, in addition to the Northern Rebels, that were planning to overthrow Orianna."

It made sense that others had been working to free their kingdom from the tyrannical ruler. She supposed the gods had favored her rightful claim to the throne. If only they hadn't…

"I need to name a new Minister of Defense?" She banished the traitorous thought.

"That's right." Sully nodded, but said nothing more.

Esme's mouth curled into a smile. "And I suppose you know just the person." She glanced at Cadwyn, who had a knowing glint in her bright green eyes. Sully would be far more levelheaded than any of the war-hungry generals she'd met in the north. And having Sully with her in the council chamber gave Esme a profound sense of confidence. She could think of no better ally. Turning to Sully, she asked, "Captain Sullivan, would you accept the role of serving as Tremaene's Minister of Defense?"

He bowed his head. "It would be my distinct honor, Your Majesty."

"Good." Cadwyn clasped her hands together, moving them along. "You'll name him tomorrow, first thing, putting any questions about the position to rest." The two of them went on to explain the specific concerns that each of the four governed territories would report on. Every one of the councilors would have far more experience than her, not just in governing territories or advising the crown in matters of trade or finances, but in basic life experience. Esme was essentially a child compared to them, at not even her twenty-fifth year. Some of the members of the royal council were likely centuries old, some older even than Sully. Therefore, until Esme could establish her own objectives for her reign, she was advised to focus instead on the goals and motivations of each member.

Quelling the overwhelming sense that she might not make it out of the meeting alive, Cadwyn assured her that while a wealth of information would be presented—information that shouldn't be of any surprise to her—it wasn't likely she'd need to rule on any specific requests. The members, like her, would use the meeting to uncover their new queen's intentions. And because her leadership abilities would no doubt be of top concern for most, Esme planned to follow Sully's instructions precisely.

She stared at the stack of papers in front of Cadwyn. They'd barely made a dent, and it was already midday.

"Should I bring up the suspected unordained priestesses?" Recalling Jaime's account, she pondered whether the women in the north had been called to serve in the same manner Orianna had.

"Not until we have more sufficient knowledge of their band," Sully advised.

"Best not to give false hope until we know for sure." Cadwyn seconded his opinion.

"But isn't the council concerned with what will happen now that the last known high-priestess is dead?"

"Right now, they want to make sure their own interests are safe."

Esme was certainly worried. Without priestesses to summon the elements, Tremaene's land would continue to die. Only the deepest rivers still flowed with water, and only because they ran through the largest cities, where magic still lingered near the temples. But the rest of Tremaene was barren, and Esme feared it wouldn't take long for it to spread across the entire kingdom.

"Though it won't be mentioned in this initial meeting," Cadwyn amended, "it will likely be brought up at some point."

Likely? Esme shoved her disbelief aside, returning to Sully's comment. "You said *more* knowledge. Does that mean their existence is more than suspicion?"

"I've asked Myles to look into the situation as discreetly as possible."

"Myles?"

"He's Cahir's partner. You never met him in Altan?" Cadwyn asked.

She hadn't. Aside from training, sleeping, and eating, she hadn't done much else in the warrior camp.

"He knows more about the Tamslo Mountains than anyone," Sully offered. "Arranged trade for food and supplies to supplement what we couldn't produce in the valley. If there are women summoning raw magic, he's our best chance at locating them."

Esme nodded, feeling somewhat hopeful.

"And what about receiving citizens?" The question had been on her mind since the one and only day she'd stepped outside the gates of the palace with her mother's crown adorning her head. Her heart had been pounding so ferociously inside her chest, it had nearly drowned out the sound of the cheering crowd.

And all she'd done was wave to the people who'd gathered to see her—their long-lost princess returned.

"Not yet." Cadwyn's voice was soothing.

Esme released the breath she was holding and looked down at her lap. "But my parents did."

"They did, though not often. A few times a year, perhaps. You needn't worry about that for some time."

"Right. Okay." *Not yet.*

The rest of the day was spent apprising Esme about the state of Tremaene, the organization of the kingdom and each region, what had happened in her absence. They discussed each of the territories at length, the varying governing styles of each lady and lord, and what each region contributed to the kingdom as a whole.

There'd be much to learn in her new role.

I can do it, Esme tried to convince herself, thinking back on her time in Periwen, on everything she'd done to survive in that faraway place. She'd made her way there. Learned to grow food. Tended an orchard. Periwen had forced her to become a different person. It'd offered a challenging, yet simple life she greatly preferred.

Never had she envisioned herself a queen. Even as a young girl, she'd hoped her parents would beget another, more suitable, heir to rule Tremaene long before they chose to fade into the hereafter.

But things hadn't worked out that way.

And there was no other heir.

Chapter Six

ESME HEARD CADWYN let herself into the other room. Her lady-in-waiting knew well that left alone Esme would choose something more suitable to gardening than presiding over a royal council.

"Oh! Perfect timing!" Cadwyn exclaimed as Esme stepped out into the main room. "I was just about to ring for you."

One of her lady's maids strode past with a breakfast tray. The other two stood waiting, their outstretched arms holding finished dresses. Leenan might not have been pleasant to work with, but Esme had to admit that the woman worked quickly.

Cadwyn excitedly ushered them into the adjoining room. The flurry of movement had Esme dodging out of their path. She took a seat in front of a neatly set breakfast and cracked the top of a soft-boiled egg.

"Thank you, Marta," she said as the final dish was placed in front of her.

"Of course, Your Majesty."

She winced. "Perhaps...Could you call me Esme?"

"Your Majesty?" Marta questioned, though it seemed more of a refusal.

Esme sighed. "Have you been here…all this time?"

Marta betrayed nothing, keeping her face impassive. She was either a very quick study, or she'd been employed at the palace before even her mother had arrived.

"I have never left my post" was all she said. It was answer enough. The things she must have seen…

But could Esme trust someone who'd served under Orianna?

Her face must have revealed her tentativeness, for the woman added, "I'm grateful that our *true* queen has returned." The dip of her chin was nearly imperceptible, but Esme noticed it.

"Thank you. And thank you for your continued service all these years."

"Of course, Your Majesty."

"Milady," Esme asserted.

Marta regarded her before repeating, "Milady."

With one task accomplished, Esme turned to her breakfast. She only hoped Marta would inform Brighid and Griselda. The *Your Majesty*'s were getting rather maddening.

Esme grabbed a leftover piece of crusty bread and stepped out onto the balcony. Her dormant nerves were beginning to wake, causing her earlier meal to churn in her stomach. She hoped the plain bread would help.

Between bites, she attempted slow, deep breaths—which ended up being rather shallow due to the constriction of her bodice. A wave of nausea rolled through her, and she glanced down at the silky purple fabric that pooled at her bare feet. It wouldn't matter one bit how queenly she looked if her gown was covered in vomit. She closed her eyes and tried to think of something else.

The simple coronet she wore was new. And a little too tight. Her hair fell in loose curls down her shoulders, with the points of her ears peeking out beside the crown. Three silver strands hung from her neck. She toyed with the crystal at the end of the longest chain, running the bead back and forth. After a few minutes, her racing heart slowed to a gentle canter.

Looking skyward, she pondered whether the gods were watching. Were they responsible for her fate, for everything? Had it all been planned from the beginning? Did she have any control over her future?

Perhaps they didn't care at all.

The waning sliver of Neve caught her eye, holding on in the morning sky as if to show Esme her support. It seemed one of the moons believed in her, even if the gods didn't.

She crumbled the bread she couldn't stomach, sprinkling it along the balustrade for the tufted titmouse who'd been eying the treat.

All nine members of her royal guard waited at the top of the stairs. Armel, Hazel, and Killian stood shoulder to shoulder in the row closest to her.

Esme mentally traced the lines of their uniforms. It was the first she'd seen them—though they were similar to those worn by the palace guards. Thin strips of interwoven gold and copper covered their torsos. Copper shoulder plates wrapped down their upper arms, with fine silver chainmail beneath. But where the gold gauntlets, leg plates, and polished black boots completed the uniforms for the other sentinels, the royal guards also donned long, pleated capes made of smooth gold fabric to distinguish their rank.

Sully stood at the end nearest the stairs, looking every bit the captain he was.

She turned as Tearlach approached. He didn't wear the elaborate armor of the guards, opting for less metal and more flexibility. Esme had insisted he have a bit of gold, only so he'd look less like a mercenary and more like her chosen protector. He'd obliged, though begrudgingly. So, in addition to the brown and black close-fitting material that covered his body, he also wore a simplified design of the gold and copper chest plate—though his thick bandolier covered most of it. She hadn't seen it on him, having delivered it to his room via footman the previous week, along with a note: *Wear this, and always think of me when you do.*

He'd probably taken one look at it, scowled, then tossed it in the bin.

She'd meant it as a joke, knowing full well he'd only agreed to wear any sort of uniform because she'd insisted. As his queen.

Thinking of the note he'd given her the other night, Esme felt a flush of foolishness for having kept the small piece of paper at the back of her dressing table drawer. Where no one would find it.

She stole another glance at Tearlach, taking in the entirety of his appearance. The chest plate looked rather fetching on him—made him look dignified, noble almost. So different from the metalsmith she'd first encountered on that back road in Debarrow. Or the warrior who'd growled orders at her in Altan.

Sully politely cleared his throat.

Esme dropped her gaze. How long had she been staring? She smoothed her hands down the front of her gown, then reached up to adjust her crown—which Cadwyn had made sure wouldn't budge even if the palace came tumbling down around her.

When she felt somewhat composed, she nodded to Sully. Tearlach moved to take his place beside her. Then, with her entire retinue, she descended the grand staircase.

The thudding of their heavy boots on the marble steps created a calming rhythm. Esme's velvet slippers gave no sound, and for a moment, she felt invisible in their midst. But the protective wall they formed was only for show. The meeting didn't pose any real danger—at least not physically.

Sully dismissed the palace guards standing sentry outside the council chamber, then turned to face her, allowing her a moment to prepare herself before she entered. Her eyes focused on the narrow seam between the intimidating doors. A moment passed, then Sully nodded for two of her own guards to open the doors.

He stepped through. Then Tearlach. When they moved to either side, Esme entered. She stopped just past the threshold. The members of her royal council stood from their respective spots around the large circular table as Esme's eyes landed on the empty chair at the far end.

Chapter Seven

THE ROOM WAS much like she remembered, though it might have simply been restored to its former state. Dozens of white flames lit the already sun-bright room, dancing in shallow silver dishes that hung from the ceiling.

Her gaze snagged on the doors along the adjacent wall—the ones that led to a spacious room with a warm hearth and a comfortable chair that was just the right size for a small child to curl up on. A room with an imposing mahogany desk. She was glad the doors were closed.

Esme steadied herself and lifted her chin an inch higher—as though she might tower over a room full of people far taller than her. She caught Sully's eye, then stepped past him, following the curved wall of windows, and breathing in the sweet scent of lemon blossoms.

Manicured citrus trees stood in tall, slender obsidian pots. Beyond the chamber stretched a terrace with a jasmine-covered wall. The tiny white flowers hadn't mattered much before, but as Esme continued toward the head of the table, she could almost smell the cloying scent that reminded her of Orianna.

Tearlach's steady voice filled her mind. *Stay here, Esme. You're safe here.*

She redirected her attention to the orange and lime blossoms as she passed the last of the potted trees, and focused on the feel of the satin skirts whispering against her legs.

After glancing at each of the council members, she took her seat. The others followed.

Her folio had been placed in front of her, though she hoped she wouldn't need to consult it.

When the heavy doors were pulled shut, Sully and Tearlach circled the room to take up positions on either side of her.

Allowing herself a more careful inspection of the people at the table, Esme noticed a man who looked rather familiar. Not the kind of familiarity that came from recognizing a face from childhood, but a resemblance rather. The man had a broad chest with long dark hair tied back at the base of his skull. If he'd been a few inches taller, with dark eyes instead of pale blue ones, she might have mistaken the man for Tearlach's brother. Thus, she knew exactly who he was. Lord Torin, Tearlach's father. Though "father" no longer described the man's relationship to her personal guard. Tearlach had been estranged from his family since his youth.

"Thank you all for attending." She began the meeting as she'd rehearsed the day before. "I know many of you have been far from home for quite some time. It is my hope that we will quickly reach a consensus about the new direction of Tremaene so that each of you may return home." The members nodded their agreement.

"Your Majesty?"

Esme turned to the man at her left. She had a vague recollection of Lord Lennox. His long auburn hair and equally lengthy beard were each bound by silver chains that ended in small faceted beads. He was well muscled, though not as tall as some of the others. Lord Lennox of Belfay had been a member of the council longer than anyone. Furthermore, he'd assisted Sully throughout Orianna's occupation.

"If I might reacquaint you with your council before we proceed."

"Please." She motioned for him to continue.

As each lady, lord, and minister was introduced, Esme repeated their names silently. Cadwyn had given her portraits to help her associate names and visages. Seeing them in person, Esme noted hair lengths and styles, jewelry and other adornments. She'd gone many years in the mortal realm without learning more than a few necessary names. But in Tremaene, with an entire kingdom under her guardianship, she was determined to familiarize herself with as many people as her mind would allow.

"Before we begin official business," Lord Torin interrupted, "might we clear the room of all servants?"

Esme scanned the chamber. There were no footmen or maids within, even her royal guards had remained outside the closed doors.

Then she realized *who* he was referring to.

There were only two people in the room who weren't members of the council, and she'd wager it wasn't Captain Sullivan's presence that was offensive to the lord of Isloran.

Esme blinked back a glare, feigning innocence. "Ah, yes. Thank you for reminding me, Torin." She addressed him without his title, a small reminder of who held the power. "Allow me to introduce my personal guard, Tearlach." Glancing over her shoulder at him, she noticed a hint of amusement play across Tearlach's face as he stepped forward and bowed to the councilors.

"Your Majesty." He nodded once more to Esme, then returned to his station.

"And I'm sure you're all aware that in reestablishing the royal guard, Sullivan here has returned to his post as captain." She glanced around the table, her sights landing last on Lord Torin, daring him to question her choice in having either man present. "In addition, I've appointed Captain Sullivan as my Minister of Defense." There were a few murmurs and chairs scuffing against the floor. If anyone voiced concerns or objections, Esme was prepared to remind the council of Sully's centuries of service to the crown, and his pivotal role in overthrowing Orianna.

When the room remained silent, Esme gestured Sully forward to claim his seat.

The meeting progressed with reports from each of Tremaene's territories and her ministries. The Western Flats were suffering the most. The citizens were confined to the three largest cities and a handful of smaller towns along the banks of the only river that hadn't gone dry.

Without rain for nearly a decade, nothing grew in the dry, brittle plains beyond. She recalled what Armel had told her about the fire that had engulfed fields in mere moments, destroying his village. The entire kingdom would soon be in danger of something even more catastrophic if nothing were done.

But instead of addressing the perilousness of the situation, the councilors continued on as if nothing were amiss.

Donellis—the territory abutting Belfay's southernmost border, with a small stretch of coast to the east—was faring better. Though it seemed only those who were wealthy enough to afford land near the large waterways that fed into the sea had remained. The rest of Donellis's citizens, she learned, had relocated to more habitable lands in neighboring territories.

Lord Lennox reported on the Belfay region that encompassed the capital city. Thankfully, due to Orianna, only the far-reaching lowlands and the uninhabited forests north of Meallán were barren. But as one of only a few places where the land was still green, Belfay was quickly becoming overpopulated.

Again, Esme listened, waiting for her councilors to voice concerns. Or solutions. None did.

Aindreas, Minister of Trade, discussed the resources native to each region—which seemed inadequate, though he didn't say. He also seemed to underreport the resources in the mountains, where the land had remained mysteriously fertile. His omission made Esme wonder if Aindreas knew but was simply protecting the information. Perhaps he could be trusted.

When he went on to recommend reallocating provisions throughout the kingdom, she knew her instincts had been correct. His view of the sovereign's responsibility to the people was much the same as hers. The grumbles he received told her it wasn't the popular opinion.

Pearce, Minister of Labor, did little to advise, yielding the floor when the minister of finance stepped into the conversation. Gwen presented a practiced explanation with a clear and steady voice, same as the others.

Though nothing Esme's advisors spoke of varied much from what Sully and Cadwyn had already explained, there was something about sitting in that room—where her mother and father had made countless decisions about their kingdom—that made it seem more official, more real.

One thing was quite clear, the state of Tremaene would only worsen, and most of her councilors didn't seem concerned in the least.

Esme scanned the room and noticed Winifred. She knew the council secretary had been listening intently, paying close attention to everything that was said. Yet Esme hadn't seen her write anything down. Perhaps the information was already known by the entirety of the group. Esme was thoroughly prepared, so it stood to reason that the other members were as well. Though it would've been nice to receive documentation on what had been said, a script of sorts that she could look through if something escaped her memory.

Keelin, Minister of Communications, discussed the Festival of Tahra that honored the goddess of land and fertility. Perhaps appeasing Tahra would help ease some of the barrenness plaguing their kingdom. But until the celebration, they needed a more actionable plan.

An idea struck. "What about water wielders?" Esme interjected. The interruption was met with various degrees of staggering looks. Either her advisors weren't accustomed to being questioned or she'd asked something foolish.

Esme decided to pay them no mind, her idea taking shape. She thought back on her short time in the mountains. Even without rain, a few water wielders had managed to keep the massive lake in the valley full, along with several streams that wound through the surrounding range. Sully had suspected that women gifted with the ability to summon raw magic—women too young to be ordained into the Order—were helping to keep the land alive. But even with the water magic from a few powerful Fae, they could—

"Your Majesty?" Pearce halted her thoughts.

Esme looked at him, then to the others. "I was thinking they might be able to bring water to the areas suffering from drought."

"I fail to see why that's necessary," he replied.

Her mouth fell open.

Pearce regarded her for a protracted moment, then nodded for Keelin to continue.

Talk of the celebration commenced as if she'd said nothing.

Esme only heard every second word until her shock finally ebbed. When the vacancy of the Tamslo Mountains lordship was mentioned, she considered which of the other territories would benefit most from an alliance.

Names of potential noblewomen and men were proposed, their families and qualifications discussed at length. Esme might have had ultimate say in all matters, but traditionally—as she'd been informed—court members voted on important issues. Adding a fifth vote would give weight to one side or the other.

The problem was, she didn't know what the sides were.

She had reservations about Pearce's motivation since he'd dismissed her query about water wielders. It was a shallow judgment, but she wasn't prepared to trust him until he proved himself worthy. Thankfully, as a minister, he held less influence.

Then there was Lady Audris of Donellis. Esme had noticed the woman several times throughout the morning, partly because she'd never seen a woman adorned with so much jewelry—every piece accented with crystals in varying shades of green to match her eyes. The slightest movement caused the chains that ran the lengths of her pointed ears to jingle. Though the woman's ostentatious display of wealth wasn't cause for suspicion, Esme had her reasons. Lady Audris was the youngest member of the council; she'd taken over the title when she was only twenty years of age. In addition, Esme had learned that the lady had joined Lord Torin's family in hiding during Orianna's reign, and Esme was hard-pressed to believe that nine years with Lord Torin wouldn't result in colluding. She might not have paid attention to politics during her youth, but everyone knew that Lord Torin believed the terms *leading* and *controlling* were one and the same. Still, she tried to quell her suspicions toward Lady Audris. At least until she'd confirmed the woman's ambitions.

Certainly in the beginning they'd all been loyal to the crown. Her father had chosen each of them personally. But after so many years of service, people changed. Especially when there'd been such a drastic shift in power. She couldn't presume anyone's intentions were purely for the good of Tremaene.

Her eyes traveled to Lord Lennox, and Esme had to admit that in spite of her untrusting nature, she did in fact trust him. Not only had he been part of her father's court since the beginning of his reign, Lord Lennox had taken great risks in getting messages in and out of the city for nine years.

Lady Pallya was seated next to him. Her territory, the Western Flats, was suffering more than any other region, but her loyalties remained in question. The woman hadn't spoken much throughout the meeting, and came across even colder than her silvery blue eyes. Not even the gentle waves of her light brown hair seemed to soften her appearance. Sully had explained that Lady Pallya had been selected to replace the previous lady of the Western Flats—a woman who'd sided with the high-priestesses over the crown at the beginning of their insurgency. Despite her air of rigidity, Esme wanted to trust Lady Pallya.

Then again, the war was long over, and much had changed in their kingdom since.

That left Lord Torin. Esme didn't need further evidence to know he couldn't be trusted. But until Tremaene was once again restored, stable, and peaceful, she couldn't risk replacing him.

When it seemed deliberations about potential leaders for the northernmost territory had concluded, Esme addressed the room. "I appreciate your recommendations, and will grant each serious consideration. Now, if there's nothing else to be addressed—"

"Your Majesty," Lady Audris chirped. Esme strived for a look of indifference as she turned to the woman. "With the utmost respect, we must attend to the issue of your...shall we say, *inexperience.*" She spoke the offending word quietly, and Esme bit back a reply about how *inexperienced* Lady Audris had been when she'd been named Lady of Donellis.

Sully caught Esme's attention and adjusted the gold and crimson crest on his chest plate that denoted his rank—a signal they'd worked out at Cadwyn's insistence.

Esme rose before Lady Audris could continue. "I hereby conclude this session of the royal council."

Sully stood before anyone could object and—joined by Tearlach—followed his queen out of the chamber.

Chapter Eight

CADWYN WAS WAITING outside with Brighid, one of Esme's new lady's maids. The woman seemed too timid to raise her gaze from the floor—though it might have been due to the eight towering guards.

"Have you been waiting out here the whole time?"

"Of course I have." Cadwyn ushered Brighid forward, who finally looked up. Cadwyn took the folio Esme clutched to her chest and handed it to Brighid with instructions that it be brought to Esme's chamber rather than the royal office. Esme suppressed an eye roll at the absurdity that a servant needed to carry her folio.

Following Sully and Cadwyn out into the corridor, Esme quietly asked about the council secretary, hoping Winifred might supply some sort of record of the meeting.

"Winifred can recall everything she's ever seen or heard. You'll have a detailed transcript of the meeting by the end of the day," Sully explained.

"Well, that's a useful talent," Esme remarked.

He smiled down at her. "Indeed."

"And Gwen..." Esme wasn't sure what to ask—or what she even suspected—but she'd noticed Gwen eying Brighid, and wondered if there was a connection between her minister of finance and her new maid. "Is she…Where is she from, originally?"

"Meallán. At least for as long as I can remember. She was away for a time, as all the councilors were, but she recently returned to her home in the city with her husband and daughter."

Daughter. The look in Gwen's eyes suddenly made sense. It was one of a sharp-eyed mother.

"Brighid, your lady's maid." Sully glanced down at her. "You didn't know?"

Esme shook her head, trying to understand why Cadwyn would've selected a lady's maid with ties to one of the councilors.

Sully pulled her to a stop when they reached the top of the stairs, lowering his voice. "We would never have extended a position if we didn't trust Gwen and her daughter. Worry not, my dear."

"But I don't understand. Why would their family need additional work?" Even though Gwen wasn't of noble birth, a minister's salary was more than mere coppers.

"Gwen and her husband are very principled in their work ethic," Cadwyn told her. "Before they…left Meallán, Gwen managed a housekeeping service in the city, and her husband owned a bakery. You remember the currant bread your mother loved so much? It was his specialty."

Esme lifted her brow in surprise; she'd always thought it had come from the palace kitchens.

"I'm told they've both taken up their businesses now that they've returned to the city. I believe Brighid had, at one time, worked for her mother. But what with the vacancies created from…well, Gwen saw an opportunity and presented her for the position of lady's maid."

Given everything, it made sense Gwen would want such a dedicated position for her daughter. It wouldn't likely be a lifetime appointment, as it was for some, but the experience would certainly expand Brighid's skills. All while Gwen kept a watchful eye on her.

Cadwyn pulled Sully away the moment they reached Esme's suite. Tearlach stepped forward, pushing the door open for Esme.

Brighid scurried out as soon as she saw them.

"Do you think I frighten her?" Esme joked. She could hardly be as intimidating as the girl's mother.

"Well, you are quite an imposing woman."

"Hardly."

"Esme."

She turned at Tearlach's potent tone.

"You are. And everyone in that chamber downstairs will soon know it." Then, with a single nod, he left her alone.

———

Esme pulled her satin robe over her shoulders and stepped through one of the arched doorways. The delicate honeyed perfume of wisteria hovered in the warm morning air. The scent reminded her of late springtime. But the persistently pleasant temperature in Tremaene would never yield to hot summer days, cool autumn nights, or frost-covered mornings.

I miss seasons, she thought.

She missed Periwen.

"Milady?"

Esme turned to find Griselda with a breakfast tray and tea. She'd initially thought her shy and timid—much like Brighid—but Griselda was proving to be far bolder, stepping into her new role with grace, and just enough enthusiasm that was telling of her younger age. Esme took in her uniform. Instead of the simple gray maid's dress, she wore a pale blue one. The indigo apron, tied with a wide satin ribbon, signified her position in the queen's service.

Esme looked at the two place settings her maid was arranging. "Thank you, Griselda, but I didn't ring for—"

"I asked if I might join you for breakfast." Killian stepped out onto the balcony, pausing only a moment before walking over to drop a kiss at Esme's temple. "If you'll have me." His eyes traveled over her, taking in the covering that did little to hide her thin nightdress beneath.

"I wasn't expecting anyone so early." She felt heat spread across her cheeks.

"First of all, you should always be expecting someone to turn up." Esme closed her eyes, realizing how right he was. "And second of all, I'm in favor of you wearing anything that does so little to cover you." He ran his fingertips lightly down the length of her arm, igniting every inch of her skin into a frenzy of excitement.

"Killian," she scolded, wrapping her arms around her chest to conceal the clearly intended effect of his touch. She dropped her voice. "Need I remind you that we're not alone?"

Killian gave her a wicked grin.

"My, that rosebush is growing quickly. It's nearly doubled in size since I last watered it," Griselda remarked.

Killian glanced at the miraculous plant that was already forming buds. "Curious." He gave Esme a knowing smile.

"The morning light must be helping it along," Esme defended weakly.

"Hmm..." Griselda seemed to consider. She narrowed her eyes suspiciously at the thorny shrub, then took her leave with a curtsy.

Once they were alone, Killian poured two cups of tea, downing his in a single swallow. She knew he'd been on duty the night before. His armor, cape, and weapons had all been removed, but he still wore the tall boots, formfitting pants, undershirt, and wheat-colored tunic from his uniform. She was more than appreciative for his effort to spend the morning with her when he could have been sleeping instead.

"I'd ask about yesterday's meeting, but I've a feeling you'd like to talk about literally anything else."

She smiled. Killian had learned to read her thoughts almost as well as Tearlach.

"It was…a lot. There's so much to do. So much to consider. I can't even begin to…" She trailed off, shaking her head and dropping her gaze to her hands.

"I'm certain you'll make sense of everything, Esme. You're intelligent and perceptive, with a clear understanding of what the kingdom needs."

She resisted the urge to look up. "I don't know why you have such confidence in me."

"I have confidence in you because I know your true nature. I've felt it. You won't allow selfish interests to fog your devotion to the people of Tremaene. You might need time to settle into this new role, but it's in your blood, Esme. Everything you need has always been inside you."

She lifted her gaze. The characteristic lightheartedness she'd come to expect from Killian had been momentarily replaced with maturity and wisdom. He seemed to hide those parts of himself, opting instead for humor or charisma to break the strain of tense situations. Sometimes Esme forgot how caring and insightful he could be.

Then his playful smile returned.

"Now that I've irrefutably convinced you of your ability to lead, I will once again attempt to distract you. Since the topic of weather won't be very diverting"—he glanced up at the cloudless sky—"what do you say we focus on art?"

She grinned, reaching for a toast point with creamy goat cheese, slivers of red onion, tiny orange tomatoes, and a sprig of thyme. "Art it is."

They spoke at length about the pieces displayed throughout the palace, particularly the glass sculptures created by extraordinarily gifted fire wielders—some of which dated back more than a thousand years. But when Killian brought his hand to his chest, rubbing his fingers absently over his invisible scar, Esme could no longer focus on art. Her mind returned to the day they'd been ambushed.

"Has Sully been able to track down all the scouts?" She'd been meaning to ask him, but every time they were alone, Sully would fall into what was becoming a customary pattern of reminiscing about Esme's youth. And every time, without fail, she'd get equally swept up in the stories, forgetting the answers she sought.

Killian glanced down at his hand, then cocked his head to the side. He placed his hand deliberately on the table. When he didn't say anything, Esme was convinced he knew something. Everyone, it seemed, was trying to keep her from shouldering one burden or another. But those efforts only reminded her of how Tremaene's horrific history had once been kept from her.

"I know he sent guards to search for them, Killian. Have they all been accounted for?"

"They have. We just didn't mention anything because—"

"Because you don't want me to worry. I know. I understand. Now, please tell me."

He nodded. "It seems Orianna was using her power to control their minds. I didn't quite understand it myself, but Sully consulted with Winifred's mother, who has a similar—albeit far less powerful—type of magic. She works with those who've experienced trauma. Her magic allows her to remove distressing memories."

Esme bit her tongue to keep from asking who the woman was and where she could be found.

"When Sully presented the information to her, she speculated that Orianna had likely bent the scouts to her will by planting ideas deep inside their minds. They followed those core directives without further manipulation. And when she was killed, the ideas perished along with her."

"What happened to them once the ideas were gone?"

"Many of them found their way to nearby towns, where local guards detained them."

"And their memories?"

"Most only retained vague recollections of the years Orianna controlled them. One described the time as a near dreamlike state or trance."

"Most? Were there some who forgot entirely?"

Killian appeared to choose his next words carefully. "We believe a few remembered their service to Orianna a bit more clearly." He paused until Esme nodded for him to continue. "They took their own lives."

Oh. Her lips formed the word.

She couldn't imagine going on after being forced to do such horrible things to one's fellow citizens. So many lives had been lost.

"What about the assassins who tracked me to Periwen? Do we know if there were others?"

"Sully confirmed that only six were sent to find you, and that Tearlach—"

"Killed them all." Her mind flashed to the alley where Tearlach had slit the throat of one who'd pursued, intent on killing her. Then came the memory of the other four, when they'd surrounded her in the woods outside Briganport. She hadn't witnessed their deaths from her hiding spot, but Tearlach had assured her that he'd taken care of them.

Esme stared down into her cup. She watched the swirling, cloudy liquid until she felt Killian beside her. Gently, he pulled her to her feet and encircled her with his strong arms. She breathed in his comforting scent and brought her hands up to rest on his chest. But as her palms pressed into the solid muscles, and her fingers moved along the defined edges, the inescapable memory returned.

Feeling Killian's deep exhale, she looked up.

"You're thinking about the iron now, aren't you?"

"How did you—"

"Everything is written on your face, love. And here I thought I could distract you." A smile tugged at the corners of his mouth.

"Oh, believe me. You certainly can." She ducked her head.

Killian tilted her chin up. "Let me put your worried mind at ease on that issue. The only iron we've recovered was found on the scouts. We assume they went through training and exposure similar to what Tearlach put himself through in order to handle the metal. Though it probably wasn't voluntary. We're confident they were the only ones who possessed the poisonous material. As for where it came from, we can't be sure. But rest assured, there are no indications that any deposits exist in Tremaene."

"If the iron isn't from Tremaene, then that means—"

"Then that means that whatever faraway place it came from is not something you need to worry about at this moment. If it's not on our soil, it isn't an immediate threat."

Killian was right. But iron was a weapon they couldn't take lightly. Eventually, they'd need to uncover the location of the mine.

When she nodded in agreement, he took her arms and wrapped them around his back. As he ran his capable hands up and down her spine, her tension melted away. Esme closed her eyes, transfixed by the soothing ministrations. His breath tickled her ear just before his lips found the sensitive spot below. Killian whispered softly between kisses—telling her how sweet she tasted, how intoxicating she smelled—but Esme couldn't think past the feel of his lips on her heated skin.

His fingers trailed down her arms. Even through the layer of satin, a familiar trail of goose bumps prickled her skin in the wake of his touch. When she shivered, his mouth found hers. He pulled her close, wasting no time deepening the kiss.

"Milady?"

Killian gripped the back of her robe and pulled his lips away, letting them hover an inch above hers. "That woman has the stealth of a lynx," he muttered.

Hearing the distinctive tapping of a soft-soled shoe, Esme glanced around Killian's shoulder to see Cadwyn. Beyond, she could see Sully waiting discreetly in her suite.

Esme burrowed against Killian's chest in an attempt to hide herself. He kissed the top of her head. "It seems you're needed, love."

As he moved to step out of their embrace, Esme held tight. "Stay," she begged.

He sighed, then made a show of glancing toward the clock inside her suite. "It seems I've lost track of time." He spoke loudly enough for Cadwyn to hear. "Hazel will be expecting me in the ring."

Liar, Esme mouthed, but Killian only winked, then nodded to his captain as he left.

Sully stepped outside. "Sorry for interrupting, my dear, but something has arrived that you need to see." He produced a letter and handed it to Esme.

"Who's this from?"

"It was delivered by messenger," Cadwyn replied. "Though it seems to have passed between several hands before it reached the palace."

"So, it would be impossible to track? Should I be worried?" She looked between Cadwyn and Sully. They must have had some inclination as to the sender, or they would've reviewed the letter before presenting it to her.

"Judging by the seal, we suspect it's from someone we've been searching for."

Esme looked at the impression in the dark wax—three curls, spiraling out from a central point. It was a feminine symbol with a number of meanings. One sprang to mind: creator, destroyer, sustainer.

Her eyes shot to Sully, then to Cadwyn. "A priestess?"

"We believe so."

Esme eased the seal away from the folded parchment.

"In addition to Myles's connections in the north, I asked Aindreas to thoroughly evaluate the resources in the region before he left Altan," Sully told her. "When his surveyors reported back, he agreed that the fertility of the land and the water supply couldn't possibly be maintained by the magic of water wielders alone—that another power had to be contributing in order to keep the land alive and thriving."

Esme nodded, her heart speeding up as she unfolded the thick, cream-colored paper. She'd been prepared to reach out to the unordained priestesses as soon as they were located. But they'd contacted her first. Though their method of sending the letter suggested a fair amount of distrust, it was encouraging nonetheless.

After flattening the inside page, Esme read through the letter. It started out cordial enough, addressing her as queen. They referred to themselves as the Triskele—the name for the symbol on the wax seal. No individuals were named, but it was clear that whoever wrote the letter was speaking for an entire sect of women. How many, Esme wasn't sure.

They'd been compelled to write after hearing that inquiries were being made throughout the mountains on behalf of the crown. One of Myles's connections or Aindreas's surveyors. But the letter conveyed— with absolute conviction—that the women of the Triskele would not be found if they did not wish to be.

Why such secrecy? Orianna was gone. Who did they have to fear?

Despite their insistence to remain secret, Esme was assured that they would continue summoning water magic in order to sustain life in the mountains—as they'd been doing since the downfall of the Order.

Only water magic? It was possible to summon only one element from the source? Esme had always been told that when it came to raw magic, individual elements couldn't work independent from one another, that all were needed—something to do with balance. But then, she didn't fully understand how priestesses were able to summon raw magic at all. Before she could respond to the letter, she'd need a stronger grasp of the fundamentals, and an understanding of the inner workings of the Order.

The sect also expressed hesitancy about expanding their range. Esme sensed it was more caution than unwillingness. If their safety could be ensured, she was confident they'd help restore life to the rest of the kingdom.

Specific instructions were outlined for sending a response, as well as a warning that if any attempts were made to track the correspondence, all contact would be severed. Esme had no intention of risking such a thing. She'd give them only reason to trust her.

Chapter Nine

THE MIDNIGHT BLUE cloak that Cadwyn had wrapped around Esme's shoulders before spelling her to sleep and sending her across the sea hung in the shadowed corner of her dressing room, untouched. Esme shrugged a long-sleeved plum tunic over her head and smoothed her hands over the beaded neckline as she stared at the cloak. It would be winter in Debarrow. Her abandoned apple trees would be bare, their branches frosted with ice, and heavy with freshly fallen snow. How she longed to feel the bite of wind on her cheek, to smell the fresh, bracing air of winter.

She tore her gaze away when Marta announced herself.

"Might I be of assistance, Milady? With your hair?"

Esme turned toward the mirror to glimpse her reflection. The sun hadn't yet risen, but even with the soft flicker of the lamps, she could see that her hair was a fright. Had she even remembered to wash it in the bath? Her mind had been elsewhere, returning again and again to the letter she'd received from the Triskele.

With a nod, Esme settled on the tufted bench. She watched in the mirror as her maid began to gently untangle the many knots that had formed.

"You remind me of a young woman I remember...from before. You look so much like her," Esme admitted.

Marta's hands stopped. She raised her gaze, locking with Esme's in the mirror before she began weaving sections of hair into an intricate braid.

Esme opened her mouth, then closed it. She watched Marta's reflection for several long moments, but her maid didn't give any indication that she'd respond. "I didn't mean to—"

"Derin," Marta said without looking up. "Her name was Derin."

Was?

Marta took a measured breath, as if warding herself against something unpleasant. "She was my granddaughter. She worked in the stables for seven years, helping to break in horses. She had a way with them."

A cold sweat broke out on Esme's skin, and the breakfast she barely remembered eating turned in her stomach. "Did something...happen to her?"

Marta gave a barely perceptible nod. Her eyes grew unfocused as her fingers continued working Esme's hair. "She was well past her twentieth year when she finally realized her way with the horses was more than just patience and an advanced understanding of the creatures. Orianna even took an interest. She doted on my Derin for weeks, asking for demonstrations. The woman seemed impressed. For such a quiet girl like Derin, that sort of attention was unsettling. But Orianna had a way, she did. Made young Derin feel admired, special. In the beginning, I suppose we all believed that woman."

Marta's hands stilled, and Esme gripped the hem of her shirt.

"Until my Derin was taken from her bed one night."

No.

"I never saw her again."

Tears welled in Esme's eyes. She swallowed, trying to form the right words. Anything that might ease the woman's pain.

With a slight tug, Marta bound the end of the braid and met Esme's eyes in the mirror—her face carefully expressionless. "If that will be all, Milady."

Esme couldn't seem to speak. When she didn't respond, Marta bowed her head and took her leave.

She wasn't sure how long she stared at where Marta's reflection had been. When she finally blinked away, she noticed the warming hue of predawn light touching the western horizon. She was about to be late. On shaky legs, she hurried to meet her guards.

"Morning, Your Majesty," Madoc greeted.

"Good morning, Madoc." Esme forced a smile. She took in the sight of him, concentrating on every feature, hoping to distract herself from what Marta had revealed.

With Madoc's hair pulled back, she realized he looked rather like Armel with his angular face, and long, lean muscles.

She turned to greet Harlow, but the woman only gave a curt nod. Clearly she wasn't a morning person. Esme studied her as well, and wondered if the braided crown she always seemed to wear wasn't simply an attempt at stylishness, but one of convenience—a way to tame her long, dark curls.

Esme reached up to touch the braid that ran down along her hairline. That Marta could create something so beautiful and precise while recounting such a horrid tale...

"Did you win last night?" Esme asked Madoc as they made their way down to the main floor. She'd overheard him and a few of the palace guards discussing plans for a card game.

"Afraid not, Your Majesty."

"I've told you, call me Esme."

"Of course, Your Majesty."

Grinning, she shook her head. It seemed she'd need a royal decree to get anyone to call her anything but.

Cadwyn was waiting outside. She held the handles of two mugs in one hand, a bundle of papers in the other. Esme carefully took one of the mugs—the earthy, herbal scent revealing that the brew was one of Cadwyn's own concoctions.

"Think we can make it?" Esme asked.

"If we hurry."

They traipsed across the south lawn, making for the wooded path at the far end. Madoc and Harlow fell back, giving them privacy.

"Coming from a meeting with Sully?" Esme gestured to the papers Cadwyn had tucked under her arm, knowing they met almost daily.

"I suddenly find myself less engaged in the mornings."

"And would that have anything to do with you finally allowing my lady's maids to handle what's far beneath your station?"

Cadwyn shrugged. "I can't say I mind the luxury of waking *after* the sun has risen. Though I suppose I've yet to break that habit." She peered at the horizon over the top of Esme's head. "Besides"—Cadwyn stepped over a low-hanging branch—"now I can make myself more available to the guards. You wouldn't believe how reckless some of them can be. Roderick came to find me yesterday with a broken arm. Apparently, he couldn't be bothered to halt the match when it happened, so it healed incorrectly. I had to re-break it." Esme winced, rubbing her own arm.

When they reached the eastern shore of the lake, Cadwyn climbed atop the wide, flat boulder, then reached down to pull Esme up. As the sun's rays pierced the treetops, and the glassy surface of the lake glowed with morning light, the tension drained from Esme's muscles. Her mind felt clearer than it had in days.

"Have you given any consideration as to how you'll respond to the letter?"

And just like that, every thought returned to pound incessantly against her skull.

"Only every moment since you left me yesterday."

"Have you shown it to Tearlach?"

"Last night," Esme told her. "We're hoping there's something in the library that will help us better understand the Order. Which reminds me, has Sully reviewed the decree I wrote?" It was largely a symbolic one since the Order no longer existed, but Esme felt she owed it to her parents, and the citizens of Tremaene, to nullify the treaty that had made it possible for Orianna to seize the crown. "Perhaps I should have Winifred take a look at it."

"No," Cadwyn replied quickly, then paused as if considering something. "There's no need. I'll see that he returns it to you soon." Then she flicked her hand toward the lake. "Remember all the nights we came out here to swim under the lights?"

Esme was fairly certain that Cadwyn was deflecting, but turned her attention to the lake nonetheless.

At the rocky shore along the southern edge, where the water was dark and deep, Esme would dive beneath the surface and feel the warmth seeping up through the bed of the lake.

A shiver ran down her spine as she thought of a different lake that was not at all comforting like the still water before her.

"I remember," she finally replied. "We were quite skilled at sneaking past the guards."

Cadwyn chuckled. "You're old enough now to know we never actually dodged any guards."

Esme turned to her.

Cadwyn cocked her head to the side, her mouth quirking up into a grin. "Did you really think your parents didn't know? Or the guards stationed outside your door, who were always conveniently absent when we slipped out? Or the multitude of guards and liveried servants between your room and the service stairs?"

It felt as though some grand illusion of freedom had shattered. Her expression must have conveyed as much, for Cadwyn's eyes softened and she pulled Esme closer.

As the sun rose over the treetops, casting its fiery reflection across the untouched surface of the lake, Esme decided it should give her a sense of security, to know that she'd always been protected—every moment of every day. She should've felt safe in that knowing.

Chapter Ten

TEARLACH PULLED OPEN one of the massive doors that led to the royal library.

"Just a moment!" called a voice from somewhere beyond the long tables and tall bookcases. Esme glanced around the high-ceilinged room until she spotted the top of a man's head through the open space of one of the shelves. His eyes went wide when he registered who'd entered the library.

The sound of books hitting the ground preceded the librarian's arrival. "Your Majesty! Your Majesty! Welcome!" Esme smiled at the sight of Kelton. The man hadn't changed in the least. His flaxen hair stuck out in all directions, like he'd been raking his fingers through it since waking that morning. He seemed every bit the easily flustered man she remembered. Anything that thwarted his routine—such as an unanticipated visit from the queen—would send him into a dither. She could only imagine how he'd been coping with the upended condition of the library.

"Come in! Come in! I wasn't expecting visitors for some time yet. If you'd be so kind as to forgive the disorder."

"Think nothing of it." Esme waved her hand dismissively. "I'd like to introduce you to my personal guard, Tearlach."

"Yes. Yes. I've heard. A pleasure to meet you." Kelton bobbed his head.

"Tearlach, Kelton is our royal librarian." Tearlach bowed his head once, and Esme noticed the slight twitch of his lips. He was clearly amused by the animated man.

"Let me clear off these tables." Kelton hurried to gather the closest pile of books, hiding them behind a tall desk. Its surface was surprisingly sparse, holding nothing more than a ledger and a polished gold bell. "I've been away for many years, Your Majesty, and only just returned to the palace this week past. You can imagine my shock at finding the library in such a disgraceful state. But not to worry, I'll have it re-catalogued in no time."

"Then we won't keep you," Esme interjected before Kelton's thoughts could further unravel. "I only intended to show Tearlach our impressive collection."

"Certainly, Your Majesty." He bowed deeply. "And don't hesitate to alert me of anything you might need. I'm forever in your service."

"Thank you, Kelton." She grabbed Tearlach's arm and led him around the corner.

Bookshelves lined three walls, with a spiral staircase tucked into the far corner that led to a narrow, railed platform halfway up. They wended around the many tables, passing doors recessed between the bookshelves. Esme thought of the many hours she'd spent in those rooms with myriad tutors—sometimes three and four times a day depending on the focus of study that month.

Reaching the farthest corner, Esme gestured to a particular section of books. "I think what we're looking for will be over there. Or...maybe not," she amended, noticing several books lying flat beside those righted on their spines. Kelton hadn't been exaggerating; everything was in disarray.

"We have to start somewhere." Tearlach began inspecting titles on the adjacent wall.

Esme rolled a ladder along the tracks and climbed up. Righting a few books that were stacked atop one another, she ran her finger along the titles until she found a small section relating to magic.

When she heard Tearlach move to the foot of the ladder she looked down to find his dark eyes staring up at her.

Arching a brow, he said, "Don't worry. I won't trap you up there...this time."

She pulled one of the heavier tomes from the shelf and tossed it at him. He caught it without effort. "You really think I'm still afraid"—she raked her gaze over his imposing build, then cocked her head to the side—"of you?"

Tearlach barked out a laugh.

The pure joy of the sound made Esme smile. "Quiet," she scolded, pressing a finger to her lips.

"Quiet? We're the only ones here. Aside from 'frazzled' over there." He jerked his chin over his shoulder.

"Be that as it may, I'll not have you disturbing the books," she mandated. Tearlach watched her descend the ladder with two books tucked under her arm. He took them from her and eyed the titles before placing them on one of the tables.

What about the Order? he asked where no one else could hear.

Right. Esme glanced around. While she'd never looked up information about high-priestesses as a child, the only reasonable place would be somewhere along the wall reserved for Tremaene's history. "Over there." She inclined her head toward the back wall. "I'll start at the top. Will you—" She turned to find Tearlach studying the books she'd pulled. With a shrug, she headed up the winding bronze staircase on her own.

But after an hour of reading titles and pulling books for Kelton to shelve in their proper places—why anyone would think *The art of raising chickens* belonged in that section was beyond her—Esme was no closer to finding what she needed.

"I don't understand." She joined Tearlach at the table. "I couldn't find a single book. Not one."

"The librarian mentioned the disorganized state, perhaps they've been misplaced."

"Perhaps," she hedged, if only because she preferred to believe they were lost amid the stacks rather than consider the possibility that Orianna had destroyed them. The woman had, after all, killed every one of her sister high-priestesses—thereby terminating the Order. But removing books about their history…What secrets had they held?

"There are a few crossover categories where they might be."

Tearlach nodded and went back to paging through the books in front of him.

When her search continued to be frustratingly unsuccessful, Esme considered searching for books about the Dark War. Any documentation regarding a war that began as an insurrection between those who supported the royal family and those who believed high-priestesses should rule Tremaene was bound to contain information about the Order. But when Esme found no volumes about the decades-long battle, she couldn't pretend to believe they'd simply gone missing. It was more likely that they'd never occupied the library shelves at all. That particularly appalling time in Tremaene's history had been kept from her, after all.

"Still nothing." She sat down across from Tearlach, glancing at the books he'd left open. "I was wondering about the Dark Wa—"

Tearlach's hand flexed, but he quickly flattened it against the table.

Esme bit her tongue. She knew it wasn't a topic he discussed. Ever. "I mean the beginning, when the high-priestesses rose up against my father," she hastily amended.

"What about it?" He didn't meet her eyes, but she knew he wasn't seeing the words on the page either.

"Did they stop summoning the elements?" It was almost absurd how much power the women had actually possessed. They could've held the entire kingdom hostage simply by ceasing to perform their duties.

"You're asking if Tremaene was as it is now? No. The land suffered only a little, and only in the beginning. The impasse between your father and the Order lasted only six or seven years before we…had no choice but to join forces." When an army wielding dark magic had descended upon them, Esme recalled Tearlach's words. "There were only two sides after that, us and *them.* The high-priestesses left the fight, returning faithfully to their temples—which were guarded by whatever warriors we could spare." Tearlach pulled over an unopened book and began flipping through it. The discussion was clearly over.

Esme contemplated what he'd said, that the land had only suffered a little. It made sense, she supposed. Nearly a decade had passed since Orianna had poisoned her sister high-priestesses. And while the magic in the land had receded to the tracts surrounding the temples, it hadn't vanished completely.

She returned her attention to the books, scanning the contents, though her mind was elsewhere. "Killian told me about the scouts," she mentioned.

"Did he?" Tearlach clipped.

Esme hesitated a moment, then asked, "What's been done with those who didn't take their own..." She cleared her throat. "What's been done with those who are still alive?" Tearlach didn't meet her eyes. "I haven't seen any conveyances, so I know they aren't being held here."

Tearlach lifted his head slowly, his eyes unreadable. After a protracted silence, he simply said, "You needn't worry about them."

"What does that mean?" She pulled herself closer to the table, trapping his gaze before he could look away. When he said nothing, she pressed, "Were they killed?"

"They weren't killed."

Esme was about to demand clarification, but Tearlach halted her by leaning forward to rest his forearms on the table.

"And they won't be," he assured in a low voice, one that wouldn't reach the other end of the library. "They're alive and well, and you shouldn't worry yourself about them."

"But—"

"Esme." His tone quelled her. "You don't need to take care of everything yourself."

"I don't want to take care of everything; I just want to know."

Tearlach arched a brow.

"Fine." She pushed away, sinking back in her chair as she pulled a book toward her. "I won't ask again." She huffed a breath, childish as it was, but was soon engrossed in the tome before her, desperate to find something useful.

When she reached the end, she slid the book down the table, frustrated. Before she could reach for another, Tearlach turned around the one he'd been perusing and pushed it toward her.

It was old—its pages brittle and edges tattered. Tearlach had it opened to a map of Tremaene. Esme examined the illustration, noting the small starburst symbols that dotted the kingdom. When she finally looked at the top of the page, she understood what they indicated.

"Channels? Are those the locations—" She stopped and glanced around. *Are those the locations where raw magic reaches the surface?*

It would seem.

But there are hundreds! I thought raw magic could only be brought forth at the sacred sites—the temples. This doesn't make any sense. She tapped her finger against one of the starbursts. She'd hoped to uncover the secrets of the Order—how future initiates were identified, the rituals they used to summon the elements—but all she'd managed to find were more questions.

Confused, she narrowed her eyes and searched for an explanation somewhere on the page. That there were hundreds of channels scattered across Tremaene seemed to directly contradict their understanding of raw magic.

A resounding bang from the main library doors drew their attention a moment before a footman rushed around the corner.

"Your Majesty." He bowed to Esme, then turned to Tearlach. "Sir, I've been sent to fetch you."

"What for?"

"The elder-wood trunks you ordered constructed have been completed. Lined with wool, just as you specified." He paused, taking note of the books strewn across the table. "I apologize, it's just...the men are anxious and we...well, we wondered if you might—"

"You want me to seal away the iron weapons."

"Yes. Yes, sir. That would be much appreciated." He nodded eagerly.

Tearlach looked to Esme, but she simply raised her brows. He was, after all, the only one who could handle the metal for any length of time.

He addressed the footman. "Send for Cahir and Roderick, then have the trunks brought to the dungeons. I'll be down shortly."

———————

Esme added the books she'd borrowed to the growing stacks that covered a table intended for dining. She'd need to remedy that soon. Clearing a small space, she pulled a few sheets of paper from the wooden box in the center. The library hadn't yielded any new information on the Order, but she needed to respond to the letter from the Triskele regardless.

Two hours and eleven crumpled drafts later, Esme wasn't any closer to figuring out how best to approach the matter.

When Marta brought in a cart, Esme realized that the sky had darkened.

She pushed aside the blank sheet in front of her and faced her lady's maid.

"Marta, I want to convey my deepest condolen—"

"I'll have none of that, Milady," Marta cut her off. "You'll not be apologizing for the deeds of that woman. Now, where would you like to take your dinner?"

Esme stared at her, lips parted. "I...uh..." She glanced at the cart of food, then over at the crumpled sheets of parchment. She'd hoped to finish the letter before dinner. Clearly that goal had been too ambitious.

From the open door she could hear the palace staff gathering in the main hall below. Music lilted up the grand staircase, echoing off the arches that crisscrossed the ceiling.

Esme hadn't left her room to dine in weeks. She rested her hand on the documents she'd set off to the side—the ones that still required her attention. Her thumb grazed the sharp edges. A break would've been nice, but she estimated nearly three dozen requests in the stack. It was imprudent to leave them. How her parents had managed, she'd no idea. Though they hadn't done it alone, they'd had each other.

The tink of glass against metal had Esme glancing over at Marta. Her maid had returned one of the covered dishes to the cart. "Dinner was just served in the hall. If you hurry, there might be some fig and hazelnut cake left."

Esme considered for a moment. "I shouldn't." She picked up her pen.

"Even your mother and father took off their crowns in the evening."

Esme sighed. Marta was right. She couldn't recall more than a few nights when either of their seats were vacant during their family dinners.

"You're younger than she was, but you've the same determination. The same strength."

A smile tugged at Esme's lips, but she kept her face averted.

When a wave of laughter drifted up from the hall, Marta insisted, "Go, and join them."

After changing into something more appropriate, Esme opened the doors of her suite, but found neither of her guards. Glancing down the corridor, she spotted Cahir and Roderick speaking with Finbarr—the tall, redheaded man who summoned the flames throughout the palace every evening.

For a rare moment, with the servants and off-duty guards occupied below stairs, and with both of her guards' backs turned, Esme found herself unwatched. Not risking a moment's hesitation, she hurried along the railing that curved toward the stairs, crossed the landing, and slipped through the facing double doors, closing them behind her quietly.

The space was dark, but the heavy curtains along the far wall had been left open, allowing the faint light from the sky to guide her.

It'd been more than nine years since she'd stepped foot in there. With a shaky breath, she made her way slowly through the sitting room, and the large dining room beyond. All the furniture had been removed. Only the window coverings remained. She paced the perimeter, running her fingers along the smooth walls. In the dim light, she couldn't discern if the color was the same.

Memories flooded her mind. She stood at the high windows along the back wall, then turned to face the empty room. Closing her eyes, she could picture the way it'd been.

When she reached her mother's suite, the scent of honeysuckle greeted her, reminding her so fiercely of her mother that it knocked the air from her lungs.

Esme reached for the wall to steady herself. Fighting back tears, she managed to cross the room and pull aside sheer curtains she didn't recognize. Creeping vines still clung to the outer edges of the balcony doors. She nudged them open, letting the familiar scent encircle her.

The ribbons of light dancing across the night sky cast the expansive room in an eerie greenish glow. She padded across the room to where her mother's towering bed had once stood. Ghosting her hands along the remembered height of the bed, she closed her eyes, imagining the feel of the embroidered satin coverlet.

She turned to the spot where her mother would sit before her dressing table mirror, and recalled a particular night, when Esme had only been eight or nine years. She'd sat cross-legged on the long upholstered bench at the foot of her mother's bed, watching the lady's maid finish setting Erena's hair. Once her crown had been placed, her mother had dismissed the servants and pulled Esme from her perch to twirl her about the room. Their laughter must have summoned her father, for Esme had spied him watching in amusement from the doorway.

Smiling at the memory, Esme turned in circles across the room. She could almost feel her mother's hands grasping her own, her father watching in delight.

The screech of an owl had her stumbling to a stop.

She looked toward the windows, blinking to right the spinning room, and saw a dark figure silhouetted against the night sky.

Chapter Eleven

"LORD TORIN," ESME gasped, making a feeble attempt to smooth the skirt of her dress. She cursed herself for not being more aware of her surroundings. No matter where she was in the palace, someone always knew her whereabouts.

"Your Majesty." His deep voice rumbled along the floorboards. Rather than offering a bow or even a nod to his sovereign, he raised his chin, looking down at her from across the room.

Esme lifted her own chin and clasped her hands behind her back. "What are you doing here?" It was a reasonable question. Only the royal family and their attendants occupied the royal apartments. Though unspoken, it was understood that permission was required for anyone else to gain access to the rooms that took up more than half of the second floor. Lord Torin had no such permission. And never would.

"I just arrived at the palace to dine with the other members of your court, thinking what a shame it was that our queen is always so busy, her schedule so overflowing with obligations, that she can't spare a moment to make an appearance."

Esme noticed a glint of light reflecting off one of his polished black boots as he took a silent step forward.

"Yet, here I find you, whirling about in a dark room like a child. Now I'm sure there's an excellent reason for such behavior." He arched a dark brow, looking so like his son in that moment.

Esme unclenched her jaw, willing her voice to be clear and strong. "I don't answer to you."

"Oh, but you do." Lord Torin took another discreet step. "Not only was I one of your father's most trusted advisors, I'm also a citizen of Tremaene. And as such, my queen must answer to me."

The desire to run from the room overwhelmed her as his presence seemed to fill the space, making it feel more confining than a linen closet.

When she didn't reply, he advanced another step. "I can see I've caught you at an indecorous moment. But I urge you, *Your Majesty*"—his voice bordered on contempt as he spoke her title—"to give Lady Audris's concern about your inexperience a great deal of reflection. It's not simply Her Lady's opinion, but that of the entire royal council. And one we all take quite seriously. I hope our queen will do the same."

Had he actually snuck into the royal apartments simply to mock her youth? To disparage her where no one else could witness?

To frighten her?

She swallowed past the tightening in her throat, realizing how much closer he was. She willed herself to stay put.

"Thank you for your concern, Lord Torin. But it isn't proper for you to be here. I must ask you to leave." She inclined her head toward the door, and the many empty rooms between her and her guards. With each second they were alone together, her heart pounded more forcefully.

"Ah, but you see, there are things we need to discuss." He leveled her with his merciless gaze.

"Then I will kindly ask that you make an appointment."

"As your attendant has refused every request from your court, I see no reason why I should inquire again."

"If you go through the proper channels, I can assure you that your request will be considered. Now, I must again ask that you leave these apartments." Her eyes narrowed, enough to tell him that he was not welcome. Not ever.

"Oh, I think we'll discuss it right now."

"I'm afraid I have a prior commitment." She stepped to the side, feeling the frantic need to put distance between them.

"I find that hard to believe." Lord Torin blocked her path to the door, and made a show of glancing around.

"And my personal guard"—she paused, calling out to Tearlach in her mind—"will be wondering where I am."

"As this matter is rather private..." He moved closer, forcing her to yield a step. "I'm sure you can appreciate that I wish only to discuss it with my queen."

"And I'm sure you understand, Lord Torin, how untoward such a request is. Again, if you'll just make an appointment—"

"No, I think we'll discuss this now."

She was vaguely aware of her retreating steps, of the door stretching farther from reach.

"You see, I'm concerned about your safety."

Her back hit the wall, and she fought not to suck in a breath.

"I wouldn't want you to befall the same fate as your parents."

Her heart slammed against her ribs, her palms growing slick with sweat. She pressed them against the wall, needing the solidity to steady her rising panic. "I can assure you"—she hated that her voice trembled—"I am perfectly safe."

"And yet, I see no guards." He made a show of glancing around the empty room, proving how vulnerable she really was. "I was able to walk right into these private rooms, undeterred, to find you utterly alone."

"Make no mistake," a deep voice came from the doorway. "Her Majesty is never alone."

Esme nearly shuddered in relief at the sound of Tearlach's voice. She didn't dare take her eyes off Lord Torin as she listened to Tearlach's unhurried approach. He had the ability to move with complete stealth, yet he allowed his boots to fall heavily upon the floor, making his size and presence known.

Lord Torin yielded a step.

"Your Majesty." Tearlach bowed his head. "An urgent matter requires your attention."

Esme stepped past Lord Torin, feeling Tearlach's protective presence at her back. She risked a glance over her shoulder when they reached the door. "Lord Torin, I believe you can see yourself out."

"Of course, Your Majesty. I have no problem finding my way around the palace." Even in the foggy green light, she could see the warning glare in his eyes. Then, feeling the ripple of Tearlach's power, she took his arm and pulled him through the residence.

Her guards took notice as Esme and Tearlach approached. Judging by their expressions, they hadn't realized she'd left her room.

Cahir stepped forward. "Sir, we didn't—"

"Later," Tearlach growled as he swung the door open and ushered her inside.

Esme didn't stop until she was behind the closed door of her bathing chamber. Avoiding the mirror above, she filled the basin and plunged her hands into the cool water in an attempt to slow her racing pulse. She splashed her face, trying to wash away the humiliation, the fear, the anger. Though she couldn't decide who she was more upset with—herself for failing to wield her power, or Lord Torin for making her forget she had any at all.

Come out. Now.

Tearlach was standing just outside the door, blocking her exit.

"Do I need to chain you to one of your guards?"

Esme pushed past him, suddenly finding a suitable target for her anger. "You forget you're addressing your queen, Tearlach." Chilled from the frigid water, she retrieved the blanket from the end of her bed and wrapped it around her shoulders.

"Am I? Because a queen would understand that dangers lurk around every corner. That no one can be trusted." She turned, ready to defend herself. "If he had—" Tearlach looked up at the ceiling and fisted his hands at his sides.

Esme's anger crumbled.

"He didn't touch me," she said softly. Seeing a muscle feather along Tearlach's jaw, Esme walked over and took one of his hands. He looked down, locking his dark eyes with hers. "Tearlach, your father was only trying to intimidate me. He might be arrogant, but he's not stupid enough to harm me in my own palace." When Tearlach didn't seem convinced, she added, "Don't worry. If he gets that close to me again, I'll strike him down with a bolt of lightning."

Tearlach's mouth curved up into a satisfied grin.

Chapter Twelve

"HOW DID YOU know I'd be able to travel safely to Periwen—that I could cross the fog?" Esme asked Sully as they settled on a stone bench beneath one of the towering sycamores.

Sully folded his hands on his lap, not at all surprised by the directness of her query. "Your mother told me, the night she created the lifeblood crystal that could bind you to another."

Esme called up the vision she'd seen of that night. She saw her mother pulling a thread of light—of life—from Esme's infant body, then coiling it into a tiny vessel shaped like a crystal.

"She knew that Tremaene might not always be safe. She told me that if I ever needed to hide you away, I should send you to the mortal realm." Sully shook his head, closing his eyes. "When I questioned her, she explained that the fog was no longer the impenetrable shield it once was."

"But how did she know?"

Sully turned to look at Esme. "Your mother...accompanied a general and three warriors across the sea at the end of the Dark War."

"She what?"

"Do you recall me telling you of the powerful Fae who used dark magic during the war, and how your mother...defeated him?"

Esme rubbed her hands together nervously, remembering all too well what Sully had told her when she'd first returned to Tremaene. But her mother hadn't killed the man. Erena had only succeeded in draining his power enough to spell him into eternal sleep.

"She crossed the fog herself?"

Sully nodded. "When they set off across the seas to seal that… *creature* away where no one would ever find him, they intended to travel south, around the barrier. But after losing their bearings one night, they found themselves heading straight into the fog. Only they didn't crash into an unyielding barricade as expected. They crossed right through it, and came to discover that the fog simply altered their magic. And their appearances."

Esme could only recall crossing the fog on her journey back to Tremaene. She suppressed a shudder, remembering the feel of the strange, tangible, shifting mass.

If Esme couldn't find a way to restore Tremaene's land and waterways, would the vulnerable land across the sea be in danger? A land that somehow survived *without* magic.

"Who else knows the mortal realm can be reached?"

"Your father was informed, and those who accompanied your mother on the voyage. But you needn't worry about them. Erena spelled the warriors to forget."

"And the general?"

"I was told he refused the king's directive, choosing instead to evanesce."

"I see." Esme contemplated the difficulty of making such a choice. It was a common practice, deciding to give up a long life, and fade from existence. She'd never witnessed the sacred ritual herself, but it was the reason her parents had been her only living progenitors. There were few of her kind who chose to remain in their bodies more than a few centuries. Instead, most decided to give up life by breaking the compact between their magic and their physical selves.

Her father had explained it to her once when she'd asked about her ancestors—their portraits staring down at her in the great hall. He'd told her that with age came wisdom. But after so many years, the wealth of accumulated knowledge began to feel more like a plague, and one couldn't help but long for the freedom of youth. There was a weight, he'd told her, in knowing life, in knowing the secrets of the world—a weight so heavy that it was nearly impossible to return to the blissful mind of innocence. After so many years, when the world had been walked a thousand times over, youth could no longer be found. And when that time came, one would choose to leave their physical form behind and begin anew. By stepping into the world beyond.

But age wasn't the only reason. Esme understood why warriors who'd survived the horrors and devastation of the Dark War might decide not to go on. And the general was no exception.

Esme wondered if one retained memories in the hereafter. Evanescing was either a final escape or an eternal curse.

"Orianna must have known as well, or at least she did once her scouts tracked me there," she reminded Sully. "Surely others know the mortal realm can be accessed."

"When they sensed your signature, they likely didn't know where you were, only the direction from which your signal originated. Thanks to Tearlach, none of them returned, so there's no reason to think Orianna even knew where they'd gone. And even if she did, she wouldn't have revealed it. She'd led everyone in the kingdom to believe you were killed nine years ago."

Esme let out a breath, feeling the knotted tension in her shoulders loosen a bit.

"The only people who know are loyal to you, my dear. Armel, Hazel, and Killian are aware."

Esme nodded. They knew because she and Tearlach had revealed where they'd been hiding all those years, not realizing that Esme's whereabouts—and the fact that she was even alive—had been kept secret.

"The generals know, as well," he added.

Right. She'd forgotten how she'd carelessly revealed the existence of iron in the mortal realm when they'd strategized about deposing Orianna. Thinking back, they hadn't seemed fazed by the mention of Esme and Tearlach's habitation during those years.

"It wasn't you," Sully assured her. "I'd already told them myself. After spending so many years lying to them, it was the only way for us to retain their trust and loyalty in the coming battle."

"I see. And...I understand. So, no one else from Altan knows?" Esme had heard whispers of speculations—that their long-lost princess had been hidden in the far reaches of the kingdom or on some faraway, uncharted island. But an official declaration had never been made. Even the other royal guards, she realized, didn't know where she'd been all those years—had never asked.

"No one bothers asking for the truth when their wild musings are far more entertaining." Sully grinned, but when he placed his hand atop hers, his serious expression returned. "And the rest of Tremaene has no reason to believe that Periwen can be reached. Do not distress yourself, My Queen, the mortal realm is safe."

She offered a slight smile as Sully rose, offering his arm.

"Do you remember the time you tried to climb the ivy on the wall outside the library, thinking it would be just as sturdy as a tree? You couldn't have been much older than three years."

Esme let her smile grow into something more genuine. "I do, but tell me again."

––––––––––––––

Thoughts of the Order returned as she climbed the grand staircase. She couldn't seem to keep them tucked away for long.

It was strange that the royal library hadn't contained a drop of knowledge about the institution when a high-priestess had ruled for so many years.

Pondering where else she might find answers, Esme halted mid-step. The image of a heavy tome flashed through her mind—its lengthy title stretching across two lines in a perfectly curved script: *Ordained: The complete history of the Order of Tremaene's high-priestesses.* And Beglan could very well have others at his bookshop.

She hurried to her room. But just as Cahir and Quinlan took up their positions outside her door, she heard Tearlach's voice. Slowly, she moved toward the low rumble of conversation, holding up a hand when her guards made to follow.

Peering around the corner, she saw Tearlach facing a woman. His head was bent toward her, his gaze soft. The woman was beautiful. A scarlet ribbon was braided through her long dark hair, holding it back from the faint golden shimmer of her face. Still in her traveling clothes, she must have sought out Tearlach as soon as she'd arrived at the palace.

Esme's mind spun with speculation as the woman's soft voice reached her. "Olan sent word as soon as he learned you were here. I came as quickly as I could. Oh, Tearlach, it's been so long." She placed a trembling hand on his chest and gazed up at him longingly.

Esme's own chest constricted at the sight, and she realized she shouldn't have been there, witnessing such a private moment. But before she could sneak away, she saw Tearlach bring his broad hand up to cover the woman's slender hand, then pull her into an embrace.

Without meaning to, Esme inhaled sharply.

Tearlach's eyes found her instantly, not twenty paces away, intruding on the moment.

He pulled away from the woman, but his eyes stayed locked on Esme as he leaned in to whisper something to the woman. He inclined his head to where Esme stood.

The woman stepped away from Tearlach, startled. She mumbled a "Your Majesty" as she swept into a graceful curtsy.

Esme was struck by the sight, no longer able to flee unnoticed.

As the woman rose, Esme apologized for interrupting. "I didn't mean to—"

"Esme." Tearlach linked arms with the woman, bringing her forward. Her eyes flicked to Tearlach at his use of Esme's given name. "I'd like to present my mother, Genvieve, Lady of Isloran."

The air was forced from Esme's lungs. Was it relief she felt? She tried to ignore the sudden fluttering of her heart as she breathed the words "His mother," then hurried over to grasp Genvieve's hands.

The woman's surprise at Esme's informality was clear. But when Genvieve shifted her gaze over Esme's shoulder, she realized that the woman had likely gone to great lengths to avoid being seen. Undoubtedly, Lord Torin wouldn't approve of his wife seeking out the company of their estranged son.

Esme glanced at the slightly ajar door of Tearlach's room. It wouldn't have an adequate seating area. And while her suite didn't boast a separate room, it would be far more comfortable. Besides, there'd be nothing amiss if the Lady of Isloran was seen entering or leaving the private suite of the queen.

It took some persuasion, but Tearlach finally agreed, leading his mother toward Esme's room with a hand at the small of her back. Once inside, he took her cloak and escorted her to one of the sofas.

Esme watched the two of them sit hesitantly, wondering how long it'd been since they'd seen each other. By the way Genvieve looked at her son, Esme guessed it'd been a long while.

After ringing for tea and refreshments—surprised that her maids weren't already privy to her guest's presence, and pleased that for once she could actually call for them—Esme made to leave.

Before she reached the doors, she felt Tearlach beside her. He gripped her arm.

"And where are you going?"

"For a walk around the grounds," she responded innocently.

"Didn't you just come from outside?"

"Tracking my every move, are you?"

"Always."

"If you must know, I was speaking with Sully and returned just now only to realize I'd forgotten to visit the east gardens." She lifted her hand and wiggled her fingers to imply her intention in visiting the plants and trees she hadn't already touched that morning.

Tearlach arched one of his dark brows, trying to detect the lie in her words. But she wasn't lying. She'd every intention of walking through the gardens. If only briefly.

"And I assure you, I won't slip from Cahir and Quinlan's protection."

After a moment and a strained exhale, Tearlach rejoined his mother.

Esme was hurrying down the stairs when she spotted Mairtín.

"Your Majesty!" His face lit up. The palace butler had a talent for drawing cheerfulness from everyone who crossed his path. Even as a child—and even when she'd been in the foulest of moods—he'd managed to brighten her day with his gleeful demeanor. She wondered if it had something to do with his attire. With more gold than the uniforms her guards wore, and black polished boots, Mairtín always looked turned out, like he could announce the arriving guests for a royal ball at a moment's notice. It was the same uniform she remembered from her youth, but there was something she hadn't—couldn't have—recognized before. He bore a striking resemblance to an illustration she'd come across while leafing through a children's book in a shop back in Debarrow. It was a story about a young boy's toy soldiers that came to life in the night.

Her smile grew as she pictured him marching down the corridor with a sword swinging at his side.

"Mairtín, I was wondering if you might assist me with something."

"Anything, Your Majesty." He stood up straighter in anticipation of the task.

"I'd like a desk to be brought to my room."

"Pardon me, Your Majesty, but wouldn't the royal office be more suitable—allow for more space?"

"No," she nearly yelped, then softened her tone. "You see, I find myself so very busy with all that must be done, and having everything close at hand will simply be…more convenient," she finished, hoping her explanation came across as sincere.

After a long pause, he bowed his head. "Certainly, that can be arranged." For a man who was bred on decorum and procedure, she admired his acceptance. "I'll see to it personally, Your Majesty."

"Thank you, Mairtín." She smiled brightly and took his hands. His eyes widened at the gesture—she really needed to stop touching everyone.

Outside, Esme hastened her steps, hurrying toward the eastern grounds. She'd assured Tearlach that she'd walk through the gardens, after all.

After swiftly walking the perimeter, she veered south, striding toward the stables.

Chapter Thirteen

WHERE ARE YOU going? Tearlach growled. Though it was expected, the vibration set Esme's teeth on edge. She'd known she wouldn't get far before Tearlach felt her gone. That aspect of their Lifeblood Oath had saved her life more than once, but made sneaking away rather difficult.

You wouldn't have let me go otherwise, she replied calmly. *And I need information from Beglan's shop.*

She shivered, feeling his fury rumble through her. Esme had never *felt* anything from him before, only the thoughts he chose to project. She wondered if it was intentional or not.

Beglan's shop is safe. And wasn't it you who searched every inch of that place when you left me there?

There was no response.

I'll be back soon, she assured. *Don't worry. Cahir and Quinlan will protect me should any book-related incidents transpire.*

Aside from another faint growl, Tearlach was quiet.

Quinlan sat across from her in the carriage, her jade eyes shifting between the two small windows. Esme sat in the center of the other velvet-covered bench, only able to glimpse the lower levels of the buildings they passed. She wanted to gaze up at the flowering vines hanging from balconies and the gleaming edges of copper roofs, but her guard wouldn't allow her near enough to see out.

Neither had challenged her when she'd informed them of her plans to leave the palace, but it was clear they didn't particularly appreciate Esme sneaking off without informing Tearlach or Captain Sullivan.

Cahir directed the driver to avoid main roads and town centers, so they wound through a maze of narrow streets. The carriage was discreet—hardly resembling a royal convoy—but the craftsmanship of the vehicle still made it identifiable as one that belonged to the crown.

As they pulled to a stop outside of Beglan's bookshop, Cahir called down for them to wait.

When he returned, swinging open the door, his traveling cloak shifted to reveal the armor beneath. They must have been terribly hot with the additional layer, but it concealed their identities as royal guards—and therefore Esme's.

"The proprietor is alone," he informed them, and Esme realized that she should've sent word to Beglan before showing up on his doorstep. She pulled her hood over her head, then stepped down from the carriage, taking Cahir's hand. He quickly ushered her inside.

"My Queen. So wonderful to see you again." Beglan shuffled to allow them entry.

Esme's eyes traveled up the large man, a smile spreading across her face. "Beglan. It's good to see you as well. And under far less dire circumstances."

He nodded, but made no comment about her previous visit—when things had not gone as planned.

"I hope you don't mind that I've stopped by unannounced."

"Certainly not. I will assist my queen in any way I can. Now, what is it you're in need of?"

Quinlan had remained outside, but Esme spared a glance toward the back of the shop where Cahir had stationed himself. Gesturing for Beglan to follow, she made her way through the rows of bookcases until she spotted the familiar spine. She slid it from the shelf and turned the cover toward Beglan. "Do you have any others like this?"

Beglan eyed the tome, considering her request. "Hmm. I haven't stocked any books on the subject for some time. After Orianna took the throne, folks in Meallán weren't too interested, you see?"

Esme nodded. "So, this is the only one you have?" The title claimed it contained the complete history of the Order, but she didn't want to rely on a single source. Though, if her previous search had taught her anything, it was to be grateful for whatever she could find.

"Perhaps..." Beglan looked over the top of Esme's head. She turned and followed his gaze to the cubbies built into the wall above the counter. Behind the sliding glass doors were books that looked as though they'd existed longer than the kingdom itself.

Beglan carefully inspected the fragile collection without inquiring as to why the new queen was seeking information about an institution that had been wiped out. Esme didn't offer an explanation either, she simply set the book on the counter and started paging through it. It didn't take long to realize that what had been titled *The complete history* was in fact not complete at all. *A vague overview* would've been a more appropriate title. It seemed closer to something new initiates were given upon joining the Order than an accurate account of the Order's history and origins.

Beglan stepped off the tiny stool that looked as though it might splinter under his weight, holding a wide book that was stitched along the short edge by a thread-thin gold wire. It appeared to be a ledger.

After carefully handing it to her, Beglan found a small table and led her into the reading alcove. He moved the comfortable chairs back to make room, then, seeming satisfied with the temporary workspace, gave Esme a bow and left her to her research.

The ancient book was, as suspected, a ledger. While the beginning pages outlined the basic duties high-priestesses performed, their connection to the gods, and their selfless servitude to the kingdom—the same story every child of Tremaene learned—the second section was a record of ordinations. Most of the early entries were too faded to read, but halfway through, the names became more legible. Along with each woman's birthplace and date of ordination, the elder high-priestess who performed the ceremony and subsequent temple assignment were also listed.

The last ordination was recorded only a few years before Orianna had...*ended* the Order. Beglan must have acquired it from someone who'd found it in one of the abandoned temples.

Esme exhaled and closed her eyes for a moment. Her people had suffered so many injustices and tragedies in her absence.

Returning to the earlier pages, Esme squinted to make out the name on the first line. The ink was too faint to decipher, so she traced her finger across the row to the date at the end, which was slightly darker. The woman had been ordained nearly a thousand years prior. Strange, Esme thought. Maybe there were other registers, or perhaps official lists hadn't been kept earlier than that date. The Order was certainly older than a mere millennium.

She glanced across the bookshop to the glass-doored shelves that housed other rare books, wondering if Beglan had any that went further back into Tremaene's history. Even a mention of the Order might give her some clue as to the origins, or how initiates were chosen. She was beginning to fear that young women destined to follow that path might only be recognized by others with similar gifts.

Beglan emerged from the back room with a tray of biscuits, jam, butter, and a silver pot of tea. The sight of food made her stomach growl, reminding her that she'd missed the midday meal.

"I thought you might be hungry."

"Thank you. I'm famished." She smiled and set the book aside.

He seemed quite eager to serve her, and Esme didn't think it had anything to do with who she was. Looking over the pair of stacked teacups and saucers, the small spreading knives, and the delicately embroidered linens that looked as though they'd never been used, she wondered if Beglan's books were the only things he had to care for in his life. She knew he was from the north; certainly he hadn't set up a life so far from home all alone.

"Beglan, do you…have any family in Meallán?"

"Not anymore." He shook his head as he arranged each cup.

Esme held her breath, fearing she knew what had become of them.

After pouring the tea, he continued. "We lived in the north when I was young. My father was a traveling merchant, always leaving my mother and me for long stretches. But he never failed to bring back special finds for us. For my mother, it was usually a bar of finely milled soap or a pouch of dried blooms. For me, he brought home books."

Esme grinned as Beglan pulled over one of the overstuffed chairs and settled in.

"He died during the war," Beglan mentioned easily as he reached for a biscuit. "He'd traveled down to Donellis, to the city of Amery, days before our town guards were pulled away to the battles that had sprung up throughout the western kingdom. He never returned."

"I'm sorry to hear that."

Beglan nodded. "My mother wanted to stay in the mountains for a while. It was our home, after all. But I wanted to see a big city, so we eventually picked up and traveled down here. We came to Meallán to inquire about vacancies in the nearby towns. I thought we'd only stay a night or two. I was worried my mother would find the noise and chaos of such a bustling place overwhelming, but she surprised me. We stumbled upon a cheese shop—you know the one a street up, across from the Bilberry Theatre?" Esme nodded and Beglan chuckled. "In all my years, I don't think I'd ever seen her so excited as she was when her eyes fell on that case in the front window. We only had soft cheeses in the mountains, and never anything as interesting or varied as they carried. Aged cheeses that needed a grater to cut. Rounds of bloomy rinds with creamy centers." Beglan hummed. "She was in paradise. I could hardly pull her from the shop when they closed up for the night."

He took another biscuit, split it, and offered half to Esme.

"I wasted no time in setting up this shop."

Esme smiled, thinking of Beglan as an eager young man.

"We had a good many years together. Until my mother was arrested for buying illegal goods at the market."

Esme frowned. "She...what?"

"She had a rare form of water magic," Beglan offered.

Orianna.

"Beglan, I'm so sorry. I can't—"

He waved a hand and lifted the nearly empty pot of tea to offer more. Esme numbly accepted. They were quiet as the minutes ticked by.

Finally, she asked, "You never married? Never started a family of your own?"

Beglan looked out the small window beside the hearth. "Books have always been my life."

When his look became more wistful, Esme wondered if he ever desired more than that. If he wanted companionship beyond the book-lined shelves.

He turned back to her. "Did you find what you were looking for?"

"Not exactly. I wonder..." She glanced around the shop. "Do you have any history books that date back further than a millennium?"

Beglan took a sip of tea, then cradled the tiny cup in his large hands, pondering the query. Esme waited. The man never seemed in a hurry.

After what felt like several minutes had passed, he met her expectant gaze. "Now that I think of it, no. Since I've been in the business these hundred-some years, I can't recall ever coming across one quite that old. Peculiar, that." He cocked his head to the side. Then, as if a memory sparked in his mind, he shot a glance to the stairs at the other end of the shop.

Without saying a word, he rose from his seat and ascended the narrow staircase, disappearing around the corner of the landing. Esme followed the sounds of his heavy footfalls as he made his way around the above-stairs room.

"There is this," Beglan said when he returned, placing a small square book on the table. It couldn't have contained more than a dozen pages between its faded covers. The title was written in a different language, but judging by the worn, gilded illustration—

Esme looked up. "A children's book?"

"Indeed. I acquired it with several others in a trade a few years back. As I don't typically carry that sort of thing, I stored it away."

"And why…"

"The printing date inside the cover."

Esme slowly lifted the cover, careful not to disturb the frayed binding. "Well, this is quite a bit older than anything I've seen," she remarked, reading the date again. It was nearly sixteen hundred years old. "Do you know the language?"

"The Old Language. I've never heard it spoken, but I've come across documents and letters that appear to use it as a sort of secret dialect. I'd always assumed it was used for confidential correspondence."

"Na Ceithre Shéasúr." She pronounced the words on the title page slowly. "Do you know what it means?"

Beglan focused on the words for a long moment, then shook his head. "They're not familiar. But, the ones below…" He leaned forward to look more closely at the line of script beneath the title. "That"—he pointed to the first word—"I believe is the word for cycles or patterns." Then, with a simple bow, Beglan left her alone to ponder the mysterious phrase.

Turning to the first illustrated page, Esme took in the delicate line drawing that depicted a scene she knew well. Though how anyone in Tremaene could even imagine such a scene perplexed her. It was drawn with dark ink that had faded to a muddy gray over the centuries. But even with the absence of color—or maybe because of it—she knew without a doubt that the image depicted a winter landscape.

Esme might not have been able to decipher the Old Language, but she suspected that the title of the book had something to do with seasons.

She consulted the printing stamp again. Next to the date was a location. Though she wasn't familiar with the city name—which in and of itself was disconcerting—Tremaene was listed at the bottom. Her initial suspicion that the book had somehow originated in Periwen and had unbelievably ended up in their realm was unfounded.

It didn't make any sense at all, but the book had clearly been crafted in Tremaene.

Unease flooded her veins as she carefully turned the brittle pages to reveal the same landscape in springtime. Instead of bare trees and hills of fluffy snow, the branches held tiny blossoms, and the hills were covered in what looked like crocuses. The summer tree on the following page was thick with leaves, which then blanketed the ground of the autumn landscape.

Why would a children's book—or any book for that matter—detail phenomena that were exclusive to the mortal realm? Seasons were a hardship found only there because the land was devoid of magic.

She flipped back to the winter scene. High-priestesses would never willingly allow such a great imbalance of the elements, especially one that would cause plants to die and lakes to freeze. Esme knew quite well the tedious labor and planning it took to survive those harsh conditions, and the months that followed of waiting for fragile new vegetation to bear fruit. It was unfathomable to think that high-priestesses would allow such a burden in Tremaene.

Esme glanced up at one of the square windows. The sun was about to set.

"Beglan?" she called out.

"Yes, My Queen?"

"Might I borrow this book for a bit?"

"You may keep it," he said without hesitation.

"Then I insist on paying for it." She looked to Cahir at the back door. With any luck, he had a few silvers she could borrow.

Beglan placed his broad hand lightly on her shoulder. "That's not necessary. How often do I have the opportunity to host the queen of Tremaene for the afternoon?"

"Thank you, Beglan." Esme smiled back, seeing the pride in his eyes. "I was wondering...why is this children's story the only book you have that dates back so far?"

He looked off in no particular direction, seeming to consider her question as though it'd never occurred to him. After a moment, he said, "I can only guess that others must have been seized or destroyed."

"Really?"

"It's the only logical explanation, wouldn't you say?"

"I suppose." Esme hadn't wanted to consider that. "But why would someone destroy books?"

"Perhaps they contained histories or stories that were best kept secret," he speculated.

Many had been kept from her. But what might have prompted such widespread censorship?

"Then why leave a children's book?"

As she'd come to expect, Beglan mulled over the question at length. "I suppose some wouldn't think a story for children could contain anything worth censoring."

She glanced down at the thin volume in her hand—a book that only one who'd experienced such conditions in Periwen would recognize as anything other than a collection of fanciful tales.

Chapter Fourteen

"THERE YOU ARE!" someone shouted as Esme led her reluctant guards down to the kitchens in search of food. A tall man strode toward them. His dark auburn hair curled slightly at the nape of his neck—the warmth offsetting the cool color of his eyes. But while he was taller than most, his narrow frame and the way he carried himself made Esme suspect he wasn't an off-duty palace guard.

"Myles, what are you doing here?" Cahir looked taken aback.

Myles. Cahir's partner.

"Looking for you. No one at the barracks seemed to know where you were."

Esme noticed color rising on Cahir's cheeks and stepped between the two men. "Myles, it's a pleasure to finally meet you."

His sapphire eyes flashed when they took her in. With her traveling cloak, he clearly hadn't realized whose company Cahir had been keeping.

"Your Majesty." He yielded a step and swept into a low bow. "I didn't— That is, I'm sorry. I wasn't aware—"

"It's nothing." Esme waved off his apology. "We were just going down to the kitchens. Would you care to join us?"

Myles exchanged a look with Cahir. "I'd love to." He offered his arm.

When they reached the ground floor, Myles leaned in, keeping his voice low. "I'm sure I don't have to tell you, but there's some serious edginess coming off your guards."

She smirked. "They're just grumpy because they missed dinner. But I'm about to remedy that."

"You really think they're going to eat while on duty?" he asked, raising his brow. She hadn't considered that.

Myles pushed open one of the heavy double doors, and a blast of steam hit Esme's face. She watched it rise up, slinking in waves over the rafters of the high ceiling before vanishing through the propped-open doors and into the night.

Rows of sinks and drying racks stretched along the wall. White towels hung limply from rods above the basins, bathing in steam.

"Excuse me," Esme addressed the sturdy woman whose arms were elbow deep in suds.

"Kitchens are closed till morning!" she called back. The man toweling off a copper pot beside her—one that was nearly the size of her small tub in Debarrow—glanced over his shoulder. His eyes widened at the sight of her, and the heavy pot slipped from his hands, clanking to the floor.

"Gareth, what in the name of the gods—" the woman barked, but was cut short when the man nodded urgently toward Esme. "Your Majesty!" She discarded the platter she'd been washing to furiously wipe her hands on the towel at her hip. "Come in. Come in." She gestured past the giant hearth. Stockpots of simmering stews and soups lined the metal grates above the flames. "I'm Rosaleen, the head cook," she claimed with pride.

"Yes, of course," Esme quickly replied, giving the impression that she knew everyone in her employ. "Rosaleen"—she tried out the name, though it didn't summon any memories—"I wonder if we might get a bite to eat; if it wouldn't be too much trouble. I was careless, and let the time escape me."

The woman raised her chin as though she might scold Esme, or throw her out of the kitchens. Narrowing her eyes, Rosaleen said, "I think we can manage that," then let out a jovial laugh. "This way." She flicked her hand toward the largest work table, which stood imposingly in the center of the space. "What kind of cook would I be if I let my queen go hungry?" Rosaleen moved around the table, pulling out stools that were hidden beneath. "Sit. Sit." She patted one of the seats.

At her command, Gareth was sent to the cellar to bring up wine. Esme watched him through the open door of the buttery as he grabbed a lantern from a hook and descended the steps at the far end. The other woman, Molly—who seemed unaware of anything aside from kneading dough—was instructed to prepare a tray of sliced fruit.

Finley quietly introduced himself before joining Rosaleen in assembling a platter of cured meats, cheeses, fresh tomatoes, and roasted root vegetables. Esme watched in amazement at how quickly everything came together.

Cahir and Quinlan both refused to partake, claiming they weren't hungry. Instead, they positioned themselves between Esme and the four entrances.

Unable to resist—or further entice them—Esme layered vegetables, cheese, and a leaf of basil onto a thick slice of crusty bread that smelled like sourdough, then drizzled walnut oil and verjuice over top. Myles did the same, adding several portions of meat to his, then leaned over and whispered, "Lie."

"What?" Esme mumbled, taking a bite with grilled purple carrots and pickled radish.

"They're lying." He took a second bite of his own sandwich, finishing it off, then gestured toward her guards. Reaching for more, he said, "Though, I'm sure you'd already guessed."

Taking a sip of wine, she glanced between Cahir and Quinlan, then back to Myles.

At her questioning look, he explained, "I can sense when people aren't telling the truth."

"Oh." She couldn't keep the pitch of surprise from her voice. "I've never…" she began, but figured most people told him they'd never heard of such a thing. "What a useful gift," she said instead.

"It can be." He shrugged.

Esme scooped a few raspberries onto her plate, contemplating the downside of being able to discern lies. It seemed like a beneficial trait.

At the clink of metal, she looked over to see Gareth arranging newly polished pots in order of size from the hooks hanging above one of the work tables. Molly continued to knead dough at the counter behind them, and Finley whisked something that smelled of vinegar, strawberries, and lavender in a large copper bowl, which he then poured into several tall jars. Esme wondered how late their shift went and when the morning crew began.

"I'm surprised I never saw you during your time in Altan." Myles drew her attention back.

"Oh. Well, that was certainly my fault. Tearlach had me following a pretty intense routine of weapons and magic training."

"I heard about that. Even so, our paths might not have crossed. That big guy over there dominated most of my time before we came here," Myles said with a wink. Esme blushed and resisted looking over at Cahir—who could no doubt hear their conversation. "Heard you have a warrior of your own."

Esme grabbed another piece of bread, slapped on a thick tomato slice, and shoved it in her mouth. Myles merely chuckled and filled his plate again.

Lowering her voice, she said, "Thank you for your help locating the… *items* we were searching for." Though she trusted her guards, she'd agreed to keep the information about the unordained priestesses private. And knew how quickly the story would spread if palace staff overheard.

"Oh, that." He gave her a conspiratorial look, but it quickly fell away. "It wasn't really me. I only sent messages to a few connections I have in the mountains. Nothing could've been easier." He popped a handful of blueberries in his mouth and smiled. But Esme could see past his modesty.

The Tamslo Mountain territory was vast, and Myles had managed to find a secret group of women who had no desire to be found. "Besides, I haven't much else to do with my time."

She hadn't thought about those who'd uprooted their lives and moved to Meallán. Aside from Cahir, he probably didn't know anyone in the city. "What do you want to do?" Surely she could help.

"Don't know." He seemed to consider. "In Altan, I arranged food trades throughout the valleys. Not much need for that here." He inclined his head to the food before them. She'd barely made a dent, but Myles was on his way to eating her share as well.

Esme thought about where his skills might come in handy, but came up short. "Well," she offered, "we'll think of something. I promise."

After she'd had her fill, she noticed the kitchen staff lingering. Their tasks had clearly been completed. Gareth was wiping down one of the work tables for the third time, and Molly had rechecked each round of rising dough more than once. Not wanting to keep them any longer, Esme thanked them for their trouble, while Myles wrapped the sandwiches he'd assembled for Cahir and Quinlan.

She bade goodnight to her guards and her new acquaintance when they delivered her safely to her room.

After clicking the door shut, she took the small lamp from the side table that flickered with a faint blue-white flame, then turned to face Tearlach.

Chapter Fifteen

TEARLACH DIDN'T SAY a word. The lines of his taut muscled form were silhouetted against the lights from the night sky.

Esme wondered if he'd waited in her room the entire night, or slipped through the passageway when he sensed her approaching.

"You knew where I was." She eased farther into the room.

"And where have you been since you returned to the palace?"

"You know the answer to that too." The glow from the lamp barely illuminated his face, but Esme could see his jaw tighten.

"It seems I'll need to have another talk with your guards."

"You'll do no such thing," she snapped, closing the distance between them. "It was my choice to visit Beglan's shop, and my choice to stop by the kitchens. Who do they answer to, you or me?"

Tearlach didn't move, but his dark eyes bored into her. When he drew a breath—no doubt ready to launch into a diatribe about her safety yet again—Esme stayed him with a hand to his chest.

But the moment she touched him, her mind blanked and her mouth went dry. She felt his heat through the thin weave of the shirt, felt the hard planes of his chest beneath her fingertips.

Tearlach looked down at where her palm rested, but made no move to capture her wrist or step away. When their eyes met again, his grew impossibly darker. Esme's head swam with confusing thoughts, but she managed a tight breath before forcing herself to slide her foot back.

Slowly she lifted her hand from his chest, unsure of why that seemingly benign gesture had stirred such—

She cleared her throat, and moved past him, desperate to put space between them. But with only the light of one lamp, the room felt much too small.

Summoning a fortitude she didn't quite feel, she whirled back around. "As I was saying"—she prayed to the gods her blush wasn't as evident as it felt—"we're not going to dispute my protection every time I do something you don't approve of. I'm not a child, and I know how to defend myself. Besides," she paused, softening her tone, "you needed time with your mother."

After a long silence, Tearlach rubbed his hand along the back of his neck and exhaled deeply.

"How is she?"

Tearlach studied her for a moment before taking two long strides toward her. Esme's breath caught at the renewed proximity, but he simply lowered himself to the sofa and braced his arms on his knees.

Esme looked down at him, then claimed the seat opposite. When she began to suspect he might not reveal anything about his mother's visit, she set the illustrated book on the table between them.

"It's been nearly two decades since I've seen her." Tearlach stared down at the book. "It's hard for her; my father rarely lets her out of his sight. But she's managed to sneak away a few times since I left home, when Torin's away. I'm not sure what excuse she gave this time. I only know that she'll be returning home soon." He looked up. "It was…good to see her."

Esme stayed quiet, hoping he might continue.

"Now"—he sat up straighter and slapped his hands against the tops of his legs—"tell me what you found."

Esme blinked at the abrupt shift, but recovered quickly and set about describing the two tomes about the Order, and how the earliest record in the ledger only dated back a thousand years.

When Tearlach picked up the book she'd brought back, she only needed to mention that no others existed from that time period for him to infer that some sort of censorship or purge had taken place. That he'd reasoned it so much quicker than she had irked her more than she cared to admit.

He examined each of the illustrations at length. But before the two of them could theorize as to why Tremaene's land had been tended so recklessly back then, the door to Esme's suite opened, and a sliver of light slashed across the floor as Cadwyn slipped inside.

"What did you find?" Cadwyn prompted as she set down a lamp with a bright white flame and plunked down beside Esme. Her white linen shirt and matching pants billowed with the movement, then settled around her as she tucked her legs under her. Esme realized it was the first time since they'd returned to Meallán that she'd seen Cadwyn in anything but a dress.

"How did you—" She stopped herself. "You'd make a good spy, you know that?"

Cadwyn smirked. "What makes you think I'm not one already?"

Tearlach closed his eyes and shook his head. "At least she's on our side." Cadwyn threw him a scowl.

Anticipating the ensuing debate about who was more committed to the protection of their queen, Esme showed Cadwyn the picture book.

At Cadwyn's confused expression, Tearlach explained how in the mortal realm, where magic wasn't summoned to regulate vegetation growth, wind, or rain, the natural world shifted, becoming a vastly different environment depending on the time of year.

"So, you mean to tell me that in Periwen the land and lakes freeze? Every year?" She turned to Esme with a look of disbelief. "What did you do for food and water?"

"It was...difficult getting used to it that first year. But you learn to plan ahead, store food. And not all water freezes. Rivers and streams continue to flow beneath a layer of ice."

"But somehow"—Cadwyn turned the brittle pages back to the illustration of spring—"it all comes back to life?"

"It does. I don't know how, but most life returns. Some plants need reseeding, others seem as though they've merely been sleeping during those cold months. As soon as the ground warms, they spring back to life, growing new branches and leaves. It takes time—months, really—before the greens are large enough to harvest, then longer still for trees and plants to yield fruit."

"Hmm." Cadwyn considered her. "Sounds like your variety of earth magic."

Esme gave a short mirthless laugh. "I was hardly responsible." Even as she said it, an image of her orchard flashed in her mind. "I don't know how life returns without magic. But somehow, every year, it does."

"So then, what happened here? If these shifts once existed as they do in the mortal realm—as unsettling as that thought may be—why don't we experience them anymore?"

Tearlach and Esme exchanged a glance. They'd been looking at the situation differently, asking themselves why the high-priestesses would've allowed the imbalance to occur. But what if the sisters had had no hand in it?

Esme thought about the register at the bookshop—the oldest ordination dating back only a thousand years—then stared down at the children's book that painted Tremaene as a completely different place mere centuries before that auspicious date.

"What if the Order hasn't always been a part of our history?" Esme told them about the register, and the date of the oldest entry.

"Certainly, there could be other records," Cadwyn offered.

"There could," Tearlach allowed. "But I believe what Esme is suggesting is that we consider that the Order might have been established around that time."

"That's absurd. The Order was forged by the gods. It's existed as long as our people have," Cadwyn countered.

"Is it possible that the gods created the Order as a response to something, to preserve our land?" Cadwyn and Tearlach watched Esme as she sorted out her theory. "What if..." She trailed off, shaking her head in frustration. There was something there, something she was reaching for, but it felt beyond her grasp.

What was the connection?

Picking up the book, she turned to the page with the spring landscape. Cadwyn's words echoed in her mind: *But somehow, it all comes back to life.*

Closing her eyes, Esme summoned the cave she'd glimpsed during their journey through the Tamslo Mountains. She hadn't quite been asleep—knew it hadn't been a dream. It was as though she'd been transported to the place where the endless magic of their world dwelled. Where it was formed.

She could still hear the gentle humming, feel the vibrations coming up through the bedrock, smell the fresh scent of spring rain and newly opened blossoms. Threads of light had danced around her, like the Loinnir Lights had fallen from the sky.

But what if she hadn't experienced the *true* source? What if it had only been a small part? Not the place where magic was born, but where it welled to the surface.

"The channels." Her eyes fluttered open.

"Channels?" Cadwyn asked tentatively.

Tearlach explained the map they'd found in the library that indicated hundreds of locations throughout the kingdom where raw magic rose to the surface.

"I don't understand. There are only five temples where high-priestesses can summon the elements. Hundreds of channels would mean..."

"Maybe the other channels were destroyed," Tearlach offered.

Esme caught his eye. *Destroyed?* she asked, but Tearlach simply shrugged his shoulders in response.

"How is that even possible?" she asked aloud.

"Nothing seems beyond the realm of possibilities at this point, love," Cadwyn said. "Now, let's think this through." She stretched her legs long, then shifted onto her other hip before tucking them under her again. "Perhaps damaging a site would be enough to block the flow of magic."

"But what would be powerful enough to cause such irreversible damage?" Esme raised.

"Some sort of calamity?" Tearlach suggested. "Quakes, floods...even a freeze that lasted too long, or penetrated too deep?"

If seasons had once existed in Tremaene—which seemed more plausible by the minute—such extreme conditions would certainly have been possible.

"If most of the other channels were damaged, and the five sites that remain to this day were...larger, more direct, stronger..."

"Say some of the channels were damaged. Wouldn't the magic simply form a new path to the surface?" Cadwyn posed.

"That seems logical. But perhaps it...can't." Esme looked at Tearlach as she considered something absurd. "What about the Heilyn Desert?"

Tearlach nodded, following the direction of her thoughts.

"The Heilyn Desert? I assume that's in Periwen."

"It is. It's a wide expanse of land with nothing more than cracked dirt and a few scrubby trees clinging to life. Any rivers that once flowed through the territory dried up long ago. It never rains in that part of Periwen." She paused. "What if the mortal realm *does* have magic, but the people there have no connection to it—no magic of their own, no one to summon it when needed. So if—*when*—channels were damaged..."

"...the humans would have no way of repairing it, or drawing up the raw magic themselves," Tearlach finished.

"But here in Tremaene," Cadwyn reasoned, "our gods could call upon those who possess more powerful magic to sustain our land with their gift."

Could it be? Was it simply that some women were born with stronger magic? And the call from the gods to join the Order was the only indication that they possessed the rare ability?

Could the origins of the Order be so easily explained?

Esme felt a small amount of optimism, though it was a precarious thing. Even if they'd stumbled upon a significant piece of Tremaene's lost history, there remained only one clear course of action: find more women who could summon the magic, or the kingdom would surely perish.

"I think that's enough for tonight." Tearlach rose and stretched his arms over his head. Esme looked away as the linen pulled tight across his chest.

"Yes. Good." Cadwyn clapped her hands resolutely as she stood. "This is good," she said again with a purposeful nod, then kissed Esme goodnight.

"Are you okay?" Tearlach asked once they were alone again.

"Oh, I'm fine. I was just..." Her thoughts kept circling the similarities between her own magic and the rebirth that seemed to happen during the spring. "I was wondering why I found Debarrow." Tearlach inclined his head, encouraging her to continue. "Of all the places I could have set up a life, why there?" Aside from the old-growth trees and wild plants that managed to thrive in such untenable soil, nothing else grew—until Esme had arrived, coaxing life back into the barren branches of the apple trees.

"If I were to venture a guess, I'd say you were unknowingly drawn to a place that needed you—that needed your gift, your touch. A place that offered a perfect opportunity for you to connect to your magic."

Esme weighed his words. Tearlach took a step closer, and in a softer voice, added, "I know the incident with the tree, and then with the wolf were...disconcerting, frightening even, but it could have been much worse. Magical awakenings are rarely painless or straightforward. I think the intimate connection you formed with the land helped ease you through the transition."

She stared up at him. He was close enough for her to feel the warmth coming off his body. She glanced at his chest—where her hand had rested earlier. Heat flooded her cheeks. She forced herself to look up.

Tearlach's eyes, though not as dark as they'd been before, looked like they were fighting a battle she wasn't privy to. But when he exhaled, his shoulders dropped, and the look cleared. Whatever his mind had been warring over had been decided. He scanned the room once more, then lifted a hand toward her shoulder.

She waited. Wanting that brief moment of contact.

But he let his hand fall back to his side.

ERICA SEBREE

Chapter Sixteen

RODERICK AND MADOC followed Esme through the palace. She was set on finding Mairtín to thank him for the desk he'd delivered to her room. But noticing more than a dozen palace maids filing out of one of the salons in the great hall, she changed course.

"Cadwyn?" Esme was surprised to find her lady-in-waiting gathering plates and sweeping crumbs from a settee. "What are you..."

"Tea," Cadwyn replied, as if it were a daily occurrence. Perhaps it was, Esme realized.

"Why didn't you tell me you were doing this? I would've made time—"

Cadwyn held up her hand. "This is merely to keep the lines of communication open with the palace staff," she said with a quirk of her deep red lips. "And they communicate much more freely when their queen isn't present."

"You mean gossip?"

"That is where truths are typically hidden, yes."

A reluctant smile spread across Esme's face. "How do you know all this?"

"You forget I called the palace home years before you came along."

"Fourteen years. You were barely grown," Esme reminded her.

"You'd be surprised at the stories I heard as a girl. People rarely think twice about watching their words when they think you're too young to understand." Her green eyes glittered with mischief.

"And did you overhear anything of interest today?"

"I might have. But I'll not have you worrying over that right now."

A protest was poised on her lips, but Cadwyn silenced it with a look. Esme huffed dramatically, then glanced around the room once more before she resumed her quest of finding Mairtín. It was the smallest of the salons. She studied the walls, looking for evidence of what it'd once been.

"This used to be the aviary," she said quietly, sensing Cadwyn beside her.

"It was."

Esme could picture the delicate wire mesh that had once divided the room in two, the perches decorating the back wall, the gilded trees in the corners. And the dozens of songbirds that had once filled the space. She could almost see them flitting about before her eyes, their feathers—an array of scarlets and deep purples, emeralds and sage greens, pale pinks and soft blues, iridescent blacks and earthy browns—flashing at the edges of her mind. She imagined the echoing melody of cheerful twitters and sharp trills of birds calling out to one another.

"Do you think they were..." Esme let the question hang in the stillness.

For several moments, Cadwyn remained silent. "It's been nearly a decade," she offered gently.

Esme nodded, choosing to believe they'd lived long lives, or had been released. She didn't want to think what Orianna might have done with them. It seemed any mark left by Erena had been wiped clean—as if she'd never existed. No matter that the room had been for Esme's enjoyment, not her mother's.

"I still don't know why they had to be kept in cages," Esme muttered, her lips flattening into a scowl.

"You don't know why?" Cadwyn asked incredulously.

"What?" Esme turned to face her.

Cadwyn stared back until amusement won out and she broke into a smile. "You really can't think why your mother insisted on an aviary?"

"I haven't the slightest idea," Esme lied.

"The maids were constantly cleaning up after that *flock*—How did you put it?—'stole into your room' one morning."

"Oh please, it was hardly a flock. A gaggle at best. And besides, I couldn't help it if they chose to fly into my room, then refused to leave."

"Mm-hmm. And what of the trail of nuts and fruit your mother found littering your floor just inside the doors that were ever so mysteriously left open the night before?"

"I know not what you speak of." Esme pressed her lips into a firm line.

Cadwyn arched one of her auburn eyebrows. "Well, I'm glad you've outgrown the desire to lure them into your room."

"Who says I've outgrown it? I'm simply not keen on waking to bird droppings all over my bedclothes. Or worse, my face." Esme scrunched her nose at the thought. Cadwyn laughed.

As the memories faded, she took in the salon's present state, noticing a few discarded dishes and an out-of-place footstool. But before Esme could reach for the closest crumb-covered plate, Cadwyn took her by the shoulders and turned her away.

"The least I can do is help you tidy," Esme protested.

Cadwyn clicked her tongue and gave her a gentle nudge out the open doors. "Off you go, now."

Esme sighed half-heartedly, but didn't argue. If she didn't soon locate Mairtín to thank him for the desk, she was bound to forget.

Roderick and Madoc found their way to her side as she marched out of the great hall. The soft, shimmering beams of midday sun angled in through the frothy panes framing the high-arching doors at the front of the palace, casting a pool of light across the cold marble floor. Stopping directly in front of the throne room.

Her gaze skittered over the sight. Her steps faltered.

It'd been easy enough to imagine that nothing lay beyond the curved rotunda wall. A space carved out of the palace. She could even tell herself that the sounds of reconstruction were coming from somewhere else entirely.

It'd been easy to pretend when both doors were securely latched.

Her eyes fixed on the one that'd been left ajar as her feet carried her forward.

Sounds of restoration drifted out. Esme crept closer to the narrow opening, thinking to spy only a glimpse. But as she neared, the sounds of hammers striking chisels, of emery cloth rubbing against stone, the chalky, mineral smell of freshly sanded marble, and the creak of suspended planks that reached up into the dome lured her closer.

Her palm pressed against the door, pushing it open before she could think better.

The view of the wrecked throne room filled her vision.

Behind Esme, one of her guards cursed quietly under his breath, before offering a quick apology. She wasn't sure who, but it occurred to her that neither had seen the destruction she'd caused.

No one, besides those who'd been there that night, knew what had transpired inside the throne room. Some of the guards who'd served Orianna—under threat of death—had stayed on as palace guards after she and her personal guard had been killed. Others had returned home.

None, Esme knew, would ever breathe a word about what had happened.

The rest of Tremaene had only been told that Orianna had been defeated, and that their rightful queen had been restored.

Even Tearlach and the warriors who'd made the journey with her didn't speak of that night. Esme suspected it was out of contrition that they'd been powerless to protect her. As such, she only confided in Tearlach when the memories forced their way to the forefront of her mind.

A high-pitched whistle drew the commotion to a halt, and the man who seemed to be in charge of the mass of workers and craftspeople came forward.

"Your Majesty." He bowed, discreetly brushing the dust from his hands. "Forgive the mess, I wasn't expecting you. Please, allow me to show you our progress." He indicated a path cleared of debris that Esme should follow into the center of the room.

"Oh, thank you…"

"Bradach, Your Majesty. Head of Palace Preservation and Maintenance."

"Yes, of course." But Esme didn't take a step farther. Her gaze swept through the rotunda. It seemed only a few columns had been damaged. Giant slabs of marble lay on the floor—which had been covered by a thick cloth, hiding the damage she'd done to the ornate tiles.

"Please, continue. I didn't mean to disturb your work." She could feel more than a dozen eyes on her before the workers slowly started up again.

A thickset man with heavily muscled forearms turned back to a half-carved block of marble. It would take several of the four-foot-tall cylinders stacked atop one another to create a single column. The man's muscles bunched with each strike of hammer against chisel, a thin sheen of sweat making his skin glisten. It took all his effort to chip away at the solid form.

And she'd destroyed it with little more than a thought.

Tearing her gaze away, she found herself staring at the concealed door at the far end of the room. The seams weren't visible unless one was looking for them. It was the door Cadwyn had used to sneak in that night. To save Esme from having to strike the final blow. To save her from the burden of ending a life.

Would that battle have haunted Esme's dreams if she'd been strong enough to do it herself? With her own magic? With her own hands?

Her skin heated at the thought—at the regret, the guilt, the cowardice she still felt.

Inhaling a breath she hoped would steady her resolve, Esme squared her shoulders, ready to leave. But her eyes trailed along the floor, coming to a stop in the center of the room. The fabric covering was a pale color, but all she could see was a pool of red so dark it was nearly black.

Her chest constricted. She couldn't bring herself to move from the spot.

A hand settled lightly on her arm, and a deep, soothing voice found its way through the cacophony of her mind.

With effort, she turned, looking up into Madoc's concerned eyes.

"Your Majesty, I believe I saw Mairtín heading toward the west wing earlier. Perhaps we should..."

Esme nodded absently, allowing him to lead her away.

After several hours of sparring with Cahir and two palace guards whose names she'd failed to learn, pushing past the pain of protesting muscles, and struggling through a short archery session with Hazel, Esme returned to the palace.

"How do you like it here?"

"I miss the mountains," Hazel replied, taking the stairs far slower than Esme knew she wanted.

"Me too. I miss...a lot of things." Tears welled unexpectedly. Maybe her fatigue was catching up with her.

Hazel pulled her to a stop when they reached her suite. "We're all here with you. This might not be the path you would've chosen, but you're not alone. You're still you...even under those fancy dresses Cadwyn keeps forcing you into."

Esme returned her smile as Hazel opened the door.

Halting, Hazel turned back to Esme. With a mischievous smirk, she stepped aside to reveal nearly a hundred flickering candles filling Esme's room.

Chapter Seventeen

AFTER KILLIAN HAD slipped out the night before, Esme had hoped a long bath would calm her racing pulse. When that hadn't worked, she'd recited the bedtime stories her mother would read to her each night. Then she'd lain awake for entirely different reasons—wondering if the book still existed somewhere in the palace, and picturing the tree where the fictional girls had discovered a secret tome of spells.

"Have you managed to take home any winnings yet," she asked Madoc.

"As a matter of fact, Your Majesty, I won three nights ago."

"Excellent!" She didn't bother to correct the title. It was no use.

"And lost it all the following night," Quinlan reminded him.

"They persuaded you to join as well?" Esme looked up at Quinlan, but the woman had fixed Madoc with a scowl. Esme glanced between them. "What?"

Madoc didn't seem the slightest bit abashed at the woman's harsh look. He stared right back and said plainly, "Quinlan's not allowed."

"Why not?" Esme's voice rose in outrage.

"Because I'm a woman." Quinlan spat the words.

Madoc barked out a laugh. "Don't believe her lies, Your Majesty. Quinlan, here, isn't allowed to join because we don't trust her. Not a whit."

Quinlan rolled her eyes. "Not this again."

"You can see everyone's next move! I hardly see how that's fair."

Esme stifled a laugh, recalling the woman's ability—a rare form of air magic that allowed her to see a few seconds into the future, making her practically invincible in a fight. As well as card games.

Quinlan scoffed, tossing her braid over her shoulder, but didn't refute his claim as the three of them strode across the great lawn in the early morning light.

When they reached the tree line, Madoc finally asked where they were headed.

"Just felt like a walk around the lake," Esme told him. She didn't need to see her guards' faces to know they were sharing a look about her oddly determined behavior.

Since the moment she woke, all she could think of was the tree from Ainsley and Ffion's story.

Only it wasn't the tree from their tales. The passage about the girls discovering a book hidden between the thick bulging roots of an ancient tree had been written with only the barest of details. Yet, when her mother would read that particular scene, she'd elaborate, painting a brilliant picture of the landscape, the knots and imperfections of the rough bark, the wildflowers scattered at the base, and the bright green grass that encircled it beyond the shade of the canopy.

Esme knew that tree. Knew it well.

Once they reached the opposite shore of the lake, she veered off into the uncultivated woods that occupied the southernmost grounds, stopping only when she reached a small clearing.

"Would you two mind waiting here?"

A look passed between her guards, but they nodded their agreement and remained at the grassy edge.

Esme approached the ancient tree that stood in the center. Harsh rays of morning light cut through the forested area, but most of the clearing was left in shadow. As she stepped beneath the wide-reaching limbs, she sensed a shift in the air. It was cooler. Heavier. It felt as though she was pressing through something tangible.

Roots arched out of the soil, covered in moss. Tufts of ferns peeked out from crevices formed between wood and earth. As she crept closer, tiny bell-shaped flowers sprang up around her. She was so focused on the tree that she hadn't noticed the slip of her magic. But her guards were surveying the already safe shelter of the woods far too earnestly to notice.

Stepping carefully up the bunching roots, she lowered herself and braced her hands. Inching forward on her knees, she reached the mighty trunk. A bright green lizard, no more than two inches long, darted over her fingers before disappearing into one of the dark crevices.

The bark felt warm, alive. Esme closed her eyes for a moment, feeling the energy of the tree as if it flowed through her.

Her mother had described the tree perfectly. And Esme suspected that she'd gone into such detail to ensure her daughter would one day understand the true purpose of the bedtime story.

She scooted around until her back was against the trunk, her legs stretched out atop the roots. With a deep breath, she let her eyes drift shut, dropping into the solidity that supported her. She concentrated on her breath for several beats until she felt a strange pressure at her hip. She ran her hand over the spot, but found nothing pressed up against her.

Esme opened her eyes to study the mountain of roots beneath her. She climbed down the swells of rough bark, moving to the location on the tree that mirrored the place where she'd felt the sensation. A narrow gap drew her attention. It seemed deeper than the others, as though it tunneled deep into the heart of the tree. With a determined breath, she reached her hand in.

Her fingers grazed soft moss before the space widened and the air dampened. She stretched her arm until her shoulder stopped her from going any farther. Feeling for the edges on either side, her hand struck something smooth. She ran her fingers along the surface until she found a corner. Gripping the object, she gently pried it from its notch.

A book. Wrapped in wax cloth.

Beneath the wrapping, the caramel-colored cover was tied shut with a knotted cord.

Even without opening it, Esme knew it was a journal—one her mother had trusted only her to find.

She clutched it to her chest, attempting to soothe the clenching sorrow she felt there. Brushing a stray tear from her cheek, she took a trembling breath. *Not here.*

With Madoc and Quinlan engaged in a hushed conversation, Esme turned her back to them and shoved the book down the front of her tunic. Her top wasn't tight enough to hold it in place, so she loosened her belt, sucked in her belly, and tucked it into the waistband of her fitted pants. The hard edges jutted out, so she wrapped an arm around her middle before clambering down to the soft ground.

Madoc turned at her approach. "Everything all right, Your Majesty?"

Esme glanced down at her arms—awkwardly folded under her breast. "It's rather chilly today, isn't it?"

"Is it?" Madoc's brows furrowed with concern. It wasn't the least bit cold outside. It never was.

Esme hastily added, "I really should have brought a cloak. Let's head back, shall we?" She didn't wait for a reply.

———————

Back in her suite, Esme found a tray of fruit, warm butter cookies, and a steaming pot of tea that smelled as though it'd just been steeped. Her maids always seemed to know precisely when she'd be returning.

But she couldn't think about food. She could only think about the book pressed against her stomach. She pulled it out and stared down at the worn fabric cover. Knowing someone might enter at any moment, she clutched it to her chest and went to hide in her dressing room.

Inside, doors closed behind her, she paused, letting the stillness sink in, bracing herself for what she might discover.

The morning light from the large circular window flooded the room in a soft yellow glow. Esme walked past the many rows of hanging garments, past the shelves lined with slippers in every color, past the drawers filled with all the accessories a queen should adorn herself with, then sat down behind the velvet ottoman at the far end.

As hidden as she'd ever be in the palace, Esme carefully unwrapped the book and unwound the ties. The smell of damp earth filled her nose as she ran her fingers along the first page. The parchment was soft from years hidden beside the roots of a tree, but the sheets were well-preserved, and it didn't appear as though the ink had bled or faded.

The first few pages were filled with notes that didn't seem related—some set apart in boxes, others underlined or starred. And while she couldn't form any connections between the random musings, Esme was certain they'd been penned by her mother.

A dozen or so pages in, there was a date at the top of a long entry. Looking ahead, she could see that similar entries filled the majority of the journal. The first several passages had been written almost daily, starting around the time her mother had joined the war effort in the Western Flats.

Esme read quickly, unable to slow herself, wanting to absorb every word her mother had inscribed. No battles were mentioned, and no fighting aside from training exercises. Erena's descriptions of the camp and her fellow warriors were scarce, but Esme still felt as though she were there, with her.

When the word "wildfire" snagged her attention, Esme read the passage carefully.

A wildfire broke out in the fields today. I reached the outskirts to find the entire village engulfed in smoke. I've never worked my magic over such an expanse before, but I managed to pull the air from the flames, extinguishing them. Only it was not enough. Three villagers perished. My fellow warriors attempted to give me solace, telling me again and again that my efforts saved hundreds. But still, my mind returns to the ones I could not save. If only I'd gotten there sooner, worked my magic quicker, more efficiently. I will carry their deaths with me.

Armel's mother had been one of the villagers who'd died. He'd had nothing but praise for Erena's bravery that day. Esme remembered his words well; they'd been filled with admiration and a deep respect for the future queen. Armel had seen her only as the savior of his village.

Still, Esme understood the burden her mother had carried for the loss of even one life. Esme carried many herself.

There was another brief passage before the entries skipped ahead several years.

We've just been informed that an unexpected force has descended upon the kingdom. Our faction will go north to join others in the fight. There are rumors spreading through camp that this unknown enemy has control over the dark magics.

Nothing was written about the end of the war, or the role Erena had played in it. Months later, she'd written about her first meeting with the king. Esme wasn't aware she'd started to cry until her vision grew blurry and a tear landed on her chest. She swiped them away, and hastily turned the page. She'd save the story of how her parents fell in love for another time.

Later, Erena had written:

Last night, I dreamt I was visited by him. The creature who was more darkness than man. I couldn't see his form, but I felt him in my mind. Perhaps it was only a memory, something reconfigured to mimic the events I forced myself to forget years ago. I've been telling myself all day that it wasn't real. That he can't reach me. But it felt real, so very real.

Esme stared at her mother's words. Not all dreams were imaginings or memories. She knew that all too well. Esme searched for more, but found no other mention of the dream.

Not until she discovered a page that bore her name as well.

I'd forgotten completely about that dreadful nightmare. It's been decades, after all. But it recurred last night. And it felt the same. Real. He returned, attempting to tunnel into my mind, to make me believe his thoughts were my own. When I forced him out, he spoke directly to me, his voice filling the room. He told me he was growing stronger, and that with time, it would not merely be his thoughts he projected across the expanse that divided us. I didn't say a word, too afraid that if I responded it would somehow give him power. Still, he went on, threatening that if I did not release him from his iron prison now, he wouldn't swiftly wipe the entire kingdom of Tremaene from the map once he regained his power, but would torture our people for all eternity. As I had done to him.

Upon waking, I entertained my fears for an hour or so, worried that if this child is a daughter who carries my magic in her blood, he will find her, haunt her dreams, lure her to him while she's young and vulnerable. But I see now that I was being foolish. It was only a dream. Nothing more. And even if, by some stretch, his mind breaches the walls of his prison, he will never escape it. The spell I bound him with is strong. I am certain. It will not weaken, not ever.

This very night, I welcomed a baby girl. As I look across the bed at her father cradling her to his chest, I'm overcome with joy. Never have I seen such a beautiful sight. I will name her Esme, as it means gracious protector. And she will be. One day, this child will protect our kingdom.

Esme shut the book, unable to read another line. Her throat felt as though a piece of stale bread was lodged in it. She stared at the perfect rows of slippers, counting them until her breathing returned to a smooth, even flow.

Though she couldn't bring herself to look at another of the heartrending passages, she couldn't help but wonder on which date her mother had written her final entry. Esme turned the book over and opened the back cover. She flipped through until she found the last page with notations. Only there was no date.

A word she didn't recognize graced the top, carefully underlined. *The Old Language?* Esme wondered.

Below what must have been a title were numbered entries with specific instructions written in the common language. A recipe, perhaps?

"No," she breathed. "A spell."

Esme's mouth dropped open as she took in the instructions on that page, and the twenty or so others that filled the back of the journal. Plants were listed in precise amounts—sometimes fresh and whole, other times dried. A few gave specific directions to face, locations in relation to natural formations or bodies of water, or timing of Neve's and Mios's lunar cycles.

Leafing through them, Esme noticed a familiar combination— one of fire, sandalwood, sage, and mugwort. And the only one that mentioned blood.

Esme couldn't discern the words at the top, but she knew the spell. With the joined lifeblood of two people, it would bind them together. In life. And in death. It was the spell that created the unbreakable Lifeblood Oath.

Scanning to the bottom of the page, Esme noticed a few lines that were jotted off to the side in a smaller script. Her eyes widened as she read the words.

The Lifeblood Oath can be broken?

She averted her gaze, feeling...Guilt? Guilt that she knew how to sever the oath when Tearlach didn't?

What would it feel like to be sundered from him? Would he leave if he were no longer bound to her, or might he choose to stay?

Esme stifled a twinge of sadness. Just knowing that the connection between her and Tearlach could be broken made her feel like she'd lost a part of herself.

She skimmed over the instructions and components of a few other spells, but being unable to translate their titles she couldn't glean their purposes. The notations in the margins were curious though. Her mother had ranked the volatility of each spell, and for those deemed particularly unpredictable or dangerous, the word "caves" was noted.

Caves? What caves?

She flipped through the pages until she reached the first spell her mother had recorded. And there, just beneath the title she couldn't read, were the words: *Highly unstable. Use the caves beneath the lake to contain until mastered.*

Esme blinked. There were caves beneath the lake?

Chapter Eighteen

AS PREDICTED, ESME didn't win a single round against Quinlan—though few ever did. When she offered a hand to pull her up, Esme gratefully accepted. Her muscles screamed in protest as she rose, but she didn't so much as wince. The feeling was familiar, and she knew it wouldn't last long.

Brushing the dirt from her pants, she thanked her opponent. Quinlan bowed her head and headed toward the adjacent training ring, no doubt in search of a better-suited partner.

Across the yard, Roderick held both swords out at his sides, inviting an attack, as Cahir stalked a circle around him, lazily twirling his weapon. Cadwyn was kneeling nearby, tightening a bandage around what appeared to be a deep sword wound on Madoc's leg. When she rose, Madoc kissed her on the cheek and bounded back into the ring to face both Roderick and Cahir.

"Excellent match," Sully remarked.

Esme choked out a laugh at the absurd comment, replacing her sword on the weapons rack. There'd been nothing *excellent* about her performance against Quinlan.

"She's difficult to best," Armel offered. "But you certainly put up a good fight."

"I tried, at least." She reached for the ties at her shoulder.

"Let me." Killian moved to help her loosen the chest plate. Free from the weight of it, she rolled her shoulders, then bent to unhook the plates covering her shins.

"May I interest you in a walk through the grounds, My Queen?" Sully asked when she straightened.

"You may."

They meandered quietly along the periphery of the woods in silence, until Esme noticed the wistful expression on Sully's face. It was the look he seemed to adopt whenever they were alone, indicating that his thoughts had turned to the past.

"What are you thinking about?" she asked.

Sully looked down at her. "The day you were born."

"Tell me," she encouraged.

He breathed in deeply, filling out his chest. "I remember waiting outside your mother's suite, awaiting your much-anticipated arrival." He paused for a long moment, looking off into the distance. "Never had I seen your mother so filled with joy. She was completely in love with you, asking me if I'd ever seen a more perfect child in all my years. I told her you were beautiful, just like her. And as enamored as Erena was, she gave you up long enough to let me hold you. You were just a tiny bundle with a shock of gold hair at the crown of your head. In that moment, holding your precious life in my arms, my whole world changed. I vowed to myself, to your mother, that I would do everything in my power to keep you safe, to protect you always."

Sully looked down at her, his eyes overflowing with so much love and pride that something shifted in Esme's perception. She regarded him a moment, studied him, then thought back to what he'd said. And what she'd read in her mother's journal.

"Sully?"

"My dear?"

Esme took a shaky breath. "Was there ever anything...*more* between you and my mother?" She held his gaze, trying not to look abashed at the accusation.

He blinked at her, then gave a soft chuckle.

Esme's eyes widened at the sound, but she held her breath.

When Sully's mirthful smile faltered, he said, "No, my dear. It's true that I loved your mother and always will, but anyone could see that Erena had eyes for only one man. And that man was not me."

Esme exhaled and looked away, embarrassed for asking such a thing of a person she'd trusted her whole life.

"But what you really want to know"—Sully's voice had gone quiet, causing Esme to meet his gaze again—"is whether I'm your father."

Her mouth dropped open.

"Let me assure you, Esme, that I am not. While I love you like my own, your father is your father." His eyes locked with hers as if he needed to be certain she understood.

"I see." She gulped. "I'm sorry for..."

Sully took her by the shoulders. "Your mother loved him more than anything in this world. Until you came along." Esme felt the hot sting of tears, but she blinked them away as Sully wrapped her in his strong embrace. He rested his chin on the top of her head and spoke softly. "Erena and I were dear friends, nothing more. I promise you that."

Esme pulled back. "You were more than that. You were our family, Sully. *My* family."

"As you are mine." He kissed the top of her head, then pulled her arm through the bend of his elbow, angling her back toward the path. "Now, where were we? Ah, yes. The day you graced us with your presence."

Esme blushed, squeezing his arm tighter. Shadows bled from the darkening woods, chasing a pair of rabbits from the underbrush. She glanced toward the palace, where the warm glow of evening flames spilled from the open doors atop the south steps.

"Your father wouldn't leave your mother's side once you arrived. I'd never seen him shirk his responsibilities to the kingdom as he did in those days following your birth. It was quite endearing, really. Your father refused to leave Erena's suite for days, despite his personal guard's urging and my own. But when both you and your mother fell asleep one afternoon, the midwife was finally able to convince him to leave your mother's bed long enough to bathe. As I recall, she mentioned something about infants being overly sensitive to—How did she put it?—unpleasant smells. I barely managed to keep a straight face at that comment."

Esme's smile widened; she'd never heard such stories of her father.

As they merged onto the path that skirted the great lawn, the rabbits darted back to their warren at the edge of the woods, right beneath the...*apple tree.*

She'd completely forgotten about the sapling she'd coaxed from the ground days after returning to the palace.

Pulling away from Sully, she ran toward it, reaching up to pluck the fruit that had taken shape.

Sully followed. "I've never seen such a tree. Are you sure the fruit is edible?"

Esme smirked as she pulled another from a low branch. "Remember the orchard I told you about?" She stepped back as Sully's look of concern turned to one of marvel. The half grin that followed told her he'd surmised the origin of the mysterious, stout tree.

He reached for one. "So this"—he held it up in one of the last rays of sun, examining it—"is an apple?"

"It is." She handed him the other, then went back to harvest the rest. "And they make delicious pastries."

Chapter Nineteen

Esme waited next to Roderick until Harlow nodded for them to enter.

A man she hadn't met previously glanced up from his hunched position over a large copper bowl, mumbled a greeting, then went back to his mixing. Esme grinned and rounded the hearth to find two faces she recognized.

"Your Majesty," both said in unison, surprise clear in their voices.

"Molly. Finley." She nodded to each. Not bothering to offer her assistance—knowing they'd decline—she set down her wrapped bundle. "I wonder if I might use one of your work tables and some of the ingredients on the back counter."

"But of course, Your Majesty," Finley answered.

Continuing their tasks, they watched as she untied the cloth, revealing a dozen ripe apples. Esme noted their bewildered expressions, but they said nothing as she went to retrieve flour, sugar, salt, and spices from the long row of canisters.

An hour later, everyone had gathered around her table—even Drummond, who'd finally introduced himself when he claimed a spot on one of the stools. Esme crimped the square edges, cut slits down the centers, then sprinkled sugar crystals along the tops of the tiny pastry pockets.

By the time they'd baked to a warm, golden brown, Esme knew morning was near. And while she hadn't slept much before a nightmare had woken her, the sugar she was soon to consume would leave her little hope of finding sleep again.

Her guards, as expected, declined to partake in enjoying the treats they'd watched her create. Was there some rule that forbade guards from eating while on duty?

After wrapping two of the remaining pastries, Esme swiped six goat cheese, tomato, and thyme tartlets from one of the many breakfast trays. Folding each into creased linens, she placed them in a basket she'd procured from the stack near the side door—inferring that they were for gathering herbs by the strong aroma of mint and lemon balm.

Roderick and Harlow followed as she left the kitchens and set off toward the barracks.

The Loinnir Lights had only begun to fade into the lightening sky, yet several matches were already underway. Perhaps they practiced at all hours.

She scanned the yard, seeing guards in various states of dress. One of the palace guards pulled a shirt over his head, then kissed Quinlan on her cheek before they strode off in opposite directions. Esme wondered what it was like to live in the barracks, with so little privacy. Though it wasn't like she had much of that herself.

She spied Killian and Armel across the central ring. When Killian lifted a tall copper mug to his lips, he caught sight of her over the rim. He gulped down its contents, then glanced around the yard before setting his mug on the long table behind him. Food was piled haphazardly on platters, as if it'd all been assembled in a rush.

Taking in the multitude of palace and royal guards out at the early morning hour, Esme pondered whether they simply woke up and stumbled outside, grabbing whatever food was closest on their way to a fight. Thinking on it, she conceded that such a regimen might actually be more effective than strong tea. Though she wasn't about to take it up herself.

"This seems early for you," Killian remarked as he joined her.

"I thought I might catch you before breakfast." She made a show of looking past him toward the mountainous spread. "But I can see I'm too late."

Killian waved her comment off. "I can eat again." Of course he could.

"Good, because I brought food. All I need is a handsome warrior to accompany me to the lake. I know a perfect spot to view the sunrise."

His brow rose with interest. "I can't imagine a better morning. Lead the way." He took the basket, then offered Esme his arm.

Her guards fell in behind them, but Esme turned and asked that they stay, assuring them that she'd be perfectly safe with Killian. When that didn't work, she respectfully reminded them that she was their queen.

"Esme," Killian chided once they reached the dark woods—the cool light from the clearing ahead guiding them through the shadows.

Without breaking her stride, she replied, "Killian, what dangers could possibly be lurking out here at this hour?"

"I don't know." Killian grabbed her wrist, forcing her to turn. "And that's the point."

A rustle in the trees had them both looking up. There were several large forms high in the branches. One moved.

"Damn peacocks," Killian muttered, removing his hand from his sword hilt.

Esme bit back a grin. They weren't much of a threat, though she wouldn't want to be in the path of those sharp talons should one decide to leap to the ground. Killian glowered at them a moment longer, then appeared to be fighting a smirk of his own.

He glanced back through the trees at the faintly warming colors along the western horizon, then sighed. "The sun will be here soon. Show me this spot."

They veered east, skirting the lakeshore until they reached the view she'd promised. Killian helped her up the wide, flat boulder, where they shared the savory tartlets and apple pastries, watching the perfectly blended gradient of orange, coral, and fiery red before the cloudless sky faded to a serene crystal blue.

Instead of heading straight back, Esme pulled Killian deeper into the woods. She couldn't resist the chirping birds, the early morning rays of sun filtering through the canopy, and the smell of sleeping flowers opening for the day. Sully had promised he and Cadwyn wouldn't be by too early, and because sleep was no longer a viable option, she wanted to prolong her time with Killian as long as she could.

By the smile Killian gave as she tempted him away from his responsibilities, he felt the same.

Not far along the fern-lined path, Esme noticed a songbird perched on a low branch. As she ducked underneath, the bird swooped, landing on a branch up ahead. *Curious*, she thought. She'd grown accustomed to birds and woodland animals following or watching, but seldom guiding. When the bird alighted on a branch up ahead, she grew confident that it wished her to follow.

The bird led her toward the warm glow of a familiar clearing. A mound of rhododendrons stretched nearly two dozen feet in every direction, reaching high enough to rival some of the surrounding trees.

Esme grinned at the sight. About to turn and explain to Killian how she hadn't been allowed to play near the thick patch of shrubbery as a child, she stopped.

Why *had* the rhododendrons been forbidden? She'd practically lived outside as a child—her maids unable to find her many forgotten shoes, or keep her in clean clothes for more than an hour before she'd dirtied the knees.

Releasing Killian's hand, she stepped closer, eying the mysterious thicket, wondering. It was the only place on the grounds where a secret entrance might be hidden.

She rounded the wild mess of branches, searching.

There. She spotted it through the fans of green leaves and delicate fuchsia blooms. The smooth surface of a boulder.

She felt Killian come up behind her as she crouched down to push aside the entwined branches.

"Killian," she whispered.

"Hmm?" He leaned down, resting a hand on her shoulder.

"This is it."

"This is what?" She could hear the uncertainty in his voice.

"The entrance to the caves." Esme pushed the branches farther aside, revealing the rocks in the center. She looked back at Killian with excitement.

Killian's brow furrowed. "You sure about that?"

"My mother used to tell me about the caves beneath the southern grounds when I was a child." It wasn't precisely the truth, but she wasn't ready to tell him about the journal yet. "Only she never told me where the entrance was."

"And you're sure this is it?" Killian moved in for a closer look, creating a narrow opening for Esme.

"There!" she gasped, pointing to a gap between two of the boulders.

"You might be right."

"Of course I am." She pushed past him. The branches snagged on her clothes before parting for her.

"Okay. Okay." Killian chuckled, clearly amused by her excitement. But when she ducked into the opening, he grabbed her wrist. "Where do you think you're going, sweetheart?"

"Inside." She shot him a baffled look, but he wouldn't let go. "We have to see what's down there."

Killian's warning look told her that they, in fact, did not need to see what was down there.

Knowing she'd never maneuver out of his grip—sweet, he might be, but Killian was still a warrior charged with protecting her—Esme glanced past him and feigned a look of alarm.

The moment Killian jerked his head over his shoulder to investigate a threat that wasn't there, Esme twisted her wrist to free herself from his grasp, then slipped inside.

"Esme," Killian growled, following her in.

Chapter Twenty

THE DARKNESS DIDN'T hinder their eyesight, but Killian lit the lantern hanging just inside the entrance. He took hold of Esme's hand as they slowly descended the rough-hewn steps.

"Don't do that again," he warned, though he made no attempt to lead her back to the surface.

The twinge of guilt she felt in tricking him faded when she saw the fascination in his eyes. He studied the walls, his gaze traveling up to where the ceiling peaked above their heads. Then the flame in the lantern flickered, shifting from a bluish flame to a soft yellow. Esme grinned. Apparently, Killian found that color more suitable to their surroundings.

They journeyed deeper. The air never grew colder, only more humid. But there was something pure about it. Though the cave was ancient, the air felt clean, new.

When the tunnel opened into a wide cavern, Esme stood unmoving, taking everything in, while Killian lit each of the hundreds of lanterns with nothing more than a thought.

She eased forward. "Killian, they're..." Her eyes fixed on the steam rising at the far end.

"Baths," he finished.

Esme approached the first of the shallow pools, letting her hand dip into the barely warm water. Each bath along the curved wall was raised slightly higher than the one before. Or rather, she realized, looking toward the opposite end, each bath was lower than the one before, allowing the hot, steamy water from the main pool to spill through narrow grooves into the next before disappearing beyond the cave walls. The main bath was larger than the others, looking as though it could fit nearly a dozen people at once. She walked toward it, then carefully climbed the steps that circled it. Peering through the clear water, she found a low shelf around the circumference, with wide dips carved at equal intervals.

"We must be under the lake." Killian's voice reached her from across the space as he took in the dome above, which wasn't much higher than the ceilings in the palace.

Beneath the lake. She could see the words in her mother's hand. "I think you're right."

She thought of the deep end of the lake along the rocky shore, where warm water seeped up through the lake bed, combining with the cool water at the surface to create a pleasant, comfortably warm temperature.

"It's like some sort of antechamber, cutting off one of the springs before it can reach the surface," she reasoned, while worrying how long it would continue to flow. Orianna had been a powerful water wielder—Esme knew all too well that the high-priestess's gift from Muirín was fearsome—but the magic wouldn't linger forever.

"How long has this been here?" Killian asked.

The stone baths were smooth from years of flowing water, but they'd clearly been made by hands or magic, not by nature. Long ago, the hot water had likely filled the entirety of the space as a sort of underground pool, before the stone had been carved away, and the water redirected.

"I'm not sure. My mother knew of this place, but she never took me down here. I think it was a secret, but I...I don't know why." She truly didn't. Even if her mother had used the sheltered space to practice spells, why would she keep it a secret from her husband, from her daughter? And furthermore, how had her mother found it in the first place?

Killian joined Esme on the step she'd claimed. "We should get back."

"Not yet." She took Killian's hand, then looked meaningfully at the hot, inviting water behind them. She wanted to slide in and let the warmth embrace her. Them.

"Esme, love, you know I'd like nothing more than to"—he squeezed her hand, then cleared his throat—"spend hours down here with you." He glanced at the heat rising from the largest bath and pressed his eyes shut for a moment. Esme wondered what image he was conjuring in his mind and moved closer.

But when he opened his eyes, Esme could see the determination behind his fiery gaze. He brought his palm to her cheek and rubbed his thumb along the contour of her lower lip. "But you know we can't. You have a—"

Esme pressed her fingers to his lips. "I know. I just wish…sometimes…"

He kissed her fingertips. "I know you do." Then he twined his fingers with hers and pulled her to her feet.

Quietly, they left. The tunnel was wide enough for them to walk side by side, their hands joined. But when the light from the entrance crept into the dark tunnel, Esme felt Tearlach. He was trying to locate her. Tension flowed through their connection, assaulting her senses and making it hard to draw breath.

She kept the hand Killian held relaxed and her steps sure, not letting on that every one of Esme's muscles suddenly felt tight and prickly.

Killian moved his hand to her lower back, letting her pass through the narrow opening first—though Esme would've insisted upon it, had he not. Tearlach needed to see her first.

The moment the branches parted at her command, Tearlach whipped around. His glare morphed from fear to fury in the span of a heartbeat as their eyes locked.

She heard her guards approaching, and Killian coming to stand behind her, but she didn't break their stare. When Tearlach didn't say anything, Esme dared a glance past him. He hadn't just brought Roderick and Harlow. The rest of her royal guard came into view as whispers were passed between them that she'd been found.

Esme met Tearlach's merciless gaze again, but before she could say anything he slid his eyes over her shoulder in a very deliberate movement.

"What in the name of the gods were you thinking, Killian?" he growled through clenched teeth. "Taking off without any guards. Putting her in danger."

"This wasn't his—" Esme started, but Tearlach held up a hand. She scoffed, then scowled, taking a step toward him. But even stretching up on her toes, she couldn't break the growing tension between the two men. Tension—she realized as she glanced behind her—that wasn't only coming from Tearlach.

"This was my choice, not his." She jutted her chin up.

Without sparing her a glance, Tearlach said, almost too quietly, "Oh, I think Killian, here, has everything to do with you leaving the palace in the middle of the night without a guard."

He couldn't possibly believe that. With her penchant for sneaking out of her room, why would he even *think* Killian could be responsible?

She spared another glance at Killian, but he didn't seem shocked by the accusation. In fact, the hint of a smirk on his lips told her he'd been expecting it. What was going on between them?

Tearlach refused to look at her again—his eyes fixed on the man behind her.

"First of all," Esme spat, "I didn't leave the palace without any guards. Second of all, it wasn't the middle of the night. And last"—she huffed a breath, but Tearlach still wouldn't meet her eyes—"I had a guard with me. The whole time. Or have you forgotten that Killian took the same oath you did?"

"Not the same one." Tearlach's reply was no more than a deep rumble. Esme blinked at the statement. Finally, he lowered his eyes to hers. "Cadwyn's looking for you."

"Cadwyn's always looking for me," she replied easily, but Tearlach didn't say anything more. He wouldn't. She knew him well enough to know she'd been dismissed.

Esme turned to Killian, eyes searching. But the look he gave her seemed to beseech that she leave it and go—to let him deal with Tearlach alone.

Fine. She slipped past Tearlach, through the heaviness that'd settled around them. Her cheeks burned with humiliation as she neared Roderick and Harlow.

"Armel and Hazel will take you back," Tearlach informed her. "The rest of you can leave."

Esme swallowed and mouthed "sorry" to Harlow and Roderick, then waded through the thick ground cover, hoping they wouldn't be punished for her actions.

The woods had gone quiet, as though Tearlach's vexation had stunned the songbirds into silence. It was unnerving. Not even the seven guards who followed made a sound.

Esme was tempted to stomp her boots. Anything to break the unnatural stillness.

When she reached the edge of the woods, the strains of a heated argument splintered the silence.

Chapter Twenty-One

MARTA AND BRIGHID were waiting in her suite after Esme finished bathing. She politely dismissed them and crossed to her dressing room. After the incident outside the cave, followed by hours of preparation with Cadwyn and Sully, she needed a few meager moments to herself.

She ran her fingers across the smooth silk of the coral dress Cadwyn had selected. The creamy color blended with a brighter orange midway down the skirt and the flowing sleeves. Far too cheery for Esme's mood.

Scanning her gowns, she chose one of slate blue brocade. The silver pattern was subtle enough so as not to make the fabric heavy. Eying the two dozen buttons that ran down the back, she debated ringing her maids back. With a shake of her head, she stepped into the gown, determined. Holding it backward, she buttoned it, twisted the dress around, then shimmied it up her chest. The sleeves pulled on with only a bit of struggle. She wrapped a length of copper chain with faceted silver beads around her waist several times, letting the ends hang at her side.

Sparing a glance in the mirror, Esme scrunched the curling ends of her nearly dry hair, then set a simple circlet atop her head. The color of the oval aquamarine diadem looked vibrant against the subdued color of her gown.

Esme closed her eyes and sighed. "Let's get this over with." She plastered on a poised expression and went to open the main doors.

Sully smiled and took his place beside her as she turned down the corridor. Tearlach fell into step with them—though he offered nothing more than a nod. She wondered when he'd address what had happened that morning. Perhaps never, which was fine. She had absolutely no desire to revisit the situation.

Roderick and Harlow followed. It seemed they'd been reinstated.

———————

Esme was barely listening. They'd been discussing the Festival of Tahra as though the celebration were in any way paramount to the many difficulties plaguing their kingdom. At least when Aindreas had relayed the trade reports at the start of the meeting, she'd had no issue taking genuine interest.

She took a deep breath and tried to focus on the absurd conversation Keelin and Gwen were having regarding the available accommodations for visiting nobility.

Only another half hour, Esme told herself. Then she could leave the encroaching walls of the council chamber. *Another hour, at most.* She could hang on for another hour. As long as nothing of import was brought up.

"If I might..." Lady Audris's piercing voice rose above the chatter. All eyes turned to her. She raised her chin and clasped her long fingers— tipped in bloodred polish—then placed them purposefully on the table in front of her. "I need to bring something of great urgency to the attention of the council. I'd hoped that Her Majesty would address this matter, but we're nearing the end of the meeting, and well...it seems the responsibility has fallen to me."

"What exactly is the nature of this matter, Lady Audris?" Lord Lennox requested with a barely perceptible hint of impatience.

The woman's gaze alighted on Esme once more. "It's quite alarming, I'm afraid."

Esme wasn't as skilled at hiding the irritation in her expression, but she motioned for Lady Audris to continue.

"It would seem"—Lady Audris paused, glancing around the table, no doubt to build suspense—"that there remain several women in our kingdom who wield the power of priestesses. And I suspect they might have been conspiring with Orianna."

Esme blinked. Conspiring with Orianna? Why would she jump to such a baseless conclusion? And more importantly, how had Lady Audris managed to find out about the unordained priestesses in the first place?

Sully straightened in his seat, as did the others at the table. Not exactly the type of announcement they'd been preparing for.

"And how, may I ask, did you learn of the existence of these women?" Lady Pallya inquired. "It is our understanding that every high-priestess in the Order was eliminated out by the very woman you claim they colluded with."

Lady Audris didn't seem the least bit put out by Lady Pallya's dispute. "One of my dear footmen informed me that Her Majesty received a missive from them directly. A warning, I'm sure."

Esme could feel everyone's eyes on her, though she kept hers trained on Lady Audris.

"What, precisely, did this message entail?" Though Lady Pallya's question was asked of Esme, she could hear the underlying skepticism directed at Lady Audris.

Before Esme could respond—though truth be told, she had no idea what she'd say—Lady Audris answered. "That Her Majesty did not think to bring such a serious piece of correspondence directly to her council was an innocent mistake, certainly. But now that she understands the gravity of the situation, I'm sure she'll swiftly turn the letter over."

Oh, how Esme loved being referred to as though she wasn't in the room.

Thankfully, Lady Audris only seemed to be aware of the existence of the letter, not its contents. And Esme wasn't about to divulge anything about the secret sect, or her plans to enlist their assistance.

With an air of exasperation, Esme leveled Lady Audris with a glare. "I'm afraid your *sources* have failed you, Lady Audris," she began as a plausible story coalesced in her mind. Esme leaned forward and lowered her voice. "I do wish you'd brought these concerns to me directly rather than wasting the time of the council." Settling back in her chair, she swept her gaze around the table. "You see, the *inquiry* I received was from a kinswoman of one of the late high-priestesses. She humbly requested that a commission be established in order to maintain the temples, preserving them as memorials to the women who devoted their lives in service to this great kingdom." Esme held back a smile, quite proud of the tale she'd so quickly spun. Not only would it detract from the truth, it would also discredit Lady Audris should one of her servants uncover another of Esme's secrets.

With Lady Audris practically seething, Esme braced her hands on the table, ready to rise and adjourn the meeting.

"Even so," Lord Torin drawled. "It would be injudicious of us to not examine this request further. I trust that Your Majesty understands the intent of the letter, but we can't be too careful, can we? Not with our kingdom in such need of women who possess the ability to restore our land and waterways. And so, I must insist, with the full support of the council"—he cut a threatening look around the table—"that Your Majesty present this letter of interest for a more in-depth analysis."

Shit.

"After all, we are not in a position to discount even the slightest possibility that any priestesses may still be alive." At the murmurs that rumbled through the room, Lord Torin held up a hand. "But let us not assume that any woman who survived the downfall of the Order would have the same despotic designs as the one who destroyed our kingdom."

Esme exhaled, relieved—and quite frankly surprised—at Lord Torin's assertion.

"Therefore, if any of these powerful women remain, they must be found. For they may be our only hope in helping our land thrive once again."

Esme resisted the urge to narrow her eyes at Lord Torin. Did he know something? The way he addressed the topic with such ease made her suspect that he'd anticipated it.

"We mustn't discount any information. If there's even so much as a whisper of the existence of these women, we must pursue those leads."

Esme feared what he might say next.

"We will seek out their hidden lairs and bring them to Meallán."

"There is no evidence of the existence of any such women," Esme reminded Lord Torin. She couldn't allow him to convince the rest of the council of his absurd conjecture.

"But Your Majesty, with all due respect, we cannot in good conscience dismiss the possibility. Lady Audris might have been misinformed about the contents of the letter—which I will remind Your Majesty to bring before the council—but she has presented an important issue, one we must investigate to the ends of the kingdom before it can be thoroughly controverted."

Lord Torin glanced at the other councilors before continuing. "If these women prove to be found, they will serve Tremaene. We'll send them to every corner of the kingdom to summon the magic. Of course, we have no way of knowing how many of them are out there, but let us presume there will be enough so that each temple may be adequately supplied. If not, we will devise a rotation, making sure to maintain all of Tremaene's territories."

Something about the way he referred to them didn't sit right with Esme. For that matter, *none* of what he said sat right with her. "For argument's sake, let us assume these women do exist and can be found. What if they've no desire to serve as high-priestesses?"

"They will."

"And if they do not?" she challenged.

"If they refuse, then we shall force them. It's quite simple," Lord Torin stated plainly.

So that had been his plan all along. Suddenly Esme was back in the war room in Altan, surrounded by battle-hungry generals who believed the only way to depose Orianna was to sack the entire city of Meallán.

"*If*"—Esme swept what she hoped was a fierce look around the room—"any women are found with such powers—and I can assure you there is no evidence of that—they will *not* be treated as slaves."

"It was a mistake to trust them before. Why should we trust them now?" Pearce protested.

"Orianna acted alone," Esme reminded him.

"But with the treaty, what's to say another won't seek absolute power through similar means?" Lady Pallya reasoned. Esme met the woman's harsh eyes, wondering if every member of the council held the same prejudices toward high-priestesses.

"The treaty has already been nullified," Esme appeased them.

Suddenly everyone at the table seemed more alert. Were they offended that she hadn't discussed it with them first?

No. She realized her error. She'd just revealed a terrible vulnerability.

When Esme had written the decree, she hadn't thoroughly considered the ramifications. Her thoughts had been only with her parents, and what Orianna had done to steal their power.

She resisted looking over at Sully, though she desperately needed assurance that she hadn't weakened her new and suddenly precarious position. Perhaps that was the reason Cadwyn had been so insistent that no one else lay eyes on the decree.

I need to leave. Esme straightened her spine, angling her chin up, and adjourned the session as quickly as she could.

When the others filtered out, Lord Torin remained.

"Your Majesty." He approached. "Have you had an opportunity to review my request to procure lumber from the mountains?"

What? Not another request for a private audience, or a thinly veiled threat?

Esme brushed her fingers over her eyebrow to hide her shock, then mentally sifted through the many documents she'd reviewed. "You need the wood to repair bridges, is that correct?"

"It is. I wouldn't otherwise bother Your Majesty with such a request, but as we do not yet have an overseer for the Tamslo Mountain territory, I'm left with no other avenue."

"Of course. I'll review it once more as soon as I'm able."

"Thank you, Your Majesty." He bowed in such a show of respect that Esme couldn't help but stare after him as he left the chamber. Something didn't feel right about the request. It was too straightforward.

When her attention pulled back, she noticed Winifred still seated across the table. Though her eyes held a soft gaze, Esme knew her ears were perked up, and that she'd likely remain in the room until everyone vacated, making sure she captured everything for her notes.

"Your Majesty? May I be of assistance?" she asked as Esme rounded the table.

"I wonder if you might deliver the record of today's meeting yourself."

"Certainly. I shall have it prepared in no more than an hour," Winifred promised.

"Excellent."

Cadwyn was at her side the moment she cleared the room. "What was that about?"

Esme knew Cadwyn and Sully would've preferred she not meet with any of the council members privately—no matter how impartial the council secretary seemed to be. "It's nothing. I just asked her to deliver the notes personally."

"I'm sure Winifred is trustworthy, but we can't be too careful. I wouldn't want her to ambush you about something."

Esme spun to face Cadwyn. "Like they did in there?" She jabbed her finger toward the chamber doors as two palace guards pulled them closed.

Cadwyn's face fell. "What happened?"

Esme dropped her head. Her patience was fraying, and she hadn't meant to unleash her building frustration on her dearest friend. She forced her breathing to slow, then counted to ten before looking up. "I'm sorry. It's not your fault."

"What happened in there?" Cadwyn braced her hands on Esme's shoulders. Her eyes were wide, searching.

"Just...speak to Sully. He'll tell you everything." She ducked out of Cadwyn's hold and walked ahead.

————————

Esme set down her cup of tea and looked over at the door. She kept expecting Tearlach to show up, to lecture her about what had happened earlier. But he didn't.

He hadn't followed her into her suite after the council meeting.

Hadn't approached her in the hour that'd followed.

Hadn't even growled a reprimand through their connection.

He'd done nothing.

Esme jumped at the sound of a knock at the door. With a wince she considered the half-empty cup of tea on the table. It was her sixth of the day. Granted, she hadn't slept much the night before, but it was quite possible she'd had enough.

Inhaling a bracing breath, she went to admit Tearlach.

Only it wasn't him.

She craned her neck out into the alcove. He wasn't there either.

"Winifred. Come in." When the woman glanced timidly down at the threshold, Esme waved her hand to lure her in. "I was hoping I could ask you some questions."

Winifred's placid expression turned to alarm, but Esme quickly shook her head. "No, no. You misunderstand. The thing is, I'm confused over a few of these documents"—she gestured to the stacks on her desk—"and I thought you might help me make sense of them."

Winifred visibly relaxed. Clutching her folio to her chest, she took a tentative step into the room.

Beyond her, Esme nodded to Harlow, who quietly shut the door.

When Winifred finally accepted a seat, Esme claimed the spot across from her and reached for her teacup before thinking better of it.

"I was wondering if you would take a look at this." Esme slid a sheet of parchment across the table that separated them. "Do you know anything about it?"

The status report made reference to detainees in Altan. She'd had her suspicions when first reading it, and assumed Sully or Tearlach—or even Cadwyn, for that matter—would try to convince her not to worry over such things. But Esme needed to know, and she had a feeling Winifred wouldn't lie to her.

Winifred scanned the sheet slowly, then kept her eyes downcast like she was rereading it—as though she hadn't memorized every single word and errant mark on the page the moment her eyes had taken in the whole of it.

"It's about Orianna's scouts, isn't it? The ones she sent to find me?"

Winifred raised her gaze, her lips a thin line.

"They're being kept in Altan, aren't they?"

"It would appear so, Your Majesty," Winifred concurred.

"Have you seen or heard anything else regarding this matter?"

Winifred allowed a slight nod, but didn't seem willing to offer anything more.

Esme waited.

"The captain and Minister Aindreas were discussing it in one of the private rooms in the royal library, Your Majesty," she finally disclosed. "I can only assume they believed the library to be vacant. It was rather late." Winifred's pale skin turned pink.

"Sully knows better than anyone that nothing said within these walls is private," Esme assured her. "Now, what else did you *overhear?*"

Winifred let out a shaky breath. "As I only overheard"—her eyes flicked up to Esme's—"a portion of their conversation, my understanding is limited, Your Majesty."

Esme seriously doubted that. "Speculate."

"From what I gathered, Minister Aindreas reported to the captain about the detained scouts who were relocated to the warrior camp in the mountains. He said that the current accommodations within the fort and the security detail were adequate. He also relayed that the additional food stores had arrived and were more than sufficient."

"Do you know why they're being kept in Altan?"

"Minister Aindreas questioned that very thing, and the captain explained that he preferred the detainees to remain far from the capital city for the time being."

"Do they pose a threat? Is their loyalty of concern?" Esme inquired.

"I don't believe that was his reasoning, Your Majesty. He mentioned that keeping them out of sight would help manage citizens' perceptions, until which time they can return to their homes and their families."

"I see." Esme sat back and stared at the far wall. It was for *their* protection, then. She wondered how many of them had families to return to. If those families would even welcome them back. "Scouts" was what they'd been called. But really, they were assassins, sent to kill her. Even if what Killian had told her was true—that their minds had been controlled by Orianna, their objectives unbreakable until she'd been killed—would they be capable of returning to their old lives?

"Thank you, Winifred," Esme stammered, shoving the unsettling thoughts to the back of her mind as she straightened, perching on the edge of the sofa. "There was something else I was hoping you could help me with."

"Certainly, Your Majesty."

"Do you recall anyone using the redwoods in the Tamslo Mountains for lumber?"

"No, Your Majesty. There's never been record of such."

"Is that because the trees are so old? Because regrowth would take too long?"

"I'm afraid that's not it, Your Majesty. There are vast swaths of sustainable hardwood forests that are used for lumber. There's no reason to use redwoods."

"Even though many of those forests are now dead?"

"The wood is still usable, though sustainability is now an issue, I agree. But pine is not used for lumber."

It wasn't? Then why would Lord Torin seek to fell redwoods if there were easily procurable sources of lumber south of the Clavlin Ridge? "I'm not sure I follow. What are pine trees used for, if not their wood?"

"Pitch."

"Pitch," Esme repeated the word.

"That's right. It's used to keep roofs or the hulls of ships watertight."

"Yes, I'm...familiar. I don't suppose it's typically used in the construction of bridges? To make them impervious to water as well?"

"Not typically, Your Majesty, no."

Esme nodded. "Winifred, I wonder if you might have time to review some other documents?"

Her cheeks flushed again. "I would be honored, Your Majesty."

Chapter Twenty-Two

"GOOD MORNING, YOUR Majesty."

"Lady Audris," Esme greeted without breaking her stride.

"I was just on my way out for a morning walk when a thought occurred to me. Have you given any consideration as to the ladies-in-waiting you'll require?"

Esme couldn't help but lift her brow at the unexpected query. "I have a lady-in-waiting."

"Yes, of course, the washerwoman's daughter."

Esme clenched her jaw and continued toward the south steps.

"I'm sure she offers...companionship. But you'll need noblewomen, certainly. At least three. I would be honored if Your Majesty would allow me to select some respectable candidates."

Women who were loyal to Lady Audris and would feed her information, no doubt. Esme spun on her heel. "There's no need, Lady Audris. I'm already considering several impeccable candidates. But I do appreciate your concern." She left Lady Audris alone in the center of the lawn without a backward glance. Esme did, in fact, have another woman in mind—though Lady Audris would likely not approve of her either.

Outside the barracks, Quinlan and Madoc left her to join the other guards as she found a spot on one of the long benches. She settled in for what she hoped would be a short meeting, then untied the small packet she'd brought. Splitting three scones in half, she arranged them in two neat rows, humming to tune out the sounds around her.

When she glanced up, her gaze immediately sought Tearlach. It was instinct, nothing more, but she was beginning to worry that he hadn't addressed the incident with the cave. She was furious with the way he'd treated her, and in front of her guards, no less. And while she wished to avoid a confrontation, the tension between them would only get worse if they didn't speak of it.

Sully began the meeting, and Esme returned her attention to her scones, scooping jam from a tiny ceramic pot onto each half. As she scraped the bottom for the last of it, she felt someone brush up against her and nearly sent her knife flying.

"Myles," she breathed, bringing a hand to her chest.

"Good morning, Your Ma—" His eyes fell on the dark red substance on the edge of the rounded knife. "Are you hurt?" His eyes roved over her.

"Blackberry jam." She grinned, bringing the knife to her mouth.

Myles exhaled, leaning over to rest his arms on the tops of his thighs. When he snuck another look at her, he began to chuckle. "Well, that certainly woke me up. Who needs tea when you can have the wits scared out of you first thing in the morning?"

Esme handed him one of the scones. "Glad I could help. Are you waiting for Cahir?"

"I am. Thought I'd catch him before he gets pulled into a match. That man can't say no to a challenge." He shook his head.

"And I thought it was just me he couldn't refuse." Esme winked. "How long have the two of you been together?"

"Since the war ended." Myles sat up, settling in for the long wait and seemingly glad to have someone to talk to.

"In Altan?"

"Yep. It was home to me, but not to Cahir. I moved there with my mother when I was young. My father went off to fight, and boy, did I want to follow. But I'm no warrior. Even with years of training, I knew I wouldn't stand a chance out there. I still wanted to help, though. So when I was old enough, my mother let me accompany a small group into the mountains for supplies. Turns out, I was quite good at negotiating agreements and finding the best solution for everyone involved. Something to do with my...gift." He tapped a finger to his temple. "I could sense when people were withholding information, knowing it would take more to earn their trust." Myles absently raked a hand through his auburn hair, making it stand on end.

"By the time the war was over, most of the citizens in the north had moved into the safety of the valley. Warriors settled there too. Cahir arrived with a few others, but no one seemed to know more than his name. You wouldn't think it to look at him now—that happy, self-assured man." Myles glanced adoringly over at Cahir. "But he was quiet when I first met him. Haunted. None of the warriors were in good shape, mind you, but I could feel the suffering in his kind soul. It took time, but he started talking to me, letting me see his pain. And then, his beauty. His love."

Esme reached over and laid her hand atop his. Myles looked over and gave her a tight smile, his eyes glassy.

He swallowed, and after a moment continued. "I used to think love was something that would make me feel complete. That when I met the right person, I'd feel nothing but happiness, and I'd finally be able to let go of all the stuff that weighed me down—the stuff I never liked about myself, all the moments from my past I wanted so badly to forget. But love isn't like that, not real love. Real love breaks you down to the rawest version of yourself, where all your pain and flaws are kept. It shines a light on all of it, exposes everything. But as scary as that is, as much as it makes you want to run and hide, you realize it's okay to feel that way, to feel vulnerable and weak. Only it isn't weakness at all, it's strength. When a person really loves you, all of you, he shows you that all of those things you don't like about yourself—the things that still hurt, the things you're ashamed of—they're still you. And you finally see that you're whole even with your imperfections. You're whole *because* of them."

Myles turned his palm up and curled his fingers around Esme's hand.

"When you find that one person who truly sees you—sees all of you—who knows how your heart beats because his heart beats the same, who loves the worst parts of you just as much as the pretty ones, well...that's love."

Esme peered into his eyes, unable to think past the erratic beat of her own heart.

He looked down, then slowly returned Esme's hand to her lap, glancing over at the guards. "Not sure where that came from," he admitted, looking abashed.

"I think you do."

Myles gave her a sidelong glance and offered a sheepish smile. "Maybe."

They fell into silence, neither of them saying what Esme was sure they were both thinking. Had she found that person? The one she wasn't afraid to show her darkness to?

She scanned the crowd again, but looked away before her gaze could land on anyone in particular. Thankfully, Sully's melodious voice broke off and smaller conversations started up in earnest, saving Esme from confronting her traitorous thoughts.

She handed the last half of a scone to Myles.

"Thanks." He shoved it in his mouth, barely bothering to chew.

Esme shook her head. Did all men eat that way?

"Those two over there..." Myles inclined his head to where Armel and Hazel were talking quietly off to the side. "There's a lot going unsaid between them."

"Oh, I'm quite aware. I'm just not sure they are."

Myles tilted his head, considering the pair. "They do. Give them time."

"Time?" Esme squeaked. "They've known each other longer than you and Cahir."

"You're right." Myles squinted as if that had only just occurred to him. "Maybe give them a little nudge, then." He patted her knee, then rose from his seat. "Thanks for breakfast, Your Majesty."

"Anytime." She smiled.

With a quick bow, he loped off to find Cahir.

Esme gathered her things, looking up as Killian broke away from the crowd.

She smiled when he reached her, but it fell almost immediately. They hadn't spoken since the cave. "Killian, I'm so sorry about—"

"Esme, it's fine." He shook his head. "Believe me. If I cowered at Tearlach's wrath, I never would've made it through the first few days with him. Don't forget, he's been my brother nearly as long as he's been my commander."

"I know, but you shouldn't be blamed for something I was responsible for."

"Esme," he reproached. "Do you really think I would've allowed you to put yourself in real danger? If I'd thought for even a second that the cave wasn't safe, I wouldn't have hesitated to throw you over my shoulder and haul you back out."

Esme's eyes widened at the forthright comment.

"Don't let these good looks fool you, love." He smirked. "I'll do what I must to protect you, whether you like it or not."

"Well, now you just sound like Tearlach."

"Never forget who trained me, sweetheart." He leaned in, his warm breath caressing the column of her neck. "But I have a softer touch." His lips pressed against her heated skin.

Her cheeks burned as Killian went to claim the next fight.

———————

As soon as Esme entered her suite, she could smell the subtle hint of mountain air. She halted her steps, hand still on the door handle, and squeezed her eyes shut.

After a breath, she shut the door and turned to where she knew Tearlach was waiting. His dark eyes locked with hers, and for a moment neither said a word.

When the tension was almost too heavy for her to draw breath, she tore her gaze away and walked over to the sofa. The sensation of being watched was more than she'd ever felt before.

She looked out the open doors to the clear blue sky beyond. It was always blue. Always clear. How long had it been since she'd seen a single cloud, or even the haze of morning mist?

Tearlach didn't make a sound as he took a seat beside her. She didn't look over, but the warmth of his body made every inch of her skin tingle with awareness.

"Esme." His deep voice vibrated through her, and she wasn't sure if he'd spoken her name aloud or in her mind. "When you weren't with your assigned guards," he began and Esme felt a jolt of Tearlach's panic—a crushing sort of powerlessness that was there and gone in the span of a heartbeat. Something he wanted her to feel, to understand.

She drew a shallow breath and turned to face him. Tearlach continued to stare straight ahead, and Esme knew he wasn't there in the room. Not really. She wondered which moment he was reliving. Was he back in the throne room, immobilized by Orianna's unmatched power, unable to protect her?

Esme slid her hand over to his, slowly, like he was a wild animal she might startle.

But with that single, innocent touch, her words were forgotten.

The warmth beneath her fingers...

The awareness it evoked...

She tried to ignore the overwhelming sensation, tried to summon the things she'd intended to say.

As fragments of her thoughts returned, Esme forced herself to say what she needed to say. "I should have let Harlow and Roderick follow. And I shouldn't have gone into that cave without telling someone on the outside. I just…"

She pulled her hand away, tightening it into a fist on her lap as she looked again to the vast blue sky. After a protracted silence, she risked another glance at Tearlach.

His attention was once again on her, not with the memories that seemed to haunt him. He held her gaze as he leaned forward to brace his forearms on his knees. "I know" was all he said. And Esme knew he did. He knew better than anyone what life had been like in that undemanding place. What it felt like to live for no one and nothing.

"Do you ever wish you could go back there?" she asked softly.

Tearlach narrowed his eyes, looking at her like she'd asked something truly bewildering. Esme wondered if anyone had ever bothered to ask him what he wanted. The silence hung between them, heavy, ripe with questions. What would their lives have been if no one had been waiting for Esme to return to Tremaene? If they could have stayed?

"Sometimes I do," he admitted, his voice rough, the words binding the two of them even more.

"Was there ever…I mean, did you have someone there, someone in Periwen?" Her pulse quickened, fearing his answer.

"What?" Confusion clouded his dark gaze.

"I was just wondering…" Esme felt her skin flush. "You spent all those years with nothing to do but watch over me. Surely you found company with…someone."

Tearlach didn't respond, but Esme noticed the slight flare of his nostrils.

"There was someone, wasn't there?" she breathed, her stomach dropping.

He exhaled forcefully and leaned back, rubbing his palms over the tops of his muscular thighs.

"What?" Her voice cracked from nerves, but she smiled through it, striving for some semblance of levity. "She wasn't interested in a stubborn, scowling, domineering, cantankerous—"

"Cantankerous?" Tearlach objected.

"—man," she finished, smiling genuinely at his indignation.

Tearlach scoffed, but didn't say anything more.

"Am I to believe that this mysterious woman could somehow tolerate your company?" Esme needled, preferring his discomfort to the unease she felt at the idea.

He arched a brow.

"So, what happened with this woman? Did you scare her off?"

"Nothing happened," Tearlach avowed.

Esme searched for a clever retort. Then her shoulders dropped as the gravity of the situation became clear. "Oh," she exhaled. Not only had Tearlach cared for someone, he'd lost her. "You had to leave her, didn't you? When we fled Debarrow, you had to...leave her behind."

Tearlach flicked his gaze back to her, staring at her for several strained moments before averting his eyes.

"I didn't leave her behind," he said quietly, almost too softly for her to hear. And before Esme could react, he was on his feet.

"It just..." He raked his hands through his hair, then dropped them to his sides in what looked like defeat. "It never would've worked. She and I. We were from very different worlds. She needed more than—" He took a slow breath as his eyes locked with Esme's. "She needed more than anything I could offer."

More than he could offer? Did Tearlach really think himself so unworthy? Truly, Esme was hard-pressed to think of a woman who'd be worthy of *him*. He was a legendary warrior, the former commander of Tremaene's forces, and by the gods, Sully had chosen him—above anyone else—to protect the future queen of Tremaene. How could he think himself unworthy?

Esme was prepared to tell him exactly what she thought of his misplaced principles, but Tearlach was already striding across the room. He vanished through the hidden passageway before her lips could form even a single word.

She sighed, sinking back against the sofa, then grabbed a pillow and clutched it to her chest. Would Tearlach ever look past his relentless loyalty and rigid code of honor, and allow a sliver of happiness into his life?

Esme stared at the wall that separated them, disheartened because she already knew the answer.

Chapter Twenty-Three

WHEN ESME FOUND *herself in a familiar clearing, she shut her eyes tight, hoping she'd imagined the place. It'd been months since she'd been there.*

She couldn't even recall having gone to bed. Winifred had arrived shortly after Tearlach left, and the two of them had spent most of the day sifting through the remaining piles of documents on her desk. Esme had been so mentally exhausted by the time they were done that she'd barely been able to keep her eyes open through dinner. She must have fallen into bed shortly thereafter.

Turning in place, she felt the soft, dewy grass between her toes. The indigo sky was moonless, the ring of silhouetted trees surrounding her unbroken. She held her breath, and peered through the fog that hovered just above the ground, praying that a wolf wouldn't emerge. When the mist remained still, she scanned the tree line until an owl dropped from a branch, gliding soundlessly toward her.

The fog swirled around her, and the clearing fell away. When it receded, she was floating in the corner of a small, dimly lit room.

A well-dressed man stepped through an arched doorway, his overcoat folded neatly over his arm.

Esme drew back, taking in more of the scene as the man took a seat across from a woman with long, plaited black hair that nearly grazed the floor.

A dark cloth was draped over the circular table, but the room was too dark to make out its color. In front of the woman was a shallow dish of water—the only item on the table.

"It's an honor to be in the presence of the infamous seer of Meallán." The man bowed his head and placed his hands flat on the table in front of him in a show of respect.

"What is it you seek?" The woman's soft, practiced tone resonated through the small room, sending a shiver down Esme's spine. Her voice sounded layered with hidden meaning and ancient wisdom.

But who was she?

Gliding around the periphery of the room, Esme tried to find a better vantage point. There was nothing particularly discernable about the woman's features— her skin was flawless, shimmering faintly in the candlelight; her eyes were cast down beneath sharply arched brows. But when Esme moved behind the man, the woman—the seer, as he'd called her—looked up.

Esme sucked in a breath at the sight of her piercing eyes. At first glance, their color seemed almost aquamarine, but upon closer inspection, Esme could see that the entire spectrum of color was contained within their primordial depths.

She forced herself to look away, realizing only then that the man had been speaking.

"...tend a small plot of land in Kearney," he was saying.

He tended land? The man certainly didn't have the look of a farmer about him. He was dressed like he belonged to the nobility. Esme peered down at his hands and the heavy gold rings that adorned three of his fingers.

Deciding to dismiss his appearance, she returned her focus to the place he'd mentioned: Kearney. Though Esme still hadn't seen the far reaches of her kingdom, she'd memorized every detail of her father's maps during her youth— every city and port town, every forest, river, and mountain range. And Kearney was a name she'd never once come across.

The seer nodded for him to continue.

"The land is suffering and I—"

His words were cut off by a muffled sound.

Fog filled the room, obscuring her view.

The vision vanished.

Esme cursed as she heard the unwelcome sound again—knuckles rapping against her chamber door, threatening to destroy her fragile state.

Refusing to let go, she spun around, slicing her hands through the mist as though she could clear a line of sight.

But it was too late. The man and the seer were gone.

Esme stared out the open doors as she ate her breakfast, barely tasting her food. She'd stayed in bed until Marta had left, too worried she'd snap at the woman for unintentionally waking her from the dream.

She speared a plum slice and glared at the bellpull hanging unused beside her bed, wondering why they bothered with them when her maids were always bringing in food before she even called for it. Before she even woke.

Returning to her breakfast, she thought through the dream again. Then again. But even after a dozen recollections, Esme was only certain of one thing—the man had been seeking guidance to aid his barren farmland. *The land is suffering,* he'd told the seer. Was that where the channels had first been damaged? Had the woman provided a solution? One that might help Esme restore the kingdom? She might never know.

Let me in.

Esme jolted at the uninvited voice.

Are the main doors broken? she snapped.

When Tearlach didn't respond, she huffed a breath and went over to the wall. Reaching under the waist-high trim, she pulled, letting the door swing open on soundless hinges.

"What if my maids had been here?" She tightened the ties of her robe.

"Then you wouldn't have opened the door," he said practically.

Esme rolled her eyes as he strode past, glad that his familiar mood had returned. Vexing as it was, she understood it better than what it had been the day before.

Tearlach was dressed for the day. With his bandolier strapped across his chest, he always seemed ready for battle. He picked up a peach and took up a position in front of one of the open doors, looking out over the western grounds. "Tell me about the dream."

So that was why he'd come to her room unseen. "You saw that?" She reclaimed her seat and forced herself to take another bite of soft-boiled egg.

"No."

She swallowed, glancing over at him. "Then how—"

"You've been so distracted by it, your thoughts have been flowing into my head all morning." He took one long stride to the table and set the peach pit on an empty plate. "It's quite irritating, really."

Esme scowled and threw a fat green grape at him. Tearlach plucked it from the air, popped it in his mouth, then took a seat across from her.

"Tell me what you saw." Urgency cloaked his previously light tone.

Setting her spoon down, she stared at her half-eaten breakfast. No amount of speculation was going to help her glean the message from her severed dream. If the owl didn't return, her only hope was to figure out the identities of the man and the seer.

She relayed everything to Tearlach, right up to the point when everything had vanished.

"It must have been long ago," she reasoned. "The name of the city is unfamiliar. I doubt either of them are still alive." Esme propped an elbow on the table and rested her cheek against her hand.

"But the seer lived here, in Meallán. Perhaps someone knew her."

"Are you proposing we comb the city for information about a woman whose name we don't even know, who, in all likelihood, faded away centuries ago?"

Tearlach gazed out at the city beyond the palace gates before looking back at her. "Get Cadwyn in here." Esme opened her mouth to protest, but Tearlach pinned her with an adamant look. "Yes, there's a less than narrow chance the seer is still alive—or that anyone even remembers her. But right now, Esme, she's all we have."

Chapter Twenty-Four

THE TENSION IN Esme's muscles eased a bit when they reached the dark, unused staircase, confident no one had witnessed their escape. But while leaving her suite unseen might have felt like an accomplishment, they still needed to sneak out of the palace and through the city to Cullen Street in the lower town. Cadwyn certainly had a talent for finding things that didn't wish to be found. She'd located the infamous seer, known as Athdara, in no more than a couple of hours.

Outside the formidable dungeon door, Esme felt her anxiety creep up again. Expecting a sickening feeling from the close proximity of the iron weapons secured down there, she was relieved when only cool, stale air greeted her as Tearlach heaved the door open.

Taking in the open cells, she wondered when they'd last been used. Had Orianna interned any of her victims down there before executing them? How long had she kept up appearances with mock trials before tossing out all pretense and simply killing those whose power she coveted? Esme peered through a narrow slit into the darkness of a cell.

"Hurry up, Princess."

She whipped her head around, her mood jumping to irritation at the title. Tearlach waited at the far end, regarding her with his head cocked to the side. She glared at him long after he turned his back to her, leading them down the cramped stairs to the lower level of the dungeons.

Tunnels spread out like spiderwebs beneath the city, but Esme hadn't realized they could be accessed directly from the palace. Hiding the entrance in a place where curious servants and guests would never willingly venture was wise, though she wondered if it was where Orianna had captured Tearlach and the others on that fateful night. She tried not to think about it as Tearlach ushered her into what seemed to be a broom closet.

She held her breath as he stepped in beside her, taking up every inch of the remaining space with his massive body. He pressed a small lantern into her hand, then gripped her shoulders and moved her farther into the corner.

Even from his stooped position in the low-ceilinged space, Tearlach was able to gain enough leverage to shove his shoulder against the stone wall. It receded, and Tearlach wedged the point of his dagger into the newly formed gap. He forced the wall aside to reveal a platform with the poles of a ladder peeking up over the edge.

They made their way easily through the dry underground storm drains and canals, emerging in the basement of a cellar she recognized. Esme did her best to block the memory of the last time she'd been there.

As they crept through the quiet building—which thankfully hadn't opened for business yet—and into the alley, Esme drew the hood of her cloak over her head. She might have recognized the neighborhood from the street, but in the alleyway, the back sides of the tall, narrow homes all looked similar. Tearlach stopped outside a door that resembled every other door they'd passed. He scanned the alley once more, then steered Esme inside.

At the end of a dark corridor was a small sitting room with a brocade divan occupying most of the space. Two wooden chairs with velvet cushions were pushed into the other corners, and a low table in the center of the room was set for tea. Nothing about the space looked like it belonged to an infamous seer.

Tearlach remained standing, alert. Esme assumed he'd already paid Athdara a visit and inspected the residence thoroughly, but his rigid posture told her he still didn't trust the situation, or the woman. His eyes shifted between the door they'd entered through and the one that remained closed.

Before Esme could take a seat, the door creaked open and an ermine scurried through, finding a perch on the curved arm of the divan. Esme shot a bewildered look to Tearlach, who rolled his eyes at the sight of the creature.

"Liffey," a stern voice warned. The animal bolted from its spot and curled into a white ball atop a tufted footstool instead.

Esme looked up as a tall, slender woman with jet-black hair and pale skin glided into the room, her layers of black and crimson skirts swishing past the furniture like a river through a canyon. The woman's primordial eyes alighted on her.

"Athdara?"

The woman dipped her chin, but only slightly. "Come. Both of you." She turned and walked back through the arched doorway without sparing a glance at Tearlach. He seemed to be expecting the woman's lack of acknowledgment, gesturing for Esme to follow.

They joined her in an even smaller room—the one from her dream.

Taking a seat across from Athdara, Esme began, "We came to ask you about—"

"You came to ask about the man claiming to be a farmer who sought help for his infertile lands." Athdara didn't even bother to look up. She smoothed the cloth that covered the table and arranged trinkets that circled a thick glowing candle in the center.

Esme glanced sidelong at Tearlach.

I didn't tell her, he assured.

Athdara slid a round obsidian stone beside a smooth, forked stick as if time was of little consequence to her.

Esme knew there was no point in denying why she was there. It was plainly evident that the woman already knew everything. "That's right. What do you remember of him?"

The seer ran her finger along the curved point of an antler, then twisted a piece of twine that bound a long iridescent raven's feather. "That was more than a thousand years ago," she said, her voice light, yet alluring. "I'm not sure how you expect me to remember something that happened so long ago."

A thousand years? Athdara had lived a thousand years? More than that if she'd been deemed an infamous seer by that time. What had she seen? What did she know? Athdara might know the origins of the Order, if Tremaene had once experienced seasonal hardships, why the seasons had suddenly stopped—

Ask only about the dream, Tearlach's voice warned. *She won't offer anything more.*

Esme exhaled, knowing he was right. Reluctantly, she reached into her cloak and produced a small purse of gold. She set it purposefully on the table before her.

The woman finally raised her head, leveling her with a measured look.

"You said he *claimed* to be a farmer. He wasn't?" Esme asked, then glanced down to find her purse gone. Hopefully it was enough for the answers they needed.

"Did he look like a farmer to you?"

Esme felt the hair on the back of her neck stand on end. How much did the woman know about her, about her dreams?

"What was his name?" She forced her voice to sound authoritative.

Athdara looked past Esme, then met her eyes again. "Dougal...or something like that. The name he gave matters little."

"Why?"

"It wasn't his true name," the woman said with a tilt of her head, as though it should've been obvious.

Esme tried again. "And what was his true name?"

"I cannot tell you."

"Aren't you a seer?" Tearlach's voice was laced with irritation, though he hid it better than Esme. "Can't you *see* his true name?"

Athdara's eyes slid to Tearlach. "There are some with strong enough minds to keep the truth locked away. Ones even I cannot penetrate." The two regarded each other for a moment before Athdara looked again at Esme. "As I said, his name is not important."

"What *is* important?" Esme asked.

"What he sought."

"Which was?" Esme gripped the edges of her cloak as if she could somehow funnel her frustration into the fabric. Perhaps she should've doled out the coins slowly—though she was fairly certain it wouldn't have mattered. The woman clearly enjoyed making their inquiry difficult.

"He sought a Fae who could wield all elements."

Esme's thoughts stalled as the weight of Athdara's voice encircled her, setting her nerves on edge. "What would a farmer..." Her words died in her throat as Athdara's eyes slitted. "What would *that man* want with someone who had such multifarious power?" Even the high-priestesses, as powerful as they were, only held one element each—two on rare occasions.

Esme ignored thoughts of her own magic.

When Athdara didn't answer her question, Tearlach rephrased it. "What would someone with that kind of power be capable of?"

Athdara arched one of her already sharp eyebrows. "One who possessed such power would bear a signature identical to the source of all magic. Such a person would be capable of not only drawing up raw magic, they would also have control over the channels themselves."

Esme's spine went rigid. *Control* over the channels? They'd speculated that the channels had been destroyed by some sort of natural calamity. But if they could be controlled...

The man who'd claimed to be a humble farmer suddenly seemed anything but.

"And you knew of someone who held such gifts?" Tearlach's tone—more command than question—caused the corners of Athdara's crimson lips to quirk up.

"There was one—a young man, Alastar of Donellis—who had a connection to each element. Barely into his magic, his power and grasp were weak, but he had the capacity to direct them all, nonetheless."

"How did you know about Alastar, his abilities?" Esme asked.

"Seeing is not my only gift."

A sensor too, then. And one strong enough to identify specific signatures, not just the presence of magic.

"So, you told Dougal where he could find the young man," Tearlach surmised.

Athdara gave a delicate nod.

"Is he still alive?" Esme pressed.

"Which one?"

"Either," Esme ground out.

Athdara's eyes grew distant, and Esme held her breath, feeling Tearlach tense beside her.

"Alastar of Donellis, no. He perished long ago."

"And the man who called himself Dougal?" Esme pushed, knowing Athdara wouldn't volunteer anything.

Inclining her head to look down even more at Esme, she answered, "That, I cannot say."

"You don't know or you won't say?" Tearlach demanded.

When Athdara didn't answer, Esme hissed a breath. "Did Dougal ask you anything else?"

"Did he ask anything else? No."

"Did you *tell* him anything else?"

The seer gave a hint of a smile. "You are a smart one, young queen."

"What else did you tell him?"

"I warned him that there would one day be another."

"Another what?" Esme snapped.

"Another who could wield all the elements—one who would not be so easily...*influenced*." Athdara folded her hands together and rested them on the table, taking on the air of a haughty professor. "You see, there must always be a balance."

"You mean someone who could reverse what he'd done?"

Athdara nodded.

"And who was this other?"

"When the man who called himself Dougal came to see me, she was not yet of this world."

"She?"

"A female, yes. To balance the power of the young man."

"So you didn't know who she was—who she would be?"

"At the time, it had not been written, so I could not see such things. I could only tell him when she would come into this world."

"And now? Has it been written?"

"It has." Athdara spoke deliberately, her piercing stare unwavering.

Esme tore her eyes away, only to find Tearlach's fixed on her in a similar manner. Growing uncomfortable, she shifted in her seat and crossed her arms protectively over her chest.

"This person who would eventually come along," Tearlach began in a careful tone. "Who would hold a similar power..."

Esme watched him, waited for him to continue. Unease washed over her when he didn't.

"Me?" she yelped, turning to Athdara. But the woman said nothing. "I can't wield them all! I can only manage earth and storm magic."

"Ah, storm magic. A favorite of mine," Athdara said in a patronizing voice that only made Esme's heart pound more forcefully against her ribs.

"I don't have fire," she asserted, even as a trickle of cold sweat rolled down her spine.

"No fire?" Athdara furrowed her brow and canted her head.

"No." Esme's voice quavered, her conviction waning.

"What, then, do you make of your lightning, young queen?"

Chapter Twenty-Five

"YOU REALLY THINK he destroyed the channels? All but five?" Esme asked once Brighid had delivered a tray of food and taken her leave. She was impressed that her maids had followed her orders not to be disturbed until she rang for them. As far as anyone in the palace knew, the queen had been in her suite all afternoon and evening.

"If the channels had been destroyed previously, by some natural occurrence, then he certainly didn't succeed in restoring them. That dream was shown to you for a reason. We have to assume that his intent in seeking such information was not benevolent."

"The timing is rather...coincidental," Esme allowed. "If he visited Athdara over a thousand years ago, it was most likely before the seasons vanished."

"And before the Order arose." Tearlach took a long pull from his goblet.

"You should have let me ask," Esme muttered as she swirled her spoon through the creamy asparagus and roasted chestnut soup.

There were many things she'd missed during her time in Debarrow. The soil had been nearly untenable—though that turned out not to matter much at her hand. Still, she'd opted for hardy plants with abundant yields, living on simple fare, while always wishing for the varied cuisine from her homeland. Esme dipped her spoon in again. It tasted delicious—earthy and creamy, with a hint of lemon. She wanted to savor it, to appreciate it, but her mind was still in that dark room with Athdara.

"Tearlach?" She waited for him to look up from his food. "Have you ever met a person who's lived more than a thousand years? Nobody chooses to live that long. She could have answered all our questions."

"That woman wasn't about to offer anything willingly. You saw something in a vision that she couldn't refute. That's the only reason she agreed to see us. But don't believe for a second that she would've opened up about any other topic, or that she'd be honest about it." He soaked up the last of his soup with a piece of bread. "You have another dream from one of your little animal friends about Athdara, and I'll gladly take you to see her again. But your visions are as far as I trust her."

They fell into silence as Esme finished her food. Tearlach remained seated, waiting politely with his hands in his lap, reminding her that while he'd spent most of his life as a warrior, he'd been raised by a noble family as she had.

Setting her napkin aside, Esme pushed her chair back. Tearlach seemed lost in thought, his eyes fixed on the silver dish of goat's butter.

"I never thought about it."

"About what?" Esme leaned her chair back, regarding him.

Tearlach looked over. "I'm beginning to think Tremaene's history has been kept from everyone. Not just you. I never questioned why there were no texts dating back more than eight or nine hundred years—and even those I never saw with my own eyes. Or why my tutors relied so heavily on oral history. They were just stories, told to make us believe that our world had always existed as it does now."

"A narrative that was nearly impossible to dispute or deviate from," Esme added.

"A narrative that kept us from discovering the truth." Tearlach stood and began pacing.

Esme watched, captivated by the sight of him. Tearlach's posture, and the way he carried his body, rarely revealed his inner turmoil. His outward appearance ranged only from dispassion to calm fury. But in that moment, he appeared unconcerned with Esme's attention on him—his steady strides across the room seeming to clarify his thoughts.

He paused, keeping his gaze straight ahead. "So, we have to assume that Dougal—or whoever he was—succeeded in destroying the channels." Tearlach resumed his pacing. "And if we're also to assume that Tremaene had, at the time, cycled through seasons, it might have only taken one winter for everything to die off and provisions to run out. Our kind would've perished quickly. Within a matter of years. And so...the gods responded, calling upon a few powerful females to summon magic directly from the source."

"And the first women who received the divine call must have been tasked with beginning the Order. They'd have used the five remaining channels to sustain the entire kingdom," Esme guessed.

Then her mind wandered farther, stretching beyond their shores. "What about the mortal realm? If it has channels like ours, why wasn't it affected?"

Tearlach halted at the far end of the table, staring at the untouched tray of fruit and pastries. He lifted a small bunch of grapes, popping one in his mouth absently as his eyes grew distant. "Perhaps," he said at length, "someone stopped him before he could reach Periwen, before he could starve the entire world of magic."

Esme laced her fingers together on her lap. Somehow, that explanation seemed too easy. And as much as she wanted to believe that Dougal had been conquered long ago, Athdara had been reluctant to confirm whether or not he still lived.

She closed her eyes as her mind spread out, her inner sight filling with visions of forests and farming villages, of harbor towns and rocky shores. The sea that had seemed endless, never allowing those who attempted to navigate the vastness to reach—

"The fog." Esme looked at Tearlach. "Even if he could've found a way to cross the barrier as we did, the fog glamours everything magical.

Perhaps even the locations of the channels. So the barrier that keeps humans from knowing about us—from finding our world—might have actually kept them safe from Dougal's destruction."

Tearlach seemed to consider her theory. "What if...the fog was never put in place to keep our world hidden?" He held Esme's gaze for a second. "What if the fog was created to *protect* humans...from us?"

They fell into silence, neither seeming inclined to explore that particular hypothesis, or its implications.

"We need to figure out how he destroyed the channels," Tearlach said instead.

"Alastar?"

"I'm willing to bet young Alastar was little more than a vessel. We need to learn more about Dougal."

"But we don't know who he really was, or his true name. Where would we even begin to look?" Esme rose, moving to one of the sofas. Tearlach claimed the one across from her. "And even if we did know who he was or where he lived, odds are he faded away long ago. We'll never find him or anyone who knew him." Defeat settled heavily upon her shoulders.

Tearlach looked past her toward the far wall, his jaw set with determination. "Do you recall the book of legends we found in the library?" His eyes settled back on her.

"A book of legends..." She strived to catch up. "Right. I remember. What of it?"

"It mentioned a place where memories are stored—every memory from every one of our kind."

"The Sacred Pool of Navlin. A myth," Esme countered.

"And if it isn't?" His gaze intensified, challenging her. "Legends come from somewhere." Tearlach leaned closer. "If we could find his memories..." He arched one of his dark brows.

———————

When the smell of apple blossoms filled her nose, Esme knew that her mind had traveled far away. Hoping she might find herself back in Debarrow, sitting between her rows of apple trees, she opened her eyes.

Instead, she found herself in a glowing cave with water circling the rock where she was perched. Shimmering lights twisted through the air. It was a place she'd seen before—a place she'd first believed to be the source of all magic, but later decided it was likely a channel.

Tendrils of glittering light drifted off the surface of the opalescent water. Esme reached down, trailing her fingers through the liquid magic that seemed thicker and heavier than water. Submerging her hand completely, she felt not only the circular current that flowed around the large rock, but an upward force, as though the water—the magic, if that was truly what it was—welled up through the pores of the bedrock.

Above were the thick, bunching roots of an ancient tree. Nothing about the channel appeared to be damaged, but there was also no clear path for the magic to reach the surface.

Esme focused on what she could feel, hear, smell. She breathed in the scent of pure, untouched magic, then reached out to pierce the veil of eddying light. Soft voices pricked her ears. Blurry images flickered through her mind.

She pulled back. After a breath, she extended her hand again. Voices. Sights that seemed shrouded in fog.

Memories, she grasped.

It was the Sacred Pool of Navlin. Magic, yes, but much more complex.

She could almost make out the individual strands floating around her, and tried to pluck one of the thin tendrils. Her fingers moved right through it.

Much as it felt real, it was only a vision. Similar to her premonitory dreams. Yet different. As though the magic itself had drawn her mind to that place.

Not wanting to waste what precious, little time she had in the dreamscape, Esme concentrated on the cave's location. Stretching her awareness, she found herself looking down at the pool. Pulling farther away, blending with the roots, the rock, the earth, her vision widened to take in the tangled branches of an ancient tree.

The tree was nestled in an oasis amid a vast expanse of rocky flats.

When she saw the sheer drop of a cliff, and a familiar outcropping far below, Esme forced herself to wake.

———————

The Sacred Pool of Navlin was in the Tamslo Mountains, directly above the place where they'd camped within the tunnels of the Northern Pass—the place where she'd first had the vision.

If they wanted those memories, they'd need to return there.

Finding the book of legends Tearlach had referenced, she paged through to the passage about the sacred pool. There was no location mentioned. No description of the place itself. The only certainty the author or transcriber seemed to have was one thing: in order to access another's memories, one needed only the individual's true name.

Something even Athdara hadn't been able to see.

Chapter Twenty-Six

DID YOU FIND anything? Tearlach asked for the dozenth time that morning.

Nothing yet, she crooned, fighting her building frustration. Tearlach had promised to help her search after seeing to a matter in the city, but Esme knew that if anyone in Meallán was likely to own long-forgotten records of Tremaene's nobility, it was Beglan.

Even though the man who'd called himself Dougal had claimed to be a farmer, Esme was convinced he was a nobleman, given his attire and air of confidence. And his noble lineage narrowed her search considerably.

When they arrived at the massive library doors, Beglan paused, his eyes roving over the ornate carvings.

"Shall we?" Esme grinned, reaching for the handle.

But the door was pulled back as Winifred appeared with a stack of books balanced in her arm. She shifted her weight to catch the heavy door with her hip, then looked up and yelped, nearly dropping the lot of them.

Though it wasn't Esme who'd startled her.

The usually quiet, collected woman blushed as her eyes entangled with Beglan's. Esme glanced at him out of the corner of her eye, unwilling to move for fear that she might disturb the precarious moment.

Offering a slight smile that threatened to break, Beglan bowed his head in greeting. "Winifred." His baritone voice dipped lower than Esme had heard before. There was no question that the two of them were more than acquaintances, or at least longed to be.

"Beglan," Winifred replied with equal formality. Then, she turned quickly, gave a mumbled "Your Majesty" to Esme, and hurried off.

"Beglan?" Esme's voice betrayed a hint of amusement.

"Hmm?" he replied abstractedly. After a moment, his eyes shot up, meeting hers. "Yes. Right. Now, where shall I set these?" He lifted his arms, indicating the books he'd brought.

Esme bit back a grin and gestured toward one of the private rooms.

————————

An hour later, Esme closed another book with a huff. Every name had been familiar, and no illustration had borne the resemblance of the man she'd seen in her dream.

Beglan glanced up from his book, but Esme only shook her head. With a sympathetic half smile, he took a sip of tea and went back to reading. She was grateful for the company.

Pulling one of the older books toward her, Esme flipped open the cover and scanned the pages about noble lineage in the northern regions. She found a curious passage about a young woman from Juverna who'd left her noble house to serve as a high-priestess in nearby Iola. The two castes rarely intersected, but Esme supposed the gods paid no heed to wealth or status.

She perused the final section. Finding nothing of interest, she closed the book, causing something to shift. A piece of aged parchment slid out from a pocket cut into the book cloth. Carefully, she unfolded it.

It was a map of Tremaene, no different than any she'd seen before. But she studied it nonetheless, ghosting her finger along the worn surface, checking the names of cities, rivers, hills, and ravines. She traced the boundary of the Western Flats—where every map of Tremaene ended, fading into the grain of the paper or truncated by a decorative frame. The map before her was no different. But where the territory lines ended, the wide, empty margin gave her pause.

The cartographer hadn't bothered to draw the natural features—the craggy mountains, bogs, and swaths of land so infertile that even the most powerful high-priestess couldn't summon enough magic to coax even a blade of grass. And yet, Esme wondered. Nothing else was as it had seemed. Perhaps there was more to the desolate terrain.

"Beglan?" She looked across the table. "The land that lies beyond the Western Flats, was it ever inhabited?"

"The Wastes, you mean?"

"That's right."

Beglan tilted his head, regarding Esme as though the answer might suddenly appear scrawled across her forehead. "Perhaps long ago— millennia ago. But if any dare to live in those harsh lands now, I'd imagine they're the kind of people who don't want to be found."

Esme nodded in agreement, then looked back at the map. If it hadn't always been so merciless, if the land had once sustained life, might it have been a habitable region, an extension of the Western Flats perhaps...

Or a territory all its own.

A territory that would've required a presiding lord or lady.

Esme glanced at the discarded books—books that chronicled centuries of noble lineage. She'd never find the name of such an ancient lord upon their pages.

Esme clutched Killian's arm as they strolled across the great lawn. Their walk around the lake had granted a pleasant diversion, and with her guards several paces behind, she let herself imagine that the two of them were alone.

Killian's breath caressed her neck as he murmured softly in her ear. Esme shied away, feeling the heat spreading from where his lips nearly grazed her skin. She was entranced and thoroughly content.

Until she spotted Tearlach.

She straightened as Killian, too, took notice of the imposing form waiting at the top of the south steps.

"You'd better go," Esme told him.

Killian merely lifted his brows.

"Really. I need to speak with him anyway."

After giving him a nudge, Killian sighed and dropped an innocent kiss on her cheek. He offered a quick nod to Tearlach, then headed off to the barracks.

Esme set her shoulders and continued across the lawn. Climbing the steps, she met Tearlach's eyes. "The guards were with us the entire time," she said by way of greeting, coming to stand in front of him.

Tearlach didn't respond, but she could feel the anger rippling off him. After a beat, he inclined his head past Esme's shoulder. She expected to see a muster of peacocks following, or any number of the furred or feathered creatures that seemed drawn to her presence. But when she turned, her eyes landed on a sprinkling of blossoms in the perfectly manicured turf.

I could see that trail from the stables.

Could he really? She narrowed her eyes at the sight. There were at most a couple dozen flowers—only the paler shades visible against the verdant blades. It was unlikely anyone would take notice.

Which means, he continued, his voice vibrating through her skull, *that everyone in the palace can see it too.*

When she faced him again, Tearlach's eyes bored into hers. *You want them to chain you up? Use you as a slave, an instrument to restore the land, the way they would the priestesses?*

Esme glanced back at the barely perceptible trail. He was overreacting, she was sure. But why?

Instead of arguing, she offered a slight nod, accepting his...concern for her well-being before stepping past him.

Chapter Twenty-Seven

SLEEP FADED SLOWLY, but Esme felt safe and content, and was in no hurry to open her eyes. Through her eyelids, she could only perceive the faintest morning light. It was either very early or her curtains had been drawn shut.

Odd, she could have sworn she'd kept them open the night before. The doors as well. She was almost completely certain she'd fallen asleep to the serenade of crickets and chirping tree frogs.

But her room was quiet.

And warm.

Quite warm actually, though she couldn't feel the weight of a blanket.

Smelling fresh, mountain air, she breathed in deeply.

Her hand was resting on something solid, firm. Its heat penetrated her skin through a thin layer of—

Esme's eyes shot open.

She was nestled beside a man. *Killian?* How much wine had she consumed at dinner that she couldn't remember him coming to her room?

Only, she knew it wasn't Killian.

Slowly, her eyes moved over his chest and the linen shirt stretched tight across his muscles. Her gaze lingered there, watching it rise and fall in a slow, steady rhythm. Her own breathing, however, had stalled. Continuing her perusal, she took in the muscles and strong tendons along his neck.

Finally, she looked up at Tearlach.

Asleep.

In her bed.

He looked so relaxed in sleep. Esme had never seen him so...peaceful, so content. He'd watched over her as she'd slept, many times. But she'd never managed to rise before him, to glimpse that trace of vulnerability.

She savored the moment, wanting to trail her fingertips gently across his forehead, his cheek, the dark stubble shadowing his jaw. His lips.

One arm was tucked behind his head, propped up against a stack of pillows that Esme was quite sure she'd tossed on the floor before crawling into bed the night before. She searched her memories for remnants of a nightmare that would've brought him to her room. But her mind could hardly grasp on to anything substantial with Tearlach lying beside her, completely unguarded.

Following the length of his body, her gaze absorbed every hard line and curved muscle. She stopped at the sight of his bare feet—one ankle crossed over the other. He was fully dressed, in the same clothes he'd worn the day before, but he'd taken the time to remove his boots.

And she couldn't remember a single moment of it.

It was only then that Esme became acutely aware of her body pressed up against his. The sheets and blankets had been cast aside at some point in the night, and her satin nightdress was twisted up around her hips, leaving her bare legs exposed.

She started to slide her hand away—the one that was draped so possessively across his lower abdomen—when Tearlach stirred.

Esme froze.

Tearlach grumbled something she couldn't decipher, then curled his arm around her back, tucking her in close.

Esme listened to his deep, measured breaths until she was sure he was still asleep, then began sliding her hand away again. If she was stealthy enough, she could grab a sheet to cover herself before—

The muscles under her hand tensed.

Esme's eyes darted up.

Tearlach stared back.

Neither of them moved. The weight of his hand against her side— and that he hadn't yet shifted it away—suddenly felt less reflexive and more...significant.

Esme's thoughts grew muddled; she didn't know whether to yank the hem of her nightdress back down or curl up into his warmth.

Their prolonged silence made the air thick and potent. Finally, she closed her eyes. "I don't remember..."

"A dream," Tearlach replied. Almost too quickly. Esme looked up at him and thought she saw a flash of panic in his eyes before he slowly removed his hand from her body.

She suppressed a shiver.

Tearlach looked like he wanted to say more. Esme held her breath, vaguely aware of a sound coming from the other side of the room. Tearlach ignored the intrusion too as they stared fixedly at one another, neither of them moving.

But the sound continued. Knocking, Esme registered as it grew more insistent. Until it could no longer be ignored.

Air rushed into Esme's starved lungs. She looked toward the main doors, expecting Cadwyn to burst in at any moment. It was Cadwyn, she knew. Her maids would never knock so incessantly.

Reluctantly, Esme slid away without meeting Tearlach's eyes, pulling her nightdress back into place as she grabbed her robe from the end of the bed.

At the door, she stole a glance back. Tearlach tucked a folded piece of paper into the front pocket of his shirt, then reached down for his discarded boots and sword belt. When he rose, their gazes collided.

Before Esme could say anything, another demanding knock startled her. She closed her eyes, wishing whoever it was would simply go away.

When she heard the barely perceptible click from the door beside her bed, she opened her eyes, finding the room empty—the sheets pulled up over her bed as if nothing had happened there.

———————

Esme's steps faltered when her foot caught the edge of the rug. She moved back to the short stretch of floor in front of the balcony doors that was unobstructed by furniture—save for her desk, which she pointedly ignored—then resumed her pacing. Sully and Cadwyn were gone, but Sully's warning echoed through her mind so clearly it was as if he were walking right beside her.

Lord Torin was up to something, he'd said. What, though, neither Sully nor Cadwyn knew. Nevertheless, they wanted her to be prepared for anything he might bring up in the council meeting later.

Her thoughts returned to the previous meeting. Lady Audris's knowledge of the letter had taken Esme completely by surprise. But then, so had Lord Torin's response. It was as if he'd had prior knowledge.

Her heart thundered, pounding up into her throat. She stopped at one of the dining chairs, gripped the tall back, and forced the sensation back down. Glancing at the clock, she felt the muscles in her shoulders relax—if only a little. There was still a little time before she needed to be down there.

In her dressing room, she absently ran her fingers across the numerous dresses she needed to choose from. Selecting the closest one—a simple gown made of raw silk in a deep teal color—she stepped into it.

Her mind drifted back to Sully's theory—that he'd long suspected Lord Torin had possessed his own plans to overthrow Orianna. Esme knew multiple insurrectionist groups had existed, but had foolishly refused to believe that one of her own council members might have been vying for her crown. *Might still be.* Would Tremaene choose to follow Lord Torin over her?

Hearing a rap at the doors, Esme swiped a silver filigree bracelet from the dressing table and hurried out, peeking again at the clock on the mantel. It wasn't yet time.

She looked down, fumbling with the clasp of her bracelet as she neared the door. Hearing a soft click, she glanced up and stumbled to a halt before colliding with Tearlach.

Neither spoke for several long seconds, and Esme wondered why he was there. She remembered acutely the way he'd looked at her that morning, as though he'd wanted to tell her something in those still, precious moments before the world had intruded.

"I thought you might want to talk." Tearlach's deep voice wrapped around her. "Before the meeting," he added, then looked down at the forgotten bracelet in her hand. He took it gently from her useless fingers. Esme tracked the movement as she begged her lungs to fill with breath.

He draped the cool metal across her wrist, but her sensitive skin warmed quickly at his touch.

Suddenly, it wasn't only her lungs that refused to work. Her heart had certainly stopped beating.

"About what Sully told you," he clarified.

Esme blinked up at him as her mind caught up. Of course that was the reason for his visit.

Air rushed back in, unrestricted, and her heart started up again, pounding loudly in her ears.

"Oh," she said aloud. "Sure. I um...just give me a moment." She spun on her heel and hurried across the room, her cheeks burning.

In the privacy of her dressing room, her eyes fell on the narrow shelves that held her crowns. Her mind traitorously returned to things she shouldn't think on as she absently plucked one of the coronets from its velvet pillow.

She found Tearlach leaning against one of the carved bedposts, and her eyes traveled down his body of their own accord. His relaxed posture reminded her of the way he'd looked that morning, lying in her bed.

She instantly hid the visual, and the feelings it summoned—hid them deep inside her mind, where no one would ever find them. She perched on the arm of the sofa, safely away from him, and positioned the coronet atop her head.

Esme knew Tearlach was waiting for her, but having no desire to discuss the countless worries she had regarding his father, she simply admitted, "It's so much more than I thought it would be, Tearlach. More than I can handle." Her muscles unknotted with the words, so she went on. "I doubt I would've been the right person for this even if my parents had been given the chance to prepare me for it." Shaking her head, she looked away—relieved to have voiced it, but ashamed nonetheless.

She rose, unable to sit still as the feeling of blood rushing through her veins suddenly became more than she could bear. She forced herself not to pace again. Instead, she flexed her feet and curled her toes, over and over, as though the movement would send all her restless energy into the floorboards.

"You wear the crown, Esme."

She looked away from her bare toes at Tearlach's confident and commanding voice.

"Let that be your anchor."

"An anchor holds you back," she argued, her brows knitting together.

"An anchor keeps you steady. Keeps you safe in a storm."

Oh. Her mouth formed the word.

"And you, Esme, of all the people in that council chamber down there, have the honor of wearing the crown."

"Honor." She hated the word, what it meant.

"Yes." He arched a brow. "Honor. Not by privilege or obligation. But by distinction." Pushing off the bedpost, he came to stand before her. "You've earned this crown, Esme." He reached up, trailing a finger along the curved metal of the one she wore. "This crown wasn't handed down to you by your father. You fought for it. You saved your people, your kingdom. And you"—he met her gaze with an intensity that knocked the breath from her—"out of everyone in your council, out of everyone in Tremaene, deserve to wear it. To lead. So no matter what they sling at you today, know that you are the only one who holds the power of the crown. The only one *worthy* of that power."

Esme nodded, but only half-heartedly, wishing she could believe the words as much as Tearlach seemed to. Shying away, she looked down at the crease of fabric she was absently sliding back and forth between her fingers.

"But above all that..." Esme felt Tearlach move closer. He lifted her chin until their eyes met. "You are strong."

The fierce intensity had faded from his gaze. But in the depths of his dark eyes, Esme could see everything he'd witnessed, every obstacle he'd watched her overcome, her strengths and her weaknesses, even his own—when he'd watched her stand up to Orianna, completely alone, without her protector, with nothing more than her own bravery. She saw admiration. Pride.

"You are strong, Esme," he said again, his voice lower still. "Know that."

She couldn't look away if she wanted to. Not even when she heard the distant sound of a door opening.

Before she could think better of it, she stretched up on her toes.

"Thank you," she whispered, then closed her eyes and placed a soft kiss on Tearlach's cheek.

She lowered back down, then lingered, pressing her lips together to seal in the heat from the brief encounter. When she opened her eyes, she found Tearlach's eyes closed. His hands had come up to grip her arms. To keep her there.

They were so close. Almost as close as they'd been that morning.

If she tipped her chin up again...

If he dipped his head lower...

Their lips would align.

When his eyes opened, Esme thought he might say something, but he flicked his gaze over her shoulder, then gently set her away. He didn't meet her eyes again, simply informed her in an indifferent tone that he'd be waiting outside.

Esme stared blankly for a moment, unsure of what had transpired. When she dared to turn around, she saw Killian standing in the doorway, his eyes fixed on Tearlach.

As the two men crossed paths, they acknowledged each other with nods that for all appearances looked respectful.

Then, with Tearlach gone, Killian aimed his sights on Esme and sauntered over.

It was only half a heartbeat, no more, but Esme was certain he'd hesitated.

A smile spread across his face as he approached. "I came to see how prepared you felt for the meeting."

Esme tried to ignore that for the first time since she'd met Killian, his smile didn't reach his eyes.

Chapter Twenty-Eight

ESME WATCHED LORD Torin out of the corner of her eye, as she had the entire meeting. But he gave nothing away. Perhaps he wasn't planning anything.

"If there are no other affairs to discuss, I move that we—" Lord Lennox was cut off.

"Actually, there is another matter we need to consider."

Esme clenched her jaw and slowly turned to face Lord Torin.

"Your Majesty, I'm afraid we must address the prospect of your marriage."

My what? Esme attempted to master the shock that was certainly written on her face.

"Marriage?" she couldn't help but say aloud. "I fail to see how that is of any concern to you or the rest of this council." Not only was it her business, and hers alone, she was far too young to consider such a thing. More importantly, *their land was slowly dying!* Marriage was the last topic she, or any of her councilors, should be interested in discussing.

A quick scan around the table revealed various degrees of surprise or confusion. Some reactions were better concealed than others. She fought the urge to turn around, wanting desperately to see Tearlach's face.

Somehow, she managed to keep her composure, even when Lord Torin leveled her with a stern look.

"This is not simply a concern of the council." He sighed, as if explaining things to his queen cost him a great deal of energy. When he spoke again, his voice softened. "The stability of Tremaene rests on your shoulders, Your Majesty. Every citizen in this kingdom depends on you—on your ability to rule in a fair and just manner. Leading a kingdom is a tremendous burden, one you shouldn't bear alone."

"Lord Torin, I don't believe—"

"I strongly urge Your Majesty to take this matter seriously."

"Lord Torin, while I appreciate your—"

"If you do not," he interjected, his callous tone returning, "I'm afraid we will be compelled to invoke the Regent Decree."

Regent?

"Her Majesty is of age," Sully asserted, his words biting.

"Of age, she may be. But earlier language of the decree states that if no male heir survives, a female may only ascend the throne under the condition that she relinquish control to a regent until such time that she is wed."

Esme nearly choked as a jolt of pure hatred shook her—a debilitating pulse that was there and gone in an instant.

She exhaled, her spine easing from the spasm. It took her a heartbeat to realize that the wave of unfiltered emotion hadn't been her own. She was half-relieved to feel some sort of reaction from Tearlach, though given the intensity of it, she guessed he'd been holding it back since the moment Lord Torin had opened his mouth.

Esme struggled not to glance back at Tearlach, though she was almost certain his face remained a stony mask of indifference.

Repeating Lord Torin's words in her mind, her own anger heated her body. *The earlier language,* he'd said. *Antiquated* seemed a more fitting description if the decree deemed an unmarried woman unfit to rule.

Don't react, Tearlach advised. *We don't know whether it's true. He may only be trying to unsettle you.*

It's working, she replied. But Tearlach was right. There was no proof.

Until Lord Torin pulled a narrow, cylindrical case from his jacket and slid an age-darkened roll of parchment from it.

Esme couldn't move, her eyes fixed on the offending document as Lord Torin carefully unfurled it.

The worn edges and faded script looked similar to the rare, ancient books Beglan kept securely locked away in his shop. How had Lord Torin happened upon something so valuable, and so detrimental to Esme's reign?

She tore her eyes away from the disturbing sight of the scroll, casting a quick glance around the room. It appeared as though her councilors were seeing the document for the first time as well. Winifred, however, wore a look of barely concealed skepticism.

Good, Esme thought.

Lord Torin spoke again. "I've heard rumors that the people of Tremaene worry about Your Majesty's lack of experience."

Esme scrutinized the ancient scroll from where she sat a few chairs away. Could it be a forgery?

"And with your unfamiliarity with the events that transpired during your...*absence*—"

"How is marrying supposed to remedy that?" Esme's indignation flared at the accusation that she'd willingly left her people, her home. That she hadn't fought to save them from a tyrannical ruler.

"Forgive me, Your Majesty"—Lord Torin's voice dripped with condescension—"I understand you may not comprehend, at your young age, how marriage will serve to strengthen Tremaene, to unite our people. Which is why we must not rush the process of finding you a strong political match. In the meantime, a regent will help to ensure the stability of the kingdom."

A strong political match?

Lord Torin turned to address the entirety of the council, dismissing her like the child he apparently saw her as. "Naturally, we'll begin assembling a list of prospective consorts for Her Majesty. But as I've said, such a pivotal decision must not be hastened. Therefore, for the time being, I propose we focus our attention on selecting a suitable regent. Let us revisit this issue when next we convene."

Esme's hands curled into fists on her lap, her nails biting into the soft skin of her palms. It felt as though her life was slipping from her grasp.

Esme. Tearlach's deep voice soothed her fevered thoughts. *Remember. You wear the crown. Not him.*

He was right. She wore the crown. She was queen. No one could force her to marry. Could they? She needed to see what was written on that sheet of parchment.

"And while I'm sure it goes without saying, I must impress upon Your Majesty how improper it would be to continue carrying on any personal relationships with...*the staff.*"

Esme flinched, unable to hide her reaction. *Killian?* How dare—

"Your Majesty." She jerked at Lady Pallya's voice. "It would be wise to consider your options when choosing a consort."

Esme held back a glare.

"I believe what Lord Torin and Lady Pallya are saying," Lord Lennox offered, "is that it's your honor as queen"—again with that word, she hated that word—"to select a husband who will not only champion the decisions you make, but challenge them as well. As Lord Torin so *emphatically* pointed out, reigning over a kingdom is no small task. And so, it is my sincere hope—as I'm sure it is of my fellow councilors— that you choose a consort who will complement you, someone who will balance your strengths and weaknesses. This, Your Majesty"—he smiled—"is what everyone should strive for when selecting a partner. But in your case, it's all the more important that you be discerning. For yourself and for the good of the kingdom."

Lord Lennox's words were a comfort, though she still had no desire to choose a husband. She was far too young to be thinking of such things. It hadn't been that long ago that she'd experienced her first kiss. How could she even begin to consider marriage?

The idea flooded her veins with panic. The sensation was not so different from what she'd felt in the underground lake—trapped in the dark, bottomless depths, not knowing which way was up, struggling to find light, quickly running out of breath—

Esme. You're safe, Tearlach reminded as her thundering heart threatened to shatter her ribs. *You're not in any physical danger. Just breathe.*

She followed his command, inhaling a shaky breath. Then another. Until the ringing in her ears quieted.

The sounds of conversation slowly filtered into her awareness. No one seemed to notice her lack of attention. Esme ground her back teeth together when she glanced at Lord Torin. Would he use the decree to seize power? Would he find a way to take the title of regent for himself, or nominate someone under his control?

With that thought, her anxiety vanished and anger resurfaced. Nausea threatened from the sway of emotions. But it wasn't solely her nerves. She could feel magic churning inside her, begging to be set free.

Esme rose from her chair, knowing the slightest thing might trigger it—much as the thought of swallowing Lord Torin in a storm cloud pleased her.

"That's enough for today. We'll resume this *crucial* conversation during our next meeting. Lord Torin"—she turned, looking down at where he sat—"I thank you for bringing the Regent Decree to my attention, and for your constant, *selfless* concern for the well-being of our kingdom."

The room was so still she could hear the pull of fabric across Lord Torin's shoulders as he inclined his head. "Always, Your Majesty."

"And you'll be sure to leave the document with Winifred when you leave."

When he didn't respond, Esme raised her brow and waited.

His jaw clenched. "Certainly."

Sully was at her side as soon as she pushed through the doors. Hazel and Armel joined Tearlach a few paces behind. No other footfalls sounded in the marble corridor. She wondered how long the others would remain in the council chamber, what they'd discuss in her absence. She was once again grateful for Winifred's inescapable memory.

When they reached her room, Sully followed her in. Before the door shut, she heard Hazel ask Tearlach about the meeting. For the first time, she was glad Killian preferred the night shifts, and that he'd only stopped by earlier to wish her luck before heading back to the barracks to rest. Esme couldn't face him just yet, though she knew he'd hear about it soon enough.

She enjoyed Killian's company. Immensely. Truly, she did. But marriage was the last thing she wanted to consider. Her only hope was that she wouldn't be forced into something she wasn't ready for.

Esme was halfway across the room before she registered Cadwyn's presence. Sully's voice hovered just beyond her awareness, his tone apologetic.

She pulled herself up onto the edge of her bed, hearing only muffled sounds from their conversation. Several times, Cadwyn looked over, her green eyes flashing with empathy, worry, outrage.

Esme turned to stare out the glass doors, though she didn't see anything. The world seemed hazy.

She wasn't sure how long she sat there, staring at nothing.

"Esme?"

Slowly, she glanced toward the sound.

"Think nothing of this, my dear," Sully told her. "We don't yet know the validity of the version of the decree Lord Torin presented. If it's even real. He could have...Well, we just don't know."

"Is it even possible?" Her voice sounded distant. "If it *is* real, can the council truly force me to give up my throne to a regent, to marry a man I..."

Cadwyn moved to sit beside her, resting a comforting hand on her shoulder.

"There are a small number of decrees designed with the specific purpose of limiting the control of a sovereign," Sully explained. "But such an order can only pass—or be enforced—with the entire weight of the council. Though I haven't reviewed the language of this version, the Regent Decree is meant to be a safeguard in the rare instance that both the king and queen are gone, leaving only a young heir to ascend the throne."

Cadwyn's hand tightened on Esme's shoulder as the reality of Sully's words hung between them.

"My apologies," he said quietly, inclining his head.

"No...no." Esme shook her head, blocking the memories of that fateful night. "It's okay. I...understand why a decree would be necessary in protecting a young child in that sort of...situation. That part, at least, makes sense. But why the marriage requirement?"

"Well, given that I'd never heard of that addendum before today, I'd wager that the earlier version was written a very long time ago, when perhaps women were not seen as"—Sully's eyes softened—"*equals* when it came to some matters."

Esme gave a mirthless laugh. "That's a nice way of putting it."

Sully seemed to relax. "My dear, do not worry yourself over this. Even if it ends up being legitimate, there may be grounds to argue that it's no longer valid. Or, we may be able to persuade some of the other councilors to join in nullifying it."

Cadwyn met Esme's gaze. "There are many possibilities, love. And we're going to do everything we can to make sure no one takes that crown from you."

"I can bring the document to Lord Lennox," Sully suggested. "He has trusted legal advisors outside the city."

"Outside the city?"

"We wouldn't want any of the councilors learning about possible gaps in the language until we're ready to act on them. Anything we find will be far more difficult to counter if it's presented, and a resolution is voted upon immediately."

Esme nodded, though she couldn't dismiss the worry creeping around in her mind—that Lord Torin was probably several steps ahead of them.

Chapter Twenty-Nine

AFTER ENJOYING A trip to the public gardens her mother had once frequented, Esme was impatient to read the pages of the journal she'd skipped over, wanting—needing—to know more about Erena's life before Esme had come along.

Book in hand, she hurried out to the balcony.

Griselda poked her head out from behind the cascading white blossoms of a potted cherry tree, and Esme slid the book behind her back.

"Pardon me, Milady." She stepped out from the tangle of foliage, long garden shears in hand. "I was just doing a bit of pruning."

Esme glanced down at a pile of severed branches, their leaves still green. Stifling the sharp pains that streaked up her arms, she pulled a smile over her features. "Thank you, Griselda. But there's no need; I like them that way."

Her maid turned a scrutinizing eye on the mess of greenery. "But it's so...wild."

"I know," Esme replied, her smile no longer fake.

"Whatever Milady wishes." Griselda nodded and bent to gather the trimmings.

Once she was alone, Esme nestled in beside the potted tree. Crossing her legs under her, she placed the journal on her lap and started from the beginning.

The shadows grew longer, and the sun set behind the palace. As stars winked into the indigo sky, the Loinnir Lights ribboned above her, brightening as their backdrop darkened. Mios was nearly full, hanging low in the sky, offering a beam of cool white light through the rungs of the railing. Neve was no more than a tiny waxing sliver, hovering straight above.

Esme continued on, determined to finish the whole of it no matter what emotions her mother's words evoked. Her resolve was strong. Stronger than she'd expected.

That was, until she saw an entry with her name at the top. Not a journal entry. *A letter.*

To her.

From her mother.

The date in the upper corner indicated that it'd been written shortly before Esme had been sent to Donellis with Cadwyn. Just days before...

Every muscle in Esme's body tightened.

It was only by sheer force of will that she kept her eyes open, staring down at the journal.

My dearest Esme,
I hope that you are reading these pages because you've grown to be a strong, self-assured woman, and that I've given you this journal with my own hands. But if I'm no longer around...well, you remember the stories I told you of Ainsley and Ffion? Those were some of my favorite moments with you. Just the two of us in your bed, your eyes wide with anticipation as I read you stories of their adventures. I began hiding the journal out beneath the tree when you were no more than a few weeks old, going out from time to time to add another entry. And if one day I'm unable to return, I want it to be safe, in a place where you will one day find it. A place that will always be ours.

She didn't return, Esme thought, squeezing her eyes shut. She didn't need to turn the page to know it was her mother's final note.

When she looked down again, it was nearly too dark to read. Clouds had gathered, blocking out the lights.

"Breathe," she murmured, trying to grip the unraveling threads of her emotions.

Slowly, the clouds evaporated, leaving a glowing haze hovering above the land. She looked down at the journal, biting her lower lip hard enough that the pain overshadowed all other feeling.

Her mind stumbled over the words.

...you are my greatest adventure...it breaks my heart that I may never see the woman you'll become...be brave...lead with your heart...

Each word struck hard. She heaved inward, her chest caving in, her head falling forward as though she could shield herself from the pain.

With a gulp of air, she filled her lungs and dared to read the lines at the bottom of the page.

I love you, Esme. I will always love you. Even after I fade from this world, I will always be yours, and you will always be mine.

Unable to hold them back any longer, tears spilled from the corners of her eyes. With every muscle in her body, she funneled her sadness into those tears, keeping a tight rein on the magic that yearned to react.

When she felt Tearlach's presence, her concentration faltered.

And the rains fell.

She wiped her face with trembling hands, though it was no use. Heavy drops pelted her skin, clinging to her eyelashes and mixing with the hot stream of tears on her cheeks.

Through her watery vision, she saw Tearlach's dark form step out from the shelter of the doorway. She clenched her eyes shut, focusing her waning energy on the magic pooled at her core, trying to stop it from spreading out beneath her skin, like tributaries, saturating every inch of her.

Lifting a hand to shield her eyes, she squinted into the bleary darkness, but couldn't discern how far the rain clouds had reached.

Tearlach lowered himself beside her. But he didn't pull the magic from her, didn't stop the torrent that fell upon them. Without saying a word, he gently pried the journal from her hands and tucked it behind him, out of the rain she couldn't stop. He didn't know what the book was, only that it'd caused her pain.

Then the weight of his arm, heavy and strong, came around her shoulders. The gesture was tender, and seemed almost tentative. Esme didn't hesitate sinking into his hold.

Tearlach pulled her closer, and she breathed in his familiar scent. There was a heavier note hidden beneath—one she hadn't noticed before, one that was distinctly male.

With each exhale, her body relaxed a little more. The rain was warm and comforting, cocooning them in a fog so dense she couldn't see beyond Tearlach's outstretched legs.

It soaked through her clothes, her skin, all the way to her bones.

She turned her face into Tearlach's chest, feeling the hard planes of muscle beneath the sodden fabric. His heart beat slow and strong against her ear. He shifted slightly, bringing his other arm around her.

With a final, trembling breath, her body released every last bit of tension, and she surrendered herself to Tearlach's protective embrace.

ERICA SEBREE

Chapter Thirty

THE SQUAWKS OF parakeets woke her. But they weren't morning calls, Esme realized as she opened her eyes to find the wall sconces lit. The glow of fading sunlight between the curtain panels told her it was early evening.

She'd slept all day.

She scanned her body, assessing every muscle and tendon from head to toe. She felt stiff, and her mind was a bit hazy. But mostly she just felt numb. Empty.

With a groan she dragged herself from bed, and made her way over to one of the sofas. A tray of food waited in the center of the table. She glanced around the room, wondering who else had come and gone while she'd slept. There were a few new stacks of documents on her desk. And the ones that remained appeared far more orderly than she'd left them. Winifred must have been by as well.

"Gods bless the woman," Esme sighed. "Cadwyn too," she added when she spotted a small vial beside the silver teapot. A note was propped against it with two words written in Cadwyn's hand: *Drink this.* Tearlach must have informed her that Esme had been...out of sorts the night before.

Steam wafted into the air as she poured the tea. Thankfully it was still hot. Then, uncorking the small vial, she opted not to smell the viscous liquid first, downing it in one, bitter gulp. She sputtered, the horrid taste clinging to her tongue. Even three sips of strong tea couldn't wash it away.

"What *was* that?" She eyed the sinister brown bottle as if it were to blame.

Wrapping her hands around the teacup, she went to draw a bath.

By the time the sudsy water reached the top step, Esme had managed to polish off every last morsel of food from her dinner tray. With a full stomach, and whatever was in the herbal tonic Cadwyn had given her warming her veins, Esme felt clearer, more alert. But not in the way she felt when she drank too much tea. The edges of her awareness were softer, her focus more mindful, as though her senses hovered close to her body instead of reaching out to take in everything the world contained.

She ran her fingers along the folded stack of towels, slid her toes into the fluffy pile of the rug, breathed in the honeysuckle and sweet basil fragrance that filled the bathing chamber. She dropped her robe, closing her eyes as the fine silk slipped down her skin. She absorbed the sensation, letting everything else in her awareness drop away.

After her bath, feeling restored and settled in her skin once more, Esme didn't startle when she emerged from her dressing room to find Tearlach pacing.

She glanced at the table where her dinner tray had been, thinking Cadwyn's herbal tonic might do him some good as well.

"Sorry, I...should've knocked."

Esme scrunched her nose at the statement. Since when did he knock?

"There's no need. Did you..."

"I thought you'd want to be apprised of Lord Lennox's progress as to revoking the..." He paused, finally settling against one of the bedposts. "Regent Decree."

"How is he faring? He's acquainted with counselors-at-law outside the city, I was told."

"That's right. He expressed every confidence that he'll succeed in revoking the antiquated addendum." Tearlach glanced around the room, taking it in, as if he'd only just entered. His sights rested on the drawn curtains. Esme wondered if he suspected they'd been closed all day. And if he'd come calling for that very reason.

"That's certainly good to hear. How soon?"

"Hmm?" Tearlach turned back to her. "Oh. A matter of days. No more than a week."

"Good." She nodded.

"Yes. Good," he agreed.

Esme's guess at the true reason for his visit solidified in the silence that followed, though she was grateful he hadn't mentioned anything about the previous night.

"I just rang for more tea, if you want to...stay." She gestured for him to sit.

Tearlach eyed the table for a moment, something clearly warring inside him. But Esme didn't want him to leave just yet.

"They always bring too much. If I drink it all, I won't sleep tonight." She went to pull out a chair for him. Tearlach watched her, then exhaled a long-held breath and unbuckled his sword belt, laying it carefully on the sofa.

Esme caught sight of a slip of paper edging out of his pocket with the movement. It looked like the one she'd seen him tuck into his shirt the morning they'd woken together. She fought a rush of heat at the reminder.

"What's that?" She nodded toward his chest.

Tearlach glanced down. He stilled before pushing it farther into his pocket. "It's nothing," he mumbled.

"Nothing, huh?" Esme felt a flicker of amusement as she approached. "Then why are you carrying it around? It's obviously important," she teased, enjoying herself more than expected. Cadwyn's tonic really had worked wonders on her mood.

He exhaled, glaring at her with clear exasperation.

She tilted her head to the side and propped a fist on her hip. She could wait. He'd invaded her privacy plenty; he deserved a little in return.

His eyes narrowed, but at last he withdrew the piece of paper. He unfolded it slowly, keeping his eyes on her. Esme didn't break their entangled gaze, but in her periphery, she caught the way he stroked his thumb across the script.

When he held it out for her to see, she realized it was the note she'd given him along with his new chest plate.

"It reminds me who to blame for that cumbersome gold monstrosity I'm required to wear," he said in a deep, brooding voice.

Esme stepped closer, looking down at the worn paper. The creases were beginning to tear, and the ink had faded. She read the words: *Wear this, and always think of me when you do.*

Suddenly, her jesting command didn't seem so...innocent. It sounded far more flirtatious than she'd meant it to. It was practically an invitation. Like she wanted him to be reminded of her every time he donned the armored plate.

Her cheeks burned, and she risked a look up at him. His eyes gave nothing away.

"But you're not...You're not wearing your uniform now," she pointed out uselessly.

Tearlach shrugged a shoulder as if that mattered little, then refolded the note and returned it to his pocket.

When a knock sounded, Esme called for her maid to enter. Only it wasn't Marta bringing in tea. Or Brighid. Or Griselda.

It was Killian framed in the doorway, with a basket from the kitchens and a blanket draped over his arm.

"Am I interrupting anything?" Killian fixed his gaze on Tearlach.

"Of course not," Esme assured, her voice rising too high.

Killian sauntered in, and Esme forced herself to meet him halfway. They embraced, but she could tell that Killian's attention wasn't on her.

She pulled away and looked between the two men.

"I was just leaving." Tearlach didn't meet Esme's eyes as he went to retrieve his sword belt, leaving her and Killian alone.

Killian ducked to catch Esme's eye. His signature smile had returned, and she couldn't resist offering a smile of her own.

"Thought you might want to join me down by the lake." His brow rose in question.

She glanced back at the dining table, thinking how her evening might have gone. With Tearlach. Finding out where he kept her note when it wasn't in his front pocket.

Painting a look of delight on her face, she replied, "That sounds lovely."

———

Esme knelt on the blanket, the soft grass cushioning her knees as she scooted into the center. Killian straightened the other edge, smiling down at her, then toed off his boots to join her.

Her mind kept returning to Tearlach's visit, and she realized she hadn't seen Killian since before the council meeting. Certainly he'd heard about the Regent Decree, that Lord Torin was trying to force her into relinquishing her crown or to marry. But Killian hadn't brought it up, and Esme wasn't about to spoil their night together.

The lake was still, save for the smooth ripples trailing a lone swan as she glided through the reflected colors of the evening lights. Crickets began to hum, and lightning bugs blinked into view within the depths of the darkening woods. The small outcropping offered some privacy from her guards, but every few minutes Esme would hear the scrape of stones as they paced along the shore.

She looked over at Killian only to find him watching her intently. She'd seen similar looks in his eyes—ones that usually led to him closing the distance between them and bringing his lips to hers.

Instead, he reclined back on his forearms to look up at the sky. Esme lowered beside him, propping herself up on an elbow to face him.

"Esme, I..." Killian took a breath, his gaze focused on the canopy of shifting lights above them.

She waited for him to continue. When he didn't, Esme leaned over to kiss his cheek, his stubble prickling her lips. He turned into her touch, their lips separated by only a breath.

She leaned closer.

"What was Tearlach doing in your room tonight?"

She pulled back. His blue eyes were deeper than she'd seen them before.

"Tearlach?" she repeated innocently, as if she hadn't been thinking about him. "He only wanted to inform me about Lord Lennox's progress on rewriting the Regent Decree, to revoke the..." She hesitated. "To revoke the marriage addendum."

Killian regarded her a moment longer, then returned his attention to the sky with a heavy exhale. Was he offended? Certainly he couldn't think she was ready for marriage.

"That was...considerate of him," Killian finally allowed. "Surely that kind of information couldn't wait until morning." He gave her a sidelong glance.

"Is something wrong?" Killian wasn't acting himself. Not in the least.

"No." He sat up and turned to face her. Esme searched his eyes, but his expression bared nothing. Finally, his lips curved into a smile, sweet and honest. "You look beautiful tonight." He brought his hand up to cup her cheek, stroking his thumb along her lower lip.

His skin felt surprisingly cool against her skin, but she savored the feel of his fingertips as they feathered along her jaw, down her neck. When he paused, Esme met his gaze. The intensity remained, though it had softened some.

Perhaps she could vanquish whatever was upsetting him altogether. She flicked her gaze to his mouth, then leaned forward to press her lips to his.

Killian seemed tentative at first. But within seconds, his arms circled her and his mouth claimed hers. Esme rose up on her knees to meet him, wrapping her arms around his neck. The familiar heat radiated between them, and Esme closed her eyes, humming with pleasure into his mouth. He pulled her closer, gripping the back of her shirt with his fists, pressing their bodies together. His lips moved to her throat, his tongue hot against her skin. She arched into his touch.

Then his lips were gone. His heat receding.

Esme opened her eyes. Killian held her at arm's length, looking down between them. His hands tightened on her shoulders, his chest rising and falling quickly.

"Killian?" she whispered.

"Esme, we..." He lifted his gaze, and Esme realized what she'd seen in his eyes earlier—regret. "I can't do this." He shook his head.

Chapter Thirty-One

I CAN'T DO this. The words clanked inside her head.

"What?" Esme's heart sunk. Tears stung her eyes. She looked away, toward the still water visible beyond the boulders. It looked like a churning cauldron with the eddying verdant and violet lights reflected in the glassy surface.

"Esme." Killian's voice was soft. She felt him shift closer. Then his hands were on her again, though his touch felt different. Slowly he slid his hands up and down her arms, the warmth both comforting and unsettling. "Esme," he said again, then turned her chin. She blinked away her tears to find him staring down at her with kind, gentle eyes. "I don't think..." He took a breath as if choosing his next words carefully. "I don't think our hearts are in this together."

"What? I don't...What do you mean?" she stammered, eyes pleading.

But Killian didn't respond with words. He let out a breath and tilted his head to the side, regarding her, a sympathetic smile curving the corners of his mouth.

She turned away, feeling the burn of humiliation rising up her throat. She had to leave, needed to be as far away as possible.

Rising on unsteady legs, she stumbled to her feet. Killian stood with the effortless grace of a man who'd spent more than a century honing his body, completely at ease in his own skin. Which only made her inexperience feel all the more prominent.

"Is this why you brought me out here? To end things with me?" She stared at him, at the contrite look in his eyes, then down at the wool blanket. A fresh wave of shame flooded her veins. How foolish she'd been, assuming his intentions had been romantic, to sneak a few hours with her.

"I'm trying—"

Esme looked up at the sound of his strained voice.

"—to do the right thing, here."

The right thing? Her mouth clenched into a scowl. "Is this because of the Regent Decree?"

Indignation flared in his eyes. "No. Of course not. Esme, I'd marry you in a heartbeat if..." He looked down.

"If what?" Marriage wasn't something she was prepared to offer, but she hadn't thought she'd lose Killian over it.

His jaw clenched, like he was keeping the words locked inside.

Esme didn't wait to hear what he might say. She bent down and yanked the blanket from the ground, forcing Killian to retreat. Twisting it haphazardly into a roll, grass and dirt scattered into the air, clinging to her sweat-slick skin. She brushed a loose strand of hair from her face, but by the feel of it, she'd only managed to smear streaks of dirt across her forehead.

Growing more agitated by the second, she turned down the path, feeling overly clumsy on the uneven terrain.

Her thrumming blood drowned out the nocturnal sounds of the woods, but it wasn't enough to block Killian's voice as he called after her.

Esme didn't look back, didn't even look up. Her eyes were fixed on the ground, on her next determined step. She could feel Quinlan's and

Roderick's concerned gazes as she passed them. Thankfully, they didn't say a word, simply falling in line behind her.

Is Killian following? Esme shook her head. She didn't care. Only wanted to be in her room, alone. Where no one could see the hurt and humiliation in her eyes, in her hurried, teetering steps.

She followed the row of sycamores around the great lawn—avoiding the countless guards and servants between the south steps and her room upstairs—realizing too late that she was heading toward the entrance of the west wing.

Without sparing a glance down the corridor that led to the guest apartments, she turned and hurried up the winding stairs, pausing after only three steps.

Two female voices echoed down from the third floor. They kept their voices low, but Esme picked up a few strands.

"...that dark hair of his. I'd run my hands through it if he let me."

"Why don't you offer to give him a massage? Help work out some of that tension?" They both giggled.

"And that stoic way he carries himself." The other woman hummed in agreement. "You know, I talked to him just yesterday."

"You talked to the queen's guard?" Her voice rose in pitch. "How did you manage that?"

Tearlach? They were talking about Tearlach? Esme eased up the curved steps, careful to keep her footfalls silent.

"We were passing in the corridor and I...well, I only said 'Good morning.'"

"And what did he say?" the other woman asked breathlessly.

"He nodded."

"That's more than I've gotten from him. And let me tell you, I've tried. But it doesn't seem to matter. There's only one woman he..."

Esme strained to hear, but their voices trailed off as they moved away from the stairwell.

Only one woman? What woman? Tearlach hadn't mentioned anyone.

Her pulse quickened, and heat returned to her cheeks. Was she jealous?

Esme scoffed at the notion as she reached the second floor. She most certainly was *not* jealous. She simply felt...protective of him, perhaps a bit possessive. That was all.

Realizing she could no longer hear her guards following—though they probably knew it was best to keep their distance—she glanced over her shoulder.

Then nearly collided with Tearlach's broad chest when she turned back.

Her breath hitched as strong hands tightened on her shoulders, steadying her.

Of all the people she'd wanted to avoid at that moment—

Then why did you take the only path that would lead you past his room? her annoying voice offered.

Reluctantly, she looked up, braving his knowing eyes. They were even darker in the dimly lit corridor, but they missed nothing. Tearlach scanned her face, then her body. She should've taken the time to brush the dirt off her forehead, the blades of grass from her shirt. But even if she had, she wouldn't have been able to hide her red-rimmed eyes.

Tearlach looked past her, gave a nod to dismiss her guards, then focused on her again.

"What happened?" His tone was even, calm, but Esme knew better than to be fooled by it.

"Nothing. I'm fine." If her disheveled appearance hadn't already given her away, then the unintentional squeak of her voice certainly would.

He dropped his gaze, as if to verify what he'd already gleaned from her appearance. "Esme?" She felt immense restraint in that single word. A muscle feathered along his jaw, and she wondered if his hands would be curled into fists if they weren't still resting, with surprising gentleness, on her shoulders.

The flickering lantern hanging above gilded one of Tearlach's dark locks that had fallen across his forehead. She'd always thought his hair nearly black, but in the warm light Esme could see hints of chestnut and cinnamon, even a bit of gold.

Her skin tingled as she imagined dragging her hands through his thick mane. Would it feel silky between her fingers? Would he—

Her eyes snapped back to his, and she banished the thought, praying to the gods he couldn't see the inappropriate desire written on her face.

Tearlach's tight expression hadn't changed, so Esme cast about for something—anything—to say. But as the conversation she'd overheard returned, she couldn't stop herself from looking more closely at Tearlach. She tilted her head slightly, seeking to look past his role as her protector, her guard, her friend, to the man beneath. A man who'd given up so much to be with her. A man who'd remained by her side since the night they'd fled Debarrow. Before that, even. For nine long years, he'd watched over her. Tearlach had left his entire life behind for a young girl he'd never met.

And once he'd escorted her back to Meallán to help her claim her rightful place on the throne, he'd stayed. Even before Armel, Hazel, and Killian had chosen to form a new royal guard, Tearlach had vowed his life—once again—to her.

"Do you miss Altan? The mountains? The life you had…before me?"

His eyes softened, then narrowed, no doubt trying to sense the direction of her thoughts.

"Are you trying to get rid of me again?" His mouth quirked up.

"No," she gasped at the thought of him leaving, then lowered her voice. "No. It's just…You left a noble life behind. And now you're living at the palace, of all places." She stopped herself before she unintentionally convinced him to leave. "I…" Her eyes locked with his. "Never mind." She ducked past him.

Tearlach grabbed her wrist. "What's wrong?"

"Nothing." She jerked her head up. But with that single word—that lie—every emotion she'd shoved down rose to the surface. Esme buried the recent memory of Killian, willing her mind to be silent.

But it was too late. Something shifted in Tearlach's eyes, and Esme saw the moment he felt her pain, her heartache.

He cut a look toward the tower she'd ascended. "Shit," he muttered under his breath. "You were with Killian." The way he said it sounded like he already knew what had happened. Like he'd actually been…expecting it?

His grip on her wrist tightened, and they both looked down at the searing point of contact. Tearlach dropped her hand instantly and took a step back. He stared at her wrist—at the place he'd touched her—then crossed his arms over his chest, like he didn't trust himself not to reach for her again.

"What happened?" he demanded.

Esme looked away. She didn't want his pity, and she certainly didn't want him asking because he felt obligated.

"I'm fine. Really." She made to move past him.

"What. Happened." His voice deepened, and Esme felt the words vibrate along her skin.

"I was out by the lake with Killian…" She forced herself to stand an inch taller, forced herself to look every bit the strong woman she was supposed to be. "I ended things with him," she lied again.

Tearlach stared at her.

Esme could feel her muscles trembling. She clenched her jaw and curled her toes inside her shoes to keep still.

The silence stretched. Too long.

Esme could almost taste the thick fog of tension swirling between them.

Then, he nodded. Let her keep the lie. Let her hold on to it as fiercely as she needed to.

He kept his eyes locked with hers, and though the intensity faded, there remained a flicker of...something.

Esme looked away and turned on her heel. She couldn't look into his eyes a moment longer. What she saw in those dark pools was fooling her, making her believe the fire was coming from within. But it was only the flickering lights reflected in his eyes. That was all. She was sure that was all.

When she reached her doors, she felt Tearlach behind her.

"Esme," he said quietly.

She paused, her hand poised above the door handle.

"Do you...need anything?"

At the precarious, almost tender tone of his voice, a smile threatened. But all Esme could manage was a soft "I'm fine" before slipping into her room.

Chapter Thirty-Two

ESME STARED AT the swirling water, wondering if she should've taken at least a bite of the breakfast Griselda and Marta had left.

Water reached her toes, and she quickly leaned down to twist the hot water knob. After draining several inches, and mopping up the water that had crested over the lip, she pulled her chemise over her head and stepped down into the bath.

Letting the heated water embrace her, Esme hoped it would ease more than her muscles. Steam threaded through the air, clinging to her cheeks. She blew ripples across the water, watching them spread out in concentric circles. Then lifted her foot, breaking the surface with a single toe, sending new ripples to collide with the others.

Sighing, she rested her head back and gazed up at the ceiling. Indeed, a bath was a fine choice, especially since she had no intention of seeing anyone for the foreseeable future.

She counted her breaths until the rhythm of her rising and sinking body with each lungful of air lulled her nearly to sleep.

But as soon as she lost count—the moment her focus wavered—the ruminations returned in full force, and the previous night played out in her mind. Again, and again.

Esme couldn't hide from Killian's words. Each time she relived the memory, his intonation changed, her mind warping the meaning. At first, his voice had been soft, caring and sympathetic, but as the words repeated, they transformed into something cruel and mocking. She knew Killian incapable of such unkindness, yet her mind persisted, coloring him a villain, twisting his words so much that all she could hear was the scorn beneath them.

Then the words weren't his at all. And the voice wasn't Killian's, but her own.

Every doubt Esme had ever felt about herself, every shortcoming and disadvantage she'd perceived, swept through her. Her heart sunk, dropping into her stomach.

Feeling a rivulet trail down her cheek, Esme brushed it away.

A drop landed on her forehead.

Not tears, she realized, blinking against the gathering mist. Esme closed her eyes and tilted her head up, letting the warm drops fall upon her skin as she listened to the soft pattering of rain against the surface of the bathwater.

When the last of her thoughts had been washed away, the air cleared.

She blinked the droplets from her lashes, then climbed out of the bath. The tiles were slick, so she grabbed the nearby shelf for balance, rattling the many bottles. Her towel was soaked through. She wrung it out and dried herself as best she could. Her robe hanging near the door at the other end was only slightly damp, so she pulled it on, the satin clinging to her still-wet skin.

She swung the door open and stumbled to a stop.

Tearlach stood in the center of her suite, fists on his hips.

Esme tightened the ties of her robe.

Tearlach's eyes were drawn to the movement, to where her hands gripped the ties.

She crossed her arms over her chest—acutely aware that the thin fabric was translucent from her damp skin.

But his gaze was already sweeping down her bare legs. Then slowly back up.

When his eyes snapped to hers, he clenched his jaw.

Heat flushed her already warm skin, and for a moment she thought he might take a step closer, that his eyes might consume her body once more.

Instead, he turned his back to her and cleared his throat. "Are you well?" he asked in a cold, unfeeling voice.

The warmth drained from her body.

"Of course I am." Esme couldn't manage the same steady voice as Tearlach. "Why wouldn't I be?" She padded across the room.

"I heard you sent your maids away, and refused to leave your room," Tearlach said as she slipped through one of the open doors of her dressing room. "Sully was forced to cancel this morning's meeting with the guards."

"Oh? Was that this morning? I thought it was tomorrow." She hoped her voice wouldn't betray her.

"Is this about last night?" Tearlach's response came from just beyond the door. It sounded quiet, cautious almost.

Esme took a breath, willing her pulse to slow. "No, this isn't about... last night." It wasn't *just* about Killian, anyway. It was about everything. She was feeling things she couldn't even decipher. Things that made no sense.

She grabbed a shirt from the top of a folded stack and yanked it over her head, then stepped into a pair of leggings.

The worst of it was, she didn't feel all that upset over losing her romantic connection with Killian. It hurt; she couldn't deny that. Being told one wasn't wanted never felt good. But it should've hurt more, after all they'd shared. She'd brought him back from death, felt his heart beat anew beneath her palms. Beating in time with hers. Beating *because* of hers. Shouldn't her own heart have stopped the moment he'd confessed he didn't feel the same? It should've killed her, seized her heart and squeezed until life slipped away.

Only it hadn't.

His words hadn't broken her as they should have.

That was the most disconcerting part. Where was the heartrending pain? Was she incapable of feeling such things? Had she seen too much, lost too much of herself?

She blinked against the nearly constant sting of tears. Fumbling with the buttons at her hip, she turned and faced the mirror. Maybe there wasn't enough room left inside her. Was that what being a queen meant? Did she only have the capacity to love her kingdom, her people?

She glanced past the open door, her thoughts returning to Tearlach.

"I just needed some time to myself. Can't I have that? Can't I have a day when I don't need to be everything to everyone?"

"No," came Tearlach's reply.

Esme gripped the comb poised above the crown of her head. She pushed the door open to find him leaning against the mantel of the hearth. "No?"

"No," he repeated, holding her gaze. He didn't look the least bit contrite for his frankness. "You are the queen." He kept his voice level, with the sort of calm she'd come to expect—and loathe. "Unless you've fallen ill and cannot manage to rise from your bed, then no, you cannot take a day." He took a step closer. Esme could only stare at him. "You have responsibilities. When you stop, everything in the kingdom stalls." He pried the comb from her hand. Esme glanced down at the impressions left on her palm. "So, if there's something going on, something personal, then you need to find a way to deal with it, to talk about it."

"There's nothing to talk about," Esme avowed. When Tearlach's gaze didn't waver, she dropped her chin, averting her eyes.

"It doesn't have to be me. If you can't—You don't have to talk to me, Esme, but talk to someone. Cadwyn or even Killian."

"Killian?" she let slip, then clamped her mouth shut.

"I thought you said this wasn't about last night."

Esme glared at him until his demeanor softened.

"Judging by your appearance last evening, I'd venture a guess that you and Killian didn't leave things...*amicably*. My advice—if you care to take it—is that you might find comfort in speaking with him about your thoughts and feelings regarding the situation." After a moment, he added, "He's a good listener. Killian."

Esme conceded with a nod, and realized that perhaps that was the reason she hadn't felt overwhelmingly crushed by the end of their romantic relationship. She knew, deep down, that Killian wasn't going anywhere. Embarrassed as she was about misinterpreting his feelings, Esme felt safe in knowing he'd still be around.

"He's a good friend."

Esme looked up at the subtle shift in Tearlach's tone.

"Killian's like a brother to me—more of a brother than my own. He's a good man, Esme."

Her eyes narrowed at the leading statement.

"But he's a guard. A...*warrior*." The word seemed like it was ripped from Tearlach's throat—like it cost him something to say it, to admit it. The broad expanse of his chest swelled with a deep breath before he continued. "And a queen can't marry a warrior. A queen needs—"

"Don't," she stopped him, knowing she couldn't stomach the end of that sentence. She saw the muscles in Tearlach's jaw flex, so she strode past him and pulled open the main door before he could say another word.

Armel and Harlow turned to let her pass, but she stopped in front of Armel. "I feel like practicing with daggers," she informed him. It wasn't a request.

She felt Tearlach come up beside her as Armel glanced over at him. "I believe Cahir and Quinlan are currently in the yard. I'm sure either of them would..."

Esme raised a brow.

"Certainly, Your Majesty." Armel nodded.

She tried to ignore the twinge of guilt at the unwelcome formality—knowing she shouldn't have pressed him for instruction while he was on duty. And in front of Tearlach no less. "I've a sudden urge to throw things," she muttered as she marched toward the stairs, leaving Tearlach behind.

Armel remained at her side as they crossed the grounds toward the barracks. Esme kept her sights trained on the trees that sheltered the yard, but felt Armel's eyes on her more than once.

"Did...Did something happen?" Armel let the hesitant question hang between them.

"No. Nothing," she ground out as Tearlach's words battered around in her mind. *A queen can't marry a warrior.* Why did it bother her so much? It wasn't as if it mattered. Killian had made clear he didn't think of her that way.

"If there's anything you need to talk about, I—" Armel stopped when she cut him a look.

"Why would I need to talk about anything?"

Armel rubbed his clean-shaven jaw in a nervous gesture she'd never seen him do before. "It's just...if something *has* happened, this might not be the best time to—"

"Not the best time to *what?*" She turned to face him straight on.

"Forgive me. It's not my place." Armel bowed his head.

Esme clenched her teeth, hating the way his subservience made her feel. Armel was a friend more than a guard. He was only trying to help. She knew that. But after everything that had happened, she felt raw, exposed. And Tearlach's comments had only made her feel worse.

A queen can't marry a warrior. Not Killian, not her royal guard, not even her friend. He was only a *warrior.* Tearlach had said the word "warrior" as if it were something beneath her. A queen couldn't be with someone like that. It didn't matter what she wanted, only what was expected of a queen. And Esme would always be a queen. So a warrior, *any* warrior, even one who...

She forbade herself from concluding that thought. Even nearing it felt like it tore at something beneath her ribs. And in that moment, she simply couldn't handle any more emotional revelations.

Armel looked like he might offer another piece of advice, so she cast her eyes down. They continued toward the yard in an uncomfortable silence. By the time they reached the edge of the central training ring, Esme's head throbbed with unspoken apologies and unfriendly remarks she knew she'd regret.

Cadwyn was across the yard—her bag of healing supplies beside her on the bench.

When Armel began unbuckling the chest plate of his uniform, Esme put a hand on his arm to stop him. "Another time," she told him. He lifted his brow in question, but Esme turned and crossed to Cadwyn before either could say more.

The following hour was marked only by the scores of daggers embedded in barkless stumps. Cadwyn hadn't offered a reply when Esme had asked for her company, she'd simply closed up her satchel and followed silently—an unspoken understanding passing between them.

Esme didn't doubt for a second that her lady-in-waiting knew exactly what had transpired with Killian. But she didn't ask. Didn't tell her how to feel. Didn't offer uninvited advice about how she was expected to cope. She simply offered silent companionship.

The scrape of metal on metal, and the shouts of fighting had at first grated Esme's nerves, but after she and Cadwyn settled into a rhythm of knife throwing, the obtrusive sounds faded into the background.

Beads of sweat slid down Esme's temples. Her shoulder ached. She signaled for Cadwyn to halt so she could pull the blades from their targets, but Quinlan reached them first, tossing Esme a glance before yanking them out in quick succession. Returning to her spot behind the mark, Esme noticed that two of the palace guards—both female—had taken up positions beside Cadwyn. Quinlan handed back the daggers before pulling her own from her bandolier.

None of them said a word as five knives struck their targets.

Chapter Thirty-Three

ESME FLIPPED ONTO her stomach, punched her pillow, then laid her head down again. She wanted to blame the stiffness in her throwing arm for her restlessness, but knew full well that it was her mind keeping her from sleep. She closed her eyes and started counting. When she reached eight hundred and nineteen, she threw back the covers and dressed.

Easing open the main door, Esme was relieved to find Cahir and Madoc standing guard. Catching the strains of conversation from the night staff below stairs, she avoided the grand staircase and started down the dim corridor that led to the servant stairwell.

Cahir went ahead of her, taking the stairs two at a time. As she rounded the landing at the first floor—with Madoc close behind—the sounds of hushed conversations and girlish laughter rose up to greet her. She exhaled irritably as her steps brought her closer to the gossip she'd hoped to avoid.

When Killian's name reached her ear, she nearly turned and went back to her room, thinking a night of restless sleep might be better than facing the rumors that were swirling about the palace.

"Heard the queen turned him down," one woman said.

"Apparently Her Majesty thinks him unworthy of her affections," another crooned.

Esme's soft-soled shoes slipped on the bottom step, but Cahir steadied her before she lost her balance. Her cheeks burned, but she managed to meet his eyes.

"Wait here while I check the kitchens," he told her in an uncharacteristically indignant tone. With footfalls that were much louder than necessary, he marched down the corridor, chasing away the snide remarks.

"Seems the path is clear, Your Majesty," Madoc said with a wolfish grin as he gestured her out of the stairwell. Esme offered a grateful smile as they crossed the abandoned corridor.

In the kitchens, three women were standing at attention beside their work tables. Molly she recognized straightaway, but the others were new to her. Rosaleen, the head cook, was absent, which Esme hoped would be to her advantage.

Molly set a cream-covered whisk down beside a large copper bowl, and stepped away from her station. She lifted her apron to the side and swept into a curtsy. "Your Majesty." She rose. "Can I fetch something for you?"

Esme glanced at the others. One woman stood rigid with a white-knuckled grip on her rolling pin; the other held a knife hovering six inches above a pitted plum.

"I wonder if I might assist with the morning preparations." She addressed her response to Molly, whose eyes went wide, like she was trying her best not to openly gawk. When she didn't reply, Esme swept a searching gaze around the space, spotting a heap of potatoes on the table nearest her.

Without a word, she swiped an apron hanging from a peg near the door, and claimed the task. She picked up a potato from the top of the mound. The freshly washed skin was still damp. A quick scan had her striding past the still-unmoving women to retrieve a knife.

As she took the first strip of skin off the potato, she looked over to see that Cahir and Madoc had taken up positions in front of the exits—surmising that her visit wouldn't be a fleeting one.

It'd been some time since she'd prepared food for herself, but the motions had been ingrained long before, and Esme was soon lost in the rhythmic flick of her wrist as she rotated each tuber under the sharp edge of the blade.

She worked her way through the mountain of potatoes until she reached over and grasped only air. She looked up—slightly bewildered by how much time had passed—and noticed that the others had finally gone back to their tasks. The woman who'd been rolling out dough had several rounds prepared and was gently lifting one into a pie pan. The other woman spooned in sugar and a spice that smelled of nutmeg, then squeezed several lemons into a bowl filled with sliced plums. She turned the contents over thrice with a flat wooden spatula.

Esme gazed longingly at the glossy sweetness of the macerating fruit. As each shell was filled, the pastry chef curved the edges of the dough up over the fruit, leaving thick slices overflowing in the center. It looked almost too perfect to eat. Her stomach disagreed, grumbling.

Perhaps next time Esme would bake something again, but that night she was content to peel and cut potatoes into perfectly round slices. To feel needed—even if her help wasn't at all necessary.

Realizing her station was covered with darkening peels, she set down her knife, grabbed the hem of her apron and swept them into the makeshift basket. Only then did it occur to her that she had no idea where to dispose of them.

Cahir caught her eye and nodded toward a cluster of tall wire bins near one of the outside doors.

Ah, she mouthed in reply, and went to empty her apron. Turning back to her work table, her eyes skidded to a halt at the open door of the buttery, her gaze drawn to the dark stairwell set into the back wall. The one that led to the wine cellar.

Esme had avoided wine with her dinner that evening. Drinking alone wasn't a wise choice, and a whole bottle to herself an even worse one. Her mind drifted back to the last occasion she'd partaken in too many cups. During the celebration in Altan—the night before the rebel army had marched out—she'd drawn one too many from the endless row of wine casks, and paid for it the following morning.

But she could practically feel the silence in the kitchens. It was wrapped so tightly around each of them that Esme decided it was worth the risk. Grabbing a lantern, she carefully descended the narrow, curved steps. Heavy boots followed. Cahir was beside her before she reached the bottom. Esme surveyed the racks and selected something light and floral that she hoped would ease everyone's rigid propriety and encourage conversation. She plucked two bottles, then turned to Cahir. "Would you mind?" She offered them up to him, then pulled another from the rack.

Esme returned and set the bottle on an empty work table, then hooked her fingers through four copper mugs on a drying rack. She turned and raised an eyebrow to Cahir as he placed the other two bottles on the table. He declined with a shake of his head and went back to his post. Madoc wouldn't meet her eyes.

After pouring a fair amount into the cups, she offered one to each of the women. Molly took hers with significant hesitation. The other two—Gilian and Abaigeal, she'd learned—seemed even less sure. Esme wondered how much longer their shift lasted. Surely one glass wouldn't impede their professional abilities all that much.

Going back to her table to slice the peeled potatoes, she heard some mumbled remarks a moment before Molly set a large bowl of cool water and another knife across from her. Abaigeal followed with a stack of shallow baking pans and a crock of goat's cheese tucked in the crook of her arm. Esme glanced back to find that their stations had been tidied and wiped clean. She watched Gilian reach up to snip several stems of thyme and rosemary from the dried bunches hanging near the jars of spices.

For a time, the four of them worked in silence. Esme and Molly sliced potatoes, tossing them into the water. Abaigeal laid them out on towels and patted them dry before lining the pans with overlapping layers. Gilian spread creamy cheese and sprinkled herbs every third layer until they reached the tops of the pans.

Wine was consumed slowly at first, but it was evident that the potato dishes were the last of the breakfast preparations, so Esme abandoned her caution and refilled their cups.

When she noticed Gilian tip hers back to finish the last of the dregs, Esme hurried to open a second bottle. It didn't take long for conversation to begin, though it was stilted at first.

Molly made a comment about a new footman. Esme could tell by her accompanying blush exactly why Molly had taken notice of him. Abaigeal joined in, commenting about a palace guard who'd recently shaved his beard. The other two hummed in agreement that the change was quite becoming. Esme grinned. She hadn't a clue as to whom they were speaking about, but it felt nice to be included.

"Kyla told me she saw Lady Audris without her hair smooth," Gilian said in a conspiratorial voice after they'd opened the third bottle, causing Esme's ears to perk up. She wasn't sure who Kyla was—a maid she guessed—but was unfortunately quite familiar with Lady Audris.

"You mean she uses..." Molly began.

"Hot tongs. Every morning." Gilian appeared appalled at the idea. "What some people do with their time. Can you imagine how long that must take?" She shook her head.

"I heard Lady Pallya's wife is coming to the palace," Abaigeal announced.

"Who told you that?" Molly asked.

"Cace. Said he heard it from one of her lady's maids."

Esme searched her mind, trying to recall who Cace was. Another footman, she thought.

"Hmm..." Molly seemed to consider the validity of the information.

"Apparently, she's quite...vivacious. And a master fighter, no less," Abaigeal added.

"I didn't even know she was married," Gilian admitted. Nor had Esme.

"Cace said the same thing when he heard. But her lady's maid explained that the two of them have been...*connected* for many years, yet only recently made it official."

Interesting, Esme thought, growing ever more curious about the mysterious woman.

"Did anyone see Minister Aindreas yesterday in his riding attire?" Gilian nearly squealed, bouncing on her toes.

"I missed it again?" Abaigeal whined.

"You know…" Molly leaned forward. Gilian and Abaigeal inclined their heads toward her. Even Esme found herself drawn in. "Bryna, who works on his floor, said she walked in on him when he was fresh from a bath."

"She just walked in?" Esme couldn't help but ask.

"Course not." Molly shook her head. "He bade her enter."

Gilian gasped. "Was he covered?"

"Only a towel," Molly answered with a glint in her eye.

"Wish I could have seen that," Abaigeal muttered. "I pity anyone who walks in on my Grady straight from the bath. Man doesn't even need a towel to cover him with all that fur!" At that, they all broke out in unrestrained laughter.

"I'd take a hairy man any day over my Padraic," Gilian countered. "Just the other day, I caught him stealing butter from my kitchen. He was being sneaky about it, so I asked what he needed it for. Do you know what he told me?" She looked each of them in the eye before continuing. "That he ran out of shaving lotion."

"Doesn't seem so bad. Would moisturize quite well, I'd think," Molly allowed.

"That's not the problem. It's *where* he used it." Gilian raised an eyebrow and they all stared at her a long moment before bursting out in laughter again. Gilian simply shook her head. "By the gods, I don't know why he wants every part of him to be smooth."

Esme bit her lower lip to keep from dissolving into a fit of giggles.

"You know who else is easy on the eyes? The guard with the honey-colored hair—the one who's always wearing such an *inviting* smile," Molly commented.

Esme looked up. "Killian?" She answered without thinking. Judging by the not-so-subtle grins that surfaced on each woman's face, they knew exactly who the guard with the honey-colored hair was.

"Ah, yes." Molly tapped her finger against her chin. "That's the one."

Esme's breath caught in her throat. She wasn't prepared to talk about what had transpired the night before. But as she looked around the table, she realized they were waiting for her to offer something. "He...has quite a smile, doesn't he?" she ventured.

The three of them hummed in agreement and Esme relaxed, letting her shoulders sink back down. She took another gulp of wine, then filled her cup and took another, letting the warmth spread through her.

"He's a good sparring partner," she offered when it was clear they wanted more.

"Oh, I bet he is," Abaigeal crooned, waggling her eyebrows. Molly and Gilian giggled with excitement, clanking their freshly filled mugs and splattering wine on the table. Thankfully the potato dishes had been completed, and were slowly baking atop the hearth.

Esme's mouth dropped open, realizing too late what she'd implied. "I didn't mean..." She trailed off, then gave into an unabashed laugh of her own. And before she could think better of it, she added, "Well, he is quite good with a sword." She clapped her hand over her mouth immediately. What was she saying?

Her regret was short-lived as they all rejoined in uproarious laughter, and Molly reached over to top off Esme's cup, grinning with delight.

"Your Majesty," Cahir said in a low voice beside her. "It's getting late—or early, rather—perhaps we could escort you back to your room."

Esme waved him off. "Not yet." She knew she was being a bit candid, but it felt so good to laugh—to feel as though she wasn't queen, if only for one night. Cahir ducked his head and stepped back.

"And that other guard of yours?" Molly inquired. "The one with the dark hair and even darker eyes."

"Tearlach," she said with a sigh.

"Mm-hmm. That's the one," Molly said with a mischievous sparkle in her eyes that Esme was coming to recognize. "He's quite a handsome man himself, is he not?"

"He's quite a *man*. Full stop," Gilian corrected.

"Never seen someone as...*devoted* as him," Abaigeal added.

Esme absently twirled a lock of hair around her finger. "He is," she hummed, feeling a rush of warmth in her chest. An awareness prickled at the back of her mind, and she fully expected to hear Tearlach's voice in her head. *It's only the wine,* she told herself, taking another sip.

Abaigeal mentioned something about a new stablehand as Esme filled her cup again, grateful that they'd moved on to someone else.

Don't you think you've had enough?

Esme choked, wine burning her nose.

Gilian patted her on the back as Esme stared down at the swirling liquid in her cup. She cleared her throat and pasted a smile on her face.

No, she told Tearlach defiantly. Taking a long swallow, she ignored the fuzzy feeling along her scalp and the tingle in her fingertips.

Chapter Thirty-Four

WHEN ESME MANAGED to open her eyes against what seemed to be midmorning light, she found herself tucked snugly in her bed. She shifted a little, trying to free her arms, but even the slightest movement hurt. After a few breaths to quell the pounding inside her skull, she gingerly pulled her arms up and pushed back the tightly secured covers. Confusion clouded her mind as she peered down at her nightclothes— a delicate linen shift with embroidered leaves along the neckline. She didn't have the faintest recollection of dressing in it the night before. In fact, she couldn't recall climbing into bed. Or leaving the kitchens, for that matter.

Though her memories were hazy, she remembered laughing. A lot. And she definitely remembered the wine. Just the thought of it summoned a wave of nausea. How many bottles had they gone through? Too many. She needed to make sure Molly, Gilian, and Abaigeal weren't reprimanded for drinking while on duty. They weren't to blame.

She glanced down at her nightdress. Her cheeks flushed at the thought of Madoc or Cahir carrying her upstairs, though she felt quite certain that both of them would've drawn the line at helping her change clothes.

Before she could further consider *who* had helped her dress, her stomach lurched. She hurried out of bed, barely making it to the other room before she was sick.

———————

After a thorough wash, a few bites of toast, and a miraculous concoction that tasted vile, Esme felt much better. Once her headache subsided, she headed out.

Spotting Armel and Madoc, she perched on the edge of a nearby bench and cradled a warm mug in her hands.

It was well into midday, but drinking her morning tea brought a small amount of comfort. And the notes of bergamot and sweet vanilla washed away the bitter aftertaste of the tincture Cadwyn had mixed up for her.

She took another sip, watching the men circle one another, daggers flying between them with such speed Esme only saw when they struck a shield or gauntlet. Armel's hand flicked another from a slot on his forearm plate, sending it across the expanse.

Madoc ducked from it, then flipped his own dagger in his hand before sliding it back into its sheath. He turned to Esme and raised a brow, gesturing between himself and Armel.

Esme inclined her head toward Armel, and Madoc brought his hand to his chest as though she'd wounded him. With a half smile, he wandered back to the barracks, plucking daggers from his shield as he went.

She was grateful he acted as though nothing had transpired the night before. Although, it was entirely possible that the person who'd helped her into bed hadn't been seen by either him or Cahir after they'd delivered her to her room.

Esme took another swallow of tea, trying to hide the sight of her heated cheeks.

Armel sat down beside her.

"He's nearly as good as you." She nodded to Madoc's retreating form.

"You should see him with an arrow."

"Better than Hazel?"

The corners of Armel's mouth lifted. "Not quite." Esme heard the undertone of pride in his voice. No one matched Hazel, not in Armel's eyes. "Madoc's able to curve an arrow's course with his air magic. It allows him to remain hidden during a fight."

"Impressive," Esme agreed, watching Armel twirl a blade around his finger.

"You wanted to practice?"

"I do. But not with daggers. At least not ones made of silver."

Armel quirked a brow, then glanced past her, surveying her retinue.

He peered back down at her, the unspoken words hanging between them—that every member of the royal guard was under strict orders not to use magic during a match with the queen unless Tearlach was present to siphon any that came too close.

Esme drained the last of her tea and set the mug aside.

Finally, Armel exhaled. "As you wish."

"Good," she chirped, adjusting the shell strapped around her torso as she marched into the center of the ring.

After securing her other protective plates, she glanced over her shoulder to where Armel still sat, watching her. Esme smiled sweetly. "Well?"

Armel closed his eyes for a moment, then rose and stalked to a position opposite her. Frozen blades appeared in his hand as he huffed past Esme.

Pulling a dagger from the batch, he turned to face her. The ice didn't seem to burn his bare skin, nor did his skin melt the ice. Armel's eyes traced Esme from across the ring, likely noting the best places to aim— places the blades would barely penetrate her armor.

She scowled, then gathered a small, gray cloud above her. Though she kept it compact, she could hear the yard go quiet. It was the first time she'd used her storm magic out in the open.

Armel looked up at it, but didn't say a word.

Esme focused on the dark, heavy cloud, feeling it stir as lightning flashed within.

When Armel raised a brow, she nodded.

The first dagger struck her in the breastplate before she even saw it leave Armel's hand. She staggered back from the impact. Her hand covered the spot just beneath the curve of the plate, coming away wet. Armel must have melted the blade the moment it touched her.

Her hands rose, her fingertips tingling with the sensation of the crackling sparks. Tearlach's lectures echoed in Esme's ears, telling her to use her mind—not her hands—to direct her magic.

She ignored them.

When Armel flicked his wrist again, a thread of purple lightning struck the dagger.

Ice exploded in front of her, and she shielded her eyes. Slivers stung her bare hand and pelted her armor before melting.

Esme looked across the ring. As soon as she met Armel's eyes, he threw another.

Her lightning was precise, shattering each blade before it could reach her—which was easy, given the steady, almost dallying rate of Armel's strikes.

Another batch of frozen daggers appeared in his hand. He plucked one, tossing it in the air.

Esme cocked her head to the side. "Armel," she growled. Her patience had been thin to begin with.

He caught the blade and glanced past her. She didn't need to turn to know that every guard in the yard had gathered to watch.

After heaving a breath, he started again.

Faster they came. Esme's mind blended with her pure, crackling magic, and everything else fell away. She pulled careful strands from the cloud, holding off the rain that threatened to douse her.

When the daggers came more quickly, Esme's precise strands became jagged bolts, blinding her as they obliterated the barrage of ice. She shifted around the flashes of light, blinking, trying to focus on the source of the attacks. But they flew too fast.

Needles of glinting ice and the swelling fog from the heavy rain cloud obstructed her view.

A dagger slipped through, its edge cutting through the haze.

Esme ducked, managed to strike the two that followed, then hit the ground. She rolled to the side to avoid another.

Armel paced the opposite way, circling her.

The next hit her shin plate, transforming back into water instantly upon impact.

She threw out her hand. A web of lightning formed in front of her. Ice splintered, but the shield wasn't solid enough to catch everything Armel threw at her.

Dropping to the ground, Esme twisted out of the way, coming up to catch the flash of a blade aimed at her face.

It exploded into liquid, the force knocking her back.

She sputtered against the frigid water. Her concentration slipped, and the cloud above opened up, drenching her with tepid rain.

She scattered what was left, spinning the clouds into thin wisps that quickly evaporated.

Opening her eyes, she found two boots an inch deep in muddy water.

"What?" she tried to bark, though it came out raspy.

Armel crouched down beside her. "You sure you want to do this?"

"It's just a little water." She brushed away his hand and rose on shaky legs, repeating the words to herself. *It's just a little water.*

Armel stood, but didn't retreat to his position across the ring. Esme risked another glance at him. From the look in his eyes, she knew his thoughts had returned to the night in the throne room, to the wave Orianna had brought crashing down upon her.

A muscle in Armel's neck tightened, but he dipped his chin a fraction of an inch and stepped back.

Esme tried to focus on the daggers that appeared in his hand, but her mind kept pulling her back to that night. She dropped her gaze to the ground. Melting ice and muddy puddles mottled the compacted dirt. Her fingers itched to sprout shoots from the sludge, to stretch vines out around her, enveloping her in their protective embrace.

Tearlach might not have been there to see, but she wouldn't risk her earth magic with so many eyes on her. He'd been right about that, to keep secret her ability to create—not just manipulate—the flora around her.

Her eyes found Armel. He lazily tossed a frost-coated blade as he waited for her.

When she nodded, Armel looked up into the empty space above them—to where a newly formed cloud should have been hovering, crackling with lightning.

"Come on," she goaded.

When a dagger came, Esme stood still, hands loose at her sides. She watched Armel's fingers twitch, ready to release his hold on the ice.

But the blade stopped short, just inches from her chest, its icy hilt vibrating from the sudden impact.

A faint smirk tugged at Armel's mouth before a dozen other blades joined the first, jolting midair as they plunged into Esme's invisible shield.

One by one, they fractured, her vines choking the magic from them. Icy chunks fell—splashing mud or sinking into the soft ground—as a new barrage of daggers embedded into her woven barrier.

When Armel started to move, Esme mirrored him, growing and reshaping the shield only she could feel. He tested her reach, prodding at her weak spots. They moved around the ring, the cold mud sucking at her boots.

Then there were no longer daggers coming toward her, but ice shards of varying lengths—some thin and long, capable of slicing through her vines, others dense and jagged, strong enough to rip through her thick, twisted strands of magic.

A vicious spike struck too close.

Esme's breath hitched. Her eyes trailed from the thick, blunt end lodged firmly in her shield all the way down to the razor-thin point that stopped a handsbreadth from her throat. She exhaled, her breath forming a layer of frost along the sharp, faceted edge.

The ice melted, trickling in down the ridges and valleys of the unseen vines.

Two dozen paces away, Armel's hand was outstretched, a column of water pulsing above his palm, ready to be formed into another wicked weapon.

Esme clenched her hands and concentrated on the feel of her vines. Sprouting more, thick as roots, she wove their tapered ends through the nearly impenetrable tangle. When she looked back at Armel, the barrier distorted his image. The sound of squelching mud was muffled as he shifted his weight.

He offered a slight dip of his chin before bombarding her with frozen, serrated spears as solid and heavy as stone.

But Armel's ice barely nicked her shield before thudding to the wet ground. Everything beyond her magic fell away. She funneled every drop of energy into those vines. But they were no longer vines. They were pure, vibrating magic. She felt it humming, pulsing in time with the lifeblood coursing through her veins.

It was a part of her. She flinched at the feel of each impact, the sensation running along her nerve endings. She poured more magic into it until Armel's ice cracked and crumbled at a mere brush against her thrumming power.

When ice exploded into a million tiny particles, the fine, glittering powder hung in the air, floating. Too light to fall to the ground.

"Snow," Esme breathed, the word turning to fog. She gazed in wonder at the thing she'd never thought she'd witness again.

Her focus faltered.

And her shield fell away.

Her tangle of protective vines gone in an instant.

She dropped to the ground, throwing her arms over her head.

Armel cursed a second before a wave of icy water crashed into Esme.

She tumbled backward, gasping. The nearly frozen water burned her skin, soaking beneath her protective plates.

Shivering, she pulled her hands from the frigid mud and rose onto her knees, wiping away what she could with her upper arm.

Don't do that again.

Esme stilled at Tearlach's voice invading her mind. She screwed her eyes shut, blocking every thought and feeling. She didn't want him in there.

With strangled breaths, she waited for the scolding she knew was coming. But Tearlach left her alone. Her mind felt unexpectedly blank. Quiet.

The entire yard was quiet, she realized.

Awareness prickled the back of her neck as she felt the many pairs of eyes focused on her. Her shoulders slumped forward, her breath heaving out as she felt every ounce of confidence she'd gained eddy into the mucky pools around her.

Why had she gone down to the yard at all? What had she hoped to accomplish? To escape the confusion clouding her mind, to forget the words Killian had said the other night? To feel something—anything—other than the frustration, the anger, the embarrassment, the...the...

Esme blinked back tears and concentrated on the cold—sharp against her skin, painful, penetrating deep into her muscles, sinking its claws into her bones. Only, the throbbing discomfort didn't distract from the humiliation of kneeling, defeated, in the mud.

Sensing Armel in front of her, she looked up. That his short dark hair was still neatly in place irritated her further.

He reached out. "Esme, I'm sorry. After what happened the other night, I shouldn't have—"

Heat flooded her chilled skin. "Shouldn't have what?" she snapped. "I asked you to fight."

"I know. But I should've realized you weren't...in the best state of mind to make that choice."

"And what *state of mind* was I in?" She glared.

"Esme," he pleaded, inclining his head toward his hand, urging her to take it.

She met his pitying gaze, refusing his proffered hand. She rose awkwardly on her own, avoiding further contact with the cold mud.

Armel nodded sheepishly and tucked his hand away. "Sometimes," he said slowly, his voice soft, "we deny what our hearts truly want." Esme narrowed her eyes. He swallowed and risked another glance at her. "And we let our minds trick us into believing we want something that feels... easy. Something that makes sense. But our hearts always know the truth."

"So, I was the convenient choice? Is that what you're telling me?" Esme fought to keep her voice from breaking. She was already covered in mud, crushed, mortified, but somehow the words stung worse.

Armel tilted his head. "That's not—"

"Are you really going to stand here and explain my heart to me when you won't even admit your own?" She lifted her chin.

"What?" Bitterness crept into his deep, consoling voice.

"You're the last person who should be spewing romantic advice, *Armel*." Esme took a step forward. "When are you planning to tell Hazel how you feel about her? Are you *ever* planning to tell her, or will the two of you just go on avoiding what you both obviously want?" She cocked her head to the side, her lips curling back to reveal her teeth.

Armel recoiled.

When he didn't respond, Esme felt an apology rising in her throat. But his blue eyes darkened to a deep indigo, and she wasn't sure if it was fury over her assertion or bafflement at her rare temper. Likely both.

When his jaw clenched and his nostrils flared, she knew which one was winning. She'd never seen the calm, quiet warrior riled.

Good, she thought, letting the apology die on her tongue. The mud sucked at her boots as she walked away.

WILD HEART OF THE CROWN

Chapter Thirty-Five

ESME TORE HER plates off, not bothering to look back for her guards. If they weren't following, she didn't care. It would give Tearlach more cause to be vexed with her. She smirked. Perhaps she'd find him before retreating to her room, burn off more of her anger with him.

Her mouth turned down. Why hadn't Tearlach come to find her? To reprimand her? After last night...after using magic when she shouldn't have...

Where was he?

"Shit," Esme muttered as she looked up to see Killian striding across the lawn.

Turning on her heel, she veered toward the woods. Her hands clenched in irritation, causing the dried mud to flake off. Away from the palace was not the direction she needed to go, but Killian would follow, and Esme couldn't fathom a worse scenario than being alone with him in her room.

"Esme," she heard barely a moment later. He was quicker than she'd anticipated. Though what had her plan been? To crouch down in the underbrush, trying to blend in with the peahens? With two heavily armored guards standing nearby?

With a huff, she stopped, though she didn't face him. Killian stepped around her, then winced at her appearance. Mud was caked onto every inch of her exposed skin. Her wet clothes hung limply. She wasn't sure what condition her hair was in, though odds were it wasn't pretty.

Thankfully, Killian didn't comment on any of that. "Can we talk?"

Esme pulled air into her lungs slowly, trying to calm her angry heart. "Fine." She nodded her guards away, then turned, letting Killian follow.

She kept close to the tree line. Having everyone with south-facing windows see a mud-covered queen was something she could do without.

"You don't need to explain anything. I understand." She didn't. But she wouldn't let Killian know that. Wouldn't let him see how much he'd hurt her.

"I don't think you do."

"You don't feel the same way about me. I get it." She struggled to keep her eyes trained on the ground.

"That isn't the—Esme, it's *not* that."

She stopped, leveling Killian with a glare. "Then what is it? I didn't have enough time for you?" Killian opened his mouth, but she charged on. "I'm trying to run a kingdom here, Killian. And I have no idea what I'm doing. So if I didn't spend every spare moment with you, I'm sorry!" She grimaced and looked back, but her guards appeared acutely interested in the peeling bark of a sycamore. "I'm sorry," she repeated quietly.

Killian closed the distance between them and placed his fingers against her lips before she could say anything more. Esme resisted the urge to close her eyes, to savor the familiar touch.

"You have nothing to be sorry about, Esme. And...you're right," he admitted. "We don't feel the same."

She jerked away from him and strode off, tears clouding her vision.

Killian caught up to her in half as many paces.

"I love you, Esme."

She nearly stumbled, but forced herself to keep moving forward.

Those words. It was the first he'd spoken them to her.

"I have from the moment you made my heart beat again. Maybe even before."

It was hard to breathe. The air felt too thin. She swallowed.

"But I'm fairly certain you don't"—Killian took a breath—"love *me*. Not that way."

Finally, her eyes sought his. "I do. Killian, I—"

He took her by the shoulders. "I know you think you do. But it's not the same."

Was he actually going to explain the workings of her heart to her as well? She ground her teeth, barely keeping a nasty rebuke from spilling out.

"If I truly felt your heart calling out to mine, I wouldn't have ended things between us. You need to listen to your heart, Esme."

"I thought I was." She wasn't sure if she was angry at the implication that her youth and inexperience made her incapable of understanding love, or at her voice for sounding so weak.

Killian shook his head. "You weren't. And I think if you really pay attention to what your heart's saying—who it's trying to lead you toward—you'll see it too." He stepped closer, forcing Esme to tilt her head to meet his steady gaze. "It's not *me* you love."

He looked meaningfully into the distance. Esme followed his line of sight, past the edge of the woods, toward the stables.

Esme drew back, gaping at him. "What?" Her voice rose an octave. "Is this about the other night? I told you—"

"I know what you said. But I can see what's going on, even if you can't." Her mouth dropped open and Killian softened his gaze. "Listen to your heart, Esme. It's quiet, hard to hear over the cacophony of thoughts sometimes, but it knows the truth." He bent to kiss her cheek, even covered in dirt.

She heard him walk away, but her eyes had already returned to the stables.

To where Tearlach was leaning against the fence of the paddock.

Chapter Thirty-Six

PEBBLES SHIFTED BENEATH Esme's boots. She glanced down to find that she'd wandered into the gardens. Feeling the pinch of dried mud on her skin, she rubbed her hands together, peppering purple cabbage leaves with brownish-red flecks.

At the sound of her guards approaching, she crouched down and plucked a thin, pale gray leaf from a lavender bush, as though the aromatic shrub had been her sole purpose for venturing over there.

She stepped over the squat bush and onto the narrow interior path. A squirrel trailed behind, halting and rising up onto his hind legs each time she twisted to look back at him. The path curved, giving Esme an unobstructed view of the paddock—and the man who once again claimed her every thought. Her hands closed around the warm, smooth wood of a plum tree. She braced her shoulder against the sturdy trunk as the squirrel climbed up over her hands, rustling the branches above as he found a suitable perch.

Tearlach didn't look over, though Esme knew he could sense her near. After the previous night, she'd expected him to at least check on her. Instead, he'd been distant.

Seeing him over by the stables reminded her of all the times she'd glimpsed him over there. She'd assumed he'd been making his rounds, speaking with the grooms and stablehands as Sully did. But Tearlach wasn't speaking with anyone. Rather, he seemed to be watching as a dark bay was shoed. Did he frequent the stables because he missed the horses he'd left behind in Debarrow?

Or maybe it wasn't the horse that drew his attention. Perhaps he envied the farrier. Tearlach's metalsmith skills were of little use in Tremaene. Bronze horseshoes and silver swords were crafted by fire wielders. Esme craned her neck, but couldn't see their workshop past the roof of the stable. There wasn't even a curl of smoke or a sharp tinge of metal in the air. Did he long for the heat of a forge, for the physical exertion needed to shape metal to his will? In her mind, Esme could still see the intricate designs of hilts and precisely crafted iron blades—both deadly and beautiful. Tearlach was a master of his own making, an artist, maybe more so than most fire wielders claimed to be.

Esme looked again toward the farrier—who'd moved to another hoof—then furrowed her brow as it occurred to her that she'd never seen a horse back in Debarrow wear anything other than boots made of thick hide. Only Tearlach's horses had worn bronze shoes—and lucky that they had, or the two of them never would've outrun the assassins.

Tearlach's smithy had been nothing more than a guise, she knew. It offered a convenient way for him to build up his tolerance to the deadly iron that existed in the human world. But it'd never occurred to her before that the townspeople's preference of leather boots might not have been a preference at all. Perhaps they'd adopted the outmoded implements in order to avoid the cantankerous metalsmith at the edge of town. Esme certainly would've, had she owned a horse.

Would she have, though? Esme had kept to herself, only leaving her plot of land when necessary. If she'd owned a horse, would their paths have crossed sooner? Before her magic had manifested? Before he'd purposefully frightened her?

If they'd met before all that, what might've happened? What would life have been like in that strange and foreign land if she hadn't been alone?

Her eyes fluttered shut as an unfamiliar warmth bloomed in the center of her chest. She gripped the tree trunk as the feeling swelled. It was light and heavy at once; it heated her skin and left a trail of chilled flesh in its wake. Her ears buzzed, and a tingle in her jaw forced her lips to curl into a smile.

Her eyes snapped open when something struck the crown of her head.

A plum bounded off her shoulder, landing near her feet. She rubbed her head, perplexed. The squirrel leapt from a branch above, descending on the ripened fruit. When another fell with a soft thud, the squirrel pounced on it.

Up in the tree, there were dozens of ripe plums tugging down branches that had been covered in nothing but leaves moments before.

Esme eased her hand off the trunk and moved away, offering glancing touches to each tree as she went to dilute the anomaly.

Settling beside another tree, she leaned her shoulder against it, careful not to touch the bark with her bare skin, then returned her attention to Tearlach. His profile was still to her. He had yet to acknowledge her presence. Likely wouldn't.

Esme sighed as the precarious contentment drained out of her.

It didn't matter what she felt. And it didn't matter if Tearlach felt the same—if he ever had or ever could. Because that life—the life she dared to imagine—would never happen. Tearlach wouldn't allow it.

A queen can't marry a warrior, he'd told her. Tearlach's damned honor, and that stupid, impenetrable loyalty he surrounded himself with, would always prevent his heart from venturing anywhere near hers. Even if he someday returned her feelings—feelings she could no longer reasonably deny—Tearlach would never think himself worthy of a queen. And by the gods, she would never be anything but a queen to him.

He would watch over her, protect her as he always had, but he'd never let anything interfere with that duty. He might be able to walk into her mind easily, to see her pain and her joy, but she'd never see his.

Esme kicked the gravel beneath her boot, sending stones skittering, then peered up into the branches. The leaves blocked out most of the ever-blue sky—a sky that never changed, that *wouldn't ever* change.

She looked back at Tearlach. He still hadn't turned. He could sense her there, so close, yet he refused.

Pebbles ground under her heel as Esme put her back to him. She set her shoulders and straightened her spine. She had a kingdom to restore. And her tangled heart wasn't going to help her accomplish that.

Chapter Thirty-Seven

ESME WALKED WEARILY through the palace, giving little thought to where she was going, the sounds of servants blurring to the margins of her mind. She forced herself not to think of Tearlach, of Killian, of the impolite words she'd thrown at Armel. Instead, she focused on what needed to be done to return life to the land, on how to rebuild the channels that had been destroyed.

If she could accomplish that, perhaps the council would excuse her lacking qualifications and let her keep her crown.

But no matter which way she looked at the problem, no matter how she tried to piece together the fragments she'd gathered, she collided with the same obstacle every time—accessing Dougal's memories.

Perhaps if she asked Athdara again…

Her mirthless laugh echoed off the marble walls before she'd even finished the thought. The woman wasn't exactly forthcoming with information. No, Athdara wouldn't assist any more than she already had. The only way Esme was going to find the answers she sought was through those memories.

Only Dougal wasn't his real name. So, his memories would remain secret, locked away in the Sacred Pool of Navlin, never to be retrieved.

Esme dropped her head, staring down at her dirty boots as she shuffled aimlessly down corridors. It wasn't until an indigo silk rug filled her field of vision that she looked up, realizing she'd wandered into one of the galleries. It was quiet in the low-ceilinged room, tucked away from the bustling sounds of the palace.

She avoided dirtying the rug, keeping to the periphery of the long room as she turned her attention to a framed painting. It was of a lake with willows dipping into the still water. She remembered it, though the painting was as unremarkable as it'd always been.

Esme bent closer, studying the intricacies of the water. From a distance, the glossy surface seemed bluish-gray, but up close she could see that very little blue paint had been used, and certainly no gray. The artist hadn't used brown or earth tones either. Even the reflections of the willow trees were created not with green, but with unexpected, entangled pigments of lemony yellow, white, and vermilion that looked as though they'd been blended directly on the canvas. The shadows were created with a dark crimson that had an almost purple hue to it. Hidden colors peeked through the many layers of paint. Some strokes were thick and textured, others thin and translucent, as though the tiny dabs of light were floating on the surface, suspended in the poppy seed oil.

Esme was careful not to touch the painting, hovering her fingers an inch above it as she traced the brushstrokes. Her eyes trailed along the arcs of color down to the bottom of the canvas. In the center, in a deep emerald green, was the artist's name and tribute to her lord: *By the hands of Olwen of Donellis, in honor of Lord Ambros.* Lord Ambros was Lady Audris's father, Esme recalled.

She proceeded through the gallery, taking her time with each piece, searching for the artist line before moving on to the next. Some were written clearly at the bottom, others were hidden within the artwork or etched into the frame itself.

At the threshold of the last adjoining room, she circled a small table that held a glass vase. The delicate creation was supported by nothing more than six thin legs that extended out toward the edges of the table— which seemed to be crafted for the sole purpose of displaying the piece.

Esme reached out and ran her fingers along the gold leaf band just below the flared opening of the vase, wondering what flowers the artist had envisioned for such an exquisite vessel.

She yanked her hand away, unsure of what had possessed her to touch it at all. Would the gold tarnish? Was it susceptible to discoloration as silver was?

Absently, she rubbed her fingers together, the warmth of the metal clinging to her skin. The gold had felt thin and worn, pitted with imperfections. The vase could have been centuries old, perhaps more.

Esme leaned in to examine the place her fingers had grazed the band, and realized the indentations weren't the result of time or mishandling. She squinted at the words debossed into the soft metal. They were almost too small to read, secret unless one knew where to look.

She angled her head until the light caught the edges of the letters. *By the hands of Cian of Kearney, in honor of Lord Luxovious.*

Esme stepped back.

"Kearney?" She repeated the word aloud. That was the city—or territory, it seemed—that Dougal had mentioned.

A territory that didn't exist on any map. A territory that no longer existed.

Only Dougal wasn't his name...

She inched forward, rereading the tribute after the artist's name.

...in honor of Lord Luxovious.

She shuddered. The name, even spoken in the recesses of her mind—a name she'd never heard nor seen before—sent a shiver of awareness down her spine.

Her lips pressed into a firm line, keeping the name trapped. Leaning in, she ran her fingertip along the letters, as if touching them might confirm what she knew in her bones to be true.

Luxovious. *Lord* Luxovious.

Could it be? The man in her dream hadn't been a farmer as he'd claimed—Esme was quite certain of that. And he hadn't simply been a man of means or influence. *No.* The man in her vision—the man with the air of authority and power about him—had been a lord.

The lord of Kearney.

Esme stood, staring unseeing into the distance. Her hand dropped to her side. She repeated the name to herself—her mouth forming the name Luxovious, though she didn't dare say it out loud.

She knew it was his name. Without a doubt. Felt the truth of it deep in the center of her being. Her inner magic gave a thrum of confirmation that resonated through her body.

Esme shivered and blinked her eyes, her focus returning to the room. She looked around, wanting to tell someone. But she was alone—her guards stationed outside.

She was alone. *Alone.*

She'd found the name on her own, without a speck of help from anyone.

The warmth she'd felt in her chest earlier rose again. Only it felt different. It wasn't the love for an unattainable man that caused her heart to swell.

A smile tugged at her mouth.

It felt rather like...confidence.

Esme glanced back at the vase, then stood tall to match its height atop the table.

For the first time in her reign, she felt the part.

Chapter Thirty-Eight

ESME STEPPED OUT of the quiet gallery and into the dining hall, her mind refining earlier presumptions and assembling new plans.

The din of servants met her ears. Silver platters of food flashed in the fringes of her awareness. Then everything went silent. She felt their eyes on her, on the trail of dirt her boots left behind. But she ignored their stunned gazes, winding her way through the palace, unseeing.

All the while, his name—the name she dared not say aloud—tangled with the thick web of conjectures in her mind. One of which—why he'd destroyed the channels—would no doubt remain a mystery. But as long as she could remedy the damage he'd caused, she didn't much care.

Until then, her priority was with the Triskele. She'd write to them and request a meeting. It would have to be worded carefully, and with great respect, if they were to trust her. And she needed their trust more than anything if she was going to convince them to help her rebuild the Order.

How long would it take? A decade? Maybe longer?

Before the fall, there'd been three high-priestesses stationed at each temple, and perhaps a half dozen younger priestesses waiting in the wings. But if there were three women, or even two, who were powerful enough to summon source magic, and Esme could convince them to travel to each of the five temples, it might be enough to stave off further barrenness.

But if she had Lord Luxovious's memories...

Her heart picked up at the possibility, beating loudly against her ribs. She brought her hand to her chest and tried to calm its frenzied rhythm.

She had nothing yet. A name, but no more.

Still, she couldn't help but fantasize what such a cache of valuable information might provide. If the memories revealed *how* he'd obstructed the channels' flow, perhaps she could surmise a method to restore them.

Esme hummed to herself, appreciating the turn the afternoon had taken. At last, her thoughts were where they needed to be.

Her feet halted her in front of a familiar door. She reached forward blindly, but a deep, rumbling voice perforated her ruminations. Her attention surfaced, and she looked down at the bronze door handles. The alcove outside her suite came into focus. She heard Tearlach's voice again.

Esme spun on her heel, set to inform him of her discovery and resulting plans. But she stopped short.

He stood in profile down the corridor. And he wasn't alone.

His arms were folded across his chest, and a woman—a maid, Esme guessed—gazed up at him eagerly, wearing a bright, open smile that rounded her pink cheeks. Even from where Esme stood, she could see the glint in the woman's eyes.

Tearlach didn't look her way, though Esme knew he could feel her nearby. Instead, he leaned in closer to the woman.

Blood pounded between Esme's ears, blocking out his words— though they must have been amusing, for the woman ducked her head bashfully and giggled.

Esme gritted her teeth at the cloying sound.

Once the woman recovered, she peered up at Tearlach from beneath her lashes, then reached out to grip his upper arm.

Esme might not have been experienced in many things, but it was clear what that gesture meant.

She wanted to back away, to retreat into her room, only she couldn't tear her eyes away from the sight. She watched the woman lean in to whisper something. Tearlach lowered his head to hers. When he chuckled at whatever she'd said, Esme stumbled back.

She turned and fumbled with the handle until a broad hand reached out to turn it for her. Without bothering to see which of her guards it was, she hurried inside and closed her eyes, her head falling back against the solid wood of the door. But try as she might, all she could see were the two of them. Heads inclined toward one another. Standing so close it would only have taken half a step for them to—

"What happened to you?"

Her eyes shot open. Cadwyn was across the room with a stack of papers in her arms.

When her question finally filtered through, Esme glanced down at her clothes. Most of the mud had dried and crumbled off. Her white linen shirt was stained a splotchy brownish red. She reached up and felt the tangled mess of her hair.

Esme pictured the woman from the corridor—her long tresses cascading down her back in perfect waves—and couldn't help but compare herself.

"I was practicing with Armel."

Cadwyn's gaze raked over her. "I hope he looks worse than you."

Esme held back a groan, remembering the words she'd thrown at him before stalking off like an ill-tempered child.

She swallowed the bitter taste in her mouth and sunk to the floor to pull off her boots.

Cadwyn turned back to the desk, shifting stacks to make room for a new set of requests.

"More?" Esme came up beside her.

"Afraid so." Cadwyn pulled her lips into a tight line. "Some are from Winifred. She stopped by to drop them off just a few moments ago. I'm surprised you didn't see her on your way in."

Esme couldn't recall anything since she'd wandered out of the gallery. Not until she'd seen Tearlach with—

She focused on the new stacks of documents crowding her desk. Esme really needed to do something to properly thank her council secretary for all her work. Glancing up at Cadwyn, she realized there were a lot of people she needed to repay.

"You were right to enlist her help." Cadwyn offered a proud smile. "I'm sorry I doubted—"

"Thank you," Esme cut her off, moving closer to scan the paper at the top of the leftmost stack. She didn't need anyone else apologizing to her, especially not Cadwyn.

Esme scanned the text briefly, noting Lord Torin's name at the bottom. She sighed, knowing she'd have to study that one thoroughly. Winifred too.

"Let me draw you a bath."

"You don't need..." Esme started, but Cadwyn was already across the room. The sound of running water soon followed. Glass bottles clinked, and Esme pulled her arm across her chest, suddenly aware of the stiffness that had settled in her muscles. Cadwyn would know which oil was best, even if the aching she felt wasn't from her match with Armel.

The earthy smell of balsam resin wafted out, and Esme halted her steps. She closed her eyes as that single scent evoked memories she'd long since forgotten. She could still see the small faceted bottle of blended oil in her mind—honey and vanilla atop a heavier base of balsam and cloves.

She'd only used the fragrance once. There'd been a ball, thrown in honor of visiting noblewomen and men from the city of Derval in the Western Flats. But all Esme could recall from the occasion was that Cadwyn had remained by her side the entire evening—dancing, sampling decadent treats, drinking punch, and helping fend off any suitors who dared approach.

Esme glanced toward the bathing chamber and breathed in the soothing aroma as it mingled with oils of frankincense and honeysuckle. Cadwyn hadn't danced with anyone else that night. It certainly hadn't occurred to Esme's fifteen-year-old mind but, thinking back, she wondered how much her selfish demands had hindered Cadwyn from having a life of her own. She had almost a decade and a half on Esme, surely Cadwyn had desired more than spending her every waking moment with a young princess.

There'd only been two occasions when Esme could recall seeing her lady-in-waiting return the attentions of a man. One had been a stablehand, new to the palace, with dark wavy hair that fell to his shoulders. The other, a musician who'd lived in the artist district. And Esme felt certain that Cadwyn had only indulged their flirtatious advances because she'd believed Esme otherwise occupied with a riding lesson or tutoring.

And even after nine years of waiting for Esme's return, it seemed Cadwyn was content to live out her days serving her queen. How long would Cadwyn put her life on hold?

"Cadwyn?"

"Hmm?" her lady-in-waiting responded distractedly, voice barely loud enough above the rushing water. She popped her head around the doorway. "Did you say something, love?"

Esme took a breath. "I just...I was wondering..." She laced her fingers together in front of her. "When you were in Altan all those years, was there ever..."

"Was there ever what?" Cadwyn cocked her head to the side.

"Did you...have anyone you cared about?"

Cadwyn's green eyes darkened, and it suddenly occurred to Esme that Cadwyn might not have mentioned a lover or a companion because it was private.

She was about to apologize for prying when Cadwyn blinked away, glancing over her shoulder—not toward the rising water in the bath, but at the far wall. Esme stood motionless, wondering what she was seeing.

"There was," Cadwyn replied softly, still turned away.

Esme exhaled, but remained quiet.

Cadwyn moved to lean against the doorframe, her eyes shifting to the floor between them. "I didn't really know anyone when I arrived there."

Only Sully, Esme remembered. At least she'd had him.

"But there was someone who looked after me," Cadwyn admitted, her voice sounding faraway.

"Who?" Esme couldn't help but ask.

Cadwyn glanced up. "He taught me how to fight, how to throw a dagger." With that, her lips hinted at a smirk.

"Thank the gods for that," Esme rushed out. They shared a brief smile before Cadwyn ducked back into the bathing chamber. A moment later, the running water ceased and the room fell silent. Esme followed her in.

With her back turned, Cadwyn spoke again, her soft voice echoing against the quartz tiles. "I don't know when it happened." She poured a generous amount of what smelled like sweet almond oil and milk into the steaming bath, which turned the water opaque. "But one day, I started to see him differently. He was no longer a warrior or a guardian, but a man." She corked the bottle and re-placed it on the shelf.

Esme nodded with understanding, though Cadwyn still wouldn't face her. Instead, she adjusted each of the dozen bottles on the shelf, straightening them.

"Did he...feel the same?"

"No," Cadwyn answered in a clipped tone, then dropped her hands. "At least"—she seemed to reconsider—"I don't think...No. He didn't. He doesn't."

Esme moved to take Cadwyn's hands, forcing her to turn. "You never told him how you felt?"

"No," Cadwyn said, though barely a sound left her lips.

"Then how do you know he doesn't feel the same? He might. He *still* might."

For a moment the only sounds were their breaths. But Esme didn't release Cadwyn's hands, didn't let her go.

Finally, Cadwyn shook her head. "It doesn't matter now."

It didn't matter? How could she possibly believe that?

Esme squeezed her hands. "Cadwyn, if you have a chance to be happy, to love someone...to be loved—"

"It's too late," Cadwyn cut her off, then sighed, her shoulders dropping.

Esme fought against the temptation to crumble, to embrace her friend and let the sorrow of unrequited love swallow them both. She pulled a deep breath into her lungs, expanding her chest and stretching her spine, doing all she could to hold them both up.

"What if it's not?"

Cadwyn didn't respond. The vibrant color in her eyes had drained, the once brilliant emerald green pale.

"You could...write to him," Esme encouraged.

Cadwyn bit her lower lip and slid her gaze away. "It's not that simple." She gave Esme's hands a firm squeeze, then stepped aside. "Now, hurry into the bath before it gets cold." She scrunched up her nose. "You're a mess."

It's not that simple. Esme repeated the words as Cadwyn left. Nothing was, it seemed. Not in love. Not in anything.

Chapter Thirty-Nine

ESME WRAPPED THE thick woolen blanket tighter around her shoulders and burrowed her feet into fleece-lined slippers as the sun crested the western horizon. She couldn't seem to let go of the deep-rooted instinct that mornings held a chill. Even in the warmest months in Periwen, mist hovered near the ground, and cool temperatures from night would cling to the early morning shadows until rays of sun warmed them.

Never in Tremaene.

After a lingering glance at the sun-gilded treetops, Esme threw off the stifling blanket and marched back inside to dress.

I need to speak with you, she requested of Tearlach in a surprisingly calm voice as she pulled her hair over her shoulder to finish a plait. Despite the tableau she'd seen of him and the woman the afternoon prior, she needed to inform him of her plans.

He didn't respond.

Esme glanced over at the door that joined their rooms, then tied off the end of her braid. She left her dressing room and began pacing, nervous energy swelling within her.

Where was he so early in the morning? Still with the maid?

Her steps quickened, like she might escape the image of the two of them.

Her bare feet stumbled, and she reached out to catch the edge of the dining table. Esme braced her hands against the cool glass surface and counted her breaths, slow and measured. When that didn't help, she lifted her gaze to the ceiling, envisioning the vast blue sky above. She considered imploring the gods for help. Perhaps they could vanquish the image from her mind, divert her thoughts to more productive ones.

With effort, Esme focused on the plans she'd formulated the night before.

Uncovering Dougal's true name had been significant. But she couldn't rely on his memories alone. While she hoped to discover a way to reverse the destruction he'd caused a millennium ago, it was possible that the channels had been damaged beyond repair, or that the magic he'd used would be impossible to replicate.

She'd need the Triskele. The women would be less experienced than even low-ranking priestesses, and Esme worried that their young, untested magic wouldn't be enough to restore the land and waterways. But what choice did she have? She'd take whatever help they offered.

The only problem was, they hadn't replied to her first letter.

On my way. Tearlach's voice cleaved her thoughts.

Her heart jumped into her throat. She knew he wasn't on the other side of the door, but still she stared at it.

After a moment, she released her breath, tamping down the words she was tempted to shout back—demanding to know where he was, who he was with.

"It's not my concern," she told herself resolutely, then pulled out her desk chair.

By the time a knock sounded—a knock that came from the main doors, which bothered Esme for reasons she refused to acknowledge—she was thoroughly engrossed in the requests Cadwyn had delivered the day before. At least, she hoped she appeared absorbed in the task. She'd been staring at the same block of words since she'd sat down.

"Enter," she called without looking up.

Hearing the door open and then close, she funneled every ounce of concentration into the request in front of her. Footfalls approached, but Esme didn't turn.

Her jaw clenched so tight, pain radiated up to her ears. Carefully, she set her pen aside and glanced over her shoulder, finding Tearlach three paces away, arms folded over his broad chest.

"Thank you for pulling yourself away long enough to see me."

Tearlach lowered his brows. "Pardon?"

Esme pushed her chair back slowly and stood. Tearlach's eyes tracked the movement.

"I'm just pleased you're enjoying the palace so much."

His confusion vanished. When he didn't respond, Esme strode past him. She picked up her tea—which had gone cold—and gripped the delicate handle to hide the tremor in her fingers. When she turned back, Tearlach arched a dark brow.

"Yesterday you seemed awfully close with..." She trailed off, gesturing toward the corridor outside her room. Taking a sip of tea, she lowered her eyes to watch Tearlach over the rim of the cup.

"With who?" His deep voice curled around her, gliding along her skin as he stalked closer.

Esme set the cup down and averted her gaze. "Well, I hope you at least caught her name before you—"

"Shouldn't the queen know the names of those in her service?" At Tearlach's smooth, mocking tone, Esme flicked her eyes toward him. "Sheridan," he told her, the name rolling off his tongue. "Her name is Sheridan."

His words held heat, but made Esme's blood run cold. "And is she that friendly with all the guards?" she forced out, the corner of her mouth twisting up. It felt more like a scowl than the smirk she intended.

"Not all of them." Tearlach's voice dipped even lower.

Esme's stomach clenched. The words upset her, but that voice...She'd never heard him use that voice before, and couldn't help what the sound did to her. How many other women had heard him use that voice, felt that seductive baritone caress their skin?

His expression shifted and the arrogance dropped away, leaving something more contrite in its place. Was that pity in his eyes? For her?

Esme turned away. She fumbled with the teapot, splashing more into her cup. Dark liquid pooled on the saucer. She closed her eyes and swallowed the contents in three quick gulps, then loosened her grip before the fine porcelain shattered in her hands.

Feeling Tearlach move closer, she carefully set the cup down.

"Esme." His voice was barely more than a whisper.

She tried to brush past him, but Tearlach wrapped his hand around her upper arm—not painfully, just firmly enough to keep her from escaping. She resisted the urge to look up at him.

He pulled her around to face him. Gentle as he was, Esme still managed to stumble into him. Her hands collided with his chest at the same moment he gripped her shoulders to steady her.

Only he didn't set her away.

She waited, but he continued to hold her.

Slowly, she lifted her chin. Her eyes traveled up his linen shirt—soft beneath her fingers—to the open collar, then up the thick tendons in his neck...his solid jaw...his mouth...

Finally, their gazes locked.

"Esme..." Tearlach's eyes searched hers. For what, she didn't know.

"We need to go north," she blurted out, needing desperately to wedge something between them.

Tearlach blinked at the abrupt subject change. The pitying look in his eyes morphed into something more akin to miscomprehension.

Using his stunned state to her advantage, Esme pushed away and crossed the room.

"What do you mean we need to go north?" Tearlach followed. "What's in the north?"

Filling her lungs, she set her shoulders, readying for the verbal match she knew was coming. "The Sacred Pool of Navlin. It's in the Tamslo Mountains. Inside them, actually."

Tearlach narrowed his eyes, advancing on her steadily. All traces of sympathy vanished from his expression. In that moment, he was her personal guard. Nothing more.

"And you know this how?"

"I saw it."

"You saw it?" He paused and arched a brow.

"In a vision." She swallowed.

Tearlach resumed his measured steps. "You know for sure—"

"I know," Esme insisted.

He stopped two paces from her and folded his arms across his chest— the chest her hands had rested against only moments before. She brushed her palms together, trying to erase the sensation.

"It's not safe." He shook his head once, as if the matter were decided.

Esme thought of Sully and Cadwyn declaring the same—not to leave the capital city until the kingdom had been deemed safe. But when would it be safe? The land was dying. People and animals were being forced into the already bursting city centers. How long until even those rivers ran dry? Until citizens started stealing, fighting, rioting?

The kingdom wouldn't be safe unless she made it so.

Esme clasped her hands in front of her and stood an inch taller. "I'm going north, Tearlach. With or without you."

Tearlach huffed a breath, then slowly gathered another. Irritation rolled off him. It was exactly what she needed—the perfect reminder of how inconvenient her feelings for him were.

"Fine, then. Let's say, for argument's sake, that we travel north." He took a step closer. "You know precisely where to find this secret place no one has ever seen?"

"I will."

"You *will?*"

"I know *precisely* where it is, yes."

Tearlach took one more step.

Esme resisted at first, then yielded, tilting her head to meet his glare.

"And when we find this sacred pool, what then?"

"I'll retrieve Dougal's memories," she said plainly.

Tearlach's eyes flared, his lips parting.

"Only Dougal isn't his real name," she appended.

His mouth snapped shut, the muscles along the sides of his jaw bulging. "And I suppose you know his true name."

"I do." Her gaze tangled with his.

When Esme didn't say anything more, she heard a growl deep in Tearlach's chest.

"Well?" he demanded. "What is it?"

"I can't say."

"Can't or won't?" he asked through clenched teeth.

"Won't."

Tearlach released another breath, taking a step back. He searched the room as though he might find something to pry the answers from her.

Or perhaps he was wondering why he'd ever thought to pity her in the first place. She could hope.

"We leave in four days' time."

He whirled on her. "What?"

Seeing his rage stoked her resilience. "Inform Sully that I'll need to meet with the royal guard tomorrow," she said in a commanding voice, then strode past him, needing to move before the tension swelled any further.

"By the gods, woman, are you suggesting—"

"I'm not suggesting anything, Tearlach," she threw over her shoulder, glad that anger had shoved aside the last lingering traces of their earlier interaction. "I'm telling you. We leave in four days."

She reached for the pot of tea—the action grounding her—pouring another cup with what was thankfully a steady hand. When she felt Tearlach draw closer, she assuaged, "I won't divulge anything about Dougal or his memories. Or the Sacred Pool of Navlin, for that matter." She added a splash of milk, then closed her eyes and drank.

Tearlach said nothing. The silence stretched until the only thing Esme could hear was Tearlach's slow, steady breathing. Finally, she set the cup down and gave him her attention.

Tearlach pinned her with the weight of his dark gaze before his eyes roved over her, looking for something. He blew out a breath and stepped around her to pour more tea into the cup she'd set down. Tipping it to his lips, he downed it in one gulp. Esme wondered if he was imagining something stronger.

"This is reckless," he grumbled.

"*This*," she punctuated the word, "is what's best for the kingdom. A queen does what's best for the kingdom. And that's what I am, Tearlach, a queen." *That's all I am*, she thought. He'd made that perfectly clear.

"Tell me, then," he challenged, leaning over to brace his broad hands against the table. "What's your plan? Are we to sneak out of Meallán, make our way across the kingdom and into the mountains, then return without notice?"

"Don't be ridiculous."

Tearlach leveled her with a glare, and Esme's lips twitched. She couldn't help herself.

The fire in his eyes burned impossibly hotter. He turned toward her fully, pressing forward until only a few inches separated them. Esme could feel the edge of the chair against her back. She blinked away, noting the white knuckles of Tearlach's fisted hands before she angled her head back up to meet his glower.

"The guard will accompany us"—she raised her brow, staying him before he could interject—"on our trip to meet with the priestesses in the north."

He eyed her skeptically, then leaned back, crossing his arms. "They've responded to your letter, then?"

"They're expecting a visit from their queen." At least they *would* once they received the missive she'd sent off before dawn, informing them of such. "As I said, we're leaving in four days."

Tearlach didn't move, didn't say anything. Esme fought to regulate the galloping of her heart—which had sensed his proximity, and ignored her demands to remain unaffected.

"That's all," she said tersely, turning away, dismissing him.

Esme could feel his eyes on her, searing her skin. But she refused to look back.

Finally, the tension in the air evaporated, and a moment later a door clicked shut.

She released a breath and gripped the seat of the chair as she sunk down onto the floor.

Chapter Forty

"YOU OKAY?" HAZEL asked quietly as they walked toward the barracks.

"I'm all right. I suppose you heard about what happened with Killian?"

Hazel nodded.

Esme looked back down at her boots. "I just want you to know that I'm sorry. I should've   "

"Sorry? What do you have to be sorry for?"

"I should've been the one to tell you, to explain myself."

"Nonsense. I should be apologizing for *him*. I heard he mucked it up pretty good." Hazel shook her head. "Such a fool," she muttered under her breath.

"Oh." Esme wasn't sure what to say to that.

Hazel leaned in and whispered, "Want me to rip him apart for you?"

Esme choked out a laugh.

"I will." Hazel's sharp brows arched, and she looked positively maniacal.

"No, I don't need you to—No." Esme shook her head as relief swept through her.

Hazel looked off into the distance, her red lips quirking up. "Well, I might anyway, just for fun." Then, as they reached the training yard, she lowered her voice and asked again, "You're sure you're okay?"

Esme thought for a moment, then nodded. "Yes. I think I am. Or, I will be."

Hazel studied her for a moment. "He'll figure it out, you know. Someday. Just give him time."

"Killian?"

"Tearlach."

Esme's eyes went wide. "Killian told you about—"

Hazel scoffed. "Give me more credit than that. I saw it the day I met you."

"How could you have known then? *I* didn't even know."

Hazel grinned. "Then you might be as blind as him. I swear, these men can't see what's so clearly in front of them."

Esme looked down, scuffing her boot through the grass. "I might have been ignoring my own feelings, but I don't think Tearlach...I mean, he's never..."

"He does," Hazel avowed. "I've known Tearlach most of my life, and he's never been anything but a warrior. That's who he is, how he defines himself. And it suits him. You know as well as I do; that man was made to defend, to protect. Don't get me wrong, there have been women over the years who've turned his head, and made their way into his bed. But he never allowed anything to go further than that. He's not like Killian, he's never allowed himself to love freely. He's had his heart locked away since the day his betrothal fell apart. He'll tell you up and down that he doesn't believe in love, in the union of marriage. I'll admit, he had me convinced. Until that day he returned to Tremaene. With you."

Esme gaped at Hazel until Armel's sparring partner drew their attention. The woman was completely mesmerizing. She didn't wield a weapon, and though she was tall, she certainly wasn't built like a fighter. Her long crimson dress hugged her ample curves, the skirts flowing out around her. Esme would've thought such a garment would impede movement during a fight, but the fabric floated along with her as though it were an extension of her. Gauzy layers of deep red and black sailed out from beneath the sleeves of her dress as her arms swept through the air.

Not through it, Esme realized, watching closely. The woman was *moving* the air. Twisting and twirling it around her. Commanding it.

She'd never seen such a beautiful dance with the elements.

"Who is that?"

"I don't know," Hazel responded in a bewildered tone.

Sparing a glance at her, Esme noticed a spark of jealousy in Hazel's captivated eyes.

When the match finished, Armel brought his hands to his knees, panting. The woman approached him, laughing jovially. Armel rose with a smile. He reached out to touch the woman's arm as she drew near, then leaned in to whisper something in her ear. The woman's laugh rang out again.

Esme could feel the tension rippling off Hazel, but when she snuck another look, Hazel's face was a mask of cool dispassion.

"Your Majesty!" a rich voice called out. Esme whipped her head around as the woman in the crimson dress sauntered over, her skirts swaying with her hips. "Such an honor." She swept into a graceful curtsy. When she straightened, a gentle wind wrapped around her long, russet-colored locks, brushing them off her shoulders.

Esme stared at the sight for a breath before meeting the brilliant blue and copper of the woman's eyes.

"May I introduce Shawndrell," Armel offered. When Esme looked to him for clarification, he added, "Lady Pallya's wife."

Esme's eyes darted to Hazel as Armel—oblivious to their assumptions about his relation to the woman—went on to explain that he'd known

Shawndrell when she was a young girl, before he'd left to join the war effort.

"I didn't realize you knew Lady Pallya," Esme said to Armel. Perhaps she *could* trust the councilor after all.

"I don't. Only in name, really," he clarified. "She never visited our village. And when the insurgence began, we heard she'd gone to Meallán to help with negotiations. But it would seem she found her way back to the Flats after the war." He turned a smile toward Shawndrell.

"She did." The woman beamed, her round cheeks warming to a rosy shade.

Shawndrell introduced herself to Hazel and Quinlan, stopping just short of embracing her guards. When she returned to Armel's side, Esme asked when she'd arrived.

"Just yesterday. I was wandering the grounds early this morning. Couldn't sleep. Too much excitement." Shawndrell's eyes shifted, taking in her surroundings. "When I noticed the fighting rings here, I sat and waited for the sun to rise." She leaned toward Esme and dropped her voice conspiratorially. "It's been ages since I've had a good sparring partner." Esme tried not to grin. "When the first guards stumbled out this morning, I went to inquire about a match, hoping I could slip in somewhere. And who do I find? None other than Armel from the Flats. *My* Armel. Then I come to discover he's a member of the royal guard." She brought a hand to her chest, eyes brimming with pride.

Esme glanced at Armel as he averted his gaze. He almost looked bashful.

"And what a strong warrior he's become," Shawndrell went on.

"Your match was quite impressive," Esme redirected, sensing Armel could only take so much admiration. "I've never seen anyone fight so gracefully."

The woman waved her off. "Pah! I felt as though I was flopping about out there like a fish on dry land. I'm quite out of practice. Now you..." Her eyes roved over Esme. "I've heard rumors about your magic."

Esme stiffened. What had she heard?

"A gift from Tuireann himself. The god of sky doesn't bestow many with storm magic. Perhaps I can persuade Your Majesty to join me in a match sometime."

Shawndrell's face was so open that Esme could find no ulterior motive, no manipulation hidden in the request. "I'd be delighted," she answered honestly.

"Wonderful." Shawndrell clapped her hands together, then seemed to notice the rest of the guards gathering near the barracks. "Well, it's about time for me to find another adventure." She turned to Esme. "Your Majesty."

"Shawndrell. It was a pleasure meeting you." Esme grasped her hand, feeling Shawndrell's magic tickle her skin, wrapping around her wrist like a cloak.

When Shawndrell took her leave, sailing past them, they all stared after her.

"I like her," Hazel admitted with a nod, then made for the barracks with Quinlan.

Esme didn't follow. Instead, she turned to Armel. His eyes were still tracking Shawndrell as she cut a crimson path across the lawn.

"Armel?"

He blinked, as though clearing something from his mind. "Yes?"

"I want to apologize. For what I said the other day...about you and Hazel. It was uncalled for."

"But not untrue," he confessed with a half smile.

Esme opened her mouth to say more, but he waved her off.

"Think nothing of it. We've all been there. Said things in the heat of battle."

"But we weren't—"

"Esme," he cut her off, his voice taking on a hard edge. "It's fine." He held her gaze for a moment, his expression indecipherable. Sully's voice carried across the yard, and Armel glanced over his shoulder. "Come on." He jerked his chin to where the other guards had gathered.

Esme hesitated, wanting to say more. But when Armel left her standing at the edge of the ring, she sighed and followed.

Finding her usual spot on a nearby bench, she settled in for what she hoped would be a quick meeting.

The sound of clashing metal had her glancing back.

Cahir barked out a laugh from his position on the ground, then reached up for Killian's hand—who'd clearly bested him. Cahir jumped up, slapped him on the back, wiped his brow, then trudged across the yard to join the others.

Esme watched as Killian dusted off his pants, then reached back to untie his hair. He took the long way around, veering closer to her— deliberately, she thought.

His pace slowed, and he offered a tentative smile as he walked past. When he raised his brow in question, Esme smiled back, hoping he'd take it as the apology she intended. His smile grew, and Esme exhaled, wishing everything could be so easy.

———————

Two rows of facing chairs had been arranged in the middle of Esme's suite. They weren't in perfect rows, which somehow helped. It made the meeting seem less formal, and managed to put her mind at ease. Somewhat.

Her guards, Sully, and Cadwyn, had all taken their seats, while Myles lingered near the glass doors nearest her dressing room. From the moment he'd walked in, finding the entire royal guard present, he'd been visibly uncomfortable, like he shouldn't have been there. Cahir kept stealing glances back at him. It was obvious that everyone in the room wondered at his presence.

Only Hazel and Quinlan wore their uniforms. Though uniforms or not, Esme's suite was filled with warriors, and the space had never felt so small. But for what they were about to discuss, her personal quarters offered the most privacy.

Preparing herself with a deep breath, Esme turned and addressed the group. "I'm sure you're wondering why I've gathered you here. I need this information to stay private until I inform the council tomorrow."

Perplexed looks jumped between her guards, even between Sully and Cadwyn. Apparently Tearlach hadn't divulged the nature of the meeting even to the captain. Esme resisted the urge to look over at where Tearlach was leaning against the opposite wall. She'd been avoiding him all morning, her eyes skipping past him. And she was fairly certain he'd been doing the same.

"In three days' time, I will require the guard to escort me to the Tamslo Mountains." The room had been quiet before, but with those words it fell into a heavier silence.

"There's a secret sect of women in the north—unordained priestesses." Esme inhaled slowly. "And I need to convince them to help restore the land and waterways throughout the kingdom."

The tension in the room lifted, and the air became charged with anxious energy.

Esme went on to explain who the Triskele were, and the letter she'd received. She told them how they'd been summoning raw magic in the north since the Order had fallen. Knowing looks were shared—with the fertile land and flowing water in the mountains, she wondered how many had suspected outside intervention.

"Myles?" Esme turned to him, hearing the others shift in their seats to do the same. His wandering gaze locked with hers and he straightened to his full height. "You'll be our guide once we reach the Clavlin Ridge. Time is of the essence, so we can't bother with the pass in the western foothills."

He stared at her for a moment, then glanced at the others. Esme waited. "They've revealed their whereabouts to you?" he asked.

"We've agreed upon a location for the meeting." *Hopefully they'll agree,* she amended silently, *once they receive my letter.*

Myles considered her for a moment, and Esme willed him to ignore the lie he so clearly sensed. "Then I'll get you there." He nodded, finally claiming the only empty seat.

"Forgive me, My Queen, but is it wise to leave during such a vulnerable time?" Sully asked the question she'd been expecting.

"It must be done. You and Cadwyn will stay behind, and Lord Lennox will govern in my absence."

He released a breath, but nodded his acceptance. She knew he didn't agree—never would when something threatened her well-being.

"The council won't like this," Cadwyn pointed out.

"I know, but Lord Lennox has been here since the beginning of my father's reign. He's the longest-standing member of the court. And we know he can be trusted," Esme defended.

"You're certainly right about that. He's more than capable. It's just... the timing isn't ideal."

"Ideal? We can't afford to waste another moment." Esme's voice rose. "The land is dying, the priestesses may not even agree to help, and—"

"Several invitations have already gone out to noblemen," Cadwyn admitted. "Their presence has been requested."

Esme shook her head and furrowed her brow. "I hardly see why that..." Then she realized what Cadwyn was saying. The noblemen were coming for her. To meet her. To *court* her.

Her stomach churned at the thought. She swallowed the bile rising in her throat.

Cadwyn dipped her head, confirming her fear. "I meant to tell you tonight," she said quietly.

"Well..." Esme took a shaky breath, then rolled her shoulders as though she could dislodge the burden. She blinked away, her eyes alighting on the furniture that had been pushed against the walls. When she lifted her gaze, no one would meet her eyes. Somehow that made it easier to pretend the information hadn't affected her.

Spinning on her heel, she forced a steady gait and walked between the rows. "Send them back home when they arrive." She waved her hand through the air as if it were nothing. "I've no intention of letting the council choose a mate for me."

"Who said anything about a mate?" Tearlach's voice halted her.

Though he was standing only a few paces in front of her, Esme didn't look up at him. Her gaze flicked to the side, catching the look Hazel and Killian exchanged before her eyes snagged on Armel. His were wide, sympathetic.

Finally, after avoiding him all morning, she looked at Tearlach. Her gaze swept up from his crossed ankles to the folded arms at his chest—a stance that looked relaxed, bored even. But Esme didn't let the familiar posture fool her.

"Don't confuse this with love," he drawled as though she were a simpleminded child, which thoroughly managed to stamp out every last flicker of nervousness Esme felt toward him.

"You're a queen in need of a consort. Nothing more."

Esme took a step forward. Then another. She crossed her arms over her chest, mirroring his stance. "Is that what I need?" She arched a brow.

"*That* is what's required. Choose a man with money, a title, political power, and be done with it," he ground out.

She heard the sounds of murmuring, and chairs scuffing against the floor, but didn't look back. Her eyes were riveted to Tearlach, the air between them vibrating with unspoken words. When she knew they were alone, Esme took a final step, closing the distance.

"And if I want more?"

Tearlach didn't move, didn't respond.

Esme's breaths became shallow as she asked again, quietly. "What if I want more?" She fought to keep the other words locked up, the ones she longed to say.

Tearlach reached out and seized her by her upper arms, stealing Esme's last breath. She wasn't sure if he meant to stop her from coming any closer, or to keep her from retreating.

His eyes darkened as he stared down at her, his grip on her arms tightening briefly. "We can't always have the things we desire." His tone was sharp and punishing, as if she were to blame for the ruination of his own wants. It was true, she supposed. But still, Esme bristled at the accusation, and pried her gaze from his.

Tearlach lifted his hands away, and Esme felt the loss acutely.

"I need to..." She took a step back, then turned, unable to face him a moment longer.

After what felt like an eternity, Esme heard Tearlach push away from the wall.

He left without a word.

Chapter Forty-One

ESME STRODE TOWARD the council chamber, thinking how foolish she'd been to assume addressing her guards would've been the difficult part. Without a moment's pause, she yanked open the doors. The sentries scrambled to catch them before they could swing shut.

Her councilors stood, milling about—no doubt surmising as to the reason she'd called a session with so little notice. She didn't bother accounting for each member as she made her way to the head of the table.

Everyone quickly found their seats, but Esme remained standing.

"I'll keep this short. I have an announcement to make. All other matters can wait until we next convene." She glanced around the room, her conviction wavering. But she had to tell them; it was the best way to keep the rest of her plans hidden. "I've confirmed that there are women in Tremaene with the power to summon raw magic. There aren't many, but those few have formed a sect in the safety of the mountains. These young women were not yet ordained at the time of the Order's collapse. I have been in communication with them, and in two days' time will be traveling north to meet with them personally."

A precarious silence hovered in the room. Then, all at once, everyone spoke.

Esme kept her head lifted, refusing to meet anyone's eyes. Most seemed to be speaking among themselves, though she heard a few *Your Majesty*'s.

When it became clear that Esme was waiting for the clamor to die down, discussions and inquiries ceased. Risking a quick glance around the table, she caught Lady Audris's look of triumph as the woman leaned over to Gwen, whispering, "I told you, didn't I?" loud enough for all to hear. Gwen had the good sense to look abashed at Lady Audris's remark.

"This is shockingly unacceptable," Lord Torin declared. "A queen does not bow to the likes of servants. Who's to say what their true motives are? They could be luring you away from the security of the palace."

Esme opened her mouth to calmly explain that it was not up to him, but when Lord Torin continued, she patiently clasped her hands.

"We must demand that they come to Meallán for questioning—or better yet, bring them here ourselves. Any priestess, especially a *young* one, cannot be trusted."

Esme arched her brow as if to say, *Are you quite finished?*, then addressed him. "I'm not asking you to trust them, Lord Torin. I'm telling you to trust me, your queen. And as a show of respect for what they—and they alone—can offer our kingdom, I will gladly humble myself."

"Are we going to discuss the real issue at hand?" Lady Audris chirped, then cast her wide-eyed gaze around the room. "Your Majesty, you lied to your own council about the existence of these women when I first brought this *serious* matter forward."

In her periphery, Esme noticed the tiny white flowers of the creeping jasmine on the terrace wall outside. She could almost smell the sickeningly sweet scent that reminded her so vividly of Orianna. But instead of turning her stomach, it strengthened her resolve. Esme had stood up to Orianna. And won.

Slowly, she turned a look of disdain on Lady Audris. "What I deem worthy of sharing with the people in this room is entirely up to me. Lest you forget, Lady Audris, who wears the crown." Her fingers twitched to touch the simple circlet she'd thankfully remembered to don before leaving her room.

Lady Audris's fair complexion turned a shade paler, and she dropped her gaze to the table.

"I will admit, Your Majesty, that your safety beyond the palace walls is worrisome," Lord Lennox deftly redirected. "But I will rightly defer to Captain Sullivan on that matter." He inclined his head to Sully.

"I assure you that Her Majesty will be well protected—escorted by her entire royal guard and led by her personal guard, Tearlach," Sully confirmed.

Esme knew he didn't fully support her decision, but was grateful he hadn't pressed the issue further when they'd met that morning to discuss the details.

"Perhaps these women can be trusted," Aindreas acknowledged. "But...Forgive me, Your Majesty, but it might appear weak for the queen to bend to the will of priestesses." Her Minister of Trade knew more about the situation than any of the other councilors, and she wondered if his comment was merely a way of not letting on about that.

"As I've said, this is a show of respect. We also have their protection to consider. They wouldn't feel safe venturing to Meallán; not after what Orianna did. These women are our best chance at restoring life to the dying countryside, and I won't have them subjected to prejudices." She leveled Lord Torin with a glare.

"But what will the people think when they see their queen leaving the palace on some frivolous trip after only recently ascending the throne?" Pearce inquired. "It will undoubtedly appear as though Her Majesty is abandoning her post during a time of great need. It's hardly the appearance of stability Tremaene needs right now."

"The people of Tremaene will not know I've left the palace. Captain Sullivan will see to it that we are not seen leaving the city." She considered reminding them that she'd already made her way across the kingdom unseen once before. "And I trust the palace staff to keep private anything they hear or see within these walls, just as I expect this council—and any of your personal staff—to do the same." Esme gave Lady Audris a meaningful look, wondering who in her service had learned about the letter from the Triskele.

"Furthermore, meeting with these women is of the utmost importance, and I refuse to delay it more than necessary. We've sat in this chamber discussing the state of Tremaene as if it were thriving, turning a blind eye to what's happening across the kingdom. The barrenness is spreading, most of our rivers and streams have run dry, and soon only those with the means to purchase resources will be able to endure the coming hardships. These women might be our only hope in restoring life to our dying land. If we don't seize this—and every available opportunity—our land will die. What then? What will a coffer full of gold buy if there is no fresh water, no land to grow food?" Esme finally took a breath.

The answering silence felt strangely like support.

"Lord Lennox will act as proxy in my absence. And the captain will keep me apprised of any urgent matters that might arise." She hurried on, ready to be done with the meeting. "Now, if there's nothing else—"

"Your Majesty?" Keelin asked timidly. "I'm sorry to bring this up, but I'm sure you're aware that several noblemen have accepted our summonses and are on their way here at this time, eager to meet you."

"Well...when they arrive, send them home."

"Your Majesty?"

"I have far more pressing issues to attend to."

"It's just that..." Keelin tried again. "I do apologize, Your Majesty, but I was told to invite all prospective noblemen—"

"Then I'm quite sorry you've wasted your time. I don't know who informed you to do such a thing, but I have no intention of playing—"

"Surely Your Majesty will want to be involved in selecting your own consort." Lord Torin's voice cut in.

He had the audacity to presume the council had a say in who she would marry?

Esme let out a breath slowly. She hesitated for a moment, wishing she could have avoided the Regent Decree—and its unjust addendum—until they next convened. But it seemed she had no choice. And perhaps it was best to address it straightaway than to fret about the vulnerability and legitimacy of her reign while she was gone.

Given what Sully had informed her of that morning, the timing was at least in her favor. Reluctantly, she sat down, cursing to herself that the meeting couldn't have simply gone as planned, then pulled her chair closer so she could rest her intertwined hands on the table.

"Lord Lennox, if you would."

He nodded and rose from his seat, removing a piece of rolled parchment from his jacket. "At the request of Her Majesty, Queen Esme of Tremaene, I propose the council revoke the outdated stipulation from the Regent Decree that unfairly requires a female heir to marry in order to retain her rightful place on the throne."

"You're wasting everyone's time, Lennox," Lord Torin sighed. "You'll need the full weight of the court to approve such a measure, and I, for one, have no intention of voting aye."

"Not so," Lord Lennox corrected, reclaiming his seat. "Since my proposition pertains to an addendum and not the decree itself, the measure can be revoked by a simple majority."

Lord Torin leaned forward, glowering at the other man. A moment passed before he sat back in his chair and turned his gaze on Esme. She held her breath and fought the urge to shy away. "Perhaps this is best," he reflected thoughtfully—though Esme knew there was no way he'd concede so easily. "But seeing as this matter has brought to light just how important a royal consort is to the stability of the kingdom, I propose a condition. Any royal marriage, from this date forward, will require approval from the council. This will apply to queens and kings alike. To be fair."

Esme caught the infinitesimal tic of his eyebrow, and she clenched her jaw. Why must they have a say in who she married? It was absurd. But she supposed it was better than relinquishing her crown to a regent until she wed.

Fine, then. She simply wouldn't marry.

Lord Lennox reluctantly smoothed the curling sheet of parchment, and proceeded to add the proposed language. He placed his pen to the side and looked to Esme. She nodded.

With a blur of hands, the amended motion passed. Unanimously.

Chapter Forty-Two

LADY PALLYA STEPPED into Esme's path as she left the council chamber. "Your Majesty, a word?"

Esme could only nod, following her to a corner of the sitting room.

Lady Pallya stood quietly for a moment, watching over Esme's shoulder. When the room fell quiet, she looked down and said, "While I don't share the same archaic beliefs as Lord Torin, I do believe that an ideal union can make a person stronger. Being joined with the right partner can bring great value to one's life...as well as great joy."

Esme waited for her to continue, thinking she meant to say something about her own wife, Shawndrell, but Lady Pallya's face remained impassive. Finally, she gave a perfunctory nod, hastened a "Your Majesty," and left.

Esme stared after her, wondering how two vastly different personalities could manage together. She was still pondering it when Tearlach called out to a woman who was being escorted into the palace by a footman.

"Cora?"

The woman looked up, and before Esme could think who the woman was, Tearlach had rushed over to sweep her up into an embrace.

Esme sucked in a sharp breath at the sight. Another woman? By the gods, how many did he have?

Although, the name sounded vaguely familiar. Thinking back, a memory surfaced in her mind—the day at sea after she and Tearlach had fled the mortal realm. He'd only spoken her name once—the only time he'd ever shared a glimpse into his past.

Cora was his former betrothed. The one woman who'd ever managed to penetrate the wall around Tearlach's heart. The woman who'd thrown that gift away for another man.

The two of them continued their embrace, and Esme took the opportunity to stare openly at Cora. The woman only came up to Tearlach's shoulder—not much taller than Esme herself. And her light copper–colored hair fell in perfect, glossy waves down the back of her pale pink gown. She was the portrait of femininity.

When Tearlach and Cora finally stepped apart, they lingered at arm's length, speaking in hushed tones. Cora looked up at Tearlach adoringly, and even from a distance Esme could see the hint of elation on Tearlach's face.

Did he still love her? Did she love him? Was that the reason for her sudden appearance? Was she there to win him back?

The pair and the woman's maid approached, and Esme couldn't think of what to do, what to say. Jealousy had taken up space inside her, leaving room for little else. Should she meet them halfway?

Try as she might, Esme couldn't move, couldn't bring herself to take a step toward them. Sully and Cadwyn remained loyally by her side, even when Esme noticed Tearlach and Cora's linked arms and struggled to maintain her composure. Tearing her gaze from the sight, she finally managed a step, prepared to greet the woman with the politeness she deserved.

But a deep, swaggering voice fractured her plan.

Tearlach visibly tensed, and Cora's eyes darkened as Lord Torin's slow, steady footfalls drew closer.

When he stopped not two paces from them, Esme couldn't help but yield a step. Her eyes tracked Tearlach's movement as he subtly positioned himself between his father and Cora.

"My son wasn't good enough for you when he was heir to the Isloran holdings, I can't imagine what you want from him now." Lord Torin looked past Tearlach's wall of a body. He didn't attempt to hide his contempt as he swept his gaze up and down Cora's form before finally meeting Tearlach's scowl.

Esme felt the heat of fury swelling in her chest, but when she slid her slipper forward, ready to defend a woman she hadn't even met, Sully's hand on her shoulder stopped her advance. She turned her head a fraction to see the slight shake of his head. *It's their fight,* he seemed to say. Esme set her jaw and remained silent.

"Though considering her leanings, it would have been a sham of a marriage anyway. At least she had the wherewithal to leave before she could disgrace our family as well as hers." Lord Torin strode away before the words had fully settled. When they did, Esme's mouth dropped open.

She glanced at Cora, concerned. The woman stared intently at the floor. Her skin had paled to a sickly pallor. Esme knew well what Lord Torin could provoke with only a few words.

"I'm sorry. I shouldn't have come here," she whispered.

"Cora." Tearlach's voice was both unyielding and soothing. When she looked up, Tearlach shook his head as though forbidding her to allow his father to have any effect on her. Cora looked past him, down the corridor where Lord Torin had disappeared. Then she exhaled so deeply it seemed to dispel the tension encircling them.

When Cora turned a genuine—if slightly apologetic smile— toward Esme, Tearlach placed a protective hand at Cora's back and introduced her.

"Again, I do apologize for arriving unannounced. But I..." Cora glanced up at Tearlach. "I have news from home." Tearlach narrowed his eyes before nodding. She didn't seem inclined to elaborate about her presence in front of an audience. Esme didn't blame her.

"Will you be staying at the palace?" she asked.

"I think...perhaps I shouldn't."

"Don't worry about Torin, he's staying in the city. And even if he—" Tearlach shook his head. "You'll be perfectly safe here; I can assure you. And I'll station a guard outside your door in case he manages to weasel his way into the guest wing." The corners of Tearlach's lips quirked up at his attempted levity, before he turned to address the palace footman. "Tomas, please show her to an available apartment in the east wing. One on the second floor."

Esme bit her bottom lip as Tearlach gave the order. He did so with such confidence, as if the palace were *his* home. Her heart softened a bit at the thought.

Tomas nodded, then gestured for Cora and her maid to follow.

Cora, even in her unsettled state, swept into a curtsy and thanked Esme. Her maid mirrored the motion, though she kept her eyes downcast.

"We'll speak after dinner," Tearlach called after her.

———————

Esme paced her dressing room, eying the row of gowns. She set her teacup aside and pulled one off its wooden rod. The weave of the fabric was smoother, finer than the raw silk she preferred, and the pastel tones made it seem all the more delicate—soft pink at the bodice, blending to a lilac purple at the bottom hem.

She couldn't stop thinking about Cora—the graceful way she'd carried herself, the way her gown that on Esme would've looked young and girlish made Cora appear poised and polished, how her hair looked freshly styled even though she'd traveled for days. The way Tearlach had embraced her.

Her hands gripped the dress as the image flitted through her mind— Tearlach's strong arms wrapped around the only woman who'd ever known his heart.

Esme cleared her throat and tossed the dress over the back of a tufted chair, then started unbuttoning the one she was wearing. It'd seemed elegant—regal even—when she'd donned it that morning.

She stepped into the new dress. The satin of the skirt grazed her bare legs. She could barely feel it—like wearing nothing more than a silk shift. She wrapped the sash around her waist, thinking how she might orchestrate a chance encounter with Cora. Perhaps she could bring over a tray of tea and sweets to make sure she was settling into her room.

Esme hummed to herself, thinking through the merits of such a ploy as she lifted the hem and sauntered over to the dressing table. Catching a glimpse of herself in the mirror, she paused, then shifted, letting the light play along the fall of the skirt. She combed her fingers through her hair, trying to smooth some of the unruly tresses into submission.

She took in the rest of her form. What was she trying to prove? With a sigh, her shoulders slumped forward.

Cora wasn't her enemy. Or even her competition. If anything, after the way Lord Torin had treated her—and Esme would venture it was the way he'd *always* treated her—she felt an odd sort of kinship with the woman. Besides, there was something about Cora that Tearlach had loved—maybe still loved—which made Esme more curious about the woman than anything. Gods knew he didn't offer up his affections freely. He wasn't like Killian that way.

But then, neither was Esme.

She looked down at the glossy fabric pooling on the ground, her toes peeking out from beneath the hem.

How much easier would it have been if she'd been able to reciprocate Killian's feelings? If she'd felt for him even half of what she felt for Tearlach.

Her eyes met her reflection.

That was why she wanted to speak with her. Cora knew Tearlach— the man he'd been before, the man who'd allowed himself to love.

Esme averted her gaze. She needed to get out of her room before she convinced herself that stalking the east wing and ambushing Cora were sound ideas.

She skimmed her hands over the bodice of her dress, then twisted her torso, trying to settle into it.

It wasn't that the dress didn't fit her. She didn't fit the dress. It wasn't her.

She rummaged through her drawers until she found something more befitting of a gardener than a queen.

———————

Esme found Hazel crouched near the edge of the ring. Madoc sent daggers curving through the air as he tried to catch Quinlan off guard. But the woman deftly sidestepped each and every one of them.

"Gods' balls, Madoc! Get your head out of your ass and fight like a worthy opponent!" Hazel shouted.

Esme choked at the remark.

Hazel glanced up at her, a smirk planted firmly on her face. "Hear that, did you?"

Esme nodded. "Very creative."

Hazel shrugged and rose to her feet. "It's been a long day; it was the best I could come up with. And he needed the encouragement." She looked over her shoulder as the two of them circled one another. "Not that it matters; he won't best her. No one can."

"Right," Esme agreed. With Quinlan's foresight, one-on-one matches would always end in her favor. "You were on duty last night?" she asked as Hazel stifled a yawn.

"With Madoc. The man wouldn't let up about some card game he'd won. I might have provoked him into this fight just to shut him up." She smirked again.

"You might have?"

"I might have."

Esme scuffed the toe of her boot against the grassy edge of the ring. "Are you heading back to the barracks, then?"

"Wasn't planning on it." Hazel crossed her arms over her chest.

"Well, if you're too tired, I can just..." Esme cast her sights around the yard.

"Don't be ridiculous. My commentary might be waning, but I can still shoot an arrow better than any man here." She raised her chin.

Esme grinned and lifted her own chin. "Actually, I was thinking we could practice with something other than arrows." Hazel narrowed her eyes ever so slightly. "Fire?"

Hazel hardened her stare, then looked pointedly over Esme's shoulder—exactly as Armel had the other day.

Esme stretched her neck and rose up on her toes to catch Hazel's eye. "He's not here."

Hazel seemed to consider Esme's request for a moment. She'd no doubt heard about her disastrous match with Armel. Might have witnessed it even. But if Tearlach hadn't bothered to show up then—or to even scold her for acting against his orders—then Esme didn't care much for his precautions.

Hazel cocked her head to the side, causing her hair—still smooth and shiny despite her night shift—to glide over her shoulder and fall across her face. "And you were planning to wield *what* against my fire?"

"I'm not sure." She glanced at the weapons rack across the yard, then back at Hazel—just as her guard swept a scrutinizing look over Esme's body.

When their eyes met, Hazel seemed to decide something. "Come on." She stalked into the ring, disrupting Quinlan and Madoc's match.

Esme offered an apologetic smile as she hurried over to the rack to grab the lightest longsword she could find.

Taking up a position three paces from Hazel, she adjusted her hold on the sword, then waited. Hazel regarded her again, her shrewd gaze fixed on Esme's grip as she absently twirled her finger at her side.

A thread of white light flared to life. The burning hot end coiled up around Hazel's arm, the other split off into thin whips of flames.

Esme stared for a long moment, mesmerized by the fiery ends as they flickered from purple to blue, then back to blinding white. She blinked away, but the outlines were burned into the backs of her eyelids. With a deep inhale, she turned to Hazel and lifted her sword—unsure of what use cold metal would be against fluid, untethered fire magic.

Hazel's fire whipped through the air. Esme clumsily ducked back, her sword hanging limply from her hand. The ends of the whip snapped at her, sending sparks dancing in the air before they extinguished into nothing.

A streak of fire cut through the air again and Esme lunged from its trajectory. Her sword slipped from her grip, clattering to the ground several paces away as she reached out to catch herself. Bits of jagged rock punctured the soft skin of her palms, but she got a knee under her and hopped up before the pain fully registered.

She wiped her scraped, bloodied hands against her pants, and looked up to find Hazel standing before her, twisting a rope of fire up over her head. Esme panted, trying to catch her breath. Hazel took her time, idly lassoing the fire in a wide circle as she glanced casually about at the many guards who'd gathered to watch.

Esme took the reprieve Hazel offered to search for her discarded sword. She hurried over to retrieve it, vaguely aware of the cheers and hollers that were meant to encourage. She wasn't sure why they bothered. What good was a sword against fire?

Hazel lowered the glowing, flickering rope, letting it glide around her as it dipped toward the ground. It hovered near her ankles, never dropping far enough to scorch the dirt.

Then, with a flick of her wrist, it snapped out lightning fast.

Esme jumped over it, but felt the prick of a spark on the exposed skin of her hand. She dodged the next strike, aimed higher. Covering the back of her head with her free hand, she pivoted, slicing through one of the white-hot tendrils with the edge of her sword.

Hazel's fire flickered out.

The yard went still.

Esme looked at her sword, expecting to find something amiss. The dull, nicked silver was only that—silver. She didn't feel any of her magic sweeping out into the blade.

Then why had Hazel dropped her magic?

Esme opened one of her palms, wondering if her hands looked worse than they felt. But the gouges had already healed—hopefully without any bits of dirt trapped beneath her skin.

Finally, she looked up. Hazel's eyes were fixed on something behind Esme.

Not something, *someone*, she realized as she turned to see Tearlach at the edge of the ring. His eyes were on her, sliding down to the sword in her hand.

Killian stepped up beside him and quickly took in the sight. They must have only just arrived.

Tearlach widened his stance and folded his arms over his chest. It was a challenge. Would Esme or Hazel answer to him first?

Esme wanted to look back at Hazel, to see what she might be thinking, but she couldn't move. She was stuck, rooted in place—those dark, fathomless eyes holding her there.

Tearlach didn't say anything. Not out loud. Not in her mind. He only stared, his expression hard and severe.

Esme had seen him look at Cora with such joy and gentleness only hours earlier. Expressions he'd never once directed at her. Would he ever look at her that way? Let his eyes soften enough that she might see past his impenetrable defenses? Or would he always gaze upon her with austerity?

Hazel moved past her and stepped in front of Tearlach, blocking his penetrating gaze and breaking their silent connection.

Esme immediately wanted it back.

Those inescapable, commanding looks weren't much, but they were all she'd ever have of him.

Hazel took Tearlach by the shoulders, said something Esme couldn't hear, then pulled him behind the line of guards. Tearlach darted a look back at Esme before reluctantly giving Hazel his full attention.

Was Hazel taking the blame? Esme shouldn't have asked for a fight, and she was beginning to suspect that she'd only initiated the match to get a reaction from Tearlach.

Killian ducked to catch her eye. "Come on." He turned her away, and Esme was certain he knew everything, had seen every one of her thoughts written on her face.

She followed Killian, glancing back once to see that the other guards had shifted away from where Tearlach and Hazel were arguing. And arguing they certainly were. Hazel's hands were planted firmly on her hips, chin jutted up into the air. Tearlach scowled down at her, then cocked his head to the side as he crossed his arms over his chest yet again.

Killian cleared his throat, and Esme turned back to him. To the flames licking up his sword.

Surprised, a smirk tugged at the corners of her mouth. She'd expected something a little more...impressive. Killian wasn't known for being prudent with his magic. "Reckless" had been Armel's word for it— though Esme wouldn't go so far as to say Killian was careless with his power. Still, compared to the precise and exacting nature of Hazel's fire, Killian's was...savage.

Yet there he stood, with a sword sheathed in meticulously even white and blue flames.

At least it's not a whip, she mused.

Esme took stock of her own arsenal and summoned invisible vines, wrapping them around her. They slithered down her arms, coiling around the plates at her shoulders and forearms like another layer of armor.

She lifted her sword. Even with the bright sunlight glinting off the smooth line of silver, it seemed dull, weak compared to Killian's. Without so much as a thought, she extended her vines down the length of the blade.

Killian looked her over, and she wondered if he could see any evidence of her magic. When he lifted a brow in question, Esme rolled her shoulders and nodded.

Her vines repelled Killian's magic, though the effect was fleeting. Each time their swords struck, his fire flickered, extinguishing in the spot where their magics collided, only to flare back to life with the next arc of his blade. Esme could barely match Killian on a good day, and with his sword hot with fire, she was even more limited. She couldn't risk any action that might expose her.

Killian attacked again. Their swords clashed and held as he pressed forward slowly, his flames dying out until their blades were crossed at their fortes, and Esme was able to shove his sword away. He retreated with a glint of pride in his eyes, then pivoted just as quickly, swiping low.

She leapt over the sweep of fire, then stayed crouched as Killian's blade curved back around, aimed high. Her sword caught his in a spray of white sparks. She ducked her head, but felt the prick of an errant spark on her neck.

Killian retreated, twirling his blade at his side—the light hovering in the air like a glowing disc.

Esme slowed her rapid breathing and glanced down at her sword. She sent more vines down her arm, weaving them into a stronger defense. The sensation of them trailing along the bare skin of her hands had her thinking of Hazel's whip. Perhaps she could...

Her eyes met Killian's as she grew a thick tapered vine around her left wrist, unfurling it down to the ground. Esme wasn't as skilled with her left hand, but knew Killian wouldn't attack if she dropped the only visible weapon from her right hand.

She advanced slowly, mindful of her sword. Her attack was direct and simple as she watched for an opening. Killian narrowed his eyes suspiciously as he parried, then riposted. Esme spun away, luring him forward. When his blade arced toward her again, she whipped her vine out, catching his sword. She yanked at it, but Killian tightened his grip, attempting to twist the blade free from the invisible vine. When he gave up the struggle, he smirked.

"Nice." His eyes flashed with admiration.

Esme released her hold, letting her vine uncoil as the magic receded back inside her. Killian looked her over once more, seemed to decide something, then tossed his sword to the ground.

Esme edged away as curiosity, and a hint of worry, threaded through her.

Fire shot up from the ground, and Esme stumbled back, sucking in a breath. A nervous laugh escaped her lips. She'd never witnessed the extent of Killian's magic. Through the flames, his eyes gleamed with mischief, and Esme wondered if she was seeing a glimpse of what he was like in battle.

Jagged flames raged before her, threatening with fervent heat. They were no longer white and pure, but wild with reds and golds—their cores so dark they were nearly black. Though she could sense Killian's disciplined restraint, there was nothing tame about his fire.

Esme sidestepped tentatively, her hands twitching with the urge to summon magic. But what could she do against an inferno?

Another wall of flames blazed to life. Heat licked at her skin. She turned, yielding another step, and saw Tearlach and Hazel edging closer.

A bead of sweat trickled down her forehead. She wiped it away and cast a timorous glance through the flames to where Killian stood watching her movements intently.

With a bracing breath, she tossed her sword, sheathed her body in thick, protective vines, then bolted.

If she could get past the flames, and reach Killian, maybe she could—

A fireball blasted toward her.

Esme dropped to the ground, then scrambled back up a split second before Killian pitched another. She reinforced the vines around her armor, stretching them further to wrap around her hands, her fingers, up her neck.

The next one was lower. She twisted, arching away as the heat grazed her. Magic sparked along the backs of her legs as the fire came close. Too close.

She could feel Tearlach's eyes boring into her, could feel the tether between them pulling tight.

Killian wouldn't let anything touch her, she reminded herself, barely dodging the next strike.

The next came too fast. Her ankle rolled under her, and pain streaked up her leg. She ducked her head, hoping it hadn't registered on her face. But Tearlach saw. His eyes were wide and furious, and Esme knew he was seconds away from calling the match.

Killian was being cautious though. He was challenging her, pushing her, but she trusted him to know her limits.

Esme flicked her gaze back to Tearlach and saw a flash of terror in his eyes.

Shouts came from behind a moment before pain seared her arm.

Chapter Forty-Three

ESME JERKED BACK around.

Ash from a guttered-out fireball floated in the air like snow.

It was a split second, but that was all it'd taken for her attention to wane, for her magic to slip from her grasp and leave her vulnerable.

She stared down at the scorched remains of her shirt sleeve. The flexible fabric of her protective garments had been burned away. Beneath the fine wire mesh that remained, her skin was red and angry. A sliver closer and it might have burned her flesh down to the bone.

So much worse, she told herself. It could have been so much worse.

Suddenly, Killian was there, gripping her by the shoulders. He turned her arm, examining the damage. When he lifted his eyes to hers, his expression was nothing short of horrified.

"Esme, I..." He shook his head, unable to say anything more.

"It was my fault." Her chin started to wobble. She wasn't sure if it was from the shock, or the way he was looking at her.

"Your fault?" Incredulity crept into his voice. "Esme, if Tearlach hadn't been here—"

"I know." She ducked her head. "I was distracted."

Esme felt Killian take a deep, bracing breath. Then a knuckle gently nudged her chin up. "No," he said firmly, then swallowed. She could feel the slight tremor in his hand. "If he hadn't been here, I might have burned you. I could have—Esme, I'm sorry. I'm so sorry. I should've been more careful." He shook his head, averting his gaze, and Esme realized what he was saying. Tearlach had siphoned Killian's magic before the fireball could strike her.

She looked over to where everyone from the yard had gathered, and saw Hazel gripping Tearlach's arm with what looked like all the strength her bow-stretching muscles possessed to keep him where he was.

Because Esme knew he wanted to charge out there. To make sure she was safe. To kill Killian, probably.

Only he didn't. He let Hazel hold him back. And stared at Esme with the same hard expression he always had for her.

Killian continued to apologize—his eyes roving over her body, checking for injuries every step of the way back to the palace. He would've followed her into her room, but Esme stopped him with a hand on his chest, insisting she was fine before shutting the door against his stricken face.

No matter how guilty Killian felt about the accident, Esme knew she was to blame. *Be aware of your surroundings.* The directive had been hammered into her time and again, from every one of her instructors.

Thank the gods Tearlach had been there.

Although...if he hadn't, she might not have been distracted in the first place. Perhaps she'd been a little *too* aware of her surroundings.

Esme sighed, shrugging out of her ruined garments. She shoved them into the dark corner of a bottom shelf—lest someone find them and worry more than they should.

Tearlach hadn't said a word to her after the incident. Not a word. Though his eyes hadn't once left her. He'd watched as the other guards had worried over her, watched as she'd finally convinced them she was well. And though he hadn't followed her back to the palace, she'd felt him watching the entire way.

———————

By evening, Esme was exhausted. She pulled on a simple cream-colored dress with a beaded scarlet sash, and hurried downstairs for dinner, telling herself she needed to make an appearance with the palace staff. It was only when she reached the hall—scanning the crowded tables for Tearlach and Cora, and finding them absent—that she realized her true motivation.

Her brush with Killian's fire magic aside, Esme's curiosity about the woman hadn't waned.

Spotting Cadwyn, Sully, and a few other guards at a nearby table, she decided to join them.

Despite the lively conversation throughout dinner, her thoughts kept turning back to Tearlach. And Cora.

Where is he? Is Cora with him? Are they taking dinner in her suite, just the two of them?

Upon returning to the deafening silence of her room, Esme extinguished each of the flames, pulling her sleeves down her arms as she moved through the space. After blowing out the last lamp, she dropped her dress to the floor and toed it over to the nearest bedpost. The room was bathed in the colors of night—deep purples, lilacs, emerald greens. Esme glanced down at her satin chemise, colored by the dancing lights.

Padding over to close the curtains, she heard something. Turning the handle quietly, she eased one of the glass doors open.

The low resonance became clearer—Tearlach's voice drifting through his open window. But who was he talking to?

As soon as the question entered Esme's mind, she heard a soft female voice respond.

Cora.

Cora was in his room.

Without a second thought, Esme slipped through the open door, sidled over to the far edge of the balcony, and pressed her back against the wall.

It didn't matter that they wouldn't be able to see her; it felt wrong what she was doing. Her heart beat wildly in her chest. But as she thought more about the violation of secretly listening in, Esme recalled just how much Tearlach had heard of her own private thoughts before she'd learned of their connection. She resisted the temptation to growl, and turned her ear toward the window.

"...and how is Alpina?" Tearlach was saying.

Alpina? The name wasn't familiar.

Cora chuckled. "Headstrong, stubborn, infuriating...beautiful, intelligent..." Cora hummed before sighing, "She's perfect." The smile was evident in her voice.

"Well, I should think so if you left me for her."

What? Cora left Tearlach for—

"Ow!" Tearlach yelped. A deep, rumbling laugh followed.

Esme could almost picture them jesting like brother and sister. Like Killian and Hazel.

With a sigh, she pushed away from the wall. But then Cora said, "I'm happy you've finally found someone too. After all this time."

Esme's heartbeat ratcheted up, filling the silence that followed Cora's statement.

"Tearlach, this is a good thing," Cora told him, her voice tender.

"How is this a good thing? It's utterly inconvenient."

Esme heard the scrape of a chair against the floor.

"Tearlach," Cora gently prodded, and Esme wondered if he'd begun pacing.

"It's interfering with...everything," he groaned. "I couldn't do my job today. I was right there. Right. There. And my head was...somewhere else."

"You're too hard on yourself. You always have been."

"I need to be."

"You don't," Cora said matter-of-factly. "Let yourself have this. You deserve to find happiness like the rest of us—like you let me have. For once in your life, just...be happy."

Be happy. The words echoed through Esme's mind as she backed away, staring at where Tearlach's window lay beyond the curve of the exterior wall. She grabbed blindly behind her, seeking purchase against the marble.

Tearlach's response was lost to the rush of blood pulsing between Esme's ears. Her hand connected with the doorframe and she pulled herself back into the safety of her darkened room. Drawing a shaky breath, she rested her forehead against the cool glass.

You've finally found someone.

That was what Cora had said, confirming what Esme refused to believe.

Tearlach had met someone. It hadn't been a meaningless flirtation with a maid after all. Tearlach cared about the woman—about Sheridan. To the point where he couldn't concentrate on his job. He felt strongly enough for her that, while he was watching Esme and Killian face off in the training ring, his mind had been "somewhere else." With some*one* else.

Expecting a fresh wave of jealousy, Esme braced her hands. But the only thing that came was sadness. *Better to know,* she tried to convince herself, *than to hope for something impossible.*

Tearlach had found someone who made him happy.

Esme straightened and stared out into the night. She'd just have to find a way to be happy for him.

Chapter Forty-Four

THEY WERE SET to leave the following day, and Esme was fretting. She'd been a bit overzealous with her strategizing. The letter would surely reach the women of the Triskele in time; she wasn't worried about that. But it hadn't occurred to her before that they might not agree to her terms—the date she'd set, that she'd be accompanied by her royal guard. Or the most contentious of her conditions—the location.

All Esme knew of the mountains were the places drawn on maps—towns and villages, all of which would be far too public for the likes of a secret sect. The only place that she assumed would be vacant was the Iola Temple, near Juverna. At least, she hoped it was still vacant.

She should've waited for a response; she knew that. But she was anxious to reach the sacred pool and retrieve Lord Luxovious's memories.

The meeting with the Triskele is merely a front, Esme reminded herself. And if she arrived at the temple with her retinue only to find it empty, she'd act as astonished as the rest that the priestesses hadn't shown. She hated the idea of lying to her guards, *again,* but it was too late to back out.

And what would she tell the council if she failed to meet with the women she'd spoken of in such high regard?

A knock saved her from having to consider that thought any further.

Armel stepped inside. "Keelin is here to see you, Your Majesty."

Esme raised her brow in question, curious why her Minister of Communications was seeking her out in her private suite. But the shrug of his shoulders told her he hadn't a clue.

Esme allowed her to enter.

"Your Majesty." Keelin gave a perfunctory curtsy. Esme hadn't noticed before that Keelin wasn't much taller than her. For some odd reason, it made her feel a sort of affinity toward the woman. "I apologize for disturbing you, but there are a few invitations that need to be personally addressed before you leave in the morning."

"Invitations?" Esme waved Keelin over to the seating area. "For what?"

"The ball, Your Majesty." She placed a wooden box on the table between them and lifted the lid.

A few? There were at least two dozen sheets of thick parchment with gilded edges inside. She looked up. "The ball?"

"Yes, of course. On the final night of the Festival of Tahra. It's not far off."

Esme nodded distractedly, recalling a few threads of conversation about the festival.

"It's customary for the hostess to write personal notes to guests of honor," Keelin continued.

"Guests of honor?"

"The noblemen, Your Majesty. The...*eligible* noblemen." Keelin gave her a meaningful look. "Though many will likely arrive before the celebration begins, the ball will provide an ideal setting for official introductions to be made."

Not this again, she inwardly groaned. Hadn't she made her position on the topic perfectly clear?

"Your Majesty?" Keelin leaned forward. "You will return before the ball, will you not?"

Gritting her teeth, Esme forced a smile and replied, "Yes. I will." She cleared her throat. "These, uh, noblemen...they won't be expecting to meet with me before, will they?" As long as she didn't have a pack of prospective consorts yipping at her heels, trying to gain her attention for weeks on end, then she might deign to dance with one or two of them at the ball.

"No! Certainly not. That would be improper. Most will take up residence in the city, though I'm sure some will request an apartment here in the palace. But they won't be introduced until that night."

"And if some arrive while I'm away, they won't know I'm not here, at the palace?"

Keelin shook her head. "They won't know your whereabouts, no. Though I'll bet a few of the bolder gents will take it upon themselves to contrive chance meetings. But I'll have a word with the staff—make sure they have plenty of excuses up their sleeves so as to lead them astray." She hummed to herself, her eyes twinkling with amusement. "I imagine it'll be quite entertaining, watching all the men scurry about looking for you," she remarked before her eyes went wide. "Apologies, Your Majesty. I didn't mean to jest."

"No, no. Don't apologize. I appreciate the visual." Esme's lips turned up into a sincere smile. "It's a shame I'll miss it."

Keelin pulled her lips between her teeth, trying to conceal another grin. "Well, I should be going. If you would? Before you leave?" She gestured toward the box of invitations and gave Esme a beseeching look.

"I'll do my best."

Once Keelin left, Esme pulled out one of the invitations. The script was neat, with a few sweeping embellishments. The royal seal was positioned with prominence at the top. And at the bottom was ample space for a personal note—a personal note to a man she'd never met. Absurd.

With a sigh, she read through the details on the invitation.

Invitation. An invitation meant the event was exclusive. Only those with wealth or status would be invited, deemed worthy of attending a ball at the palace.

It'd always been that way, she knew. Though in her youth, celebrations merely meant an opportunity to sneak sweets with Cadwyn before the festivities commenced. She recalled a lavish tower of glazed, sparkling confections designed to honor the goddess of fertility.

Esme scrutinized the invitation in her hand. It felt like a sham. How could they celebrate the gift of fertility as barrenness spread across their land?

But then, it wasn't really about the goddess Tahra. Festivals never truly were. At least not in Tremaene. They were simply an excuse for the nobles throughout the kingdom to flaunt their wealth.

Another memory pressed to the front of her mind. It was of the harvest festival back in Debarrow, where everyone would come together to enjoy one another's company, to share in the bounty summer had granted. A true celebration.

———————

Esme scooted her chair forward and stared down at the stack of invitations. She'd drawn the curtains so the eddying lights in the night sky wouldn't divert her attention.

She'd skipped her meeting with Sully and Tearlach to discuss details about the trip—claiming she'd had too much to do. She trusted whatever decisions they'd make, so long as they got her into the mountains. But in truth, she hadn't attended the meeting because of Tearlach.

After hearing his conversation with Cora, Esme had resolved to get over her problematic feelings. And she would. It would simply be easier if she wasn't in such close proximity to him for a while.

Then, after successfully avoiding him all day, Cadwyn had swept into her room with a cart laden with food and drink, followed by Armel, Hazel, Killian, Sully, and Tearlach.

Luckily, she'd been saved from so much as looking in Tearlach's direction by Killian's lively retelling of his match against Roderick's fire daggers.

All Esme needed was to keep Killian by her side the entire journey, which—she glanced at the clock on the mantel and let out a breath—was set to commence in a matter of hours.

She eyed the numerous invitations that each required a personal line. Setting the first one in front of her, she aligned it squarely with the edge of the desk and poised her pen above the empty space near the bottom.

Minutes ticked by, but she couldn't lower her pen.

A drop of black ink fell onto the thick paper. Thin rivulets spread out along the grain. Esme stared at the strange pattern it made, then pushed back her chair and strode across the room.

She needed something comforting. Just for an hour. Then, she swore she'd return and finish the job.

Harlow and Cahir came to attention as she swung open her doors.

"I thought I might go downstairs to the—" She paused at the sound of distant voices. Ones she recognized.

Taking a few tentative steps forward, she peeked around the corner of the alcove. Only the flicker of evening flames lit the space, but Esme could clearly make out the man with the large build at the end of the corridor. And the smaller woman standing before him.

The woman reached over to grip Tearlach's crossed arms, her golden hair glinting in the shifting light as her head tipped up.

"Are you sure?" Sheridan's voice rose with concern.

For the second night in a row, Esme strained to hear a conversation that was not meant for her.

"There's nothing to worry about," Tearlach's deep voice rumbled.

"But what if there's danger? You'll put your life on the line—for your kingdom. How can I not worry about that?" Sheridan pleaded.

Tearlach didn't respond right away, and Esme worried he'd become aware of her presence. She was only a few paces outside her room, surely he couldn't sense the exact spot where she stood. Could he?

"If it comes to that," he admitted. At Sheridan's responding gasp, Esme gritted her teeth. "If danger befalls *my queen*, then yes, I will."

Hearing the emphasis of his words, Esme's lips parted. It was *her* Tearlach had sworn his life to, not the kingdom, not even the crown. *Her.*

If a bound protector was all he could ever be to her, it was enough. More than enough.

It had to be.

"But you'll be back before the ball? You promise?" Sheridan practically purred, her earlier worry so easily forgotten. She rose up on her toes and placed her hands possessively on Tearlach's chest. "I think I might be able to sneak away that night, what with all the fuss going on."

Esme jerked her gaze away as a bitter taste crawled up the back of her throat. She batted away the image of the two of them stealing away to a linen closet—or worse, his bedchamber—and made a dash for the stairs. Her soft-soled slippers were silent on the marble floors, and she hoped Tearlach wouldn't notice or sense that she'd ventured away from her room until she'd reached the kitchens.

Can I order him not to leave my side the night of the ball? Esme scolded herself for the unseemly thought.

Although, she considered more seriously, having Tearlach beside her might keep others from approaching. Like eager noblemen. A smile tugged at her lips, but she grimaced the moment her guards started down the stairs behind her—their not-so-silent footfalls loud enough to alert everyone in the palace.

Chapter Forty-Five

HEARING HER NAME again—or her title, rather—Esme forced her eyes to open. After blinking several times, she recognized Marta looming over her, holding a cup of tea.

She scrubbed her palms over her face. Her mind was blurry. She'd only gone to bed an hour earlier. Reluctantly, she pushed herself up to accept the tea, praying it was strong.

It was still dark outside, but Marta had brought up the flames in her room.

Brighid hurried out from the dressing room, murmured a greeting to Esme, then planted herself beside the open doors, twisting her hands in front of her. The air about her was frenzied, and Esme's pulse sped up. They must have let her sleep as long as they could. Perhaps the kitchen staff had alerted them about her late-night baking.

With one last swallow, she finished her tea and padded across the room. Marta held out a thick slice of buttered toast. Evidently there'd be no time to sit.

Brighid helped her into a set of plain clothes, then ushered her out before she'd even finished with the ties on her belt. Marta offered another cup of tea and a small packet that smelled of herb and goat cheese pastries. She hummed her thanks and gulped down the tea, her gaze skidding past the untouched invitations on her desk.

She handed the cup back to Marta, and accepted a dark brown cloak from Brighid. Throwing it over her shoulders, Esme told her maid, "Fetch Keelin from the west wing. Have her meet me at the stables." Brighid nodded and ran from the room.

Esme's strides were a good bit slower. Her heart was pounding with nervous energy, but her legs hadn't yet caught up. She joined Madoc and Harlow outside her room. Both wore nondescript armor and muted-colored traveling cloaks similar to her own.

"Milady," Marta called out. Esme glanced back to see her maid disappear into the dressing room before rushing back. "Your hair." She handed Esme a narrow strap.

"Thank you."

"You're welcome, Milady. And…good luck." Marta punctuated her words with a nod.

Madoc and Harlow flanked her as they hastened down the stairs. Esme wove her hair into a braid, then tied off the end and tucked it into her cloak. Her hair wasn't particularly distinct, but, combined with her exceptionally petite stature, made her identifiable.

She'd expected the palace to be quiet and empty at that hour.

Quiet it was. Empty it was not.

It appeared as though every servant had taken it upon themselves to rise and begin their tasks early. Hours early. The corridor was busy with hushed activity—a broom sweeping invisible dirt, a rag dipped into clean water washing an already sparkling patch of tiles, arms laden with fresh sheets and blankets to make up beds that would still be occupied. Outside, the groundskeepers seemed equally ambitious. Apparently, the hedges that bordered the south steps had grown so much during the night that waiting until sunrise to prune them was unthinkable.

Esme grinned at the sight, but kept her head down. At least they distracted her from the fluttering anxiety in her stomach. She unwrapped her parcel and started on one of the pastries as they approached the stables.

The gravel yard was teeming with grooms, stablehands, horses, and guards. Due to the mountains, they wouldn't travel by carriage, so every mount was weighed down by supplies.

Madoc and Harlow went to ready their own horses as Esme popped the last bite of pastry into her mouth, looking back to search the dimly lit grounds for Brighid and Keelin.

"Hagen has your mount ready," Cadwyn called over. Esme turned, taking in Cadwyn's calm, collected appearance as she breezed past. But seeing the deepened hue of her green eyes, Esme knew she was anything but. "The one with the trilby hat," she threw over her shoulder before Esme could ask which one Hagen was.

She found said man holding the reins of a silver mare with a dappled neck. Even if she hadn't known who Hagen was, she would've guessed that the shortest mount was for her.

After Hagen introduced her to the horse, Esme stroked her cheek slowly—allowing the animal to get accustomed to her. She admired the long, dark lashes that framed her big obsidian eyes, and contemplated suitable names.

A blur of motion caught her attention. Brighid raced across the packed earth of the paddock with Keelin following close behind. The councilor's arms were wrapped around her midsection, keeping her cloak from revealing what Esme could only assume were nightclothes beneath.

Brighid stopped a few paces away and Keelin stepped past her. "Your Majesty," she greeted, slightly out of breath.

"I'm sorry to have woken you at this hour, but I needed to speak with you before I left."

"You didn't finish the invitations." Her voice implied she'd already suspected as much.

"No, I didn't. But that's not it." Esme smoothed her hand along Edlyn's coat—deciding Edlyn was a fitting name—then faced Keelin. "I've decided to open up the celebration—the ball—to the entire kingdom."

Keelin's eyes went wide. She blinked. Then blinked again.

Esme waited.

After a moment, Keelin ventured, "It won't go over well with the council."

Esme gathered a deep breath, ready to explain her decision. Then she noticed the gleam in Keelin's eyes.

"Consider it done, Your Majesty."

"I...uh...thank you."

Keelin curtsied as best she could with her cloak wrapped so tightly around her, then set off toward the palace with Brighid in tow.

After letting out a long-held breath, Esme returned to her horse, feeling more at ease. But as she moved her hand down Edlyn's neck, brushing aside her thick mane, she looked to the saddle.

The last time she'd been on a horse had been with Tearlach, which had hardly been a leisurely promenade. Prior to that, she hadn't ridden since the age of fifteen. Suddenly, Esme regretted all the hours she'd spent in the training yard instead of the stables.

Her eyes traveled down the thick straps to the foot loop at the end. Edlyn might have been the smallest mount, but every horse in Tremaene was bred tall and sturdy. She frowned at the loop, dangling several inches higher than her foot could possibly reach. As Esme searched the paddock for a groom or stablehand to help her up, Tearlach marched over.

Without preamble, he ordered in a low voice, "You'll stay close to me during the journey."

Esme stared at him for a breath, then nodded and returned her attention to Edlyn's shiny coat. She understood that Tearlach would use his magic to shield her. Still, she gritted her teeth at his mandate. It was a precaution he wouldn't bend on, no matter that it impeded greatly on her plans to keep the entirety of the royal guard between her and Tearlach.

"Do you really think there's any danger out there?" she questioned pointlessly.

"There are always dangers," Tearlach answered in a rough, gravelly voice that made Esme wonder if he'd slept at all the night before.

Banishing the thought of what he might have spent his night doing, she spun around, folding her arms at her chest. "Fine," she bit out.

Tearlach held her gaze, his eyes narrowing slightly. Esme debated telling him the truth about the Triskele just to break the building tension, but resisted. Better to wait until they were well on their way.

Lifting his eyes, Tearlach openly surveyed her horse, then returned his attention to Esme.

"What?" she snapped. "Don't I get my own horse? Or do you want to strap me to yours again?"

"I never strapped you in," he corrected evenly.

"Strange. I felt like a prisoner on that journey." Esme inched her chin up.

The muscles in Tearlach's jaw bulged, and the air between them seemed to vibrate, prickling the exposed skin on her neck. Finally, his chest heaved with an exasperated breath. He inspected the horse again.

Esme opened her mouth, set to protest whatever objections he had about her mount, then yelped when he grabbed her by the waist and swung her up. Her hands flew to his forearms reflexively, feeling his muscles tighten beneath her palms before the backs of her legs connected with the saddle.

When he released her, Esme could only stare back.

Tearlach's gaze raked over her once more, snagging at her hip.

Esme looked down. Her cloak had fallen open, revealing the dagger she'd tucked into her belt—the one he'd given her in Altan. The one he'd had crafted for her. Just like the slightly charred protective garments she wore beneath her plain clothes.

Their eyes locked once more before Tearlach stalked away.

It was only then that Esme realized she was stuck on her horse, and would remain there for the foreseeable future. Tentatively, she circled Edlyn around, getting a feel for the reins.

Sully approached, a smile claiming his features. "It's been an age since I've seen you on a horse." He looked her over as he patted Edlyn's shoulder.

"I think you mean a filly." She smirked.

"Well, she might have been. But I see you've managed without the double mounting block this time."

Esme huffed a laugh, then grew more serious. "Sully, I think I've been too hasty." She glanced around to make sure no one would overhear.

Sully moved closer. "What is it, my dear?"

"I haven't received confirmation from the Triskele. About the meeting." She held her breath, but to Sully's credit he didn't ask why she'd proceeded with her plans without one. And she wasn't prepared to tell him about the sacred pool just yet.

"The truth is, I only sent them the letter a few days ago. I told them when and where to meet. I...well, I assumed they'd agree, that there'd be no point in waiting. But now...I'm worried the letter might not reach them in time, or that they won't agree to my terms. Sully, what if—"

"I'm sure they'll receive your letter," he soothed. "I know they seemed circumspect in their correspondence—and for good reason—but they've kept the land alive in the mountains. They formed a sect for that sole purpose. They want to help. And once they hear that you're coming to them—that you've left the palace, and are venturing to the northernmost reaches of the kingdom solely to meet with them—they'll be humbled. I've no doubt they'll receive you." He took her hand. "Have you told anyone else? Tearlach?"

"No," she breathed.

Sully gave a solemn nod.

"If they send a reply, will you deliver it to me?"

"The moment it arrives," he promised.

Esme exhaled, feeling her shoulders relax.

"Now..." Sully released her hand and patted the top of it. "Stay vigilant out there. And let your guards do their job." He gave her a meaningful look.

"I will."

"Come back soon, my dear."

A whistle drew her attention. Tearlach rode toward the eastern service gate, then brought his mount around to face their group.

Esme looked back down at Sully. "You won't even notice I'm gone." She winked.

He gave a tight smile that didn't meet his eyes before stepping out of her path.

Her own smile dropped as she walked Edlyn forward, listening to Tearlach's quiet, yet assertive orders.

Cadwyn caught up with her before she reached the others. "Be safe," she ordered, reaching up to grip Esme's forearm.

"I will. I promise."

Cadwyn pursed her lips together, then went to stand with Sully.

When Esme joined the others, Tearlach gestured Armel and Killian forward. Killian led Madoc and Harlow through the gates, heading north, while Armel veered south with Roderick and Cahir.

Esme ducked her head and pulled the hood of her cloak up, hiding her features in shadow. When she looked up, she found Tearlach watching. He shifted his attention to Quinlan, who joined them at the front. Her ability to perceive events moments before they happened meant she'd likely remain at the head of the line for the entire journey.

Myles sidled up beside Esme, offering a crooked, slightly tired, smile.

Tearlach craned his neck to see past them. Esme glanced over her shoulder at Hazel, who gave a curt nod. Tearlach turned and urged his mount through the gates. The rest of them followed. They kept their formation tight as they wended through the sleeping neighborhoods.

Esme offered up prayers to the gods Muirín, Tahra, Tuireann, and Aeveen that she'd find the sacred pool, that the women of the Triskele would meet her at the temple, and that she and her guards would return to the palace safely when it was all through.

As they exited the city through the eastern gates—the city guards conveniently absent from their posts—Esme scanned the horizon and spotted a lone wolf standing at attention near a copse of tall oaks. He seemed to be watching, as if he'd ventured out of the woods just to see her off. At least, she hoped that was the reason for the rare sighting. She needed a bit of luck.

With the city wall behind them, Tearlach spurred his horse on, setting a clipped pace. Esme leaned forward and held tight to her reins. They rode hard for nearly a quarter hour before she caught sight of the other two factions closing in. She exhaled with relief, her hands already aching from her tight grip on the straps. But Tearlach merely glanced at Armel, then Killian, before returning his focus straight ahead. Without slowing his pace.

Esme whimpered and adjusted her grip.

Chapter Forty-Six

THEY HEADED WEST, the lights of the night sky casting everything in shades of muted green. Esme hadn't before seen where the vegetation faded, but when a tingle of magic began creeping up her feet and legs, she knew there was only barren dirt beneath Edlyn's pounding hooves. When they reached a wooded area, she looked up and saw only silhouettes of bare, twisting branches cutting through her view of the sky.

The further she got from Meallán, the more she felt the trapped magic. It called to her. She pushed against the building pressure. With so many hundreds of channels destroyed, she feared the magic would do anything to reach the surface. Even seek another outlet.

The Loinnir Lights faded into a dull, purplish-gray sky as they reached the northern boundary of the woods. The sun rose in the west. The simple gradient of warm colors in yet another cloudless sky seemed bland, uninspired. Once they resumed their fast pace across the bleak countryside, Esme embraced the speed, feeling the magic chasing her beneath the dried, tamped grasses.

Her breaths shortened as the pressure increased. She fought it back, grateful that the control over her magic had improved so vastly since last she'd traveled over the barren land, when life had sprung up freely in her wake.

Not only that, her magic was stronger too. Battling Orianna had awakened her abilities fully. She just hadn't realized how closely connected she was to the source of it all.

The raw magic beat against her in waves, trying to force its way through her. But Esme held strong.

When they stopped midday, she was exhausted, her muscles aching from the constant strain. The others unpacked food beyond their corralled horses, but Esme stayed atop hers, unable to move. She took several deep breaths and stared down at the dried, matted scrub. What would happen when her feet hit the ground?

Something touched her knee and Esme flinched.

Killian lifted his hand. "I called your name. More than once."

"Oh. I'm sorry. I..." Esme looked at him for a long moment before Killian gently pried her hands from the reins and tossed them over Edlyn's mane.

"Are you okay?"

She shook her head. "No—I mean, yes. I'm okay. Just tired...I suppose." She shook her head again. It'd never been so difficult to form a sentence.

Killian pressed his mouth into a line and gave her a nod, even though he looked like he didn't believe her claim.

Esme didn't protest when he reached across her to grab hold of her waist. He set her down gently, but didn't release her right away. Her legs were certainly fatigued from riding, but that wasn't why she could barely stand. Her bones were vibrating, and she worried the building pressure of the magic might erupt from her at any moment.

But then...why couldn't she let it out? She trusted her guard, didn't she? They were far enough from any village or farmstead that no one would witness the display beyond her party. And it would revive a barren swath of land. There was no reason not to.

Carefully, Esme relaxed her hold.

Pain tore through her. She barely managed to stifle a cry as her knees gave out.

Killian caught her, lowering her carefully to the ground. "What is it? What happened?" he asked frantically, running his hands over her face and arms, looking for the origin of her pain.

Esme clenched her teeth so hard she feared they might break, but she managed to force the magic back once again. She took a shaky breath, then felt the cool patch of newly grown turf padding her knees. "It's my," she croaked. "My legs."

"Oh, you poor thing." Killian gave her a sympathetic half smile. "I guess you're not used to this kind of riding."

She closed her eyes, trying to quell the rising nausea.

"Come here." Killian moved his hands under her arms and started to lift her.

"No," she yelped.

Killian stopped, his eyes going wide.

"Just…let me sit here for a bit." His eyes clouded with concern, so she added, "I'm fine, really. Go and join the others."

"You're sure?" He leaned back, but didn't look like he wanted to leave her.

"I am. I'll be over in a minute."

Killian stood, assessing her. When she forced a smile, he reluctantly turned away.

Esme pushed back into a crouch. Thick blades of grass crowded the dried brush beneath her. Beyond, bright green shoots poked through the dead, knotted brush, spreading out nearly three paces in every direction.

She rose slowly, then ambled over to a large clump of brittle yellow stalks. They pulled free easily from the loose dirt. Esme grabbed two handfuls and went back to cover the evidence.

She was fairly certain that only Killian had witnessed her pain, but Tearlach might have felt it. And if either suspected what was going on, they'd try to send her back, deeming the trip too dangerous for her.

Which, she realized, it was.

If she opened herself up to the pressure that had been building for nearly a decade again, it might very well kill her.

———

By the time they stopped for the night, Esme's legs were numb, her bones ached, her ears were ringing so badly she could barely hear, and her skin felt feverish. The uncomfortable prickling sensation had only intensified, feeling like sharp talons clawing their way under her skin.

She couldn't dismount. After fighting back the indomitable invasion for an entire day, she didn't have the strength to touch the ground, to risk the connection. She feared one touch would break the dam she was barely keeping in place, and kill her instantly—not to mention what the eruption of raw magic would do to everyone nearby.

Esme only had one choice.

Reluctantly, she summoned Tearlach. *I need your help.*

Not a second later, Tearlach was at her side, looking her over. "What's wrong?"

"I need you to—" Esme pulled in a strained breath, then unclenched one of her hands, reaching out to him. "I need you to take some of my magic," she whispered, her voice quavering. "As much as you can."

Tearlach opened his mouth, then closed it. He looked at her trembling, outstretched hand, then at the other one gripping the reins so hard her knuckles were white.

His eyes dropped to the barren ground.

"Does it hurt?" he asked, almost too quietly.

"It'll hurt more if I let it through me."

Tearlach didn't need to touch her to siphon her magic, but he took her hand anyway. Blackness filled her vision as her magic drained, leaving her feeling weightless and dizzy. He drew every last drop, until no trace of her magic remained. Without it, her connection to the source was temporarily severed. And she could finally breathe.

Esme slumped forward, her pain vanishing. Her cheek—wet with tears—pressed against Edlyn's coarse mane as her eyes closed. But before sleep could claim her, Tearlach swept her off the horse and into his arms.

Through the haze of exhaustion, she registered him rummaging through her horse's pack for a bedroll. She blinked several times trying to come awake, and gripped his arm before he could reach for her tent.

"Tearlach."

He glanced down at her, mouth a firm line.

"You need to put me down."

He reached for the tent poles.

"Tearlach," she said louder, forcing him to stop. "I can't have you carrying me into camp like this." She waited for him to realize that she was right. "I'm okay, really." At least, she needed to appear so if he—or any of her guards—was going to allow her to continue the journey. "Besides"—she tried to wriggle out of his hold to no effect—"I need to eat something."

With a great sigh of reluctance, he set her carefully on her feet. Esme's legs were still unsteady, so when Tearlach slowly released her, she swayed and placed a hand against Edlyn's flank.

Tearlach eyed her intently, his hands hovering inches away, prepared to catch her again. But she managed to straighten away from her horse.

Tearlach tucked the bedroll under her arm. "Eat quickly, then go and lie down before you collapse," he ordered.

Esme clambered toward the glowing embers of a perfect fire that only Hazel could have summoned. The smell of warm bread made her stomach rumble and had her footsteps quickening.

She was ravenous.

Chapter Forty-Seven

THE MORNING SUN cast a warm glow inside the confines of Esme's tent. A tent Sully had been adamant about. She'd refused at first, but with the pleading look he'd given her—as if a canvas sheet could somehow offer the kind of protection her nine guards couldn't—she'd relented.

Stretching her arms over her head, she wondered at the time. The sun was up; why hadn't anyone woken her? Then the smell of oversteeped tea and oatcakes wafted in, and Esme knew she hadn't overslept much.

Tearlach's silhouette took up an entire panel of her small tent. Had he been standing there all night? She couldn't recall much after stumbling inside the evening before. Pulling her knees up, she realized one foot had been sticking out beneath one of the flaps, and that both of her boots were still on. Her jacket too.

Tearlach was gone by the time she emerged. A few twists of her pant legs, and a tug at her shirt had her looking almost refreshed. The restful night had helped, though she still felt like she could sleep through the day, and perhaps into the next.

She stood for a moment taking in the surrounding area. No wonder she hadn't woken with the others. Aside from the clattering of cups and pots, and sporadic conversation, it was far too quiet. There were no birds to herald the morning, no woodland creatures scampering through the brush, no flowers opening to the sun. There was nothing. Only remnants of a once thriving forest.

Feeling the same kind of emptiness inside her, she reached for her magic. But her well was still depleted. Tearlach must have pulled more from her when he'd sensed it replenishing. It felt strange without it. Though she'd only had her magic for less than a year, it'd become a part of her, an extension of her. Without it she felt a bit lost.

A feeling she'd need to get used to.

With a sigh, she went to join the others around the cold fire pit. A pot of tea was being passed around while Roderick cooked oatcakes on a copper skillet with his bare hands.

By the time she finished eating, she felt better. The food had managed to fill some of the emptiness inside of her. Sitting back, she watched Roderick scoop the last of the batter onto the hot skillet, and remembered the pastries she'd packed.

Returning a moment later, she unwrapped the small, rectangular pastries and asked if Roderick could warm them. Not one for words, he merely grunted, brushed the leftover crumbs off the skillet and held it out for her. Esme placed them side by side, and Roderick settled the skillet between his hands. Esme watched as though she might see the magic radiate from his skin. But aside from the auburn streaks in his messy locks that complemented his talent quite nicely, Roderick simply looked like a man holding a skillet. The sweet smell of cooked apples filled the air as the edges browned a touch more. When steam escaped from the slitted vents, Roderick raised an eyebrow in question.

"Perfect!" She clasped her hands together and grinned. "Try one."

Roderick picked one up. The pastry looked tiny in his hand, and disappeared in only two bites. Esme smiled as his eyes closed in bliss.

Needing no encouragement, Killian and Myles each reached for one. "You made these?" Myles managed before he stuffed the whole thing in his mouth. Killian simply gave her a knowing look.

Madoc leaned over to Quinlan and quietly asked, "What kind of fruit is this?" He eyed his half-eaten pastry with suspicion.

"Mmm…" Quinlan took a small bite as if to savor it. "Who cares?"

Tearlach took a seat on the log beside her, his hair wet from washing. He grabbed the last plate of oatcakes, and Esme offered him one of the pastries. When he bit into it, he gave her the same knowing look Killian had—though Tearlach's might have veered slightly more toward frustration.

His hand brushed against her hip as he stole the copper cup balancing on the log between them. Taking a too-large gulp, Esme squeaked in protest.

He handed it back to her, his nose scrunching in distaste. "Can't you just drink it black like the rest of us?"

"Can't you just enjoy the simple delight of a little sweetness?"

He shook his head without looking up from his plate. Esme took a sip and hummed in pleasure to irritate him further. When it provoked a growl, she smiled.

Killian caught her eye as she brought the cup back to her lips. She glanced at the others. They were all staring. Killian flicked his eyes toward Tearlach—who still hadn't looked up from his food—then cocked his head to the side meaningfully.

Esme felt her cheeks go warm. "Where's Hazel?"

"She's with Harlow and Cahir," Killian offered, licking apple filling off his finger with a smirk. Myles jerked a thumb over his shoulder, indicating the direction they'd gone.

Esme snatched one of the remaining pastries, and almost tripped over the log in her attempt to escape.

The dry, brittle undergrowth crunched under her boots as she searched for Hazel. The quiet had become disconcerting. Even in the coldest months of winter in the mortal realm animals were active, birds chirped, rivers hummed beneath a thick layer of ice.

But around her, nothing lived. It felt eerie. Unnatural.

Esme found Hazel not far from camp, leaning her shoulder against a tree with gray, patchy bark.

"I thought you might want—"

Hazel lifted her bow and soundlessly pulled back the string.

"Oh—" Esme started, then lowered her voice. "I...Sorry, I..." She didn't finish, her eyes drawn to where Hazel had her arrow aimed.

Esme squinted at the cluster of bare trees in front of a small outcropping, searching for her guard's mark. But saw nothing.

Harlow was positioned a dozen paces away with an arrow nocked and aimed at the same location. Esme looked between them, then at the outcropping again.

Hazel loosed an arrow at the same moment Esme saw something shift in the smooth surface of the rock face. *Cahir.*

The arrow hit solid rock and splintered. Hazel cursed under her breath.

Esme widened her field of vision, watching for the subtlest of movements. Her eyes flicked to the right, but it was only Harlow taking up a new position, her bow trained on the wide trunk of a tree.

"That for me?" Hazel asked.

"Huh? Oh, yes," Esme answered, remembering the pastry clutched. Amazingly, she hadn't crushed it.

Hazel traded Esme her bow and took the proffered treat, devouring it ungracefully. Esme held back a grin and glanced in the direction Harlow seemed to be tracking Cahir, though she still couldn't find anything amiss among the boulders and trees.

"Hmm. Was that...cardamom?"

Esme smiled, remembering that Hazel used to work in the kitchens in Altan. "That's right."

Hazel looked her up and down. "Not bad."

"Thank you." She nodded as Hazel turned her attention back to Cahir's whereabouts. "Listen, Hazel, I've been meaning to ask you..." Esme trailed off, watching Harlow creep closer. The woman's eyes were locked on the ground near one of the larger rocks. She risked another step and pulled her bowstring back. But a vine—brittle and brown—whipped around her, binding her arm.

The bow fell to the ground, out of reach. Harlow growled in frustration and threw something with her other hand. Esme felt the ripple of her air magic a moment before something heavy crashed to the ground beside a tree. Cahir unblended from the crumbling bark, where a dagger was embedded an inch above his shoulder.

"Should've bound them both," Harlow taunted, wiggling the fingers of her free hand as she gave a cocky grin. Cahir sighed and reached up to pull out the dagger.

"Did you need something?" Hazel asked, releasing the string from her bow. Esme furrowed her brow until Hazel looked up. "Earlier. You started to ask me something."

"Oh. Right..." Esme paused, reconsidering what she'd intended to ask. Hazel wouldn't want the position, would she?

But then, maybe she would.

Or she'd laugh at her.

Yes, Esme decided, that was the most likely outcome.

When Hazel cocked her head, Esme exhaled heavily and asked anyway. "I want you to be a lady-in-waiting."

Hazel pulled back and lifted her chin, staring down at Esme. "You don't want me." She shook her head and swung her bow and quiver over her shoulder.

Esme suddenly worried she'd misread everything. Maybe they weren't growing closer. Maybe Hazel was only being genial because of who Esme was.

"I'm...not noble-born," Hazel clarified.

"What?" Esme gaped at her. That was her reason?

Hazel ducked her head, but Esme could see the color rising on her cheeks.

"Cadwyn wasn't either. Her mother worked as a laundress in the palace. She was fourteen when I was born, but still the closest in age to me. When I was older, we became friends. A few years later, my mother appointed her to the position."

Hazel averted her gaze. "I didn't know that about her." She faced Esme again and scrunched her brows together. "Would I...have to wear dresses?"

"Only if you want," Esme rushed out, then fought the smile that threatened.

With a cautious nod, Hazel told her, "I'll think about it."

Chapter Forty-Eight

IT TOOK TWO more days of hard riding for them to reach the Clavlin Ridge. As the evening light began to fade, they stopped to make camp. Esme dismounted Edlyn easily, looking toward the rocky escarpment beyond the trees.

She spared a glance over her shoulder, then picked her way through the dead undergrowth. The ridge in that place wasn't a sheer wall of rock as she'd previously seen, but the continental divide was still imposing, and there was no indication of a passageway. She looked off to the east, worried they were too far from where she believed the sacred pool to be. How long would it take her and Tearlach to reach the site?

It'll be fine, she told herself. Even if the detour took longer than anticipated, the others would never know. She took a deep breath, inhaling the scent of dry wood and decaying leaves. If only there were a chill to the air, she could convince herself that winter was coming.

Esme raised her eyes to the dim glow of the Loinnir Lights. Night hadn't quite fallen, but she could still tell that the lights were weaker, without even a wisp of color through the milky swirls. There was little magic to reflect—nothing from the land, nothing from her.

Movement caught her eye, and Esme looked just as a hawk took flight from a high branch.

Sully?

She hurried to the tree and looked skyward, trying to see the direction the hawk had gone. Something crunched under her heel. Lifting her boot, she found a small folded piece of parchment amid the blanket of moldering leaves.

Esme darted a glance to where the others were setting up camp, but no one seemed to be watching or even looking in her direction. She crouched down to retrieve it. The symbol on the outside fold was that of the Triskele.

For some reason, the relief she expected to feel didn't come. Had they agreed to her terms? Refused?

After staring at the letter for a prolonged moment, she managed to shove her worries to the back of her mind. Turning her back to the camp, Esme opened it, fingers fumbling over the many folds.

She scanned the text, barely reading the words. When she reached the bottom, she clenched her eyes shut and exhaled, clutching the letter to her chest.

They'd agreed.

After reading it through twice more, she returned to find Killian and Hazel arguing beside a freshly dug fire pit. The image was familiar and oddly comforting. Before their squabble progressed any further, Roderick stepped forward and summoned the fire. Esme bit back a grin at the ferocious looks Killian and Hazel threw at their fellow guard.

The sharp cry of a hawk drew everyone's attention, and Esme turned to see Sully diving toward the ground. With a flash of light, he shifted into his Fae form, landing lightly on his feet.

Esme started toward him, but Tearlach reached him first. With a sigh, she settled in front of the fire and grabbed a loaf of crusty bread. Onions, root vegetables, and dried lentils went into a large pot. A hunk of cured meat was set off to the side. It wouldn't go in until she'd gotten her portion. As Esme sawed thick slices of bread from the loaf, her eyes darted over to Tearlach and Sully. She tried to discern the tone of the conversation, but could only see Tearlach's face. And as always, his expression was impassive.

When they finished, Esme hurried over, eager to catch Sully alone.

"What was that about? What's wrong?"

Sully chuckled and took her by the shoulders. "Everything is fine, my dear. The kingdom is in good hands with Lord Lennox."

Esme let some of the tension leave her body.

"Winifred asked that I assure you of her progress. She explained that most of the requests that have come in since you left the palace have been substantiated. They need only your signature upon your return."

"Most of the requests?"

"She expressed concern about two documents, and plans to review them with you personally."

Esme nodded. Only two? That wasn't bad.

"You chose well, inviting Winifred to assist in such matters."

"She's...been most helpful. You all have."

Sully bowed his head. "Now...I do have a few requests from Keelin." He offered a reluctant grin.

Esme groaned. "Tell me."

Sully pulled a small roll of paper from his jacket. "Keelin would like to know what *theme* you've envisioned for the cuisine. She can have the kitchens prepare the traditional fresh or lightly cooked options to honor the goddess Tahra, but wondered—since you've opened the ball up to the entire kingdom"—Sully's mouth curved up at the corners—"if you'd be amenable to a broader representation of the delicacies offered by each territory. She also requires a decision about the color scheme. She's listed—let's see—seven combinations for you to—"

"Sully," Esme stopped him.

"I know. Let's say I ask Cadwyn about these."

"Yes. Thank you. But...don't let Keelin know. Tell her the choices were mine."

"Consider it done, My Queen."

———————

They packed before the sun had even crested the western horizon. Myles took the lead, guiding them farther west until he found what he was looking for—a cleft that was barely wide enough for one horse. Tediously, they removed saddlebags and passed them through. Thankfully, after a hundred yards or so, the narrow path widened slightly.

The trail—if one could call it that—curved and cut back, never straightening for more than a dozen paces at a time. But it was undoubtedly more direct than the wide pass through the gentle sloping foothills farther west. The Northern Rebels had taken nearly a week to traverse that route, which was time they didn't have.

When the incline grew too steep for the horses, they were forced to dismount and hitch the animals together. Myles maintained his position at the front of the line, but Esme was moved between six of her guards, with Tearlach directly behind her. Roderick and Madoc—both of whom rivaled Tearlach in build—took lead of the horses. If any of the horses stumbled, Esme didn't doubt the two of them could hold the entire line. Cahir brought up the rear, and she wondered what he might do to the rock beneath them should something more go wrong.

The incline became increasingly difficult for Esme's small stature. She stretched each stride as far as she could just to keep pace with the others. For the first hour, she'd caught looks from every one of the guards in front of her. It seemed no one believed she'd be able to keep up, and were ready to offer their assistance. But eventually the muscles in her legs grew accustomed to the deep lunges required to hoist herself up the rocky terrain. In time, her mind wandered to the Triskele. She thought about what she'd say to them when they finally met, how she might convince them to help restore the land, and what she could possibly offer as repayment.

When the path hooked sharply, Esme raised her foot onto the ledge, pressing her hand to the top of her thigh for leverage.

Her foot slipped, her ankle twisting.

Her hands shot out to break her fall, but she was yanked back.

She slammed into Tearlach's chest, and the breath was forced from her lungs.

As her feet dangled uselessly, her hands instinctively fisted in his shirt. He'd pulled off his chest plate halfway up the mountainside, which left only a thin layer of fabric between them.

Slowly, she lifted her head. Her face was only inches from his. But her eyes didn't make it past his jaw. It was rough with two days' growth, and Esme wanted desperately to know how it felt beneath her fingers, against her cheek. Would it be prickly or soft?

She felt Tearlach's breath against her forehead, and realized he still hadn't loosened his hold on her.

When she dared to look up, his gaze bored into her, intense and focused. His grip tightened even more, and she felt every inch of his body aligning with hers. They'd never been *that* close before. She could count the number of times they'd touched—every moment he'd gripped her shoulders, her arm...the morning she'd woken with him in her bed, his heat close enough to touch...when he'd swept her off her horse only days before, cradling her in his strong arms.

But none of those compared to what she felt in that moment, with their bodies flush together. Close enough to share breath. Close enough for their lips to meet.

Was he thinking the same?

The look in his eyes softened, though the intensity didn't wane. It was a look she couldn't quite decipher. One she'd never seen before.

The moment stretched until Esme slowly became aware of the quiet that surrounded them.

The others had stopped, the horses halted.

Her lungs started to burn, and she sucked in a desperate breath. "Thank you," she said in a rush, but Tearlach didn't set her down.

When the sounds of scuffing boots and shifting metal armor drifted over, it seemed to pull him back to the present. He blinked once, his eyes refocusing on her, like he'd only just realized he was still holding her up off the ground. Then, after drawing a slow, deep breath, he slid his arms down her back to grip her waist. Taking a step forward, he set Esme on top of the ledge, met her gaze once more, then gestured for Myles to resume his lead at the front of the line.

———————

They reached a small valley shortly before sunset. After scouting the surrounding area, it was deemed safe to make camp. So safe, in fact, that no one had given her a second look when, after dinner, Esme waved off Myles's offer to set up her tent and unrolled her mat on the bare rock.

Tucking her feet under her, Esme closed her eyes and waited for the sounds of conversation and clanking dishes to fade into the background as she attempted to summon a vision of the Sacred Pool of Navlin. It took a while, but when it finally appeared, she spread her senses out and tried to place its distance and direction from the camp.

All she could feel was a weak pull to the east. It was enough to go on. She only hoped they wouldn't have to search the vast mountain range for the lone tree that marked its location.

At the sounds of others settling in for the night, she glanced around and saw Tearlach surveying the perimeter. Luckily, they'd all agreed that the area was secure enough to warrant only one guard for the watch that night, or they might've had a problem.

———————

Esme stood in a clearing with an empty indigo sky above and dewy grass beneath her feet.

She breathed in the cool, damp air, and trailed her fingers through the thick layer of fog that came up to her thighs. When nothing moved in the mist, she exhaled, grateful the wolf hadn't appeared since her battle with Orianna. At least she could rest assured their journey would commence without conflict. The physical sort, anyway.

She looked instead to the dark trees that circled the glade, then turned in place. Before she'd made it halfway around, the silent wings of an owl skimmed past, rippling the air against her cheek. The clearing vanished.

Killian came into view, his sword slicing through the night air. The green from the Loinnir Lights limned his blade as it clashed with another. Esme watched Killian's heel grind into the dirt. Even with the greenish tinge of night, she knew it was the color of cinnamon, and that he was in the palace training yard.

Tearlach stepped into view, swiping his blade low before whipping it around to catch Killian's.

"You still haven't told me why you did it," Tearlach said, parrying Killian's next strike.

They circled each other. "You know exactly why. And don't even pretend you're upset about it."

Tearlach attacked with a growl.

Killian blocked, smiling.

Esme wondered what they were talking about. She examined their clothing, hoping to determine when the conversation had taken place. It was futile though. Their attire never varied much.

"Now those councilors will get their claws in her, force her to marry someone of their choosing."

That was answer enough.

"She's smarter than that, and you know it. She's not about to fall prey to their manipulations," Killian defended.

When Tearlach didn't seem convinced, Esme scowled. Did he really think her so easily influenced?

"If you don't like it, why don't you do something about it?" Killian smirked as he attacked.

"There's nothing to be done," Tearlach gritted out as he ducked clear of the sword's edge.

"Oh, there's something to be done. That's for damn sure."

Tearlach glared, then thrust his blade toward Killian's chest.

Killian blocked it, laughing.

"Esme is queen," Tearlach stressed.

"Ah, is that the reason, then?" Killian parried again, but didn't bother with a counterattack. "Funny, you didn't seem to have any qualms about her station when she and I were together."

Tearlach attacked again. When Killian did nothing more than block, Tearlach let the grip on his sword relax.

The two men stared at one another.

"She might be queen, Tearlach, but she's also a woman."

The muscles in Tearlach's jaw bulged noticeably, and Esme wondered how long he'd been denying that fact.

When Tearlach stalked off, Killian frowned, shaking his head.

A hand closed over Esme's mouth.

Her eyes shot open, but it was only Tearlach leaning over her.

When he seemed satisfied that she wouldn't startle, he released her and sat back on his heels. Their eyes met, and Esme wondered again when the conversation from the dream had happened. Before or after Tearlach had been so adamant about her choosing a consort?

It's time to go, he told her, sobering her instantly.

Esme stood and glanced around the camp. Everyone was asleep. Even the horses.

Chapter Forty-Nine

HOW LONG WILL they stay asleep? Esme asked, trying to forget the dream that emerged in her mind every time she looked at Tearlach.

As long as I wish.

She glanced over as he arched one of his dark brows menacingly.

Which way? He tightened one of the straps on his pack. Esme gestured east and Tearlach nodded. *Ready?*

For what?

It's time to move, Princess.

Esme scowled at the title. But when Tearlach took off across the flat crest of the mountain range she groaned, and quickly tightened her own straps before racing after him.

It only took a few dozen strides for her breaths to become labored. She concentrated on keeping a steady rhythm as she shifted her sights between her foot placement and Tearlach up ahead.

Aside from a few sprints in the ring, she hadn't run a notable distance since the night assassins had tracked her down at her home in Debarrow. Esme never allowed herself to linger on that memory, but as she struggled to keep up with Tearlach—feeling like a mortal herself—she let the terror of that chase drive her.

They skirted valleys, keeping to the ridges and slowing when the terrain became rough. All the while, they remained quiet. The heavy silence of night only made it worse. Even the fresh mountain air felt tight, strangling. Inevitably, Esme's thoughts returned to the dream, to the words Tearlach had spoken.

Was it possible? Did he actually feel the same about her? She darted a glance at him, then back to the ground—just in time to avoid a patch of loose stones.

If he did, then he was rather skilled at hiding it. Esme nearly laughed at the thought. He was perhaps the most inscrutable man she'd ever known.

After another quarter hour, Esme halted Tearlach. "I need to—" She took a long swig from her canteen, trying to conceal her panting. "I can't sense the pool at this pace. Give me a moment." Without waiting for a reply, Esme loosened the straps on her pack, swung it to the ground, then sat down beside it. She closed her eyes, taking slow, measured breaths until the pounding in her ears lessened.

Even without her magic, she felt the ancient power. The pull was strong. She opened her eyes and pointed slightly south of the direction they'd been heading.

When they reached a rugged incline that looked nearly impossible to traverse, Esme knew they were close. It was a place not meant to be found. But the Loinnir Lights glowed bright and vibrant above, confirming the presence of strong, concentrated magic.

As they climbed the uneven surface, littered with loose rocks, Esme kept her eyes trained on the path Tearlach established, careful not to wedge her boot into one of the narrow crevices.

At the top of the ridge, Tearlach reached back to take Esme's hand and pull her up.

Her breath caught in her throat as she took in the valley below. It only stretched a few dozen paces in either direction, but every inch was filled with lush greenery. An oasis amid the vast tract of rock.

Vines covered the gentle slope into the basin. Tufts of dark green grasses, wide purple leaves, and feathery fronds harmonized with the colors in the night sky. In the center, the thick foliage gave way to a tree so ancient it might have stood since the beginning of time. Its twisted, knotted branches reached out like a parasol—some dipping low, rooting back into the ground, others stretching wide.

"I...wasn't expecting this," Tearlach admitted. He kept his voice low, like he might otherwise disturb the stillness.

Esme looked up, finding his face a mixture of amazement and disbelief. She watched him for a moment, captivated, then glanced down at their hands, still clasped together. Tearlach hadn't released her after helping her up. She wondered if he noticed.

Her palm was warm, tingling with sensation—an awareness that felt both familiar and exciting. Something she craved.

Memories flooded her mind as she stared down at their joined hands—the ancient tree forgotten.

She remembered every moment they'd shared, every lingering touch and fervent gaze.

The dagger Tearlach had given her...

The morning she'd awoken to him in her bed...when neither had moved apart.

And later, when she'd risked kissing him on the cheek, how he hadn't pulled away. How he'd almost...leaned into her touch.

Her mind returned to the present, to their encounter on the mountainside earlier in the day. She could still feel the way Tearlach had tightened his hold on her after she'd slipped, like he couldn't bear to let her go.

Even the protective garments she wore beneath her clothes acted as a constant reminder—the small metal octagon with his initial always pressed against her skin.

But the metal tag wasn't there to warn her of the consequences of failing to wear the armor, she finally understood.

No. It was a way for him to be with her, to be close to her in some small way when he…couldn't. Its purpose had never been to protect her in the training ring. It was simply the only gift he could give her.

The only gift a guard could reasonably give his queen.

Esme lifted her eyes to Tearlach's shirt pocket, wondering if the worn note was still there, secretly tucked away, next to his heart.

She thought back on the night she'd asked if he'd been involved with anyone in Debarrow—during those long years spent alone, with nothing to occupy his time but watch over her…

Her lips parted.

I didn't leave her behind, he'd said.

Tears stung her eyes.

"You didn't leave her behind," she breathed. *You didn't leave* me *behind.*

Chapter Fifty

"WHAT?" TEARLACH TURNED. He looked down at their joined hands and released his hold instantly. When he met her gaze again, all Esme could do was repeat the words.

"You didn't...leave her behind."

Something flared in Tearlach's eyes. A spark of understanding.

How long had he stood by and watched her, wanting her? Unable to have her.

"Tearlach?" Esme risked, her voice near pleading. She moved closer—only a half a step, but he moved away, casting a glance down into the valley, toward the ancient tree.

Esme split her attention between him and the destination of the journey. It was so close—everything they sought, every answer they needed. Yet she suddenly had no desire to reach for it.

Not when Tearlach was standing beside her, making no denial of what she knew to be true.

"The pool." Tearlach still wouldn't meet her eyes. "Where is it?"

"The pool?"

"The sacred pool, where is it?" He finally turned to face her. She noticed the rise and fall of his chest increasing, the clench of the muscles along his throat.

"I...Right. It's..." She shook her head and surveyed the valley. "Beneath the tree. In the center, there." She pointed. "The pool is in a cavern beneath the tree."

Tearlach nodded and made his way down to the valley floor.

Esme watched him in what should have been disbelief, but really wasn't. What exactly had she expected of him? It was Tearlach, after all. He didn't think himself worthy of her, so why had she thought he might admit to something he'd never allow himself to act on?

Esme shoved those thoughts away, even though she knew they'd push their way to the forefront anyway. She needed to focus on why they were there.

With unsteady feet, she climbed down the rocky slope to where Tearlach was waiting.

He didn't acknowledge her, just pushed through the foliage the moment she was at his side.

The magic was close. She could feel it pulsing through the rock, up through the soles of her boots. Esme brushed away vines that curled at her touch. Tearlach moved aside stalks and fronds with a gentle hand, but the broad leaves sprang back, reaching for them both. Tall blades of grass swayed into their path, skimming their legs as they passed. It was almost as though they craved touch, like they'd been alone so long they needed to feel the strange new presence in their secret world.

If Tearlach noticed, he didn't say.

Esme was worried he wouldn't say anything for a good long while.

They ducked under one of the branches, stepping into the shadow of the tree. Esme stared at the wide trunk in the center, while Tearlach moved with purpose, circling it like a puzzle that needed solving. When he stopped and braced his hand against the tree, Esme came up beside him and pressed her own palm to the rough bark. It was warm to the touch and vibrating with magic.

"How do we get down there?" he asked in a brusque tone.

"I..." Esme lifted her hand away slowly. "I don't know," she admitted. Afraid of what she might see if she looked up into Tearlach's eyes, she stepped back, searching the moss-covered ground for some sort of entrance, a small opening, anything.

The pool was right there, beneath her boots. It was so close, yet she had no idea how to access it. Once again, she envisioned the sacred space. There was no tunnel leading into the cavern, the smooth stone walls broken only by the bunching roots at the apex.

"I think I need"—she swallowed—"some of my magic."

Tearlach narrowed his eyes at her when she looked up.

"Just a drop," she placated. "I think it needs to...recognize me."

The muscles in Tearlach's neck strained, but he didn't say a word.

"We'll need to wait for it to replenish."

Tearlach took a step closer. Esme's breath caught as his gaze raked over her. When his eyes fastened with hers, he released a long exhale and brought his hand up to cup her cheek.

Esme couldn't help but close her eyes and lean into the warmth of his hand. Every thought eddied from her mind, her awareness narrowing to his touch. She felt like she might melt into him, might—

Magic swelled inside her.

Gasping, her eyes shot open.

Tearlach pulled his hand away, curling it into a fist.

For a moment, she could only stare at the hand that had touched her as the familiar sensations of her magic spread through her body. It was only a small amount, not enough to summon a storm or grow vines from the soil beneath her. Not enough for the raw magic to mistake her for a channel. She hoped.

But that wasn't why she felt disoriented.

"You...kept my magic?" she murmured.

"Only a little," Tearlach said through clenched teeth.

Why would he keep *any*? Why hold on to magic that wasn't his? He'd sworn he'd never done such a thing—never would.

Orianna's power flashed in her mind—how the late high-priestess had thieved magic, hoarding it until she could wield untouchable power.

Tearlach's gaze became fierce, like he was silently begging her to understand why.

He's not like that, she reminded herself as her stomach soured for even considering him capable of such malice.

He couldn't be further from that greedy, tyrannical woman.

But then, why had he done it? Kept her magic?

Esme studied him. The intensity of his stare didn't waver.

Finally, she knew why. Understood his need to keep it.

So he could feel what she felt. Even if it caused pain—the pulsing summons from deep inside their world, the constant pressure of raw magic trying to invade his body with every step. He'd endure it a thousand times over, if only to have a piece of her.

Was that all he thought he could have? A drop of her magic, hidden away where no one could see?

He can have all of me, Esme confessed to herself, then clenched her teeth in an effort to stop the tears that threatened.

"Well..." She cleared her throat. "Good. Thank you. We won't...have to wait, then." She stepped back, forcing herself to concentrate on the return of her magic. On the true purpose of their journey.

Circling the tree slowly, she let the beat of the magic guide her. The closer she was to the trunk, the louder the droning in her ears became. She inched forward and reached out.

Her palm pressed against the bark.

Then pushed through it.

Her eyes widened. The tree shimmered like the surface of a lake, and for a moment she thought it might have been an illusion. But when she fluttered her fingers, the tree felt fluid, rippling around the intrusion of her hand like a current.

Tearlach's eyes were fixed on the place where her arm disappeared into the tree. When he reached out to touch the same spot, his hand collided with the surface—still solid.

Esme yanked her arm back, her eyes snapping to his.

Neither said a word. But they both knew.

He couldn't follow her in.

Chapter Fifty-One

IT DIDN'T MATTER if Tearlach held an ounce of her magic, or all of it. It wasn't enough. He wasn't *her*.

The tree only recognized her.

Tearlach stepped back, his chest expanding slowly. Esme felt the tension rippling off him, knew he wanted to rage at the ancient tree for blocking his entry, for not letting him follow wherever she went.

Finally, he gritted out, "Be quick," crossing his arms over his chest and widening his stance.

Esme nodded and turned once more to the tree, forcing herself to ignore the wealth of emotion contained in that brief command.

She pushed both of her hands into the tree. It yielded, making space for her. She sucked in a breath, held it, then closed her eyes and stepped forward.

It swallowed her, forcing the air from her lungs, like there wasn't room for more than just her inside the strange, magical place.

She couldn't open her eyes, couldn't move. Like she was being pulled under by a strong swell.

Just before her panic mounted, she felt solid rock beneath her feet.

The cloaking pressure vanished, and Esme inhaled a desperate breath.

She opened her eyes to the place she'd seen in her visions. The wide, flat rock where she stood was surrounded by a gently swirling pool. The water was clear, with white, glittering sand lining the bottom. She breathed in again, smelling the magic. It reminded her of spring, of growth.

The cavern glowed with a warm light, though she could find no source. Nor could she see the threads of memories floating through the air.

A chill swept through her. She had no idea how to retrieve Lord Luxovious's memories.

Lowering onto the rock, she studied the space. She wasn't sure what she expected—a placard of instructions nailed to the rock wall?

Tearlach, she tried, but her voice only echoed in her ears. She was truly on her own.

Deciding she had nothing to lose, Esme closed her eyes, and summoned the only image she had of Lord Luxovious. When he was clear in her mind, she wet her lips and said his name aloud. For the first time.

"I wish to see the memories of Lord Luxovious of Kearney," she enunciated carefully.

The lilt of the words reverberated off the cavern walls, drifting toward the root-covered peak before tumbling back down. Esme heard the water ripple, as though absorbing his name.

She opened her eyes to find thin strands of light floating in the air, orbiting her slowly. Each thread looked slightly different. Some were thick, glowing brightly. Others were thin, fraying. Some intertwined, then pulled apart. The soft murmur of voices reached her ears. The same voice, all of them. *His* voice.

Esme leaned back, trying to see them all at once. There were thousands. How would she ever find the memories she needed? And with only a matter of hours, she couldn't possibly view them all.

She rubbed her forehead, then dropped her hands to her lap. Not wanting to waste time with anything that wasn't relevant to the channels, she decided to start with something she already knew—a vision she'd already seen. Esme called upon the dream that had shown Lord Luxovious portraying himself as a humble farmer, seeking answers from an infamous seer.

The vision appeared in her mind, and before she could pose a question or ask to be shown a memory, a shimmering ribbon slipped away from the others and floated down, coiling neatly in her open palm. She lifted her hand, inspecting it. The thread wiggled slightly as it settled, but did nothing more.

Esme looked up at the others, then back down at the one in her hand. Slowly, she curled her fingers around it.

Her eyes were forced shut.

A memory flashed in her mind.

But it was her own. She was kneeling among rows of pumpkins and squashes, pulling weeds from the tangle of thick, fuzzy vines. It was from the year she'd spent at the Dogherty Farm, back in Periwen. Esme took in the garden, and the farmhouse in the distance, remembering the life she'd had there.

After a moment, she blinked her eyes open and smiled at the pleasant memory as it lingered in her mind.

She drew her brows together, confused, as she felt the slippery strand still in her palm.

That wasn't the memory she...

It began to fade.

Esme tried to recall what she'd just seen. Tried to imagine the feel of the soft dirt sifting through her fingers. The warmth of late summer. The smell of freshly turned soil and ripening vegetables.

But it was vanishing. Slipping away.

She chased the last echoes of it until the memory was gone.

Gone.

Until all Esme knew was that she'd lost something. Something she could no longer remember.

Something important...she thought.

Looking down, she opened her fingers to see the glowing strand in the center of her palm, and understood its cost.

Her own memories. For his.

Chapter Fifty-Two

HAVING ALREADY PAID the price, Esme curled her fingers around the strand once more. Closing her eyes, the vision she'd sought appeared in her mind. It was the same scene from her dream, only she was seeing it through Lord Luxovious's eyes. Athdara's room was as she remembered. The questions and responses were the same. And when the man who'd called himself Dougal paid Athdara and left, the memory ended.

Esme looked down and opened her hand. There was nothing there, nothing left of the strand. Her shoulders slumped forward as she stared at her empty palm, wishing she hadn't wasted one of her memories on something she'd already seen.

Lord Luxovious's memories continued to float through the cavern, waiting to be observed. Esme turned her mind to the information she needed—what *precisely* she needed—determined not to squander anything more than was necessary. Straightening her spine, she cupped her hands in her lap and organized her thoughts.

First, she needed to understand how Lord Luxovious had damaged the channels. Closing her eyes, she formed the question in her mind. Even before she finished her query, images flickered behind her eyelids.

*...Killian leaning in to tuck a loose strand of hair behind her ear...
Tearlach reaching across the boat to hand her a pouch of dates when
they'd crossed the Sea of Muirín...Cadwyn clutching her hand as they
ran down to the lake under the night sky when they were young...*

Memories emerged, then vanished. Almost too quickly to grasp.

*...a hawk taking flight from a high branch...a folded note in her
hand...her mother's arms wrapping around her...her father kissing
the top of her head as he whispered "good night"...*

His voice faded with the rest of the memories.

Tears clung to Esme's lashes as she slowly opened her eyes. What had
she lost? Looking down, she saw tangled threads mounded in her palm.
More than one, she realized. She held them in one hand and angrily wiped
the tears from her cheeks with the other, giving the memories a pointed
glare for what they'd taken from her.

"Better be worth it." She clenched her hand into a fist. Images darted
through her mind—images that thankfully weren't her own.

*...a large room...a long table covered in instruments, books, herbs,
powders...a hanging cauldron, cold and empty...the hem of a long,
black cloak grazing the stone floor...a young man with frantic eyes,
restrained to a chair, gagged by a cloth band...*

Alastar. The young man who possessed all the elements. Esme ground
her teeth, cursing Athdara for giving Lord Luxovious the boy's name.

The scenes came faster.

*...a glowing sphere suspended in the air...specks of light dotting the
vaporous surface...*

The channels, Esme guessed, noting the familiar coastline of Tremaene. The globe appeared to depict the channels across the entire world.

Only, Periwen was dark. As if no channels fed the land. Or, perhaps she'd been right about the magic of the mortal realm being concealed by the fog. A small comfort.

...steam rising from the cauldron...dark, viscous liquid pouring into small, round casts...four colorless, glass-like orbs...chanting, a hand moving over them—the skin pulling taut, darkening, finger bones lengthening, knuckles protruding...shadows slithering within the orbs...

Esme tried to make sense of what she was witnessing, memorizing every detail before each memory faded.

...Alastar stumbling down into a pit where the stone floor had been excavated...moving toward a silver rod with copper banding that plunged down into the churned earth...

It looked like he was being controlled, the way Orianna had immobilized Tearlach and the others. Esme struggled not to relive her own memories, and only barely resisted the urge to open her eyes and look away. She had to know what Lord Luxovious had done.

...Alastar convulsing in pain...reaching out to touch the rod...crying out as he collapsed onto the ground...his hand opening...an orb rolling into the dirt...no longer transparent, but opaque, concealing the shadows lurking within...lights winking out across the surface of the globe until only five channels remained...

Esme's eyes shot open as the final image disappeared.

Lord Luxovious hadn't damaged or destroyed the hundreds of channels across Tremaene. He'd used Alastar to seal them off, to block the magic from reaching the surface at all but five of the sites.

What, then, were the glass-like orbs? Esme thought back, recalling how they'd been formed. Lord Luxovious's hands had moved over them, imbuing them with something. *Dark magic?* Perhaps, given how the joints of his fingers had buckled with the intonation, how his skin had stretched and blackened. And after Alastar had held one of the orbs as magic was forced through him, it appeared changed, more solid in its opacity.

If Alastar had truly been able to funnel source magic into the orbs, perhaps they could be used as instruments, or keys of some sort.

And if Lord Luxovious had used those keys to impede the flow of magic at all but five of the channels—as evidenced in the suspended globe—then couldn't the orbs reopen the channels as well?

Hope bloomed in Esme's chest. If she could find them, she might very well be able to revive the dormant pathways.

Only, she had no idea where the orbs were located. Had they been lost? Or hidden? Destroyed?

Esme recoiled as her eyes were forced shut again. Memories were wrenched away, gone before she even realized what she'd asked.

Gathering a breath, she blinked her eyes open and found a knotted mess of strands in her palm. There were so many. She bit her lip hard, horrified by how many of her own memories were taken in exchange.

...a hammer shattering the orbs into glossy shards...a gnarled, blistered hand dropping them into molten silver...an artist presenting illustrations of the gods and goddesses...robes and silver adornments organized neatly into sets...a stone replica of a temple...calendars, lists, and drawings of the four gods papering every wall of a large study...three high-priestesses joining hands around a circle of blue flames, chanting words from the Old Language...

The scene faded, and Esme struggled to find the connection between them. While she'd never witnessed a summoning ritual herself, she was fairly certain that was what she'd been shown in the final scene. But why would Lord Luxovious have memory of such a sacred and *private* happening?

The adornments the high-priestesses had worn were the same ones she'd seen in Lord Luxovious's study. And they were all silver…

Silver that contained splintered pieces of the broken orbs.

Lord Luxovious had given the instruments to control the channels to the high-priestesses?

Esme stared unseeing at the swirling memories as a new, larger picture took shape.

What if high-priestesses hadn't been blessed by the gods to summon raw magic? And what if the Order hadn't been created as an organized effort to replenish the dwindling magic across the kingdom?

What if…

Esme could hardly believe what she was considering. Still, she had to think it through.

What if Lord Luxovious had formed the Order as a way to *control* the world's magic? To control the entire kingdom?

Esme shuddered as more pieces fell into place. The temple replicas she'd seen hadn't been replicas at all, but concepts for temples that hadn't yet been built.

Because Lord Luxovious had *made* the gods.

It'd all been a lie. Every part of it.

A chill spread across Esme's skin. It felt like the truth, as unnerving as it was. But one aspect didn't quite fit.

If Lord Luxovious had once held complete control of the boundless magic inside their world, he could have dominated the entire kingdom without the Order. Why hadn't he seized power himself? Why create an institution with little political influence?

The memories drifted slowly around her, and Esme supposed they could only reveal *events* from Lord Luxovious's life, not his motives or intentions. Looking up at the bunching roots of the tree, she wished she could reason things out with Tearlach, ask him which questions would yield the answers she needed.

Then again, she reconsidered, Lord Luxovious *hadn't* held all the power. Not really. The power to summon source magic actually belonged to the orbs. As she again visualized Lord Luxovious's hands while he'd created the vessels—the way his skin had become gray and scaly, sinking into the bony hollows—she knew it had to be the result of dark magic.

Pure magic wouldn't corrupt its conduit. Perhaps, after creating such powerful objects, he couldn't risk putting the orbs to use for fear of infecting himself in some irreparable way. And if he couldn't wield them himself, it would've been crucial for him to keep the truth of their purpose hidden.

What better place to hide such powerful objects than within a sacred institution devoted to the gods?

False gods, she had to remind herself.

So then...what had his intent been?

The pieces of the orbs were surely gone. Hidden or lost. The true origins of the Order had been concealed, possibly from the sisters themselves. High-priestesses summoned the elements as needed to sustain a constant state of growth; they never withheld magic.

Or at least...they hadn't.

Not until the insurrection.

Might Lord Luxovious have lived that long? Had he somehow compelled the priestesses to rise against Esme's father?

She stared at the gentle ripples lapping against rock, sifting through everything she knew of the insurrection. Those who'd supported the high-priestesses hadn't succeeded. In the end, they'd joined forces because—

Esme inhaled sharply as another memory was ripped from her.

Then another.

When the images faded, she peered from beneath her lashes to see a thick, ragged thread in her hand. She swallowed, hoping it was the last memory she'd have to witness, then closed her eyes and wrapped her fingers around it.

...arms reaching, looking more creature than man...legs long and twisted...dark, scaly skin stretched tight over the bony ridges of a hand...black, curving claws...

A shudder ran through her as she struggled to keep her eyes closed, to keep watching, horrified by the sight.

...legions of lesser-formed creatures swarming the mountainside, blackening the land, felling Tremaene's armies with sickening darkness...cries of dying warriors...battlefields coated in blood...charred bodies...ash...death...annihilation...

Esme forced her eyes open. She inhaled a shuddering breath, but all she could smell was burning flesh and the heavy tang of blood swamping the land.

She didn't need to see where the vision would lead. She knew. Knew exactly who that dark, twisted creature was.

"The Dark War." Her voice trembled. "He was...Lord Luxovious was the one who..." She shook her head, trying to clear the memory that would forever be seared into her mind.

It hadn't been some unnatural force that had devastated the kingdom after the insurrection had begun. Not simply some wicked monster her mother had battled in the end. *No.*

The man who'd stolen magic from the land—from her people—had turned into that...thing. That *creature.*

Only he hadn't been defeated. Not completely.

Esme didn't need to see another memory to know how the Dark War had concluded, where Lord Luxovious had ended up. Where he remained to that day.

Locked in an iron box across the sea.

Able to reach her mother through dreams. Threatening to torture the people of Tremaene should he one day escape his eternal sleep.

Her mother's magic had been strong, but the magic that had trapped Lord Luxovious—the same magic that could release him—flowed through Esme's veins too.

Sweat coated her palms. She rubbed her hands against the thick fabric of her pants, then clenched them together tight. She wouldn't dare open them to another memory. The screams of dying, burning warriors echoed in her mind. She couldn't bear to see another horror. Didn't want to think that the creature who'd devastated her kingdom might someday find her. Reach her.

"I don't want to see any more," Esme whimpered, tears clouding her vision.

Chapter Fifty-Three

BEFORE SHE REGISTERED the soft earth beneath her feet, Esme was crushed against Tearlach's chest as his muscular arms engulfed her.

She sunk into his protective embrace, breathing in his scent. He tightened his hold on her, to the point where Esme couldn't draw breath. She didn't care; she didn't need to breathe. She just needed to forget every nefarious thing she'd seen. She just needed Tearlach.

She wasn't sure how she'd made it to the surface. There'd only been an unsettling sensation of being immobilized before Tearlach had caught her up in his arms. And then the cave was gone, as if it'd never existed.

But the memories...They remained. Infecting her mind. As though *his* memories were hers.

Esme wrapped her arms around Tearlach, fisting her hands in the back of his shirt. For a moment she let herself forget. For a moment only they existed.

When her thundering heart finally began to slow, Tearlach pushed her back—abruptly. As though he'd suddenly become aware that he was holding her. So close.

Esme stumbled, taking in her first full breath, but Tearlach kept his grip on her shoulders, holding her at arm's length. His eyes roved over her, inspecting every inch. When his gaze finally met hers, she saw the last remnant of fear before it vanished from his dark eyes.

Carefully, he removed his hands, but didn't look away.

"What?" she managed, her voice weak. "What's wrong?"

Tearlach didn't respond, he only stared down at her. Had he seen everything she had? All the appalling memories?

Esme's heart started to beat more rapidly under his heavy gaze, and she forced herself to turn away. It was still dark under the canopy, but soft, honey-colored light filtered in through the branches.

Daylight.

How long had she been down there?

She spun back around, eyes wide.

"I couldn't reach you in there, couldn't go after you." The low rumble of Tearlach's voice sent shivers over her skin. "I couldn't...feel you."

Esme stared at him, unable to speak. She wanted to tell him that time hadn't passed as quickly down there, that to her it'd been no more than an hour since she'd left him. But telling him wouldn't alleviate the powerlessness she knew he felt.

"I didn't know if you were..." Tearlach exhaled, then ducked his head.

Esme wanted to close the distance between them. She wanted to put her arms around his neck and tell him she was safe. But when his eyes swept back up, locking with hers, a crash of emotion forced its way in, surging through her body, her mind, her heart.

It only lasted an instant—a flash that was there and gone in a second—but it stole her breath. She couldn't move, couldn't think past the ferocity of what Tearlach had felt when he couldn't protect her, couldn't get to her. Thunderous rage. Desperation. And the faintest hint of something deeper, something...softer. Something a warrior shouldn't feel for his queen. Something Tearlach felt nonetheless.

But it wasn't the emotions that had her staring at him. It was that he'd allowed her to feel those vulnerable parts of himself. *Wanted* her to feel them.

Before she could react, Tearlach began pacing, his long strides eating up the space between the wide trunk and the curtain of branches.

Esme watched, transfixed. The echoes of his unrestrained emotions flickered through her, making her skin prickle with sensation, soothed only by the underlying, endless devotion he had for her—a need so strong her heart faltered before kicking up into a wild beat as the remnants rippled through her one last time.

If her mind doubted before what her heart knew to be true, it no longer did. Whether Tearlach would ever admit his feelings to her or not, she knew.

"What did you find?" Tearlach's firm, detached voice sounded so at odds with what Esme knew was roiling just beneath the surface.

"What did I find?" she repeated, her mind slow to comprehend his query as she tracked his movements, back and forth.

When she said nothing more, Tearlach ceased his pacing. With two long strides he was standing in front of her, eyes searching hers. "What did you find down there?" He lowered his voice, clenching his fists at his sides. She wondered if he was fighting the temptation to touch her, to prove to himself that she was there, within reach.

Esme stepped away, letting him keep his burdensome emotions tethered. She set off, tracing the path Tearlach had tamped, suddenly understanding the merits of pacing when one's mind was crowded by demanding thoughts.

Tearlach backed away and crossed his arms over his chest, watching as she had him.

"What did I find?" Esme repeated to herself as she circled back, sifting through every piece of information she'd learned.

Everything her people had believed as absolute truth for more than a thousand years had been nothing more than a carefully crafted deception.

Lord Luxovious had not only manipulated their people with myths of all-powerful deities, he'd seized control of their world's magic as a means to gain ultimate power over the people of Tremaene.

And while there remained a chance of unlocking the channels, Esme had little hope that the pieces of the orbs had survived the fall of the Order.

"I saw what he did. I saw everything."

The horrific images threatened to surface, but Esme forced them down, realizing only then that she might be irreparably linked to the malevolent man through the memories she'd bartered for.

Her breath quickened at the thought.

"Who?" Tearlach demanded.

"That...that *man*." Her voice wavered. "Who visited Athdara...all those years ago. The one I saw in the dream."

"Dougal? You learned who he was?"

"I did." She paused, wishing she didn't have to tell Tearlach the rest. "It's *him*. From...the war."

Tearlach's gaze darkened and Esme averted her eyes.

"Tell me."

"He's the one who...who led..." She looked up. "The one who used...dark magic."

Tearlach inhaled a measured breath, turning his ire toward the thick trunk of the tree, as if the monster himself might be found trapped inside the ancient bark.

His eyes snapped back to her, and the intensity thieved Esme's next words.

He stalked closer as Lord Luxovious's memories overwhelmed her.

Epilogue

A PLAIT OF golden hair slipped through the perpetual darkness. He pulled away from the deep chasms where he dwelled, drawing nearer.

And who might you be? Luxovious drawled.

It had been a time since he'd had a companion. The last one had failed him. And after he'd gone to great lengths to find such an exemplary prospect—one who possessed a wealth of power, but was easily swayed by the promise of more. An immense disappointment that one had been. Greed had gotten her—not that Luxovious could blame the ambitious priestess. So much power within reach could be tempting. But without careful action, without patience, it could slip away just as quickly.

His attention returned to the glimpse of woven hair. Taking his time, he savored the dips and curves of the braid, delighting in the play of light along each strand. The silken locks fanned out, their paths broken only by the point of an ear. He followed the shell to the pale shimmer of skin beneath.

What of the appearance of his own skin? Had it remained dull and scaly? Stretched thin over twisted bones and joints? Perhaps years of endless sleep had rejuvenated him. How long had it been? A hundred years, he thought. Maybe more. Maybe less. Not that it mattered greatly.

Time was of little consequence. And he'd been quite content with his stretch of dormancy.

But here you are, come to find me. And I shan't turn you away.

At least not until he'd determined her usefulness.

Luxovious beheld his new companion, tracing the features of her face. Her eyes were the color of wet earth. He lingered there, drinking them in. Great power dwelled within those dark eyes. They'd seen things. And yet, they were unquestionably young.

Familiar, almost.

Though his new companion was too young to have witnessed such things, her eyes bore the same haunted look he'd seen on battlefields as warriors pleaded for their lives.

Luxovious hummed as he sifted through his stores, searching for a satisfying recollection. As he summoned them one by one to the forefront of his mind, he could almost taste the succulent fear of his prey as they were slayed. He relished the coppery tang of blood as it spilled upon the land. Smoke and ash burned his nostrils, singeing his skin, as he trailed fire in his wake.

He savored those memories.

But as he reminisced, he noticed a slight shift in the air. A presence.

As though he wasn't alone in remembering each moment.

He called forth his new companion. The image had become clearer, more complete. He pulled back to find her hiking along a rocky expanse. Another kept pace beside her. Luxovious couldn't make out more than a vague outline of the girl's escort—a well-built man from what he could tell. But he had little interest in that one.

The girl, though...

There was something about the girl.

Yes, he decided. She'd do quite nicely in keeping him company.

And I shall be the most gracious host, he purred.

Surveying her again, he considered her stature—quite small compared to the one she traveled with. Yet, she wore the attire of a warrior. Interesting.

Then again, he wasn't sure why that singular aspect surprised him. It wasn't as though the woman who'd trapped him with her vile spells had been heavily muscled or of formidable build. And she'd been powerful beyond measure.

Luxovious growled, the sound resonating through his skull. Perhaps he wouldn't have underestimated her ability if she hadn't appeared so...diminutive.

But underestimated her he had. She'd been impervious to every offer he'd made. That woman—that crafty, cunning woman—had managed to trick him, to bind him in eternal sleep.

No matter, he mused. He'd find another. One who would appreciate the extent of his reach. One who was worthy of the gifts he would so generously give.

The question was whether his new companion would become such a recipient.

How, pray tell, did you come to find me? he wondered. Luxovious lingered on the features of her face once more. So familiar.

Those eyes.

They looked up then.

She peered straight at him. Through him. As though she could somehow see him from wherever she dwelled a world away.

There was something of *his* in those eyes. Something she'd taken.

Oh, you are no guest, he growled.

Searching the chambers of his mind, he searched for threads, trails, remnants she might have left behind. But she was not there. Had not been there. He could find no shadow or haze of infiltration.

Yet somehow, she'd seen inside. Seen things she was not meant to see. Things no one was meant to see.

He gazed into her eyes again. Dark and knowing, afraid. And so familiar.

So like those that had bored into his during the final moments before darkness had taken him into its comforting embrace.

Eyes he'd never forget.

Eyes that were looking back at him.

A daughter. He'd always wondered. It seemed his captor *had* managed to keep something hidden from him.

But no longer.

There'd be no need to search for another. The one who could free him from his confines, and wake him from sleep had come right to him.

Laughter rang through his head.

Couldn't keep away, could you, my dear? Luxovious crooned.

DEAR READER

Thank you so much for reading *Wild Heart of the Crown*! This storytelling journey started many years ago, and I'm so grateful for every reader who wants to explore the little world I've created. If you enjoyed *Wild Heart of the Crown*, please consider writing a review. Something as simple as "I liked it" helps a book gain visibility through searches, newsletters, and *Also Bought* lists. If you have a moment, help new readers find the Wild Heart fantasy series by leaving a review on Amazon, Goodreads, or BookBub.

Esme's journey continues in Book Three:
Wild Heart of the Magic

COMING SOON!

ACKNOWLEDGMENTS

I lost my dad a couple of weeks before *Wild Heart of the Storm* was set to release. To say I wasn't fully present for the launch is an understatement. This time around, I want to express how much he meant to me, and all the wonderful qualities he passed on to me.

I have him to thank for my creativity (he was a woodworker). My tendency toward organization came from him as well, though I'm still not sure if that's a good trait or a bad one. He also instilled in me a sort of resourcefulness. Why buy something new when you can repurpose something you already have? I wish I could say that I inherited his love of cooking—preparing good food for the people he cared about was certainly his love language. I think mine might be storytelling, and I'm grateful that I was able to share some of my stories with my dad.

Thank you to my fierce fan club of friends who continue to encourage and celebrate every step of this daunting publishing journey. Jen, Jim, Deborah, Brianne, Annie, Diane, Matt, Dorothy, and Roy, you've somehow convinced me that my writing doesn't suck. Please keep doing that!

To my family—who've understandably had a rough go of it these last several months—thank you for being proud of every little accomplishment I've made with these books. I appreciate it more than you know.

Chris, my editor and proofreader extraordinaire, you've once again hunted down all those sneaky typos! Thank you for not only offering suggestions to make the story better, but for truly enjoying the world and the characters. I couldn't have asked for a better editor.

And finally, thank you to Volodymyr at MiblArt in Ukraine for the stunning cover! I'm thrilled with how beautifully you brought my vision of the Meallán cityscape to life.

ABOUT THE AUTHOR

Erica Sebree lives in Austin, Texas, where she works in public service as a graphic designer. She reads too much romance and drinks too much tea—usually at the same time. She makes frequent attempts at gardening, and will happily talk to any animal who crosses her path. She believes lists should be written in colorful ink, and dreams of one day having a farm sanctuary with many adorable cows. When she escapes into fantasy worlds, it's to places where magic is vital, animals are guardians, and a stubborn bodyguard's only weakness is the fierce, reluctant heroine he's sworn to protect.

Find her online:

ericasebree.com

facebook.com/ericasebreewrites

twitter.com/erica_sebree

instagram.com/ericasebreewrites/

goodreads.com/erica-sebree

bookbub.com/authors/erica-sebree

Newsletter:

bit.ly/WildHeartMail

ericasebree.com

* 9 7 9 8 9 8 6 6 1 1 8 3 9 *